WITHOUT A WITNESS

A HIDDEN SHIFTER ROMANCE

THE MAFIA ARRANGEMENT
BOOK TWO

JAEGER ROSE

BEARLY CONTAINED ROMANCE, LLC

E-Book ISBN: 978-1-971642-97-0

Model Paperback ISBN: 978-1-971642-98-7

Discreet Paperback ISBN: 978-1-971642-99-4

Editing - Jeanine of Indie Edits with Jeanine

Proofreading - Nay of Nay's Notations

Book Cover - Katelyn of Designs by Kage

Model Photograph - Lindee Robinson

Chaos Coordinator - Kelsey Schneider

Without
A WITNESS

A NOTE FROM THE AUTHOR

Distinguished guests,

We have come here today to formalize a union between stalker romance and shifter romance. Their joining signifies all that is good and bountiful in paranormal romance, under which such things as morally gray, Mafia, and alpha males find their home.

This union is a powerful commitment in which you may find many wolf-shifter romance themes. There will be gruesome events such as on-page physical violence, murder, and biting. In addition to wolf-shifter romance violence, this does stay well within the realm of Mafia romance. There will be more realistic acts of violence, such as guns, knives, and fists used against individuals.

However unlike its predecessor, *My Solemn Vow,* this book takes a more cybersecurity twist. Book two in The Mafia Arrangements, *Without a Witness,* is a tale of stalking and possession unseen before in this world.

As in many dark romance relationships, there will be events that, outside the pages of this novel, would be abhorrent and grounds for divorce and a protective order. But here in the darkness, we say 'Yes, sir' and 'Please, give me more.'

In the event you find yourself uneasy with things that happen in the dark and you're looking for confirmation that this darkness is, in fact, safe for you, please read the list of generalized events, available on my website.

If upon reading the list, you find yourself further questioning this book and its handling for you . . . I might suggest you reach out to the author so she can disclose additional information that others may find to be spoilers.

You may find the content advisory list or/and contact information at www.authorsarahjaeger.com

Your mental well-being is important and should not be compromised for the sake of fiction.

For those who do first
and ask forgiveness later.

CHAPTER ONE

BOY GENIUS

LETICIA D'MEDICI:

You're NEVER going to guess what Nona Isabella told me about Cousin Violetta and the De Bonna boy Nicolas.

No, really, you'll NEVER guess.

I can't help but open the messages on the cloned phone I'm working on. *What aren't we guessing?*

LETICIA D'MEDICI:

Violetta and Nicolas are getting MARRIED.

Well, that was less thrilling than I hoped for. I sigh and set down my newest assignment, the cloned phone of my brother's new wife, and scrub my hands down my face.

I always thought I'd be at my brother's wedding — second wedding — and do the whole best man thing again. And this time I'd give a much better speech about how his new wife is a great addition to our family. This time, though, through an arranged marriage, I'm not exactly sure that's true. I haven't even met her.

Not that it entirely matters. Instead of at the church, I'm safe and sound deep in our territory, at home in my parents' house. Today, I'm the designated sole survivor in the event of a tragedy at the wedding. The biggest truce in the history of our family is culminating in the most archaic rites of two funerals and a wedding.

After today, the Irish Mob and Italian Mafia will officially be partners.

That didn't stop our family from preparing for the likely event of a double cross. Death and total annihilation are what the arbiters promise for breaking the truce after the deal has been struck. While personally, our family would never risk the penalty, we don't know the D'Medicis' morals well enough to place a bet on their desire to stay alive.

The phone vibrates again. I shouldn't be so damned interested, but the heads of the family literally made it my entire job to snoop through all the information I gathered from the D'Medicis' operation.

I'm not saying our Italian enemies are bad at crime.

I'm saying if it was so easy for me, a Cavanagh and, until recently, sworn enemy, to simply stroll over to one of their SUVs, climb into the back seat, and clone Antonella's phone they left right out in the fuckin' open, the Feds could do the same thing.

It's a wonder they were winning the war between our feuding families. Maybe it doesn't take brains to smuggle drugs, broker in information, and launder money . . . only large numbers of 'made men' willing to do the labor on the cheap.

Antonella D'Medici, my older brother's new wife, was an only child, but every one of her aunts and uncles has at least three children.

It's probably why she has over three hundred contacts in her phone, all with very similar last names. D'Medici, D'Angelo, Bonetti, De Bonna . . . I think I recognize a handful of the people with last names that aren't outright Italian and aren't also labeled with qualifiers such as 'professor' and 'Eastwick Elementary' or 'grad school' following the names.

This texter, though, the only one sending her any messages

today, is her younger cousin. Leticia is the real principessa mafiosa and apparently has nothing better to do than text Antonella at least ten times an hour.

I open the phone up and look at the new messages.

LETICIA D'MEDICI:

They're getting married because Father Domingo caught them in the rectory together. Like, TOGETHER together! AT CHURCH!

Nicolas, I can understand he's . . . De Bonna . . . but VIOLETTA?!

I almost text her back. I want more details. *What does that mean, 'he's De Bonna'? Why do we not believe this of Violetta?*

The drama is always so much better when it isn't your family's to deal with. I can imagine, though, that for Antonella and Leticia, this is probably pretty run of the mill, given all the cousins.

My fingers twitch.

I look up the family tree I've pieced together from the contacts and some genealogy websites that I may or may not have hacked into.

Violetta is Antonella's third cousin, and Nicolas must be . . . Stop. I close out of the tab on my monitor. If it were a Mafia-related marriage, I'd probably let myself dig more, but kids getting married because of puritanical reasons isn't what I'm meant to be looking into.

"Leticia." I speak to the phone, knowing she'll never hear me. "Couldn't you tell me something about what's going on at the funerals?"

LETICIA D'MEDICI:

Also, Berto is MAJOR UPSET.

I love the way she keeps using caps lock for emphasis. Most girls have a favorite emoji, but Leticia seems to use caps in their place.

"Tell me about Berto?" I'm talking to the phone. I've clearly lost my mind.

My wolf has locked in on my interest with a lazy yawn, trying to determine whether it's worth waking up for or if he'll go back to sleeping inside me.

LETICIA D'MEDICI:

I think Berto is mad you got married before him. Not that he'll ever admit to that, but he's really upset that you went through with this and are now a Cavanagh.

Also, when did the Cavanaghs get so HOT? I do not remember anyone being this attractive in the photos that Dad showed us of people to be on the lookout for.

I roll my eyes.

LETICIA D'MEDICI:

Maybe Royal is ugly to make up for how attractive Valor is?

"Ouch." I push the phone over on the desk. "Rude."

I ignore the next few messages when they come in, transitioning to working on tracking software installation rather than information gathering. But it takes all of two minutes before I crack and check what the Mafia princess has to say next.

LETICIA D'MEDICI:

Nope, he's hot too. I looked him up. He was at a fundraising event for women in STEAM.

I smirk and then do the same thing Leticia did . . . look myself up online. I don't do it a lot. But from time to time, I search for myself, Mom, Dad, my older brother Valor, and his daughter Kerrianne, and scrub any of the top search results from the internet. Luckily, since our family is small, it doesn't take a lot of time to expunge the unnecessary posts from the World Wide Web.

Attending and being seen at some galas and events are societally necessary for networking, but we prefer to keep our wealth less flashy.

I have to scroll through three pages of images before I find one of me tagged at the particular fundraising event she's referencing.

She spent all that time looking us up? My wolf yawns, paying attention again. *What is she like?*

Why do we care? I set my phone down on the desktop and stare at it.

Call it curiosity? My wolf rolls over to the side and then starts pushing images of outside and rolling in the grass before hunting through some bushes.

Yeah, yeah. Outside, touch grass. I know, I know. I shove him down, out of my mind, but I give in and start searching for Leticia D'Medici.

She isn't hard to find. Public social media profiles, photos at all sorts of fundraisers and events. The camera loves her.

Leticia is . . . stunning. Uncharacteristically blonde hair stands out in stark contrast to the dark browns of her family. She's smiling in every single picture, and in ninety percent of the photos, it looks genuine.

With one click, I examine one of the photos that doesn't have a genuine smile. When it opens up, not centralized on her face, it's not hard to figure out why she's not smiling as brightly. Leticia stands sandwiched between Gregorio D'Medici, leader of the Italian Mafia, and her older brother Berto, his heir. Gregorio's grip on her wrist looks damn near bruising.

I download the image and view its digital backmatter before I start doing my standard scraper to pull it off the internet. Normally, I'm thorough and dive deep with every search. Something tells me to leave the proof there though. That somewhere, there needs to be public record of this likely abuse.

It's so natural to just remove images and scrub an entire existence from the internet. Our family values privacy and operates a whole major corporation under pseudonyms. But I don't know Leticia. She's not my family, yet I'm deleting the image nonetheless.

"I can't imagine what that's like, Leticia," I whisper, deleting all but one image from the internet.

The phone buzzes, and guilt rakes through me. *I shouldn't have meddled like that.* But I can't help but look at the text messages anyway.

LETICIA D'MEDICI:

I'm sorry we couldn't talk. I love you. I miss you so much. Dad is being Dad. It's like the truce means nothing and you're dead to him. He's said terrible things, and I didn't want to cause a scene. God I hope you're getting these messages.

You're my only fucking friend, and it's not fair that they're taking you away from me. I hope the Cavanaghs let us stay in contact. If it's up to Dad and Dad only, then our goodbye was something blue in your bedroom this morning.

My wolf's attention shifts to Leticia, and he lets out a low growl.

It feels protective in the way he interprets her words and latches on to her.

Something gnaws on my heart, my chest aching at her words. So many of those feelings I know and understand. Worrying about being disowned, what life would be like if your family didn't love you, and not wanting to be the talk of gossip is such a heavy burden to carry.

"Let me know you're okay, Leticia." But I have a feeling there won't be a response.

A text message doesn't come.

I wait, staring at it for longer than I should before setting it aside and going back to work.

I've been tossing and turning all night.

Leticia never messaged me again. Never messaged *Antonella* again.

I keep my eyes closed and try to focus on the soft whir of the cooling fan on the smallest server I keep here at the house. It sounds perfect, running like it should, a little technological hum.

Normally, two minutes of focusing on the brownish-white noise and I'm headed off to sleep, but I can't. Not with my brain this wired.

Defeat isn't something I accept regularly, but after three hours and not sleeping, I get out of bed and go to my desk.

The problem is the look in Leticia's eyes in that photo. It's in the words of those text messages. It's because I can't do anything about it. Maybe in the future, but not just yet. For now . . .

Be the hunter, my wolf says the same time I plop my ass in my computer chair.

The leather is cool against my bare back, sending a shiver up my spine and adding to the thrill of the chase. *Find her.*

Images of dark alleyways, stalking a blonde-haired woman, come into my mind, and I'm quick to push them away. I refuse to stalk someone that way.

It's a lot of proprietary software.

It's a lot of keystrokes.

It's more than a lot of luck.

The tracking shows that the D'Medicis took Antonella's phone back with them into their house. I assumed they would since the information we gleaned showed that Antonella moved in with her uncle, Gregorio, the head of the D'Medici Mafia, when she returned from New York.

The D'Medicis didn't turn Antonella's phone off when they took it back to their penthouse. So through the clone, I have access to everything.

I take it back. The D'Medicis are bad at crime.

Immediately I gain access to their home network.

There isn't even a firewall protecting shit. Their internet password is their last name with the year Berto was born.

Their home security system is . . .

I scrub my hand down my face and squint at the screen to be sure I'm reading this right. *Shit.* Maybe *we're* bad at crime.

All this fuckin' time, one of our conglomerate's baby corporations has been doing the security of the D'Medici penthouse?

Then again, who would approve the hours for me to go through every single client record of every single baby corporation we own? An audit that size would mean way too much manpower to convert all the systems to talk to each other. Plus, the contract process to look over and make sure we even had the legal authority to do so.

Not that what I'm doing is legal. But I'm a criminal, so it's fine.

I open camera after camera. My wolf and I scour every feed and every room. We're checking all the angles of each room. It's not enough. But I can't admit that I'm doing anything more than snooping. I can't admit that it feels as good as a hunt does. It's the same though. My heart is beating hard, and my wolf is right there on the surface with me. Ready to go.

Where is she? My wolf growls as I flick through the screens again. His curiosity has intensified with narrowed eyes.

I don't see her. Sitting here and watching the feeds won't change that.

My brain is moving a hundred miles an hour.

I go to county records and grab floor plans for the building. Then I start mapping out the cameras and the viewpoints, trying to find dead zones. I flick into the feeds on the second floor. None of them are labeled like the downstairs ones were. But there are a lot of cameras.

Big trouble. My wolf says it first.

I open the city planning map for the second floor, and it looks like all bedroom suites.

"Maybe they're door cams." I cringe as I click onto the first feed.

A bedroom suite comes into view. It's appointed with fancy, expensive furniture and is blessedly empty.

"It's not creepy to have live streams in bedrooms, not at all." My sarcasm doesn't make the creepy crawlies across my skin any better. Seeing how high tech and advanced these ones are with their night vision only makes it worse.

But I have absolutely one objective in mind.

First, I remotely disable the sound in every bedroom camera before I click into them one by one. The first three are empty rooms.

My hackles rise as I click into the next room. Berto is sleeping, ass up and naked in his bed. I close out of that as fast as I can and move to the next one.

Leticia is curled up under the covers on her bed. Her blonde hair spills across one pillow, and she clings to another like it's anchoring her through a storm.

She's perfect. My wolf perks up, his attention zeroed in on the image. My skin prickles like he wants to get a closer look in the flesh. *Gorgeous little angel.*

We're violating her privacy. I scold him — and myself — but my hand falls off the mouse when I go to close out of the feed.

Her phone lights up on the nightstand next to her, the screen illuminating the room. I instinctively look at mine. Four thirty. It's late, or early, depending on how you look at it.

Leticia stretches for a minute before, in a practiced maneuver, sliding off what must be the alarm.

Where are you going, gorgeous? My wolf cocks his head.

My finger twitches like it's trying to zoom in.

"I really should close this feed out and then destroy the camera." But I can't help myself, watching as Leticia goes to her closet, then the dresser, then to the adjoining bath.

Does she know about the camera?

I know for a fact this is a discreet model and it's free of any indicator lights, so there's a chance she knows it's there, but she'd have no idea if anyone was actively monitoring it.

Leticia emerges from the bathroom a few minutes later. She's wearing a long skirt and a fluffy blouse. She grabs her phone off the nightstand and then takes an apron off the back of her door and pulls it over her shoulders before tying it up in the back.

There's only one camera in the hallway, and it's not of the same quality as the ones in the bedrooms, but I follow Leticia's shape as she migrates to the staircase. Then, clicking camera by camera, I track her through the massive penthouse until she gets to the kitchen.

She's graceful as she maneuvers around in the low light.

We work together — her in the kitchen and me re-coding the camera in her room.

I could disable it entirely, make it so that it overheats and burns itself out. No one would be able to watch her room then. But I can't bring myself to do that.

What if they buy a new one?

My wolf reminds me that I can make the camera appear offline rather than removing it from the menu. I put the setting back on, then throw on a heavy-duty password encryption to that video feed and test that it works.

Leticia and I yawn and stretch at the same time. She has loaves of bread in the oven, and I have the peace of knowing that no one will be watching her bedroom.

I hate that I can't make her safe. But I can watch her.

Two more keystrokes and I lock down their system.

The D'Medicis will have to do a password reset to get it all back online, and given that I changed the protocols and made the system more complex out of habit . . . It'll be a long time before they sort out that Leticia's camera is automatically and permanently locked.

They'll never be able to detect that I'm here and watching them all. They'll never know I'm watching her.

My wolf wags his tail in small, brisk whips back and forth. Sleep finally calls us toward bed.

CHAPTER TWO

THE SAFE AND SCREWDRIVER

The overhead door is closing as I open the entry door from the house to peer out into the garage, which is empty of the cars that normally occupy the space. "What's the deal? You took my favorite little pest because we're doi— oh, okay, so when Mom said 'something loud' I thought she meant drilling or excavating, not Valor's job."

A male human is tied to an old wooden captain's chair, which is set on tarps in the center of the garage. He's unconscious, his thick head of brown hair slumped between his shoulders.

Yesterday a wedding, today a man tied up in the garage. It's always something.

"I didn't want to bother your brother when it's something so simple." Dad's chest is proudly puffed up as he admires his handiwork.

"Yeah, I don't think you remember, but it's your other son who has a hankering for blood. I'm more of an information-in-the-form-of-computers kid." I close the door to the house behind me, my nose wrinkling at the scent of blood already thick in the air.

"It'll be easy," Dad says, walking over to his tool chest.

Unlike Valor's, which is full of implements hand selected to cause harm and maim without killing, Dad's is filled with actual tools, like screwdrivers and shit.

"So what exactly is so simple and easy that we can do it?" I slide on my ratty old sneakers I wear for jogs down the driveway to get the mail.

"We need him to give us the combination to a safe." Dad grabs a flathead screwdriver out of the toolbox. "I'll show you how Neil and I used to do it back in the old days."

My whole body cringes at the thought of what we're about to do. "Where is said safe?"

"In the back of my truck." Dad shrugs and approaches the guy, grabbing hold of his hair.

"Why don't I crack into the safe, and we can save the time torturing the guy?" I walk toward the side door to the garage.

"I already had our usual guys take a stab at it. They couldn't get through." Dad huffs. "I'm not that old. I tried the path of least resistance first."

"But you didn't come to the kid genius with a massive tech budget who bought some safe-cracking tools last year." I point out and open the door. The cool late autumn air tickles my skin.

Dad sighs to himself, but I don't hear any screaming as I close the door, so at least maybe he's waiting a little bit. I see the rather sizable safe sticking out of the back of Dad's truck before I even open the tailgate. It's covered with what looks like concrete, as if it's been ripped out of the side or floor of a building. But the mechanism on the front is something I've been meaning to practice on and most definitely fit for the equipment I bought.

I head back into the garage and find that Dad woke the guy up.

"What safe?" The guy's eyes dart between me and Dad. "I don't know anything about a safe."

"You don't know anything about the safe that was in the back of your restaurant?" Dad holds the metal of the screwdriver in one hand while tapping the handle against his other palm.

"Dad," I bark, "I've got the tools. Give me five minutes before you start making the body disposal that much harder."

His eyes cut into me, but he gives me a single nod in approval. With a yawn and a stretch, I cross the garage and head back into the house and down to my lair. The tools are stacked neatly on a shelf in my storage room, waiting for their opportunity to shine.

When I get back into the garage, Dad has backed his truck inside and closed the door. The stranger's face is now inches from the end of the tailgate.

"And this is where Valor gets his unhinged from." I sigh as the engine cuts off.

Walking behind the guy in the chair, I roll it back out of the way, leaving it still on a corner of the tarp.

"Damn, I missed him," Dad grumbles. "Well, hurry up and get into it then. I don't have all day. Your mother wants to go antiquing."

"No, she wants to torture *you* by taking you to antique stores because you said her potatoes were a little bland last night." I correct him before setting my tools on the tailgate and scaling up alongside them.

"She's not that upset over one comment." Dad furrows his brow. "Is she?"

"Yeah. How is it in forty years of marriage you haven't figured that out yet?" I turn to look at him, cocking my head, but Dad stays his stony self, and I turn back to the safe.

Silly alpha. My wolf giggles.

"I've never seen that safe before," the guy stammers.

It takes only a couple minutes to set up the safe-cracking software and hook up the mechanical spinner on the safe door itself. All the while, Dad tries to press the guy strapped to the chair for more information about what's in the safe.

Within five minutes, the safe is open, Dad knows no new information, and I'm packing up my equipment.

"Well, that was easy," Dad huffs, and I hear that very distinctive gurgle of blood like someone's throat was just slit.

I clench my eyes shut but take a quick peek to find dark red pooling on the floor under the chair.

At least he didn't get tortured for something so stupid. Not that bleeding out is a short process. I pinch the bridge of my nose and step back. It's not like there isn't a time to torture people for information, and maybe the guy was a bad person, but this seems a little too . . . trivial for that sort of bloodshed.

I look at the contents of the safe. It's stuffed with cash, guns, and files of paper. I reach for one of the folders. "What is this?"

"Don't touch it!" Dad barks, and I snap my hand back. "It's

evidence we'll be planting on a competitor." His words become calmer and more well-mannered.

"Oh." I take a healthy step back from the safe. "Well, alright then. Did you need anything else?"

"I don't have anything for you. I won't make you deal with this." Dad gestures to the chair with a bloody screwdriver.

My stomach lurches under the hefty realization that he slit a guy's throat with the same screwdriver he uses to fix practically everything.

I close the door to the garage and rest my weight against it. The bag of equipment in my hands feels like the anchor holding me to the floor.

You have no problem killing rabbits but other prey? My wolf sighs.

I let him have more space in my brain, and he helps ease the discomfort of my stomach.

I'm halfway down the stairs when a flurry of text messages hits my phone.

VALOR:

Can you text me the dumbed-down version of what happened while I was gone?

Easy enough. He was only gone for a week, and sure, our whole world changed, but the events are pretty straightforward.

VALOR:

Why didn't you catch that Antonella was a D'Medici?

Rude much? I hate that not catching a single personnel file — in an elementary school full of staff — makes me look incompetent, but it's not like he caught it either.

VALOR:

Need a phone for Antonella. Clothing too. Was that negotiated for at all? Can you investigate that or get Mom and the pack ladies to get her outfitted accordingly?

I put my cool, and proven useful, toys back on their shelf and answer him, one message at a time.

ROYAL:

Sean died. The arbiter was called in. D'Ms demanded you marry A. Funeral planning. Taught K how to play Texas Hold'em.

I wonder if he'll comment on the fact that the only way I know how to play Texas Hold'em is by counting cards.

ROYAL:

Didn't catch because her documents were tight. Now that I found the flaw, double-checking everything else. Won't happen again.

Embarrassment flames my cheeks. I'm better at background checks than Valor. He didn't catch it when he reviewed the school prior to Kerrianne's enrollment, but I should have when I was looking into Kerrianne's new teacher.

School has been in session for months, and that's months that Kerrianne was in the same building as someone from a rival family. I'd be devastated if Kerrianne was hurt because of me. Granted, Antonella and Kerrianne have only been in the same classroom together for a little over a week, but he has every right to be taking the crappy, direct tone with me rather than asking.

We've already had this guilt. We looked at her documents again and again. There is no way to know that the D'Medicis had papers this good. My wolf stops me from beating myself up.

And I know he's right. Less than a week ago, I was already berating myself for this. But now that my older brother has caught up with my fuckup, I'm hating being seen as subpar.

Can't stand seeing blood, guts, and death. Missed Antonella's paperwork. Not to mention, we had access to their house through a subsidiary all this time and no one knew to look.

I plop down at my desk chair and send off one more text.

ROYAL:

10-4 phone, negotiations, and lady stuff.

I open my chat with Mom.

ROYAL:

Antonella needs clothes and things appropriate for the future alpha's wife. Valor asked for help. I'm working on his new bride's phone, but could you handle the wardrobe?

Mom sends back a thumbs-up and an emoji of a shopping bag and then the smiley face with a money tongue before my phone stops vibrating, and I set it down on the desk.

You're not bad. My wolf reassures me. *We're smarter in other things. Imagine Valor trying to get into the safe.* My wolf thinks of Valor's wolf trying to chew on the knob and ultimately peeing on it and walking away.

He has a point. But it doesn't stop me from throwing myself into doing a better job and getting all the technology locked down.

Leticia

CHAPTER THREE

THE PRINCESS IN THE TOWER

"I'm, for one, super excited to graduate." Brittany sighs. She's staring at the engagement ring on her hand like it's bigger than a one-carat stone.

I know it's not right to judge, but she likes to talk a big game about money, and I know the truth. Brittany's family is in big debt to mine. I shouldn't know that, women aren't meant to know family business, but I overheard Dad talking too loudly to Berto. And two days later, Berto asked me why I was hanging around with 'the undesirables.'

It's three heiresses: Kiersten, Ashton, and Brittany. Berto was happy to see I was buddying up to Ashton, but not so much Brittany and Kiersten. When I asked for more information, all he said was that it was business and I shouldn't worry about it beyond becoming friends with Ashton.

They're nice to me. Probably only because they know I come from money.

"You're excited to be married." Kiersten corrects.

"Well, I did say ring by spring." Brittany waggles her fingers back and forth, the small stone catching the light. "Finals, another boring semester, finals, graduation, and then a June wedding."

Ashton catches my attention and rolls her eyes. It draws a smile from my lips, but only at the drama of Brittany's fake swoon.

"Are you walking for graduation, Leticia?" Brittany directs her question to me, but it's clearly not graduation we're talking about. Even more evident when she says, "You seem to be in the same place when we started the semester. Waiting on Mr. Right?"

"I'm not waiting for Mr. Right." I shrug and dismiss the question entirely because how do you tell your acquaintances that you're waiting for your father to marry you off like some princess in a fairytale? "I don't think I'm walking at graduation either. We normally go to the villa in the spring."

Ashton rests her head on top of her hands, supported by her elbows on her desk. "Okay, but seriously, there are tons of guys who would love a date with the infamously unavailable Leticia D'Medici. Or girls, if that's your thing."

With a sigh, I stop the nonsense the best I can. "Stop being silly. We don't have long to work on this project."

We're seated midway up the lecture hall, and groups all around us are wrapping up their projects, while I feel like we've gotten nothing done on ours. It isn't even that complex of a project.

"Don't worry. I'm tackling it this weekend." Kiersten yawns. "I've got a date with Addy."

Addy, as in Adderall. If I didn't hate this class so much, I might argue that we should all work on it together, but Kiersten is the best at statistics. It might be easier to let her do the work and accept taking the credit.

It's not like I'm in this class because I'll be using it someday.

I was stalling the inevitable: being married off to the highest bidder or for the most influence. It just so happens that I made an argument that I'm more valuable with a degree. Ridiculous, but it worked. A degree in communications can't hurt when it comes to cooking and cleaning someone else's mansion . . . and being shown off on someone's arm as their 'adoring' and 'grateful' wife . . . but the analytics behind the communications won't matter. Not that I'd ever let myself dream of working for some big fancy brand or doing social media for a cause I believe in. It can't happen, so I don't waste hope.

I hate that I'm so immune to the crushing weight of Mafia life and the expectations of my future. But since I was old enough to understand how our world works, it's become a fact of life and one I don't argue about anymore.

Sometimes, though, like right now, everything starts to feel pointless. Why bother trying for good grades? They only matter to me, and no one wants my opinion anyway.

"Alright, next class is here in five minutes. Everyone out," the professor shouts from the lectern.

I slip my laptop into its plush green sleeve before tucking it into my sleek brown leather tote bag. I probably have a dozen different colors and patterns that I coordinate with my outfits. But it makes me smile to control something, and this, coordinating my accessories to my outfit, is about as good as it gets.

The group of us mosey slowly, mixing with the others out the door and into the foyer of the business building. I'm shrugging on my thigh-length trench coat when we reach the large open atrium, which is practically a glass fishbowl out to the streets of Chicago.

"Did you want to go grab coffee?" Ashton offers as we both take a moment to feel the brightness of the sun on our faces.

The early morning, two-hour lecture and winter weather leave much to be desired in the way of seeing daylight.

"That'd be nice, but I'll have to check with the bodyguard. I don't think we're due home right away." I dig through my bag, looking for the durable fern-colored phone case I slipped it into this morning.

"I thought my parents were strict about having me go with an armed driver, but your family is so intense." Ashton sighs. "Are we doing the Christmas market this year?"

"Uhhh." I don't know how to let her down politely.

It's not that I don't want to do these things with her, but I'm trying to save all my good graces and asks to do things to see Antonella and get out of going to Italy for Christmas. Asking to go to the Christmas market right now would foil those plans.

"Leticia," a guy says as he approaches.

I vaguely recognize him as one from the front row of our statistics class.

"See, told you," Ashton murmurs, bumping me with her shoulder before taking a respectful step away for the illusion of privacy.

"New bodyguard?" Brittany gestures in the opposite direction as she nudges me away from the doors and closer to the guy who said my name.

The man she's gesturing to is dressed in what they're always dressed in. Black suit, black tie, and a scowl. Except it's not a bodyguard.

"Worse," I huff, adjusting my tote bag on my shoulder. "Older brother."

I'm torn between obediently following the daily protocol of going home with my bodyguard or being polite and hearing what the guy from the front of class has to say.

"Oh damn." She hums, keeping her voice down, but wags her eyebrows suggestively. "And what exactly is the family fortune in . . . you know, and is he single?"

The guy from the first row walks between Berto and me as he talks at me rather than to me. "Leticia, I was wondering if you'd maybe like to go out and get some coffee before my next class."

Berto steps to the side, back into my line of sight, and taps on his watch, rushing me along.

I focus back on the man talking to me. He's cute, young looking for his age, nearly boyish. In a world where I could pick a partner for myself, this guy wouldn't be in the running. Just . . . not my type. Luckily for him, it's not personal.

I start delivering the tried and true rejection lines. "I'm sure you're really nice, but I —"

"Move." Berto positions himself to stand next to me, wrapping his arm around me.

The guy from the first row looks between us, jaw going slack. "Oh, I didn't realize you had a boyfrie —"

"Don't be gross. I'm her brother. Now beat it." Berto opens up the side of his suit jacket, and I don't need to look to know he's flashing a look at the pearl handle of his gun in a chest holster.

To be polite, I give the well-intentioned guy a small wave and let Berto redirect me to the doors.

"Wait! Did you want to go get coffee?" Ashton calls, repeating the request from before. Maybe it's her attempt to get me out of the brisk removal from campus.

"Sorry, he's in a rush. I have to go, see you in class." I can't hear what she says as I get herded out into the vestibule first and then outside.

No students are milling around, only four of Dad's best and

most loyal men. They stand shoulder to shoulder, blocking a clear path straight to the blacked-out SUV.

"What's going on?" I seethe, looking between Berto and his darkly dressed henchmen.

I look like a beacon of brightness in the tan coat and fern-green scarf I chose this morning.

"It's not for you to worry about," Berto snaps.

He grabs hold of my wrist, and I'm led to the SUV waiting for us. My heels click on the pavement as I descend the four stairs to the street level.

The driver opens the door, and I'm pushed in first, climbing all the way across to let Berto in behind me.

"Berto, what's going on?" I rub where Berto held my wrist and hope that in the enclosed space, he'll be more forthcoming with answers.

"You need to be secured. Someone threatened your safety. That's all you need to know," Berto grumbles, tapping his phone screen furiously.

Of course it's all I need to know. What's new? Damn, I wish Antonella was here. He'd tell her.

For a while, it was easy to believe Antonella would be back. Maybe she'd work on Dad and Berto so that they'd tell me things. Slowly and single-handedly, she'd take down the misogynistic bullshit, and I'd get to know things and be more than a glorified pawn in this game. But no sooner had she gotten home and started with her life than she was ripped away from me again. Arranged marriage, family business, and I only know half the details because she told me.

I'm back to being in the dark, again, and alone.

Antonella calling the truce was what was best for the families but the worst thing for me.

I can't believe it's only been a week since she did, ending a billion-year-old war between the Cavanaghs and the D'Medicis. Our world moves so fast that she's been married off and completely moved on with her new life.

Meanwhile, I'm stuck being told nothing, as usual, by my older brother. I'm carted around like an inconvenience. I know siblings are supposed to have some tension between them, but honestly, I think Berto would prefer I not exist at all.

It feels like a crapshoot. But I pull my phone out and send a message.

LETICIA:

Toni, if you're getting this. Just know how much I love you and miss you.

Leticia

CHAPTER FOUR

MORE THAN THIS PROVINCIAL LIFE

"Leticia, I don't know how many times I have to tell you it is not up to me what your father decides he wants for lunch." Mom huffs as she tucks her scarf into her jacket.

She begins adjusting the little beret hat on her head and checking her makeup in the hallway mirror.

"All I'm wondering is, did you tell him that I already had lamb marinated and ready to be eaten?" I grip the ties on the back of my apron. Arms crossed painfully hard behind my back, it keeps the anger from boiling over.

Mom turns to look at me. She drops her shoulders slightly and raises her chin. "Leticia, your father wants a calzone. I know for a fact you know how to make one."

The conversation is over, and she turns to the elevator. Her chauffeur stands in the lift, holding the door open for her.

It's been four days since what I finally learned was an apparent attempt to kidnap me at the university. But you'd never know I was a near victim of the Mafia life because my life is as it always is: cooking, cleaning, and ridiculous last-minute requests to appease the patriarchy. I may get called 'princess,' but it's been made abundantly clear that I need to be able to 'manage' a house to impress whoever I'm married off to. But since Mom manages our house, I've been relegated to the menial tasks with the 'learn by doing' method.

"Yes, Mamma." I drop my arms, bringing them in front of me as I spin to go.

One time, she saw the angry marks I'd made on my skin before it had lightened, and she scolded me for making myself 'look ugly like that.' Now, I do better to hide them and pray for patience when dealing with her and Dad.

My phone is right where I left it in the kitchen, but now it's blinking. I tap the screen, and the notification shows a preview of the message.

UNKNOWN NUMBER:

Hey, it's Toni. Are you still alive?

My mouth goes dry, and I look away from the screen only to make sure I grab my drinking-water cup and not my dough-water cup from where I'd been letting the filtered water come to room temperature.

My thirst is quenched by the time the next message arrives. It's an image, and the warning on my phone pops up — 'Do you know this person' and 'Possible sensitive content' — but I click through it anyway.

Please be her, please be her.

The photo is of a hand creating a half-heart shape. The nails, manicured but short, a small speckling of flour. I'd know that hand anywhere.

I take a picture of my opposite hand so that they'll kinda sorta match up in the texting feed to make the heart image.

LETICIA:

OH MY GAWD. YOU'RE STILL ALIVE?!

I know I'm being melodramatic with that one, so I follow it up with something a bit less dramatic but still conveying my heart.

LETICIA:

I miss you so much. Ugh. It's been so weird without hearing from you.

Tell me what you can without getting killed.

I love you so much.

I instantly save her number into my phone and add it to the favorites. I should have known she'd get a new number. I feel silly now for sending all those texts that probably went nowhere. There have been days of random jabberings that are out there in the ether for someone else to come across.

Sadly, I can't stand and stare at my phone until I get a little more work underway. I have a whole calzone to just 'whip up' for Dad's lunch, because of course I do. But I leave the screen up where I can see everything.

TONI:

It's weirdly nice. Don't get me wrong, it's only been a little bit, but I'm not sure this was the worst decision I've ever made.

LETICIA:

That's great! I miss you so much. It's been so weird not having anyone to talk to. Sarena is moving on with her life and now you're . . . well I will SPARE you some of the words Dad has called you. My finals are soon.

Now Mom isn't pleased with the housekeeping staff. ALLEGEDLY they have something to do with the security system acting funny? Now she's breathing down my neck all the time.

It's like I'm being punished. Cleaning AND cooking all the meals. Luckily next semester my classes are heavier so she will HAVE to accept hired help.

TONI:

Leave it to Francesca. I'm so sorry. I wish I was there to help you.

Tears well up in my eyes. Antonella wasn't home long. She was in New York, getting her master's degree and teaching before coming back this year to teach here in Chicago.

I shouldn't be this emotional. If Dad were to see me crying, he'd list it as another reason he's done with me. Anything is possible ammunition for 'it's time you have a husband' and 'it's not proper for girls your age to be unwed' and all that misogynistic bullshit.

The walls are closing in on me. My college graduation date looms in the near future, and an arranged marriage will be quick to follow.

Toni's message gives me hope though. Maybe being married off to whoever Dad picks won't be so bad after all. It surely can't get much worse than the work I've been doing since I graduated from high school. Getting my bachelor's degree was a huge compromise to his plan. So, the last five years, I've been dragging out progress on my degree, 'learning' to manage Mom and Dad's entire house, and cooking practically every meal everyone eats.

Maybe I'll get lucky, and it'll be a charming prince instead of some beast of a crime boss. I snort at my own joke and flour my hands so I can get back to work.

With the small bit of relief that my cousin is safe in her new life, I breathe a little easier and go back to rolling dough.

My phone beeps.

TONI:

Could you dehydrate some starter for me? Buns from scratch for the rest of my life with instant yeast will be the death of me.

I giggle and go to the refrigerator where the family starter has been chilling in her antique glass jar. Something told me when I woke up this morning not to feed the sourdough starter, and here it is. Toni needs me to get her some.

"Okay, Nona Agnesia, it's time to make you a new daughter for a new home," I tell the little glass jar as I set it out in the warmth of the kitchen.

I'll still finish making Dad's lunch first, but giving the starter some fresh air and warmth before I feed and divide her feels better than keeping her in the cold fridge.

In the family for forever, everyone calls the starter Nona Agnesia. Even back in Italy, everyone refers to the starter as Nona. As the grandmother of the family, she's been told all the kitchen secrets. She's heard everything before, and I think it's why she's so spirited.

Mom doesn't believe in all the 'nonsense' I do. Like how Nona knows when the family is upset and rises more quickly as if she wants us to make more bread.

I made the mistake of telling Mom about Nona Agnesia and how she works. It got me one of *those* looks that only mothers do so well. She calls the things I say like that 'witchcraft,' and has made me go to extra catechism classes in the past for all the 'blasphemy' I bring around her.

She can say what she wants, but I can tell if she's been banging around in the kitchen. Everything feels more hostile. Nona Agnesia knows, too and doesn't bubble as pretty. Heck, I would go so far as to say the produce tastes more bitter and less sweet because of her rage.

LETICIA:

Nona has started making a daughter for you.

So, in OTHER news. There was another attempted kidnapping. I swear, I cannot for the life of me figure out why Berto doesn't come out with it and say it. He and Dad have used the same code for it since the one time they took me ice skating at the winter carnival.

TONI:

You're kidding me. The least they should be doing is telling you so that you know what to be on the lookout for.

LETICIA:

Instead I get lectures about how I must stay vigilant and the two of them talking in code about dragons coming to take the princess.

I'm twenty-three not twelve.

No, you know what, not even cousin Martina would fall for that bullshit. I'm twenty-three not eight.

Toni sympathizes with me, but it's no longer her place to try to talk sense into Berto and Dad, so I don't expect her to offer.

Fifteen minutes later, I'm in the middle of talking with Toni through text about Violetta and Nicolas and cousin Sarena's engagement plans, when the hairs on the back of my neck rise. The feeling of being watched creeps in, but it's not the malicious kind. Not the kind of being watched that makes you want to hide under the covers or put your back up to the wall so no one can sneak up on you.

We weren't supposed to know about the cameras in the house. But when it becomes your responsibility to clean, you're not doing a very good job if you don't notice things like cameras.

When I brought them to Dad's attention, thinking they were from federal agents or our enemies, he laughed in my face and told me to 'stop being so silly' and not to worry my 'pretty little head about men's work.'

It's not my fault that my 'pretty little head' told me to look up the model of the security system. I found out it came from this little subsidiary, which I then found to be owned by the Cavanagh technology corporation, Clark Enterprises.

Since no one wanted me, a woman, to talk about the cameras, I didn't think it was worth arguing over. And I let the information I discovered about the company go. Maybe it's Valor showing Toni that they've been keeping tabs on us and still plan to.

Dad was so desperate to win the war with the Cavanaghs, and maybe it's because he knew they were already so close to victory ahead of him.

The truce goes both ways. We're supposed to play nice with the Cavanaghs, and they're supposed to play nice with us. There really isn't a reason Toni and I can't hang out together anymore. I'll have to make it happen myself.

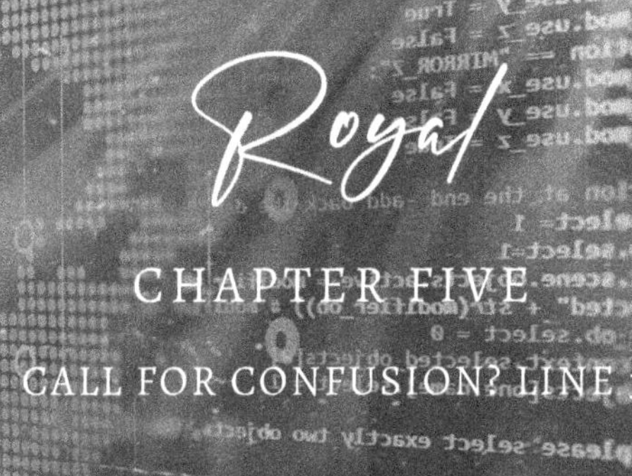

Royal

CHAPTER FIVE

CALL FOR CONFUSION? LINE 3

Margret knocks on my office door. "Royal, I'm so sorry to bother you."

I'm only in office at Clark Enterprises because there was a shareholders' meeting, which ended three hours ago. I'm trying to pack up and get out of here for the day, but it's one metaphorical fire after another.

"You're not bothering me. Unless . . . Did you eat the last donut out of the conference room?" I squint at her, and it gets the sour look on her face to soften.

"No." She cants her head and shakes it with a light admonishment. "I have a person on the phone, and I'm not sure how they were routed to me, but they swear they're a vendor who has been personally working with you on a project that's highly classified. And they're giving me all sorts of technical specs but refuse to be transferred to the technicians—"

"Margret. I've got it, you're okay." I demonstrate a big breath for her, and after she mimics me, I pick up my headset. "Go ahead and route the call to my phone. I'll take over from here."

The call comes through a few moments later.

I throw on my sweetest customer service voice. "Thank you for calling Clark Enterprises, this is Reuben Clark. May I know the person I'm speaking with?"

"Oh, thank god." A woman's breathy voice comes over the phone. It's followed by an overdramatic sigh. "I knew if I kept trying, eventually I'd get a Cavanagh."

It comes so naturally to use my pseudonym with that voice, I don't even think twice about it. But it's odd someone would know that the Clarks are really Cavanaghs in disguise.

I don't confirm to the caller who I am. "Miss, you are?"

"Leticia D'Medici and you're Royal Cavanagh," Leticia says, and I can practically hear the smile in her voice.

It's her. I sit back, a little shocked.

"I wouldn't peg you for a Reuben." She scoffs.

"Hey, what did a Reuben sandwich ever do to you? They're delicious." I'm quick to defend my cover identity.

"Mmm, no. No. No, they're not." She disagrees with ferocious adamance.

Strong-willed. My wolf is all the way forward, waiting with me for more from her.

Silence takes over the line, so I fill it. "So . . . you're not a vendor, and we're not working on a project together, let alone a highly classified one. What on earth were you reading to Margret for technical specs?"

"Oh!" Leticia giggles, and a smile pulls at my lips. "The manual to the toaster."

"Who keeps a manual for a toaster?" I relax into the seat, at ease, smiling at her actions. *That was a clever use of resources.*

"Mmmm, my mother, but worse yet, we don't even own this toaster anymore. The manual is from the eighties. And I'm not allowed to get rid of it."

"That manual is older than both of us? I'm impressed." I drum my fingers on the desk but can't help myself.

I flip open my laptop, access the system to Casa D'Medici, and flick through the camera feeds. I find Leticia in the kitchen, sitting on a stool in the corner, with a pamphlet unfolded in her lap.

She's wearing her blonde hair in a high ponytail, anchored with a bow, and a beautiful blue dress.

Radiant. My wolf focuses on her.

He's not wrong.

"It's more impressive if you see the stack of manuals from every appliance ever owned in this kitchen."

Leticia can't possibly know I'm watching her, but she pulls open a cupboard door down by her thighs. I can't see into the cupboard, but I assume it's full of every manual known to kitchenkind.

"Well, if you're not calling for the aforementioned nonexistent highly classified project, may I ask, what gives me the honor of talking to our very own Mafia princess today?"

"Oh, ew, no. Don't call me that." Leticia wrinkles her nose. She's shaking her head, and the movement sends her hair flicking back and forth.

"No, not princess?" I repeat it, and she shudders.

"Not a princess." She sighs, and her voice goes quieter. She brings her hand up to muffle her words. "But I was calling to try and get a hold of Valor."

I lean forward, looking at the screen more intently. *Why would she need to hide that?*

"Well, I can pass on a message for you, but he's preoccupied today." The honest truth is, I don't know where Valor is, and I'm too enamored with her to take the time to look up his coordinates.

"Can I trust you to really do that, or are you trying to get me off the phone?" Leticia drops her hand away from her face and picks up the toaster manual. She looks defeated.

"You can trust me." I assure her. "I'll get him the message today. I won't promise before the end of business, but I will promise before midnight."

"I'm big on promises." She warns me as she stands up from the stool and squats to put the manual away in the bottom cupboard. "I want to see Antonella. An invite to dinner would be a really good place to start."

"All you had to do was ask nicely. I'd be glad to take you to dinner." *Please don't take that as creepy. Did I say that creepy-ish?*

She lets out a gasp and snaps up into a standing position. Her fist clenches at her side. "Well, I would never."

"Never go to dinner with me?" I wince.

My wolf takes a cowering position, and the secondhand shame is a lot to bear.

"Would never invite myself out to a meal with someone." She lets her fist go, and I relax a bit.

"But you would invite yourself to dinner with Valor and Antonella?" I clarify.

"Yes." Leticia sounds annoyed. She goes to another cupboard and begins to pull out something from inside. "Because it's different when Antonella would be the one cooking the meal."

"So, not at a public restaurant." I note the specificity of this demand.

"That would be too weird." Leticia sets a large mixing bowl on the counter before spinning to another counter space, this time opening up a drawer.

"Too weird, got it." I watch as she moves about the kitchen.

We could be eating with her too, my wolf demands. We're both enthralled with her dance as she gathers things and sets them on the counter. *You could pretend to cook more than one meal. Make her come visit.*

My cheeks heat at the thought. Mom made sure Valor and I could cook at least one meal enough to impress a girl. It's not that she hasn't tried to make me learn how to cook more, but I'm much more inclined to snacking and easily made foods than a whole meal.

"So . . ." Leticia grabs something from a cupboard, and I instantly recognize it as earbuds. She slips one in and then the other before speaking. "What should I bring to dinner at Valor and Antonella's?"

The quality of the earbuds is fantastic. Her voice floods into my brain at a new wavelength and sends shivers down my spine.

"Nothing," I answer out of reflex.

You're never supposed to show up at an alpha's house with a gift unless you're a visiting alpha, and Leticia definitely doesn't qualify. Valor isn't *exactly* the pack alpha. That's my dad, but everyone treats my older brother as alpha too.

She scoffs and makes a tutting noise. "You can't show up to someone's house after inviting yourself and come empty-handed. It's rude."

"One could say it's rude for them not to have invited you over already." I try a redirect because Valor would graciously accept something but then spend the next six months trying to figure out how to reciprocate with something she'd appreciate. It's quid pro quo on steroids with him.

That might be funny to witness though. My wolf supplies.

I'm undecided in that department.

"You know what, you're right!" Leticia huffs, straightening her spine and raising her head, her fluffy ponytail flopping. She's standing so tall and strong. I expect a hand to go to her hip with sass. "I won't bring anything on the principle I should have been invited over already."

"Yeah! You tell 'em!" I agree, feeling her self-empowerment through the phone.

She sighs and slumps back down, measuring things out to put them in her big bowl. "You're sure he won't think it's rude?"

"Positive."

I can feel the seconds running out on this phone call.

Get her number! My wolf whines, picking up on my anxiety.

"Let me get your number; that way I can be sure Valor follows through." I slide open my desk drawer and make sure to hold the pen up toward the microphone when I click it so she knows I'm serious.

"Leticia!" a woman shouts shrilly. "You better not be messing around, there is so much work to do!"

"Ope, gotta go. I'm counting on you!" she says before rattling off a phone number and disconnecting the call.

It was too fast to catch, but I didn't need the digits. I only needed permission.

Leticia pulls the earbuds out of her ear in a hurry, stashing them back in the cupboard, barely getting back to the bowl before a woman with dark raven hair comes into the kitchen camera view.

I don't need to turn the sound on to watch her get scolded.

There's finger pointing and wide gesturing. The strength Leticia bolstered herself with when thinking about telling off Valor falls out of her body, leaving her making herself smaller. She's all but cowering behind the big bowl.

Guilt sinks a rock in my stomach that rolls around with anger. *She doesn't deserve that.*

We could make it so she doesn't have to deal with that. My wolf starts putting together the idea of playing house with Leticia.

It soothes the anger to agree with his fantasy, but that's all it can be. Leticia D'Medici is, as much as she doesn't want to be called such, the real D'Medici princess, and there is no way they'd ever let her be with a Cavanagh, let alone be seen with one.

CHAPTER SIX

THEY'RE BROTHERS

Valor is assembling firearms with a couple of pack members when I find him at the warehouse. "What now?"

"You know, for a guy who just got a new wife, you're grumpy. Shouldn't you be on a honeymoon or something?" I poke back at him before turning to our cousin, Gavin. "Has he been this pissy to everyone today?"

"No, just you." Gavin laughs as he keeps assembling.

His laughter goes up in a puff of condensation into the cold air of the warehouse. The recent cold snap has left everything down below freezing.

"Well, shit. Sorry to break up the party." I try to step into the line. My fingers brush the cold metal surface of the table before I pick up a frigid piece and start putting in a firing pin. "I see the heat isn't any better here than last winter."

Valor snatches the work out of my hands. "Stop. What do you want?"

"Ugh, you never let me play with your toys." I moan and groan, but it's mostly to rile him up.

"I swear to God, I never wanted a younger brother. Why was I cursed with one? What do you want, Royal?" He turns to face me, and we lock eyes. His wolf rises to the surface to meet mine.

"Gimme five minutes and I'll let you go back to playing with your guns." I gesture back to the door I came from.

"Go." Gavin shoos us with his hand. "We've got it from here. We don't need you involved with literally every shipment."

Valor draws a calming breath. "Yeah, you're right. Thanks, Gavin."

He and I don't speak on our way out of the warehouse, but once we're outside, it's like Valor is a different person.

We brush shoulders as he asks, "So what did you really need?"

"I received a call today from a person of interest." I lead the way back to one of Valor's many offices.

Valor waits until we're inside the office with the door locked before pushing me for more information. "Oh?"

The heating in the offices is much better than the freezing warehouse, and I start stripping out of my winter coat so I don't die from overheating.

"Mmhmm." I nod, sinking down into the worn pleather chair. The green vinyl is cracking and old but really insanely comfortable.

"Are you going to tell me who it was, or are you doing this ridiculous make-me-guess game?" Valor pinches the bridge of his nose.

"Yes, I'll tell you. Though you'd never guess who. Not in a million years." I scoff, taunting him, but he doesn't try to guess anyway. I give it another second of pause before letting the information out. "Leticia D'Medici called, and we had a lovely chat. She's coming to your house for dinner. You're to message her with a day that works for you and Antonella."

Valor's jaw drops. He closes it and shakes his head as he starts to shrug out of his peacoat. "How did you manage that?"

"She called Clark Enterprises and managed to find a way to talk to Margret, who patched her in with me." I shrug, wishing it had been more exciting than it was.

"And she voluntarily wanted to come to dinner at my house?" He cocks his head to the side like I'm the one who is insane.

"Literally, that was almost the entire call." *Shit. Almost slipped.* I don't try to backpedal, hoping he misses it.

"And what was the rest of the entire call?" Valor leans forward, pressing me for more information.

Busted.

"We talked about how she used jargon to confuse Margret to get to me. I clarified that it had to be at your house and not a restaurant. And she insisted that it had to be with you and Antonella for dinner."

"So you were flirting." Valor rolls his eyes and leans back.

"Was not!" I scrunch up all my features. "I would never. She's a fuckin' rival family's princess. She's a significant bargaining chip at a table I'd never be invited to, and I'm the second son of the alpha. We're not the same. And she'd never see me as worth flirting with."

"Mmhmm." Valor digs his phone out of his pocket. "What's her number? I'll set it up. But you were totally flirting. You're probably just bad at it."

"Are you done being mean to me, or do you have more?" I pull my phone out to give him Leticia's number. I have it memorized, but I don't need him to know that.

If he knows that, he'll know I was up late doing some stalking with her cell phone number. Which is the fastest way for my brother to figure out that I have a new person to obsess over for a little while.

It happens. Valor's wolf is built for the kill, and mine is built to stalk. It comes out in our everyday personalities. He's scary, and people just know he's a killer. I'm personable, and when the wolf and I latch on to someone, or something, it's not easy to just let it go.

Valor takes the number and sends a text before answering me. "You're right. I'm sorry. I don't mean to be such a dick. I'm . . . Don't get married to a stranger. She's so fuckin' nice and agreeable all the time. It's messing with my head. This isn't how it's supposed to be."

"You realize you're complaining because you like your wife, right?" I scratch my head for emphasis.

Valor scrubs his hands down his face. "I know. But I can't help but wonder if there isn't some dark secret going on. Is it a trap?"

"Well, I mean, dinner with her cousin will probably open up some more information. Like if her cousin shows up with another D'Medici in tow, there's reason for alarm . . ." I pause for effect. "Or maybe, you married a school teacher who is a genuinely good person."

Valor doesn't even acknowledge that last bit. I knew he

wouldn't. He's so used to looking for something to go wrong that he won't ever settle into the happiness of something going right.

"How often does Antonella text her cousin?" Valor slides his phone back in his pocket, not having gotten an answer to his text right away.

"Some. Their communications are frequent but inconsequential." And because it's who I am, I read them fourteen times, looking for some hidden meanings and couldn't find any, so I'm *fairly* certain that I'm right about them being inconsequential.

"Were we able to recover the messages from before the wedding?" He immediately jumps into the next question.

Deny. My wolf immediately raises his hackles. *Protect her.*

"No, I didn't get all the message history. However, I get the feeling these two are close but that Leticia probably doesn't know anything about what happens in our lives or even really inside the D'Medici home. It's not like Mom and her being into everything." I pepper enough information into that sentence, hoping somehow he doesn't ask more questions.

"I don't remember the last time I had humans in my house," Valor grumbles.

"Other than your wife?" I huff a laugh.

"That's different, she's stuck with me." He heaves a massive sigh. "I have to get Kerrianne prepared to behave. What do we even talk about at dinner? Couldn't this have been like coffee, or I don't know, some sort of outing where we're not confined to the dining room?"

"You have a built-in distraction with my favorite niece. She's practically a whole night's worth of conversation. I don't think you'll have an issue getting through a single dinner being civil." I try really hard not to invite myself to dinner.

I need to keep my distance from Leticia. Even if our circumstances were different and I could explore my attraction to—and my wolf's obsession with—her, this level of attachment to someone I barely even know is unhealthy.

What's a little stalking? My wolf is obsessed already.

"No," I say aloud to scold my wolf, and it cuts off Valor before he even starts the next question he was going to ask.

"You don't even know what I was about to say." Valor raises an eyebrow at me.

"I know you well enough to know you were about to ask me to spy on Leticia and figure out what angle she's playing, and I know enough to tell you no. That you need to be open to the merger of the families. It happened. Get over it." I hope my stab in the dark is in the right direction.

It was because Valor folds, slouching further. "Fine."

"Tell my niece that I'm ordering the last pieces for her robot. So we can do that later on during break." I get out of my chair before I can do something stupid like mention to Valor what's going on in my head.

"You know she's obsessed with building robots, right?" He laughs.

"Oh, I know. She messages me all the time asking if I think a robot could do any number of things. Surprisingly, though, she's never asked if it would do her homework." I smile.

"She really likes Antonella as a teacher," Valor muses, and I can feel the undercurrent of something more.

My brother and his kid are falling in love with his new wife. The arranged marriage isn't as bad as he keeps trying to make it out to be.

Maybe an arranged marriage wouldn't be so bad? Mom and Dad have always left marriage up to me. But even the second son could have some pull for an alliance.

My wolf walks away, disgruntled, thinking of Leticia.

I've always wanted everything I'm not supposed to have. Why wouldn't I want her? It's just that this time, I can't have her.

Probably.

Leticia

CHAPTER SEVEN

VERY SUPERSTITIOUS

It's been a rough day, and it's only one in the afternoon. Mom is on a trip to Entitled Island today, and it's a product of her own doing.

I duck into the second-floor utility closet and draw a deep breath, wishing it didn't smell so much like cleaning products but knowing it's one of the few places she won't think to look for me.

The dark closet is such a reprieve to the current 'stressful situation,' which Mom has made for herself. We're preparing for an 'impromptu holiday get-together' for all her high society friends. An event that isn't happening today, but one that I have to get the house ready for, nonetheless.

The cleaning people left two hours ago, and yet Mom insists I go over every inch of the house again and 'double-check' that they didn't miss anything. Which wouldn't be such a chore if she wasn't breathing down my neck.

If it's not her, it's that should-be-but-isn't-creepy 'someone is watching you' feeling I get every time I'm alone lately. Alright, not every time, but it feels close to it.

My phone vibrates in my apron pocket, startling me, and I jump, almost knocking over one of the many mops, brooms, and dusters leaning up in the corner. Quickly, I right it and hold it still. Even though it's dark in the closet, I close my eyes to hear better. *One Mississippi, two Mississippi, three Mississippi* . . . I count like the disturbance is lightning and Mom's the impending thunder, but I don't hear her rushing toward the sound.

Carefully, I slide my phone out of my pocket and, blinking against the brightness of it, find a text message.

UNKNOWN NUMBER:

Hey Leticia, it's Royal. I was checking in to see if you'd heard from Valor. He should have sent you a message yesterday or the day before about dinner arrangements.

That was so thoughtful. I save his number in my phone and reply.

LETICIA:

I did. Thank you! I appreciate you being so thorough. We're doing dinner tonight!

I don't expect a message back, but my phone vibrates almost instantly.

ROYAL:

You're most welcome. I know the holidays can be a difficult time to schedule something. I hope you're doing well.

Kitten heels clicking nearby against the terrazzo floors snap me back to my current task of hiding.

"Leticia?" Mom calls.

It sounds like she's by her bedroom. I quickly turn on the cleaning closet's light, using the overhead chain, and hurry, grabbing a microfiber duster and polishing supplies.

With a little bit of adjustment, I step out into the hallway as she gets to the closet.

"There you are." Mom looks me over from head to toe. "You're filthy. Your father and I are doing dinner at La Fatal Piedra. You're welcome to come if you get yourself presentable. We're leaving in twenty minutes."

I'm sweaty, gross, and need way longer than twenty minutes to make myself presentable to her standards. Plus, I have a whole three-course dinner, which they requested, practically done cooking downstairs in the kitchen.

I fight the frustration from my voice. "Oh, no, you and Dad go. I was going to Antonella's for dinner, remember?"

"Well, if you're sure you'd rather dine with *them* than us."

Mom doesn't even wait for me to confirm that I'm sure. She whisks away toward the staircase, all the while musing to herself, nothing that's loud enough for me to hear.

When the clicking of her footsteps stops echoing, I know she's on the rug in the living room and can't hear me anymore. I open the closet door and put the cleaning supplies away.

It's the feeling of eyes on me that has me pausing. I look beyond the door to see if I missed hearing Mom come back up the stairs, but no one is there. Back the other way down the hall, no doors are open and no one is standing there.

I'm going insane. Actually insane. I shake my head and close the closet.

But the feeling of being watched doesn't stop.

Or maybe we're being haunted.

Leticia

CHAPTER EIGHT

NO GARGOYLES

The driver is cautious on the driveway, maybe too cautious given it looks well plowed and maintained, but it's not like I drive a car, so how would I know?

The house is massive with big stone work and a high roofline. But it doesn't look as uninviting as I expected it to be. I tried to look it up on the navigation website, which shows you what the street and surrounding area look like, but you couldn't see the house from the road. Suspiciously, the guard shack and guards were edited out of existence. Or, maybe they're new?

The driver opens my door for me, and I step out into the cold, briskly walking over to the door.

Antonella opens it before I can even knock.

I squeal with delight, throwing my arms around her. Antonella hugs me back, squeezing tightly and demurely. But I'm quick to remember myself and take a small step back to appear polished. Valor must be lurking around here somewhere.

"I can't believe you live here," I whisper to her as I look around the house while I unzip my jacket.

The flooring is a mix of wood and carpet with rugs. The furnishings are a curated collection of traditional and more modern pieces. It's so different from the Romanesque style Dad and Mom decorate with. It's warm and welcoming, like you could actually touch the furniture and not get in trouble.

When Antonella takes my jacket and hangs it on the hook, I point back out the way I came. "I'm pretty sure there are gargoyles on the roof."

Antonella stifles a laugh and whispers with me. "No gargoyles, but there is a tortoise."

"On the roof?" I unzip my boots. *That's a weird house ornament.*

"Solarium." Antonella sighs and shakes her head.

She hooks my arm with hers, leading me deeper into the house. I get the distinct feeling of being watched and can only assume it's Valor behind us. I don't turn to look, afraid of seeing nothing. *Like the feelings I get back home.*

But Antonella does glance back over her shoulder and questions, "Okay, will you tell me how you planned this?"

I chance a look back and find the dark-eyed, dark-haired 'inquisitor' of the Irish Mob staring back at me. *The Valor Cavanagh.* Antonella's new husband is there behind us.

"That was all me." I giggle, trying to hide my fear. I draw a deep breath and pretend to be excited to tell the story and not scared out of my mind. "You see, it wasn't enough texting you every day, so I called up the Clark Enterprise office and pretended to be a vendor, started reading a bunch of technical jargon off the internet." I lie, trying to sound more intelligent than grabbing a random toaster manual. "And asked for answers or the person who would be in charge of this sort of top-secret project."

Antonella's head is pulled back in shock, and she's giving me the look that she gives Berto when she's finally getting the answers she's asked for. It's stunned but equally curious.

I talk faster, trying to finish the story. "The receptionist, after like, thirty minutes, transferred me to Royal, who was surprisingly nice and informal, and with a little flirting, I got him to have Valor call me back."

"Ha." Valor laughs, breaking some of the tension.

It's not even a full laugh, but instantly I feel more at ease.

I attempt to add some sass, putting my hand on my hip and giving him a look up and down. "What of that wasn't true? Because your receptionist, Margret, is very nice and, I say, deserves a raise if she regularly puts up with that bullshit."

"No, it's just that Royal was positive you weren't flirting with him," Valor explains while stooping in front of a wine fridge. He takes out a bottle of wine, offering the label out to Antonella.

She shakes her head and opens the fridge before pulling out three beers.

Oh, thank god, not another stuffy meal with wine pairings and small talk. I gesture to the bottles of beer with hopes I can have mine right away. If anything, to settle the remainder of my nerves. "You're going to make it so hard to go home if you spoil me like this."

"Beer goes better with the pork I'm making," Antonella explains to Valor and hands him a beer first.

He opens it without protest and then offers me the bottle.

"Thank you." I remember my manners, but the first sip doesn't dull my nerves quite fast enough.

I take more time to admire the large, but not entirely spacious, kitchen and the attached living area with views toward what must be outside seating and a patio. The walls are white but not stark. It feels like a home without being lived in.

I smile at Valor before directing myself back toward Antonella. "This is nice. A lot brighter than I was expecting, not that I would know because you're like the single-word answer queen." Tears threaten to breach my eyeballs, but I fight the urge. With a steadying breath, I relax a little more. I've always been vulnerable with Antonella, even if I can't help it. I lean into humor but express my real fears. "I'm not lying when Valor told me he had no problem with me coming to dinner tonight. I thought he was full of shit, and you'd be gone or something. Maybe chained up in the basement."

"I should have made it clearer that you were supposed to talk with your cousin." Valor's still smiling, but there's a crease in his brow. He looks between the two of us and takes a small step back, like we intimidate him. "Should I maybe give you two some space?"

"No," Antonella and I answer at the same time.

Hers is a bit snappier than mine. But I don't want to be accused of secret telling or for Antonella to be accused of hiding something from him. *Is she worried about the same thing?*

"Well." Valor nods slowly. "Leticia, you're welcome here anytime." He turns his attention to Antonella.

I swear to God, the way this man looks at her like she's becoming the love of his life melts my soul. *How can an arranged marriage lead to a love like that?* It's something I don't think will happen for me, but a tiny little butterfly of hope finds my heart.

"And, Antonella, anytime you'd like to see Leticia" —Valor gestures between the two of us— "you two can meet up in public if you'd prefer. I don't trust Gregorio or Berto and don't want you at their home without me, but I have no problem with you two speaking and getting together."

He's absolutely, one-hundred-percent correct that Dad and Berto can't be trusted. Valor doesn't need to know the bad things they've said about him. I don't know how this truce works, but if saying bad things about the other party violates it . . .

I hold the beer up, slightly blocking my mouth, and speak through clenched teeth with a cautionary melody. "It's so weird."

Antonella looks at me, cocking an eyebrow.

I keep my voice low while keeping my eyes trained on Valor. "He's almost normal. Toni, are you sure he's a Cavanagh? Did you look at his driver's license? Did you marry the wrong rich guy?"

Valor softly huffs, but Antonella answers with an eye roll. "Oh, I'm pretty sure he's the right rich guy." Her voice turns almost wistful as she finishes. "The Irish do things differently."

"Clearly," I accidentally mumble and cut off the rest of my thought—*because Dad would totally have Valor in the basement of the building, in the torture room they don't think I know about.*

"Daaaad!" a little girl calls from somewhere deeper in the house.

"Yes, Kerrianne?" Valor echoes back.

"Can I wear pants?" she shouts down the stairs.

"I told her one time that she had to wear a dress when company came over, and now we go through this every time she meets someone new," Valor explains, pinching the bridge of his nose for a moment before letting go. He answers back at a louder volume. "Yeah, pup. Pants are fine."

"Pup?" I squint. *What sort of nickname is that?*

Valor's face pales, not a lot but enough to let me know that I'm right to question it.

"Term of endearment. Kerrianne is kinda unique." Antonella is quick to explain but then tries to redirect. "You'll like her."

"Nope." I shake my head, looking between the two of them. "Bullshit meter is off the charts." I point to Valor. "He stiffened."

And I look Antonella over. I've known her forever, and it's obvious she's hiding something. *Something is wrong. Something is different.* I draw a steadying breath and pressure her. "You're about as subtle as a freight train. You're not actually offering an explanation. I wanna know."

The two of them share a series of looks. Something literally flashes in Valor's eyes. They almost turn a whole new color for a moment.

A gasp escapes my lips. *What the fuck did I see? What is going on? Is he on drugs? What's in this beer?*

The fight-or-flight part of my brain is currently flicking back and forth, unable to settle on a response. *What should I do? Calling Berto is absolutely out of the question. He only makes things worse.*

I feel hot all over and fluff my hair, trying to cool myself. *Keep it together. You're not in immediate danger. They're all the way in the city. It takes an hour to get here.*

"Leticia," Antonella calls, and I take my eyes off Valor for a second to watch her, hoping for an explanation. "Not tonight. But we will tell you later. When have I ever lied to you?"

Never. The answer is never, and she knows I know that's the case, but this is suspicious.

I narrow my gaze on Valor and pull out the scary voice that I always want to use with Mom. "I don't like this. I saw your eyes do something. If you're getting her messed up or on some shit, I'll be really pissed. I may have absolutely no skills to take you down myself, but don't think I can't come up with something."

"I swear to you, the only trouble Antonella will find herself in is whatever she chooses to walk into. She will always have a choice for an out." Valor steps closer to me, offering his hand. "I'll tell you in two weeks when you come back for dinner again, you have my word."

First, I didn't know I was coming back to dinner in two weeks.

Second, why do I believe him?

I move my beer from my right to my left hand and eye him with hopes that he'll see me as serious and not some woman he can brush off. I take his hand, and we shake. "Deal."

Awkward does not cover the way silence has filled the room. It's like that one time during church when Father Erickson forgot to mute his microphone and was in the sacristy complaining about Mrs. Bernsmith's cooking and how he was invited to dinner, again.

A small, brown-haired child comes running into the kitchen and breaks up our silence. She slides on stocking-clad feet, swinging her arms in big circles as she comes to a stop.

With a quick up and down look, she mimics her father's tense eyebrows and narrowing features. "I thought you said she was Antonella's cousin."

"I am." I pull my long blonde hair over my shoulder and then stand exactly the same way Antonella is, with my elbows bent and off to the side, demonstrating the similarities we share.

The little girl, Kerrianne Cavanagh, that Antonella called the truce over . . . is not impressed. *I want her to like me.*

I try to quickly come up with something a child might like to talk about, but I resort to my default for any conversation starter. "I like your outfit."

"Thanks! Tortoises are my favorite." Kerrianne holds out the corners of her T-shirt to show me better.

It's adorable with little tortoises mixed into the paisley print.

"I heard there's a tortoise here. Is he yours?" I set my beer down on the counter, hoping to see this mysterious tortoise for myself.

Kerrianne nods excitedly. "Let me introduce you to Captain! He's amazing."

With my hand snatched into hers, she leads me through the house. On one long wall in the hallway are dozens of family photos. The gallery-style wall features one big photo in the center.

I stop, consequently stopping Kerrianne on her path too.

She explains the picture. "That's Grandma and Grandpa and then Royal, he's my favorite uncle, and then me and Dad. We took that picture at Easter before our run. Grandma says it's her most favorite one we've ever taken."

Run? As in marathons? That hardly seems worth hiding.

I recognize all the faces but somehow get stuck looking at Royal's a bit longer. He's handsome with brown hair, and in the sunlight of the photo, it has a slight red tinge to it. It's a little lighter in color than Valor's, and he has striking greenish-brown eyes. He's tall and of medium build. In this picture, I can see how thick his arms and shoulders are.

Kerrianne pulls on my hand but lets me walk slowly so I can take in the photos. There are a lot of Kerrianne and Royal together. It's clear he's a big part of their lives and really is a bright spot. He's smiling in every photo, and it looks so genuine, not the forced smiles of a family playing nice.

Why can't I have that? My soul craves that light and positivity. *If Antonella can have it, why can't I? Why can't it be this way?*

I force my attention off the photographs and happy families and back to Kerrianne. She chatters about the tortoise, and I try to keep up with the facts as they come hurtling at me at a million miles an hour.

We get to a large glass door with what looks like a tropical oasis on the inside. A distinct reptile smell hits my nose as Kerrianne pushes the door open.

She drops my hand and walks over to her tortoise. I follow her, watching my step for anything unsavory.

Captain is as adorable as a tortoise might be. He takes a big bite out of some romaine lettuce, looking at me slowly as if he's judging me.

"Captain is old, like super old. Like double how old you are." Kerrianne explains, crouching down and running a delicate hand over Captain's shell. "Wait, how old are you?"

"Twenty-three," I reply automatically.

"Yeah, so at least one times twenty-three." She shakes her head. "But I don't know two times twenty-three. I'll have to ask Antonella later."

"That's a good plan." I nod. I'm incredibly out of my depth looking at the little creature, realizing maybe I'm not a pet person. And as nice as this expedition is, it's not why I'm here. "Captain is very nice, but it looks like he's enjoying his dinner. I bet our dinner is done. Want to go see?"

Kerrianne leads the way back to the kitchen, where Valor and Antonella are standing a little closer together than you'd expect from near strangers. They've only been married for nearly two weeks.

Valor's arm is wrapped around Antonella, and his hand is definitely down below her low back, their chests pressed together. I can feel the sexual tension from here. That sort of connection isn't something I've seen outside of movies. I'm not sure they want Kerrianne to see such 'love' in the air. Maybe she wouldn't understand it, but better safe than sorry? Quickly, I move to try to put my hands in front of Kerrianne's eyes to block her view.

"Ope! Looks like I was wrong and dinner isn't ready yet," I call out loudly before us. My offhanded inner thought slips out. "Though your dad might eat Antonella if it isn't done soon."

Kerrianne stops walking, and I nearly run into her. She looks up at me with a giggle. "We don't eat people."

No one addresses that statement, and that doesn't sit well with me. *Pup? Eating people? What. The. Fuck.* Something isn't right here. I want to ask again, but I shook with Valor. This keeps getting weirder. *Are they some sort of cannibals? No, she said they don't eat people. Maybe it's a kid thing? No. I can't see any of our cousins . . . No, Donovan would totally say something like that.*

"Kerrianne, do you want to set the table?" Valor is waving Kerrianne over in what feels like a distraction.

"Okay." Kerrianne holds her arms out in front of her in a dramatically begrudging way.

I follow her, crossing the kitchen and offering my arms equally stretched out to help.

Valor looks at me, almost confused.

Before he can get sassy, I cut him off, hand going up to my chest for a moment. "What? In the last year, I've cooked all but five of the family meals. The least I can do is set the table."

Valor hands me a stack of silverware, and I shrug. "Thank you."

I follow Kerrianne into the dining room and circle the table with her.

"I like you. You're funny, and you make Dad stop talking sometimes." Kerrianne smiles up at me. "Are we going to be friends?"

"Well, we're already family. I don't see why we can't be friends too." I offer my hand out to her, and she leads me back toward the kitchen.

That is, unless you're lying about the eating people thing.

Leticia

CHAPTER NINE

THE PRINCESS RETURNS TO THE CASTLE

I didn't want to put my coat on to leave, but stepping out into the cold night air, I couldn't wait to get into the warm SUV. Dad's driver arrived the standard twenty minutes early, but Antonella and I have been doing the Midwestern goodbye for thirty minutes.

With the promise of getting to see her again, it's the only reason I agree to leave.

I look at my phone. After a full three hours of not looking at it, you'd assume I'd have a bunch of notifications or at least some concern or worry about how dinner is going.

Nope.

I have three notifications.

Mom, reminding me that I need to make fresh pasta for her 'get-together.'

Berto, asking if I needed backup, but he never followed up when I didn't answer.

The third though . . .

ROYAL:

Did you have fun at the boring Cavanaghs' house?

It's not the funniest sentence in the world, and yet I'm already smiling.

LETICIA:

Thank you, I had a lovely time. I'm sorry I didn't message you back. I was caught up in something.

ROYAL:

Well, you could make it up to me by texting with me now?

That feels almost scandalous when he puts it like that. My eyes flick to the driver up front. He's listening to the sports channel on the radio and thankfully doesn't notice my cheeks flushing.

LETICIA:

And what on earth would we text about?

ROYAL:

Well, I'm so lonely I would be glad to listen to more of your manuals if you have one with you.

I stifle a snort and try to come up with a response. Valor's statement comes back to my brain and shuts down the fun. *Royal was positive you weren't flirting with him.*

We're extended family. I text with extended family all the time. I'm probably bad at flirting because I don't ever get to do it. I could really use a friend though.

LETICIA:

Well, sadly I'm away from my manuals. Though I bet I could get the car specs out of the glove box if you'd like.

ROYAL:

It's a coffee maker I'm in the mood for, I'm afraid. Water elements and filters, maybe a self-contained heating element.

I roll my lips between my teeth to stop my smile from spreading and alerting the driver to something 'unusual' happening. I quickly type back a response.

LETICIA:

Sorry, fresh out. Still heading back from Valor's. I'll be home and in the kitchen though in about an hour.

He doesn't respond right away.

Did I do the wrong thing telling him that? My heart skips a beat seeing him finally texting me back after too many minutes of silence.

ROYAL:

Sorry, didn't mean to leave you on read. You're headed into the kitchen after you get home? Did Valor forget to feed you as part of 'dinner at his house' or???

I swear I can't let him do anything by himself.

LETICIA:

Antonella is a great cook. Dinner was divine, but I have food prep for an event for Mom and her friends.

I'm already dreading it. But if I premeasure all the ingredients and get them ready to go for all of me, myself, and I in the morning, the special get-together will be much easier. On me anyway.

ROYAL:

Do the D'Medicis not use caterers?

I snort, covering it with a cough so the driver doesn't ask questions, and roll my eyes before answering.

LETICIA:

Catering? For authentic Italian food served in the most esteemed Gregorio D'Medici's home? It doesn't matter that La Fatel Piedra is an authentic Italian restaurant. No, it all must be made by a D'Medici to be real.

After I send it, the realization that I may have said too much rises up from my toes to my head, and I go to send another message to clarify that I'm not complaining, but Royal beats me to it.

ROYAL:

I'll stay up with you, if you'd like. I'm up working on a project too. Mine is more boring. If you want, we could even call.

It'll be almost midnight when I get home. Surely, he doesn't mean that. But it would be rude to not text him back.

LETICIA:

You want to stay up well after midnight while I prep ingredients for tomorrow morning? It could take hours.

There's a lull in texting, and I'm sure Royal has realized the insanity of that. Though a small part of me liked the possibility. My inside joy feels squashed and discarded.

A few seconds later, a notification lights up my phone.

CALENDAR INVITE:

Late Nite Bytes with R&L

A late-night virtual soiree of Italian food in byte-size pieces hosted by the second siblings of Casa D'Medici and the Illinois Irish.

To confirm your reservation send "YES"

"Everything alright back there, Miss D'Medici?" The driver examines me in the rearview mirror.

Did I laugh out loud? I quickly cover it up. "Yes, everything's fine, just a funny meme."

He turns his eyes back to the road, no longer concerned.

"You could turn the radio up a bit if you'd like." I leave off the sassy 'I don't mean to disturb you' that I want to snark.

This guy is Dad's driver, and he doesn't work for me. He works for Dad and will probably report back everything that happens.

The volume goes up almost immediately.

I let my fingers hover over the keyboard. I should say no. But everyone will be asleep, and I know for a fact that you can't hear anything blaring in the kitchen up in Mom and Dad's room. In his room, Berto can't hear anything coming from the kitchen either, especially not over the three fans and his television.

LETICIA:

YES

ROYAL:

Tap the link when you're home and ready. Can't wait to hang out with you.

Another message comes in with a link for a well-known conference call software.

Heat brushes my face and neck. I wiggle my toes in my shoes, venting the schoolgirlish giggles that I have. *Why does this feel like a date? It's just a phone call.*

My reaction is irrational and completely uncalled for. I'm not allowed to date, and if I was, it certainly wouldn't be with Royal Cavanagh.

I don't even know if he likes me. It could simply be him being nice.

It's two acquaintances hanging out in the late hours of the night.

Logic can call it that all it wants, but the butterflies in my stomach say otherwise.

CHAPTER TEN

LATE NITE BYTES

She said yes. I can't believe she said yes.

Obviously she was going to say yes. My wolf wags his tail in anticipatory excitement.

Some dumbass started his thirty-hour 3D print job in the morning rather than in the evening. Which means said dumbass has to be up late when the custom modifications on an order of high-caliber sniper rifles finish cooling to start another load.

It's me. I'm the dumbass.

Out here in one of our warehouses, I have a temperature-controlled office specifically for these machines. The setup is similar to my main office, but it's not as fancy and has the various 3D printers. Being away from home late at night isn't great, but there's only so much room in Mom and Dad's basement.

The cool-down timer is keeping perfect time, but my brain is making it seem as though seconds are dragging. I check the camera feed in Casa D'Medici again. The SUV hasn't pulled up to the parking garage yet.

I absolutely hate that I can't track where she is. I'm so used to having everyone I care for at my fingertips that now with her, I feel reverted back to the time of dial-up internet that cut off the telephone to the house, playing video games with a wired controller, and, god forbid, printing driving directions.

Should I feel guilty for putting spyware in the link I sent her for this call? I don't feel guilty. When she clicks the link, I'll have access to her phone, everything she does on it, and her location at all times.

It's necessary. My wolf doesn't care about guilt, only that we have the access.

I look at the screen, watching the parking garage again.

If I should feel guilty, I absolutely don't. It's not like I'll sell her data to a third party.

The timer on my printer beeps, signaling that it's done, and the door auto unlocks. I start to unload it and quality inspect each piece. After every piece, I look for the SUV I saw on Valor's home security system to turn up at the parking garage.

I've packed up the entire batch when the SUV finally pulls up out front of the skyscraper that the D'Medici's own in Gold Coast. The driver opens her door for her, and she steps out, the black parka covering her beautiful blue dress. Her blonde hair spills out over the dark fabric, and it catches the artificial light, making it look like liquid gold.

In a few short steps, the doorman opens the front door to the building. I didn't expect her to use the formal front entrance, but it makes more sense when I flick to the lobby's interior camera view.

Berto and Gregorio are standing in the lobby waiting for her.

The hair on the back of my neck rises. *Why hadn't I thought to check in on them while she wasn't home?* I force myself to forget that thought. I can't monitor everyone at every second of the day.

"Dad? Berto? What's wrong? Where's Mom?" Leticia looks back and forth between them.

The lobby camera is doing its job flawlessly.

"She's in bed, let's go upstairs." Gregorio gestures for Leticia to lead the way.

They bypass the front elevators and head straight to the penthouse executive one. The elevator camera doesn't have sound, but it doesn't matter because no one is talking.

They don't make it two feet into the house before they pounce. The foyer camera picks up the video feed and collects audio as it bounces around the space in an echo.

Her brother demands first, "What did you learn at dinner?"

"Valor's house is nice and Antonella seems happy." Leticia

answers quickly and quietly. "Is that all this is? You're questioning me because I had dinner with Antonella?"

"And Valor Cavanagh." Gregorio, her father, adds to her statement. "What did you talk about?"

"Antonella's job, what it's like learning to spell a new last name, Kerrianne's tortoise, and how good the food was." She rattles off the highlights of dinner.

And us. My wolf tries to add. He should see the conversation for what it is: an interrogation.

It sets my jaw tight.

"Don't be silly. Surely he pushed you for information on us." Gregorio narrows his eyes as he steps toward her.

Why should she tell you what they talked about? Is it a truce or isn't it, Gregorio? I debate starting a recording.

See how she handles it first. My wolf encourages me to have faith in her.

"Honestly, I don't think Antonella gives two cares in the world what you're doing. You're the one who forced her to be married off when she called the truce, and she's forgotten your existence." Leticia is fierce, making her dad take a second and putting him on his heels.

Atta girl. I smile but then see the cracks in her armor. Tight shoulders and clenched fingers. It's false bravado.

"Surely she asked for any information at all." Berto wraps an arm around her and leads her from the foyer to a formal sitting room. I bring up the camera feed and hear what must be the tail end of a question. "Even something small like how we're doing?"

"The only time you came up was when she asked if I was still going to Christmas in Italy or if I was staying home." Leticia shrugs him off and, with a yawn, perches on the arm of the sofa.

"Of course you're coming to Christmas." Gregorio tosses his head as if insulted.

"But do I have to? I don't exactly travel the greatest." Leticia is different at that moment. Like she's lying.

Making excuses to stay home? My wolf cants his head, first one way and then the other.

"I get so sick, and you're only gone for two and a half weeks. I'll spend most of the time puking my guts up and being exhausted."

Leticia places her hand over her stomach as if to prove her point. "It's hardly any fun for anyone."

"This is true." Gregorio paces back and forth across the room. "We can't have that. You should stay home."

Leticia stiffens. Perhaps surprised?

I lean in to watch more closely.

Then she looks at Berto, it's just the slightest move of her head, maybe to not draw attention. Suspicious maybe?

But when neither man moves or makes any corrections, she gestures off into the penthouse toward the kitchen, stepping away from the two men. "Well, that's settled then. Am I dismissed? Can I prepare for tomorrow?"

"Yes. I'm off to bed." Gregorio draws a deep breath and lets out the most exaggerated yawn I've ever seen.

I split my monitor view and follow Gregorio and Berto as they head to the second floor of the penthouse, presumably to their bedrooms, and Leticia as she walks through the grandeur of the first floor to the kitchen.

After a few steps, she heads back to the foyer, takes off her jacket, hangs up her purse, and pulls out her phone.

In contrast to the beauty of the flowy dress, she crouches down to almost her knees and lurks around the staircase, nearly getting down on all fours and going up to the top to look down the hallway.

She sees what I see — closed doors and family members tucked away.

She pumps her fist once before sneaking back down the stairs and, at the bottom, dusts off the dress skirt and walks much more confidently back to the kitchen.

Smart girl. My wolf thuds his tail and lies down, less alarmed by the ambush she walked into.

But will she still call? An empty ache settles in my body. I leave the volume on for the call system I sent her the invite through, but rather than wait and be disappointed, I busy myself with setting up the next print run.

The generic call alert filters through my speakers right as I open the container of cleaning solution. I almost drop it when I rush back to my chair. I click accept as fast as I can but try to compose myself.

"Hello and welcome to the air. I'm your host, Royal." I try to play the funny guy on the radio station, but now I'm wondering if she'll understand the joke.

"And I'm Leticia, and this is Late Nite Bytes." She finishes as if we've done this a dozen times before. She pulls her phone away from her ear, and I see the telltale tap of selecting speakerphone.

"So, Leticia, how's your night? Get home okay?" I try to probe without being suspicious.

She sighs, and I open up the view of the kitchen, where she's tying on an apron.

"I'm fine. Home is fine. I got the third degree from Dad and Berto when I came home, but that's expected. They can't accept that the truce happened and there is no ulterior motive anymore." Her voice isn't as crisp through speakerphone.

There isn't? I keep that as an inside thought. She doesn't need to know that I still plan on helping Valor get revenge for some of the terrible things the D'Medicis have done. They don't relate to her.

"Well, no ulterior motive here. I'm glad to have someone to keep me company."

I double-check that the malware I sent to her phone is capturing the data I need while sliding on my headset.

"Yeah." Her voice leaves the speakers and transmits through my headset. "What are you doing up so late? Or is it a classified type project?"

"I'm doing a 3D printing run on some metal pieces for a modification on— It's parts for guns." I opt to avoid overwhelming her with unnecessary information.

"Hey, you don't have to simplify it for me. I've got a complete understanding of mechanical kitchen gadgets," she sasses, and it's the adorable, fun kind, not the defensiveness that she has with her father.

"It's a modification for a sniper rifle's trigger system that causes less wear and tear on the gun and helps maintain accuracy. The other modifications like it on the market aren't much better than the original product, but I found a way to alter it so that it's a steadier squeeze rather than a sharp jerk." I explain the basics without trying to brag.

"Dang, cute and smart," Leticia says softly.

She said we're cute. My wolf preens.

I look at the camera and see her with a scale and bowl, measuring something. "Cute and smart? Are you talking about yourself?"

"Pft," Leticia huffs, and she blows her bangs out of her face. "No, I hardly count for either of those things. Just now I forgot to put my hair up before opening the flour container. Luckily, I caught it before I got dirty." Mesmerized, I watch as she puts it first into a ponytail and then into a messy bun. "And now to put you in my ears."

"In your ears?" I joke, but I know she means her earbuds, and I long for the more crisp sound of her voice.

"There. Much better," Leticia says before a soft yawn.

"So, what are you cooking tonight?" I force myself to turn away from the monitor and get back to work. Otherwise, I'll be here literally all night.

"I'm doing the prep work for tomorrow morning. It's too early to start most things, like the fresh pasta. But I get it all measured out so it's dump and cook." She makes a clanging noise on her end.

"What are you cooking tomorrow?" I just want to hear her voice.

But I also think Leticia is probably a fantastic cook, and maybe I can order something similar tomorrow for food and pretend like we're eating the same thing at the same time.

For a moment, Leticia hums a little melody I haven't heard before, but I immediately love it. "Three kinds of ravioli, two different sauces, two fresh salads, a soup, and mini panettone."

"Oh, is that all?" I'm floored by the sizable task at hand. "Who are you, Juliette Child?"

"That's not— You know what? Never mind." I can imagine her waving a hand dismissively at my error. "But of course not, she didn't care for Italian cooking anyway."

I want to look over at her and watch her speak, but I force myself to stay turned away from the screen.

Leticia helps by continuing to explain. "But this is Mom's big event for the season. She throws something almost every year and acts like it's this total surprise and then is totally last minute about it. I guess what's worse is I just let it happen. I pretend it isn't happening and then rush around on her timetable to make it all work. She likes to go all out. Now that I'm old enough — trusted enough — to make it happen, I get the kitchen to myself."

"So you like cooking for everybody?" I keep wiping down the machine I'm working on, clearing the dust and debris away.

"I don't hate it, but it would be nice if, once in a while, someone told me to take the whole day off." She seems so sad.

I look over at the screen and find her having weighed out multiple bowls of flour and moving on to the next task, which looks like packages of meats from the refrigerator.

We can provide for our mate. My wolf shakes with delight. *You will learn to cook.*

I drop the rag I was wiping with and knock over a small stand of tools. Everything clatters to the ground around me.

Excuse me, our mate? We— I—

"Everything okay?" Leticia's voice pitches with worry.

"Yeah. Yup. Mhm." My voice is all over the place, and I put a hand over my racing heart to try and focus. I get better control over myself and answer her better. "I was clumsy and knocked over a cart of cleaning supplies."

"Oh gosh." I look over at the monitor. She places a hand on her heart, and we're doing the same thing. "Had me worried there that something bad happened."

Our mate is worried about us. My wolf uses that damn word again.

"Nah." I brush it off and try to reassure her of our safety. "A materials cart. This location is safe. Deep in Cavanagh territory. Someone would have to be really stupid to come all the way out here. We don't even keep inventory here."

We haven't even met her. We can't be her mate. Most of the time, humans don't have wolf mates. I try all the arguments, flimsy ones and real ones, but my heart is siding with the wolf. Before I can even stop the decline down the slippery slope, it feels like I'm already at rock bottom.

I want her.

Bad.

"What's it like living in the country?" Leticia asks innocently and completely unaware of my brain going full meltdown mode.

"It's nice." I force myself to move and start cleaning up what I dropped. "I like the open spaces, it's really good for running."

"Mmm. I never understood running as a hobby. Kerrianne said you're a whole family of runners. Marathons or what?" I look over at her on the screen. She's measuring out spoonfuls of something into a plastic bowl full of meat.

"I mean, it's more like we enjoy nature walks but fast-forward?" I leave out the 'with four feet' and 'hunting' part of the usual family activities.

"Oh, well, that could be fun. But doesn't the running scare the furry woodland creatures?" Leticia keeps working on the screen, and her ability to multitask is clearly better than mine.

We could show her furry woodland creatures! My wolf is so excited over the idea. He starts picking out the best trails in the nature preserve.

We're a furry woodland creature, you nitwit. I keep picking up and finally finish the wipe down I had started as I answer Leticia. "Nah, you have to be quiet about it. Most of them don't care as long as you leave them alone."

"Good to know," Leticia says before she lets out a big sigh. I don't have long to mull it over because she groans, "Ugh. Do I slice the romaine tonight or wait until tomorrow?"

"How much prep do you have left?" I look at the twenty minutes or so of work I have left to do, even though I know deep in my soul that I'll stay up with her as late as she does.

"A lot." Leticia sighs. "I've done the measuring for the pasta and the filling for one of the ravioli. I have time to do one of the fillings tomorrow because it has bacon I need to fry." She lists off her work, and the more she talks, the more tired she sounds.

"Save the lettuce for tomorrow. It'll be better freshly cut anyway." I wish I was there to help her, but showing up there in the middle of the night would cause way more questions than I'd like to answer.

Just tell —

I'm not telling her that I'm her mate. She doesn't even know you exist. I cut him off.

"Good plan." Leticia yawns softly. "Alright, I have to prep the soup, then."

"Let's do it. While we do it, what do you do in your spare time? Aside from reading old appliance manuals." I snap open one of the panel doors to check filament levels.

"Mmm . . . Well, now see, here's the thing, you've caught me. That *is* all I do in my spare time." She giggles for a minute before I hear the chopping of a knife against a cutting board. It's fast and efficient, but I don't turn to look. "But I listen to audiobooks while I'm cooking and cleaning. I'm studying to get my bachelor's degree, but that'll come to an end soon enough."

"Oh, what's your degree in?"

I should know this about her by now. Her GPA, her teachers, her class schedule, the buildings she goes to . . . It frustrates me not to know it. But with my workload for all the jobs I do in a day, I'm running on fumes and don't have time for passion projects and in-depth stalking. *Just the bare-minimum surveillance kind.*

It's not stalking if it's your mate. My wolf supplies. *It's concerned observations.*

I try to shut him out of the conversation. *Enough of that mate talk.*

"Communications. I know it's silly, but I knew it wouldn't be too hard, and it was something to do so that Dad wouldn't marry me off right after high school." She sounds annoyed and on edge.

"Sore subject?" I probe, filling the last filament and moving on to the next machine.

"I don't mean to dump on you." Leticia tries to brush it off, but there's undeniable tension there.

"It's not dumping if I asked."

I want to beg her to tell me. I want to tell her that communication isn't a silly degree field and that I want to hear everything about her. *Don't scare her, Royal.*

"I don't want to be someone's wife. I know logically that's what I'm destined for. But part of me wonders if there isn't something out there I could do that doesn't involve being a made man's wife."

I stop what I'm doing on the second machine and sit down in my chair to watch her work. Leticia is putting one slow cooker next to another on the counter.

How much soup is she making?

"I can't imagine what that's like, not knowing what the course of your life will look like."

"It's not the same for you? You're not just waiting to be married off at the first opportune moment for a good deal?" Leticia's laugh is dry and humorless.

"No, our family kinda believes in soul mates." I way overgeneralize.

Oh, so you get to talk about mates? My wolf rolls his eyes with disapproval.

"But Valor had an arranged marriage?" Leticia starts dumping what looks like homemade meatballs out of a gallon bag into each slow cooker.

"It's a little different when your kid is on the line." I play with the desk's chipping fake-wood surface.

Leticia keeps working, pouring containers of liquid into the pots. "That makes a big difference. What about you though? Waiting for *the* one?"

Found her. My wolf pushes hard at the idea. Practically begging me to tell her.

"Yeah, something like that. You know how it is, your world is so small in this life." I hope what I'm saying is relatable to her, despite my double meaning. "So few people get to know about what it is we do and who we are. It makes it hard to find *the* one among such a finite number of people."

"Mmmmm." Leticia is tying twigs of spices together. "And then you get all these people who want to be with you because of who your parents are and get all weird about it?"

"Yes!" I relax into my chair, happy with her understanding. I know we're talking about completely different worlds, but at least some things — nepotism — are a universal language.

"How much work do you have left?" Leticia puts the lids on her slow cookers.

"All done." I lie. I've got another ten minutes left, but she looks too tired to stay up much longer.

Leticia pulls her apron off over the top of her head and hangs it on a hook. "Are you sure? I can stay up for a little bit."

"No, chef. I'm sure." I throw in one last joke. "Get some sleep, you've had a long day."

"Oh." Leticia hesitates, tapping her phone screen, then drumming her fingers on the countertop.

"Well, if you want to talk some other time, you have my number. Just say the word." I reassure her.

Anytime. All the time. My wolf agrees.

"I'll do that." Leticia is much more upbeat. "Good night, Royal."

"Good night, Leticia." I let her disconnect the call.

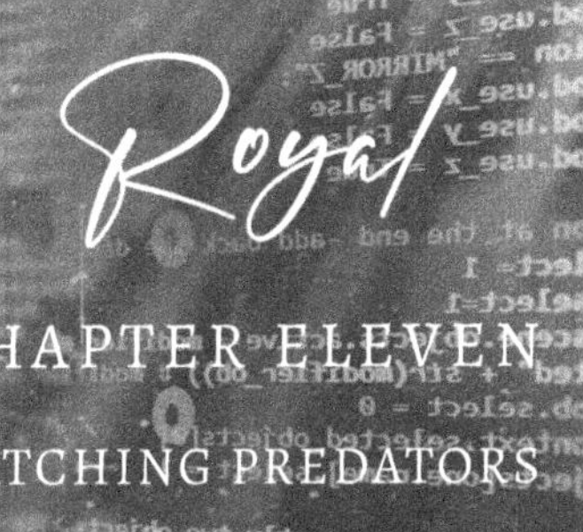

Royal

CHAPTER ELEVEN

CATCHING PREDATORS

It's well after noon when I roll out of bed. The small clock on my desk, illuminating the numbers, tells me I've way overslept.

I was too wired to sleep after talking to her, so I stayed up to start additional print jobs to have a fuller inventory. I'm paying for it now though. I find the small remote on my nightstand and press the first programmed button. It pulls the bottom of my blinds up in small intervals every couple of minutes.

I'm a wolf and can see in the dark, but if it's dark, my brain will let me sleep until it's not dark anymore. Without looking, I feel around on the nightstand for my phone, but it's not there. Shuffling, I look for it amid the sheets and comforter but groan when I remember hearing a thud when I finally flopped into bed. Looking over the edge, I see the device. At least it's plugged in and charging.

It takes some effort, but I manage to hook the corner of it with my middle finger and pull it close enough to pick up.

On a normal morning, I can wake up to anywhere between ten and two hundred notifications. Depending on what I sleep through.

There are the usual three or four from Mom and Dad, with their plans for the day and asking me if I'm alive. Two quick replies clear those off the pile.

There are a couple from Kerrianne asking about her robot, along with a picture of Captain. I agree that Captain is dashing in his radish hat and let her know that I'll have more info on the parts later.

Valor sent me a 'honey-do' list of projects he's working on and what parts he'd like me to take care of. I give him a thumbs-up.

Notifications regarding several tech upgrades having been completed and a dozen or so from the 3D print shop get deleted without looking, and I make it all the way to something I didn't expect to find.

LETICIA D'MEDICI:

Thank you for last night, it meant a lot to me.

Not if that sounded weird though. I didn't mean it to be weird. If it sounded weird, I just mean thank you.

There is something about dinner that's bugging me . . . could you tell me what the family secret is? Valor said he'd tell me in two weeks, but I'm getting super frustrated every time I think about it. There's something weird about Kerrianne saying 'we don't eat people' AND Valor calling her pup. I don't know if it passes the vibe check, and I'm hoping it's not cannibalism or something. We're friends and late-night cohosts, so you should tell me.

Or at least give me a heads-up so I don't show up next time and get eaten or look stupid thinking the worst.

We could eat her. My wolf salivates, and I try to push the dirty thoughts of Leticia out of my mind.

I read her next text instead of indulging him in that thought.

LETICIA:

Please tell me you're not cannibals and it's just something funny Kerrianne said.

I snort and click into the three images she sent a few hours later. They're pictures of beautifully plated Italian food.

Now, I'm the one salivating.

Our mate could cook us that? We could –

I shove the wolf down. We haven't met her in person. We can't be sure we're mates. He's overly attached. This is attraction to a beautiful woman, and the chemistry will change when we meet face to face.

I go back to the third message. *Valor is going to tell her the family secret? How the fuck did he mess up that badly?*

A rock sits in my middle, and it's cooling me from the inside out.

Mom, Dad, and Valor have no mention of it in their messages. Kerrianne didn't note anything off about her dinner with Leticia.

I let those thoughts ruminate as I stretch and slowly make my way out of bed. But by the time I've stretched out and stared at my closet for a minute, trying to remember what clothes are, I don't have any answers, and I push them out of my brain to focus on joining the rest of the world.

"Royal. You never answered your brother back." Mom sighs as I ascend the stairs to the kitchen in search of food.

"I sent him a thumbs-up that I'd start working on his to-do list," I say as I head toward whatever she's working on to see what I can steal.

Mom bats my hand away from the food, raw green beans, in front of her. "These are for dinner, or did you forget we're doing Thanksgiving dinner again tonight. The redo."

"I remember." I don't, but no way am I getting caught slacking on everything. "What's got Valor's boxers in a bunch?"

Mom stops working and turns to face me. "You didn't read that message at all."

"I was going to grab a snack and then go down and start working." I raise my hands in defense.

"Christ, Royal." Mom grabs a towel off the counter and chucks it at me.

"What?!" I snatch it out of the air but grab my phone from my pocket before she throws something heavier.

VALOR:

Take the information you gave me yesterday from the guy, Marc, and work backward. The guy has videos circulating on the internet of teenage girls changing. Antonella is included.

Find me where they've been distributed and who I need to dispose of.

I want this done: yesterday.

My blood turns cold. Doing recon on someone Valor was pressing for information was just supposed to be mundane work. I knew Valor planned to use the guy as a warning to others who might double-cross us, but to show Antonella his darker side . . . That is wholly unexpected.

"Jesus." I tuck my phone back in my pocket, fighting off a shiver.

My wolf is already pulling a mental list of codes and things we'll need to get the job done.

My appetite is now completely gone.

"I'm going." I turn back toward the basement, tossing the towel on the counter as I go.

Time to hunt. My wolf wags his tail, all too excited about stalking a new kind of prey.

Three hours into deleting videos of teenage girls changing and showering from hard drives all across the city, state, and country, I feel dirty for having to live in a world where this happened to start with. With a ring of disgusting individuals being tallied up and added to Valor's list of 'next to die,' he won't stop at those who have seen his wife. My older brother has zero tolerance and will go as far and as deep as necessary.

No one deserves to have videos of themselves like this floating around on the internet. Antonella is, from what I can tell, kind and compassionate. It's absolutely not a question for me to take the time to do this for her.

I've set up a spy bot that goes far beyond what Valor noted, deleting and stripping files from every linked perpetrator on Marc's 'friends list,' dating back over a decade. Some of these predators go back a lot longer than that. It catalogs their names and locations as well as how much was deleted from their computers . . . in case Valor wants to be creative with his pound of flesh, so to speak.

I've been so dedicated to working quickly and thoroughly that I blocked out the entire world, including my wolf. But an alarm starts blaring, and I rip myself out of my chair, rushing to the wall where I have three tablets set up for different perimeter securities.

On the alarming tablet, I flick to the open notification.

The camera feed of a security panel at one of our weapons caches, on one of the farthest edges of our territory, comes into view.

Fuckin' Uncle Neil. What is he even doing out that far? I turn off the alarm since he's fat fingering the code as he attempts to punch it in . . . again. *Why does Dad keep him as pack second if he can't handle a damn passcode? Valor would do a much better job.*

"Thanks, Royal," he says with a wave to the camera as he gains entry.

I microphone in. "Welcome. Text me next time. You about gave me a heart attack with too many wrong attempts like that."

"Will do, kiddo."

I groan at the nickname but walk away from the wall.

What the fuck is he doing out at that cache?

My wolf is back, alert and in the forefront of my consciousness. *Our mate will make us feel better.* He pushes me to look at my phone.

But without logic, I pick up Antonella's clone first, which Valor had me set up to keep tabs on his new wife.

She has a few texts from other people, but I don't bother reading those. I home in on Leticia's texts to Antonella.

LETICIA TO ANTONELLA:

Mom is driving me literally insane.

Dad already said I don't have to go to Italy, but she's insisting that I do.

Is there any chance I could get invited to Cavanagh Christmas as some sort of good faith . . . joining-of-the-family type deal? Cause I REALLY don't want to go to Italy.

You should see the dress Mom bought me for Christmas Eve Mass. It's like she thinks I'm a little girl. It. Has. A. Bow. ON. THE BUTT.

On the butt? My wolf tries to pull mental images of what Leticia's backside looks like from all the security footage we've watched of her.

I wish I wasn't on his side of trying to remember what it looks like. But we've mostly seen her in soft, flowy skirts and nothing that gives either of us an idea of the curves.

She sends a picture of a shapeless kind of frock with what looks to be a big red satin bow somewhere toward the lower midsection.

"Yikes." I cringe.

Don't get distracted by the dress. My wolf is nudging me to close out of the picture that he just demanded I open. He changes his focus so quickly my head is spinning. *Our mate wants to see us for Christmas.*

I set the cloned phone down and pick mine up to send her a message.

ROYAL:

I'm the worst cohost, and friend, for not texting you back this morning. Got pulled into an awful job first thing.

Forgive me?

I don't expect a message back, but it doesn't stop me from hoping.

I stretch and move my desk to the standing position, opening up the D'Medicis' penthouse cameras on my second computer's monitors.

The facial recognition software I use starts flicking through cameras to find her when my phone buzzes.

LETICIA:

You're forgiven. But seriously . . . It's driving me crazy. Family secret?

Smiling to myself, I send her a message back.

ROYAL:

How crazy?

She's not on any of the main camera feeds. I hesitate for a minute. *Invasion of privacy. The reason you locked this camera was so people wouldn't be able to watch her.*

My own logic doesn't stop me from throwing the password into the locked channel and instantly pulling up her bedroom's feed.

Seeing her safe in her room warms my insides and awakens the parts of myself I've deadened to get work done. After a few seconds of watching her, I'm already feeling lighter.

I take in her room and try to find changes. The most obvious is the ugly Christmas dress in plastic, hung up on the back of her bedroom door.

Leticia is flopped down on the bed, like she walked over and threw herself butt first onto it. Her feet hang off over the side, her phone held up above her face.

I look back down at my phone and find what she must have sent.

LETICIA:

I mean, not enough that it's distracting me from getting stuff done, but I'm definitely not not thinking about it.

ROYAL:

I don't know, are you ready to handle the truth?

What if we're a secret cult and there's some naked moon dancing involved? Are you ready for that kind of truth?

I don't love lying to her, but it's not my place to tell her the family secret, and it's not something Valor mentioned to me directly. For all I know, he'll manufacture a fake secret to get her off his case. Thus, the two-week comment.

LETICIA:

Bahaha, fine. You win. Don't tell me. What did you do today?

ROYAL:

Working on some dark web shit. I really don't want to talk about it. Distract me?

Make me forget there's anything bad in the world. The thought unsettles me in a new way. *What if there's more than simply keeping an eye on the newly minted family 'friend' and more to do with . . .*

I look at the phone screen and see an indicator of typing. The bubbles show up, and I expect a message to come through, but the dancing dots stop. On the monitor, Leticia has rolled to her stomach and is shuffling forward on to the bed.

It's not a sexy maneuver by any means, but her, in bed, has my blood pumping, and now, with her skirt flat at her sides, it's clear her ass doesn't need a big bow to draw attention to it.

When did I get to be such a horndog?

She looks at her phone for another moment before tapping a spot on the screen.

A message comes through.

LETICIA:

Well, you've asked the most boring person in the world to distract you. I left my user manuals in the kitchen.

With a smile, I know exactly what to say. I disconnect the laptop from the displays and take it, with her room's feed on display, over to my bed. I mimic how she's lying before sending back a message of my own.

ROYAL:

Ahh, so you escaped the kitchen?

LETICIA:

Fortunately, I've escaped until at least tomorrow morning. If I'm lucky, until tomorrow afternoon. The parents have other brunch plans before their flight to Italy and Berto is busy.

Mimicking her position is incredibly uncomfortable for me. I roll back over, choosing to look only at my phone rather than both screens. Dragging down the top corner of my phone, I check the clock. It's only two hours before dinner, meaning Valor and Kerri-anne will be here soon with Antonella.

A little downtime with our mate won't make the computer run the program slower. My wolf argues.

I had been assisting the bot and running other tasks, but it's nothing I need to be doing right this second.

And the truth is . . . with the shit I've seen today, I need a bright spot, or I won't be in any shape for dinner.

Want to see her. My wolf pushes toward the laptop. I roll to my side and click around a little until my screen goes dark and my projector takes over. A large version of Leticia's bedroom is now painted across my ceiling, giving almost a more immersive experience.

Lying here, looking at her, seeps into my consciousness. I look forward to my interactions with Leticia. She's not just an acquaintance, a potential ally, not anymore.

ROYAL:

What do you do when you're not in the kitchen? What do the couple of hours, assuming you sleep 8 hours, look like for you?

Leticia jolts, sitting up, and I try to figure out why. She's staring at her phone, hands covering her mouth like it did something bad.

My hackles rise. The wolf stands at attention, trying to decipher the threat.

I pick up my laptop again, leaving her bedroom on my ceiling. I check other cameras, the one in the hall, the one on the stairs, but there's nothing.

I reactivate the sound on her camera, hoping it'll pick up whatever happened that startled her. I try so desperately to figure out the problem, but all I see is the beautiful blonde looking at her phone.

She picks it up and shakes her head before dropping it back to the bed, defeated. "I can't believe I sent that."

I look at my phone and see the notification I missed, distracted by her reaction.

LETICIA:

Honestly, I normally throw on some TV and try to forget.

Forget what? My wolf pushes, still unsettled.

I wish it was harder to figure out. Adrenaline falls out of my system, and exhaustion starts to settle in.

ROYAL:

Forget? Forget who you are and what life is?

Cause honestly? Same.

I try to be relatable. But the image I scrubbed off the internet has me afraid I'm going to learn something a lot darker about life in the D'Medici penthouse.

Leticia picks up her phone. Delicately lying it flat in one hand, she taps it open with the other. As she reads the message, her shoulders slacken and she sits back, curling herself up into a ball.

LETICIA:

I've never told anyone that before. I don't feel like this all the time. I try to be positive about it.

But sometimes the reality that I'm just the next Mrs. Mafia Wife crushes everything I love about myself.

ROYAL:

No matter how good we are at living our lives, we can't ever truly forget we're the children of mobsters.

I've been working on stuff today outside my normal scope. I mean, it's still hacking and technology so that's not –

What I'm saying is: I'll never understand what it's like to be you, but I'm here.

We can distract each other from the bad. Like right now, texting you is the highest point in my day.

I feel weird spamming her with text messages. So I stop and lie back down, looking up at her bedroom again.

Leticia flops down on her bed kinda like I'm lying. She types for a little bit, and then my phone pings.

LETICIA:

I really am glad I'm not alone. I've never really had a friend before. I've had family, and Antonella is absolutely a friend, but at the end of the day she had to help me because we're blood related.

Those words hurt me on her behalf. My wolf growls. That isolation would never happen in our life. With our pack, someone's always around. Someone's always available. Even though I mostly prefer to work alone, I always have someone to talk to.

We'll be the friend she deserves. My wolf assures me.

CHAPTER TWELVE

A DISTRACTION

LETICIA:

Would you want to do something together tonight?

I feel so childish asking that question, but alone in my room all night doesn't sound as appealing as it normally does.

ROYAL:

What do you have in mind?

LETICIA:

We can start watching the same show at the same time and text about it?

Or I saw one of those cool websites where you can play games and stuff together?

Or we could call and talk about nothing, pretend like we're not from rival families and wouldn't get scolded for talking to each other.

But I don't text him that. I don't send it because, despite being our reality, 'friends' with Royal feels a whole lot easier than being 'friends' with Ashton or the girls from school. I've never had sleep-overs or girls' nights out, but I don't think it should be hard to talk to people you call friends, especially since it's not that hard to talk to Royal.

ROYAL:

I can't. I have to watch some screens. I could talk though. I understand if maybe you can't call. Rules are different for princesses than they are for the second-born son.

Ugh. That word. Princess.

A knock comes to my door, and I freeze. I draw a slow breath. "Who is it?"

"Who else would it be?" Berto huffs. "You opening the door or not?"

"I'm changing." I lie on instinct, but I know my cheeks are pink from smiling as I talk to Royal, and I don't want Berto to shove question after question down my throat, all because he notices my face is flushed.

"It's fine. I'm headed out. There's a problem we're handling before we take off for Italy. Mom is in bed, she took her medication and a glass of red. Dad is where I'm going. We won't be back before we go to Italy. There's a little heavier security, so you'll be safe until your flight later after finals. Unless Mom changes her mind again and you really do stay home," Berto rattles off.

He doesn't even wait for a response before his footsteps retreat.

No goodbye. No love you. No frills.

But it does change my answer to Royal.

LETICIA:

I can call. But only if you promise to never call me princess ever again.

ROYAL:

I swear on my favorite computer mouse's life, I will never call you princess again.

I call Royal, not wanting to dance around the whole 'you call,' 'no, you call' routine, and it doesn't even trill through the first ring.

"Hey, Leticia." The way he says my name, velvety and smooth, makes me pause.

I try to pull it together, but my stomach is replaced with a giant butterfly swooning for no reason. "Royal, hey."

"It's good to hear your voice," he says softly with a chuckle. "Now, let me put you in my ears as they say."

"Ditto."

I know he's making fun of me for saying it, but it doesn't feel malicious. I find my second set of earbuds, tucked underneath my mattress, and pop them in one at a time.

"What's the difference between a jeweler and a fisherman?"

Royal's question catches me off guard.

"Oh, I don't know."

"One sees watches and the other watches seas."

I laugh. The joke is actually kind of funny. "Ooft. I haven't heard a dad joke like that in a long time."

"Thank you, I'll be here all week." Royal announces himself like a cheesy stand-up comedian.

"Leticia's distractions and side quests at your service." I keep the humor rolling with an odd voice, nasally and nothing like my own.

Royal laughs, and it's warm but also kind of forced. "What sort of distractions do you have on the services menu?"

"Well, we have the basic packages: twenty questions, two truths and a lie, and would you rather." I offer the first three things that come to mind.

"Hmmm, very standard. What else have you got?" Clicking and typing sound in the background on Royal's end.

"The gold packages include things such as polite small talk, readings from textbooks, and explaining plots of Italian movies you've never seen before."

"Tempting. Very tempting. But I don't fancy myself a small talker." Royal hums for a moment. I hear more clicking, this time like a mouse tapping. "Maybe something less structured but conversation deep?"

"Okay, but I warn you, the diamond package is usually reserved for longtime friends and trusted allies." I rack my brain. *Anything deep to talk about. You can do it. Just come up with a subject.* "It includes offerings like: advanced would you rather, childhood trauma, and dreams, goals, and aspirations."

"Hmmm, advanced would you rather? I didn't realize that came with tiers of difficulty." Royal stops typing. "Let's try it."

"Don't say I didn't warn you." I go over to the stack of textbooks on my desk, open the folder for my psych class, and pull out the list we had been given. I pick the third one down on the page. "Would you rather never be able to celebrate your birthday again or be forced to have a big party each year?"

"I thought you said these were hard. I'd rather have a big party each year." Royal answers quickly like that was an easy decision for him. "The Cavanaghs are really close as a community. I couldn't imagine not having a celebration that didn't involve everybody."

"Really?" I shake my head, not like he can see me. "I could never. Like, sure, I have all these cousins, but after you turn sixteen, there are no more birthday parties for you. And honestly, I didn't like the attention. I was eager to turn seventeen and not have the —"

"The?" Royal prompts.

"Well, this falls outside the 'would you rather' game territory." I warn him.

"You don't have to tell me if you don't want to. I just like hearing your voice." There's more typing on his side of the phone.

It feels easier to tell him knowing he's a little distracted. "And not have the pressure of being a well-behaved birthday girl and the fake happiness. It's so much work trying to be perfect for appearances. Even from a young age, it was always 'Leticia, no man will want a woman who doesn't' — insert a laundry list of expectations."

"That's gross." Royal's words are harsh and unexpected. "Grooming, I'll never understand. You didn't deserve that. You don't deserve that. I'm so proud of you for recognizing that."

"It's life." My face heats, and I try to dismiss the conversation.

He's proud of me? I can't remember the last time someone said that to me.

"Doesn't make it right." Royal pauses for a beat, and the clack of a bunch of keystrokes sounds over the line. "So does your family go all out for Christmas and Easter?"

"Ugh, yes. We do Christmas in Italy every year, and I can't stand it. I don't travel well. I get serious jet lag, and my stomach gets super upset. Plus, it's with all the cousins, and for the first couple days it's like 'Do I even speak Italian?' because it's been almost a year since I last spoke it. Whether I'm going or not this year is still up in the air. Dad said I didn't have to. Then he and Mom talked, and she said I had to go." I cut my ranting off.

"Yikes. We do Christmas, but it's more low-key. Lots of food, the community gets together a few days beforehand and has almost a little festival-type deal, but actual Christmas is just the nuclear family."

"That sounds incredibly nice. I'd love to experience that sort of calm," I muse, glaring at the ugly Christmas dress hanging on the back of my door.

I can't believe I'm expected to wear the monstrosity. *Maybe Mom won't get her way, and I'll get to stay home.*

Ripping my gaze off the dress to quell the anger, I focus on the next question from the sheet. "Would you rather be loved for everything you're not or liked for everything you are?"

Royal lets me move on without pushing back. "I don't know how hard these questions are because I'd rather be liked for who I am. I don't need everybody to love me. Acceptance is good enough."

"Why are you so well adjusted?" I blurt out on accident.

I scrunch all my features, waiting for a reprimand. It doesn't come.

"Well" — I can almost hear a shrug in his voice — "I guess it probably has to do with my parents not being the traditional good Catholics and Irish mob bosses that you'd expect. I came out at dinner one night, and rather than one of those horror stories about coming out, I got 'That makes sense' and 'Which pride flag should we buy?' I think Valor was the most offended, and it was because I didn't tell him first."

"Oh." *Is he gay? How did I not know this?* My shoulders fall. *I mean, it makes the 'friends' thing a whole lot easier.* "I know for sure my parents would be the horror story about coming out. You're lucky to be Irish."

"So they say." Royal snorts.

"Which pride flag did they buy, then?" I feel awkward asking, but it's easier than the question I really want the answer to.

Why does it matter if he's attracted to women, Leticia? You're not allowed to fall in love.

"Nah, I told them that the pan sexual flag was ugly and we should get a flag from one of my favorite movies instead. That was vetoed, and the front of the house remains flagpole-free," Royal answers so casually and unafraid to share these details with me.

I can't imagine being this free with information. Surely not with the girls from college and never anyone from high school.

"Oh, I have one." Royal pauses typing for a moment. "Would you rather always feel understood or always feel appreciated?"

I've never been either. How am I supposed to know?

Clicking resumes on his side of the call, and after a few seconds, it stops. But I'm still waffling, trying to figure out what those words really mean.

What would it look like to be appreciated? What would it look like to be understood?

"Leticia?" His voice is a little louder in my earbuds.

"I'm here." I draw a slow breath. "Is it dumb that I don't know if I've ever felt either of those things before, so I don't know what it'd be like? I mean, surely, Antonella understands me a little, but then again, she's always been able to push for things and change her own life. And I know she's accepted my help in the past with projects and stuff, but it was never something she couldn't do alone."

"You really look up to her." Royal hums.

"Until very recently, she was my only friend." I realize I've been standing, holding a piece of paper dumbly for the last few minutes, so I carry it with me to my bureau to pull out pajamas.

Should I change while on the phone? It's not like he can see me.

"Well, I'm honored to be one of your friends. Especially when I stand with such an interesting and selfless woman in that category." Royal sounds pleased.

"I'm surprised, truthfully, that you seem open and genuine about this truce thing." I sigh and give up changing my clothes, dropping the pajamas on the bed and walking back to my desk.

"Oh." He clears his throat. "Well, the truce happened. I could be mad about it and waste energy, upset that we're now in a truce and needing to merge businesses."

I start tucking the paper back into my stack of school stuff.

"Or I can spend time getting to know people I missed out on years of knowing because some long-dead people couldn't get their shit together."

"That's a good way of looking at it. I don't think Dad and Berto see it the same way." I freeze, realizing I said that aloud.

Royal doesn't say anything for a long pregnant minute. "I don't think Valor sees it entirely the same way either. Though I think he likes getting to know Antonella. He's always more suspicious than I am. But I really don't want to talk about Valor."

"Oh, right. Too much like work." I assume and reach for my ponytail, where my hair has been up all day.

"Not too much like work." Royal sighs. "It's just complicated."

"Complicated?" Relieving the tension from my scalp feels so good. I try not to be rude and groan. "Complicated how? Oh, you don't have to tell me. We were trying to change the subject. Sorry. Uhhh."

My mind goes blank, and I look at the stack of school supplies, trying to remember the questions left on the sheet that would give me anything to talk about that doesn't feel totally inappropriate.

"Royal!" A girlish squeal comes in the background.

"Kerrianne, no woo girl." Royal scolds, and I hear a huff of air. "I'm on a call, gimme a second to say goodbye."

"Okay," Kerrianne says quietly.

"I'll text you after dinner?" Royal offers.

"I'd like that," I answer.

"See you later, Leticia." Royal almost sounds pained saying goodbye.

"After while, Royal," I answer, and he disconnects the call.

I sigh, running my fingers back through my hair. I can't believe how honest I was with him. Worse than that, I can't believe how good it felt to say things and not worry about being judged.

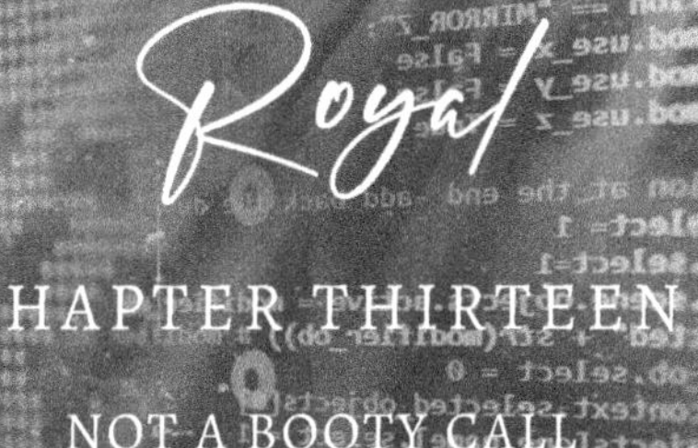

CHAPTER THIRTEEN

NOT A BOOTY CALL

Dinner ran late, so by the time I get back to my lair, it's after ten o'clock. While I know the rule is that nothing good happens after midnight, is now too late to text Leticia back? *Probably.*

Answer is always no if you don't try. My wolf pushes, thinking about my phone. *We talked to her late into the night before. Maybe she's a night owl like us.*

It's not like he doesn't make a solid point.

ROYAL:

Sorry it's so late. Dinner ran long. I promise, I wasn't trying to stand you up.

The shower I wanted to take before dinner is now screaming my name. I head into my bathroom and bring my phone into the glass-enclosed shower, sticking it to the magnetic clip where it always goes.

It's not that I'm addicted to technology, but the shower has some really good acoustics for listening to music. With a few clicks, I turn on a playlist of relaxing tones, trying to flush the frustration and exhaustion out of my system.

But I'm halfway clean when my phone beeps with a message.

Maybe it's her. My wolf presses.

I keep rinsing, but he keeps nagging.

I turn and tap the screen. It's definitely Leticia.

LETICIA:

Ooooh, standing me up . . . I thought we were JUST friends.

Just friends? My wolf snorts. *You have to tell her. She needs to know.*

It's been literally four days since we started talking to her. There is no way in hell I'm telling her we're mates. That's not happening. Now shut up about it. I push hard, trying to shove him out of my front-of-brain consciousness.

I type out a message about how we never said the word date, but I was pretty sure that's what it was, before deleting it. I go with something a little more tame.

ROYAL:

Well, I wouldn't go so far as to say JUST friends. Friends are a pretty big deal.

Regret hits when I send that message. It's not rational to want Leticia like I do. The mountain of shit standing between me and her is too high to contemplate climbing for the chance to be together. I should stop messaging her and let it go.

But I can't. This is what happens with me . . . I can't pull myself away from her. Maybe it'll be a hyperfixation, and I'll lose interest, but when this level of obsession sets in . . . and my wolf calling her our mate? I doubt Leticia will ever leave my mind.

LETICIA:

Well, that's true. Seeing as how I have one . . . it is kinda important to keep him.

What are you doing right now?

I snort, looking at the shower around me.

ROYAL:

Right now? I'm about to get out of the shower.

LETICIA:

Pictures or it didn't happen.

Holy fucking shit. That was not within the possibility of any answer I expected from her. I can't believe she said that. I wipe the overspray water off my phone screen and look at it again.

LETICIA:

I can't believe I said that. IGNORE IT. Delete that message, it NEVER happened.

I step back under the stream. *What if I don't want to ignore it?*

Angling the camera just right, I take a picture. Droplets cling to my hair and trail down my chest. But I make sure there's no trace of the family jewels in the photo before I send it to her.

Then I send one more message before I lose my nerve.

ROYAL:

Is there anything else you want to see?

Please reply. Please reply. It's only been two days of serious talking with her. I probably pushed this too far. My phone is quiet, and I turn off the shower and start to dry off.

LETICIA:

Well, you definitely are not good at following directions. Should I feel weird that the first pic I've gotten of you is naked and in your shower?

ROYAL:

Well, I'm out of the shower now. Would you feel better if I sent you one while I was wearing clothes?

A message comes through at the same time I send that out. It's an image file.

In the photo, Leticia is lying down. With her phone above her face, a shadow is cast across her jaw and some of her blonde hair, which is fanned out over her shoulders and the bed around her. Those soft, kissable light pink lips are centered in frame, and it's a perfect look right into her blue eyes. She's the definition of beauty.

"Hello, gorgeous," I say to myself while I try to come up with a witty retort, but I don't have one. And then an idea hits.

ROYAL:

New game if you're up for it? Picture for picture. Whatever you're comfortable with and the first thing that comes to mind when the other person sends.

Leticia takes a minute but responds.

LETICIA:

Deal

Unfortunately for her, I'm absolutely going to cheat. With my towel wrapped around my waist, I head to my bedroom. Flicking my wrists, I straighten the covers on my bed and fluff the pillow so it looks inviting and not like I rolled out of it this morning without straightening the sheets.

With the bedroom light's adjustable controller, I make the space seem warm and cozy, then I send off a picture.

I pull on a pair of boxers and sweatpants before turning on a computer screen and bringing up her room's camera feed. Leticia is pushing up on her bed and looking around at her room. She raises her phone and takes a picture, I'm guessing of the room facing the camera.

Before the image comes in, I start grabbing food wrappers and unnecessary items off my desk, binning or putting them away appropriately.

Leticia's photo comes in, and it's exactly what I expected. A partial tour of her room. And I scour the image, looking for where that camera is hidden. I know it's there, because I have the feed, but even with my trained eyes, I'm not seeing it.

Frustrated with not being able to figure it out, I start turning on monitors and set them to my winter-blues setting, essentially turning my wall of monitors into a panoramic forest.

I send her another picture, adding a message shortly after.

ROYAL:

Welcome to my office.

LETICIA:

Well, hardly fair. I'm not going down to the kitchen right now. You'll have to settle for this.

I flick the monitor with her room back over to see her opening a bureau. The camera doesn't get a good look, but it's okay because Leticia sends me a photo of its contents.

There are phone cases, laptop cases, and piles of folded fabric. Everything is organized by color and type.

ROYAL:

What am I seeing, other than kick-ass organization?

LETICIA:

All my phone and laptop cases, my aprons, and my hair ribbons. I really like to coordinate. Berto calls it frivolous and obsessive.

"Berto is a fucking dick," I mumble.

The only problem is . . . what I want to reciprocate with drastically changes the innocence of this game we have going. Then again, maybe it isn't so innocent after all.

ROYAL:

I don't think it's frivolous and obsessive. I think it's creative and kinda sexy that you put so much thought into the mundane. I've had the same case for probably a year. I like that you change it up.

I want to send you another picture, but I want to make sure you're okay with things getting more intimate and that this is a judgment-free zone.

I glance over at my dresser before turning my focus back to the screen. Leticia is closing the bureau doors. Her lips move as she reads the message, and I turn the sound on to hear her.

"— would I start judging you now?" She types back a message.

LETICIA:

Judgment-free zone.

Like every piece of furniture in my bedroom, the dresser is completely custom. The top raises up on hydraulics, and the drawer pulls out, with power cords set up in the back. It's probably overkill. *I know it's overkill.*

I open it up, and the LED lights illuminate the area where I keep all my toys. The different sex toys include cock sleeves, dildos, plugs, and vibrators of various shapes and sizes.

Part of me knows, given my moderately Catholic upbringing, that I should feel some shame for this collection. But my belief in God doesn't align with the Christians who somehow find prejudice in the messages of love and acceptance of the Bible. And the whole no-sex-before-marriage thing was clearly designed to stop the spread of disease among humans. Not applicable being a wolf.

I'm all about *not* following rules, especially those that don't apply to me.

But does Leticia feel the same?

I hesitate. I could send her a picture of my servers instead. They're equally organized.

If she doesn't appreciate this, then she's not our mate. My wolf surfaces a bit, encouraging me.

Hesitantly and with squinted eyes, I take a photo of my toy drawer and send it to Leticia.

No reply comes through right away, and I wait a few more seconds to see if maybe she'll respond.

Tension coils in my stomach, and I close the dresser and flop backward onto my bed. *I've ruined a good thing.*

I check my phone again. Still no new messages from Leticia. I turn on the overhead projector to view the night sky before turning off the rest of the lights in my room.

It's been almost five minutes, and I'm giving up on Leticia messaging me back, so I decide to look and see what she's doing.

On the monitor across the room, her bedroom is empty. Her phone is on her bed, but Leticia isn't in the room.

I scramble off my bed to the monitor wall and flick on a few others. I scroll through different camera feeds until I find her.

Leticia

CHAPTER FOURTEEN

THE PAWN OF THE PLAN

I'm about to open a photo from Royal, but Dad bellows from somewhere in the main portion of the penthouse.

"Leticia!"

Berto said he and Dad weren't coming back before they left for the airport . . .

Is Berto okay? I rush down the stairs as fast as I can.

Dad is standing at the door to his study wearing his usual look, the same one Berto has adopted, black suit with a white shirt, no tie, and his shoulders back. This time, though, his fists are clenched, and I hesitate to approach. He's always been so unpredictable, but it's been a while since he's even really raised his voice at me. It's been since before Antonella came home that he last hit me. Almost a year maybe?

"I don't have all night, Leticia." He gestures toward his open office door.

I am *never* invited into Dad's office.

I'm allowed to deliver items to him in his office, but I'm never there for any intentional business purpose.

Well, tonight's the night, then.

I straighten and cross the open space, my flats beating against the cold terrazzo floor all the way to his office, and then I try not to wince as I step across the threshold.

Berto is staring out the large window, which looks out at Lake

Michigan, with a pensive expression and his glass of malt liquor halfway to his mouth. It's dark outside, so I don't even know why he'd bother looking out at it.

"Take a seat, Leticia." Dad's voice is low and harsh as he points me to a chair.

Stiffly, I perch on a chair across from his desk, my skirt protecting me from the cool leather of the seat. The rich oak arms feel like a cage, and I don't dare lean back into it.

Dad takes a moment to sit. The wood and leather of his chair creak in protest as he settles in. For a moment, the room is quiet with dreaded anticipation.

Or maybe that's just me.

"Why is Ian Cavanagh inviting us, and you, by name, on a hand-delivered invitation to Christmas at their home?" Dad slides an invitation across the desk.

I don't pick it up, but I glance and see all four of our names, not just mine, spelled out in a fancy metallic font.

Why wouldn't they invite me? I want to question and be assertive, but that's not me. That's Antonella.

I shake my head. "I don't know."

"Then who is it that you've been exchanging texts and phone calls with? It started within the last two weeks. One of them, I'm assuming, is Antonella, but there is this other one you speak to at all odd hours of the day and night." Dad presents the phone bill from across the desk.

I don't reach for it either.

"Royal Cavanagh," I answer honestly and quickly.

The truth will come out, and there's no shame in it. We're just friends.

Berto sputters on his next sip of liquor. "What?"

"Royal Cavanagh? Leticia, now is not the time for one of your silly little jokes." Dad talks down to me.

"I'm not joking." But I also don't remember the last time I told a joke. I don't bring that up. "I called Clark Enterprises to get someone to give me Antonella's new number, and I connected with Royal. We've been chatting since then. He's nice."

"Nice." Dad scoffs. He narrows his eyes at me, pinching his lips tightly. "Hardly."

"Leticia, he isn't nice. He's using you." Berto speaks with false sympathy that's amplified by a pitying scowl.

"He's not using me. There's nothing to use. We don't talk about anything family related unless talking about what I'm cooking for dinner is some sort of secret now." I force myself not to clench my fists.

"Leticia." Dad scolds me, and I expect escalation. But he draws a breath and sits back in his chair. His voice holds a cutting precision. "You've said nothing about anything we do here? Even a small detail."

"Are you kidding?" The question slips out with uncalculated frustration, but I push through and try taking a page from Antonella's book. "What would I even know to tell him? No one tells me anything. I didn't figure out until dinner the next night that someone had attempted to kidnap me from the university. What could I even know to tell Royal?"

Dad's jaw drops, and he looks at Berto. Since he's looking at Berto, I look at him too.

Berto shrugs. "She has a point."

"This has to stop." Dad swings his gaze back to me. "It's a risk, and it's improper. You're to be pure for marriage."

My fists clench despite my efforts to stay calm, but this accusation of impropriety cuts. "We're just friends. There is nothing improper about it. We determined there is no risk because I don't know anything."

I gasp, swallowing it down. *I can't believe I did that.* Eyes wide, I look between Dad and Berto, waiting to be reprimanded.

"Leticia, you'll be married soon. And it will be to someone worthy of what you are: a princess to my empire." Dad starts with the lecture.

No. No. No. I chant it in my head, hoping that somehow this isn't him taking away the tiny bit of joy I have in my life. But I cling to false hope like I clung to Antonella when she first came back home from New York, tight and begging for it not to go away ever again.

"You need to not spend your time talking to strange men." Dad looks down his nose at me.

"And they don't get any stranger than that weird Cavanagh nerd. The second son probably wishes he'd been born a girl rather than simply the spare heir." Berto rolls his eyes. "Then he'd be worth something."

"True," Dad mumbles.

I bite my tongue, stopping myself from defending Royal, his uniqueness, and how loved he seems to feel. *I can't believe how mean they're being.*

"Wait —" Berto holds a finger up in the air. "What if we use this?"

"Use what?" Dad gestures to me broadly with an open hand.

"They'll never suspect Leticia as a spy. She's a woman. They may not be as careful about what they say to her. She could find out more about their entire operation." A sly smile crawls across Berto's lips.

I shake my head. "I thought we're in a truce with the Cavanaghs. Why would we need to spy on them?"

Dad lets out a huffy, heady laugh before picking up his own cup of amber liquid. He pauses to take a sip. "Just because we're in a sworn truce, sealed by your cousin's marriage, doesn't mean we can trust everything they say or do. Surely they don't trust us."

"It'll be so easy." Berto smiles as he sits next to me. "All you have to do is listen and report back what they say. You're good at remembering things. Maybe be indirect and ask that punk Royal what he's up to."

"We don't talk about his work." I warn them, but I see an opportunity to get out of going to Italy, and I'm not missing it. "But I could try. I know Mom really wants me to go to Italy, but if I stay home, I could maybe meet up with their family more. It'd be great to see Antonella. Surely everyone will be there at Christmas. Maybe the more I'm around, the more comfortable they'll be?"

"You're awfully eager. Are you sure you're up to this?" Dad's eyebrows are raised, and he purses his lips. "What happens if they ask why you want to know something?"

"It's curiosity. What's the worst that could happen?" I fail to stop myself from shrinking into the chair. "They won't answer, and we'll move forward with conversation."

"I don't like it." Dad shakes his head. "They don't call Valor all those dark and terrible things for no reason. It's a small miracle he hasn't turned his knives against Antonella already. He's a bloodthirsty killer, and the worst that would happen is that he'd kill you." Dad's tone is sharp, cutting, and there's a fire in his gaze as he stares at me. It's deep, and for a moment, I think it softens. But then he adds, "You're too valuable."

"It's the best opportunity we've gotten." Berto argues on my behalf. "If you're serious about wanting an in to make sure that they're not doing anything against the treaty, then sending her to their house is the best bet. Their guard will be down."

Silently, Dad mulls over the decision. He swirls his glass and takes a sip. Then he turns toward the window overlooking the lake. He stands from his desk and crosses the room to look out as if a few feet will help him see the other side of the expanse of water.

After a few more seconds of loaded silence, he turns and glares at Berto, shooting daggers at him with his eyes. "Alright, but at the first sign of danger, you're coming home to be with your sister and keep her in line."

"Understood." Berto nods and turns to me. Through gritted teeth, he warns me. "Don't fuck it up."

"I won't." I shake my head.

My brain is buzzing, and I can hardly believe what is happening.

"Go get your mother up. She can leave with us tonight," Dad orders, and I don't hesitate.

I dismiss myself and walk as hurriedly as I can to the staircase and then up toward her bedroom.

They're one hundred percent letting me stay home for Christmas.

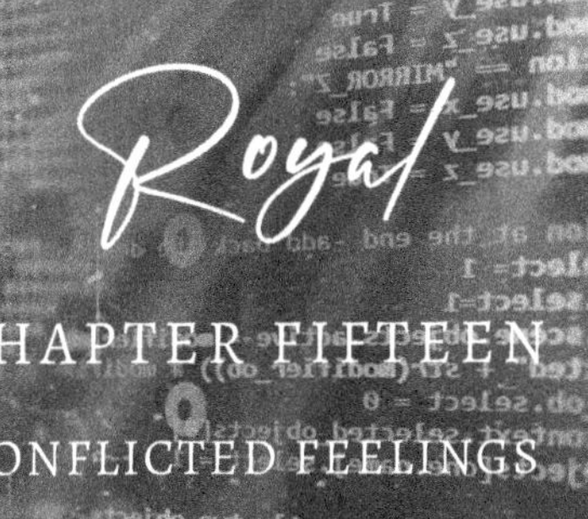

CHAPTER FIFTEEN

CONFLICTED FEELINGS

What Leticia will do is more important than what she agrees to with her parents.

I try to reassure myself, but while watching her, I slump back into my chair. I don't want to believe what she's agreed to do. *She won't do it. Right?*

The truth is, I don't truly *know* Leticia. And as much as I want to trust her without a second thought, I lock down her text messages to her dad and brother, so all the texts will have to be approved by me. The system I created runs off the phone I cloned when we did Late Nite Bytes and has the ability to override her real phone.

I go through the communication history back from last spring when they went to Italy for Easter and check to see if they used any other phone numbers.

Weirdly, they don't use different lines when traveling.

Give our mate a chance. My wolf encourages me. He stands and stretches.

I should do the right thing. Informing Dad what I learned and telling Valor is the protocol-based response. It's my job, working in technology, to share when there's a potential data breach.

But I don't know if she'll breach confidentiality or not. She had every opportunity to tell them we have a family secret and that Valor promised to tell her what it is. Leticia stayed quiet on it.

My wolf pushes in my brain harder again. *Our mate will be loyal to us.*

Maybe he's right, and Leticia's loyalty doesn't lie with the D'Medici family. Maybe she can be won over to our side.

We could protect her from her family. My wolf wags his tail. *We can make her someplace safe here.*

I'd previously flagged the cell phones connected to the D'Medici Wi-Fi, so I set up a program to track the ones I've attributed to Berto and Gregorio, who should be leaving the country, to make sure they get on their flight tonight.

I check that it's working before looking back to Leticia's room on the monitor closest to me. It's still empty. The hallway camera shows her being rushed back from her mother's room as Francesca D'Medici shoos her daughter out of the way, dragging a carry-on suitcase behind her.

Leticia ducks into her room, and I split my attention between screens, watching her family get into the elevator and down to their SUV, where my tracking software will follow them.

My phone buzzes, and I pull my attention from the monitor for a moment.

LETICIA:

Please don't be offended that I don't know what those are.

Don't know what they are? I squint at the notification.

The conversation we were having comes barreling back all at once, slamming into me and shaking me out of the worry about whether Leticia will cause trouble, and I'm back to the terror that I showed something so intimate to another person.

But now the question of how to respond is begging to be answered.

If I tell her, 'That's okay, you don't need to know what they are,' and we keep playing the game, it'll probably bother her like Valor not telling her the family secret.

On the other hand, if I do tell her, that means we'll have to have a more sexually charged conversation.

On that same hand, if we have that conversation, maybe it will shut down any further communication between us altogether, and I won't have to worry because there won't be anything for her to tell her family.

I choose my words carefully.

ROYAL:

Not offended, surprised. They're sex toys.

I'm too anxious to not watch her on the screen. I have to know what she's thinking. I have to see her reaction in real time.

She's laid out on her bed again. This time not as gracefully. Her legs are spread, and her skirt has hiked up from around her ankles all the way up to her thighs.

My cock twitches seeing the extra skin. *Don't be such a predator. We don't even know if she's . . .*

Leticia brings her hand to her mouth, and I expect her to freak out, but instead, she opens the picture back up, the telltale bright blue of the picture on her phone screen illuminating her face. Leticia pinches and zooms on the photo before texting back.

LETICIA:

That's SO cool. I've wanted one, but there is no way to hide it. Mom would find it for sure.

I'm hard just reading that. Throbbing in my pants at the idea of her getting off. I look at her on the screen as she looks back at the image again.

My wolf salivates, wishing she'd roll over and wondering what that skirt might do with the movement.

ROYAL:

It must be hard having restrictions like that. Do you get any privacy?

Is that creepy? I try to check in with my wolf, but we're back to staring at her in the monitor again. Which, I think, proves I'm being a total stalker and probably shouldn't be worried about what I'm texting her.

LETICIA:

Honestly, no.

There are cameras everywhere. Even in my room.

I get this feeling of being watched a lot. Like someone is right there looking over my shoulder. For a while, I thought maybe we're haunted, but now I'm pretty sure it's the cameras.

How do I respond to that? My cock steadily begins to behave, and I try to come up with something that doesn't acknowledge I know the truth while reassuring her she's safe from anyone with bad intentions.

But my intentions, which *I* don't think are bad, are at the heart of her concern, whether she knows it or not . . . someone watching her while she's at her most vulnerable, someone who would gladly take the opportunity to watch her pleasure herself.

I should probably feel guilty about it. I should probably shut the camera feed off and try to assure her that no one would waste time watching her room.

And while I don't feel guilty about my obsession with Leticia, I also won't lie to her about no one watching.

ROYAL:

I can't imagine what it's like to not have any privacy.

Too bad we're not THOSE kinds of friends. I'd share my toys with you.

That last one might cross a line, but the gorgeous woman returned to the photo and zoomed in again. She took a closer look. Curiosity is there.

Our mate won't back away from this. My wolf watches the screen just as intently as I do.

Leticia goes to a dresser and begins pulling some clothes out before picking up her phone. She types off a quick message.

LETICIA:

Very generous. But I don't even know what I'd like.

How far can I push this?

ROYAL:

Well, if you ever want to learn, I'd be glad to offer advice.

I set my phone down, the possible fallout waiting in cyberspace as the message pings from one satellite to another.

Glancing back at the screen, I do a double take. Leticia unzips her skirt and shimmies it off over her hips, revealing the most adorable blue underwear with some sort of pattern too small for the camera to discern. They're a fuller-coverage piece, like a boy short, that hugs her ass tightly.

I'm fixated on the screen, salivating over every inch of skin uncovered. I adjust my cock where it strains against the fabric of my sweats.

Casually, she flicks the skirt into a laundry hamper and pulls on what looks like soft, cozy joggers. The material is thin and dances around her legs as she wiggles them over her butt before tying the strings into a petite bow.

She wraps her fingers around the hem of her shirt and pulls it off, and I'm treated to a fantastic view of her half-naked form — her soft stomach and her bra, the same color as the panties — as she turns the shirt right side out and also tosses it into the hamper.

Leticia pulls a long-sleeved shirt over her head, leaving her bra on.

That can't be comfortable to sleep in. My wolf is taken aback.

It's not too long, though, before Leticia reaches back and unclasps her bra. She shimmies her arms in and out of the sleeves before pulling the bra out through the neckline of her shirt.

She does know she's being watched. It makes sense she'd protect herself. That doesn't change how hard I am again.

LETICIA:

Don't they come with user manuals? I'm quite proficient at user manuals.

I laugh out loud reading her text message.

LETICIA:

Though . . . who knows, maybe I've never been meant to know what an orgasm feels like. Could be at the mercy of someone who doesn't believe in the female orgasm.

That sobers me fast. *Never? As in, never have I ever?*

My wolf growls low at that. We're both a little hedonistic in the way we chase all the good things of the world.

ROYAL:

Are you meaning to tell me you've never, ever had an orgasm?

Leticia is pulling back the covers of her bed, phone on the nightstand, when I see it light up with my message.

She picks up her phone before walking back to the light switch by the door. When she turns on her phone flashlight, I stop.

Human, Royal. She's a fuckin' human, and you're attached. Not in the least bit disillusioned, I do nothing to disentangle my attachment as I watch her walk hurriedly to her bed and pull her feet up quickly.

Why? My wolf tips his head back and forth, trying to unscramble the mystery of her behavior, but I don't have an answer for him.

When Leticia pulls the covers up around her chest, she turns off the flashlight. The camera takes a moment to refocus in night mode.

LETICIA:

I didn't MEAN to tell you that, it just kinda came out.

And that's enough embarrassment for me for the day.

How was dinner?

Jealous of how cozy Leticia looks, I stand from my desk chair, go to the back of my door, and pull on the plaid flannel I keep there.

Now's the time to test Leticia's loyalty to her family.

ROYAL:

Food was delicious, we had Thanksgiving again since the first one was kind of ruined with work and then a wedding and some funerals.

Company, however, just wanted to talk about work and get on my case about getting shit done.

LETICIA:

So I take it your family doesn't have a 'no work at the dinner table' rule? We do, but that means a lot of meals are silent because Berto and Dad don't know how to talk about anything else.

ROYAL:

Nah, we talked about rugby and some other stuff too, but there are some urgent things going on that need my attention.

I click my work mouse, and my usual nightly scans are running as they should. No new notifications on Antonella's phones for anything that would be suspicious. No new disasters out at my 3D printers. There is a warning for a storehouse with a couple attempts to get into it, but it's Uncle Neil's number again.

What is it with him and passwords, and why is he so busy lately? I thought we were slowing down business operations with the truce and the holidays?

My phone vibrates, drawing me away from verifying the daily log entries.

LETICIA:

No talking about work.

Would you rather have a secret that you couldn't tell anyone or have to tell someone everything?

I drum my fingers on the desk, looking at my phone. *If I pushed hard enough, would she tell me that her family wants her to spy on us?*

ROYAL:

That one is hard. It's a 'it depends' for me. What kind of secret? Who is the person I have to tell everything to? All my thoughts? Everything I do?

I'm leaning toward having to tell someone everything. At bare minimum, there's a chance they'd go down with me as an accomplice or accomplice after the fact. Best case scenario: I get a friend who takes some of the icky off some of the work I do. I wouldn't be alone in some of the trenches.

What about you?

I just gave her so many opportunities to ask probing questions and figure out more about what we do — what *I* do — so she could report to Gregorio and Berto.

LETICIA:

Can we call?

Unexpected. My wolf tries to weasel his way closer to the screen, like getting closer to the monitor will put us closer to where she is.

ROYAL:

Of course. Call when ready.

The temptation arises to put her on surround sound in my room so that I can hear her voice all around me, but I slip my earbuds in instead.

When the phone rings, I hesitate. *Should I record this call?*

"Hey." I answer before the second ring, pushing the recording idea out of my head. I can always start it if I need to.

"Hey." Leticia's voice is quiet but also small, almost vulnerable.

"You okay?" I watch on the screen as she rolls onto her side, the phone resting on the pillow next to her.

I'm jealous of her phone.

I'm jealous of a little bit of plastic and metal because it's in bed with her and I'm not.

My feelings for her are getting out of hand. I'm becoming obsessed with her. I force myself to minimize the camera feed in her room. I twitch, wanting to reopen it again.

"I'm just feeling funny, and my answer to the 'would you rather' is complicated. It'll make more sense when I talk it out rather than type it out." Her voice is a little stronger.

"Yeah, texts don't have tone, I get that." I settle back into my chair and go back to double-checking the nightly report for errors.

"I also can't pick between the two. Because on one hand, it'd be nice for someone to tell me something, a secret, that I can guard. Something I get to know that not everybody else does. It's like every conversation around me ends abruptly with statements like 'It's not for women to know' and 'It doesn't concern you.' But on the other hand, sometimes I get so incredibly lonely that maybe telling someone else every thought or thing that I do would be kind of nice." Leticia sighs, and my hand jerks to go to the computer that will bring up her room again.

I stop myself, gripping one hand with the other, squeezing so tight that I could hurt myself.

"Sounds like we're both just looking for the right connection," I answer and physically move my chair down the desk, away from that monitor.

"Connection would be really nice." She agrees before falling silent.

I look for something to fill the silence, but it doesn't feel tense, more like we're hanging out.

"Can I ask you a weird question?" Leticia says after a minute.

"Always." *What sort of weird?*

"Generally speaking, do you think it's a turn off that I haven't had an orgasm?" Her whole sentence sounds like she's wincing, and again, I'm dying to see her.

"No." I answer too quickly, so I draw a slow breath and try

again. "No, it's not. It makes sense, and for me, it's alluring. To be able to unlock that with a partner could be really intimate, and I really want that for you."

We want her. My wolf corrects. *We want to do that for her.*

But I don't correct the statement aloud.

"You make it sound so magical."

"It kinda is." I laugh and focus for a second, typing in a line of code through a program patch. "A good partner can make you feel a lot more than just an orgasm."

"Are you a good partner?" Leticia's voice is soft again.

My restraint crumbles. I slide my chair back and flick on her room feed. She's looking at the phone screen.

"If I say yes, do I sound conceited?" My cheeks and neck heat.

We'd make her come so hard. My wolf is salivating at the thought.

"No." Leticia gives me the smallest little laugh. "I wanted a good partner someday, but now I'm afraid I'll go through life and never experience the good stuff. I should have done so many things already."

"There's always time to change." I try not to push her, and yet, feeling selfish, I do. "You can experience it tonight, if you want."

"But what if someone is watching?" she whispers.

"Most of your basic security cameras don't have night vision, and if you stay under the covers, no one can see anything." I almost let it slip that no one is home, but she didn't tell me that information. I knew from stalking her.

"Feels weird talking to a guy about this." Leticia is a little breathy.

"Yeah, it can feel a little weird." I attempt to soothe her. "I want to give you permission to take something you want for once instead of waiting for someone else. Wouldn't want them to deny you."

"What do I even do?" Leticia gives off a low groan, and the lump of covers moves as she pulls them over her head with the phone. "Not that you even have the same parts I do. Why am I asking such weird questions? Never mind."

"No, not never mind." I stop her panicked, almost frantic words.

"Not never mind?" she squeaks.

I smile, holding in a small laugh while watching her. She's so perfect and oblivious.

Reassurance. My wolf agrees with me. *She needs reassurance. We can help her.*

"It's not weird. There's no shame in not knowing something." I settle back into my chair. "I've had femme partners before. If you want, I'd be honored to walk you through how to come."

Leticia's side of the phone is silent except for her breathing.

"Or if you'd rather, you can experiment on your own, and we can call this good night?" I try to be okay with that possibility.

Tell her it's better with a friend. Remind her what we said. My wolf urges with his territorial side, trying to overcome my self-restraint.

"What if I try alone and decide I need help?" Leticia is extremely hesitant, each word drawn out or delivered with a pause.

Rejection stings like a tearing bite, ripping open a wound of self-pity. "I'll be up for a long time. There's no rush."

"Promise?" Leticia's voice peaks.

"Promise." I draw slow, steady breaths, controlling myself for a beat. "Call me if you need me. I might miss a text."

Liar. My wolf snorts. He turns his back to me, pissed off that I gave her an out.

"Good night, Royal." Leticia's voice wavers in what I assume is uncertainty.

"Good night, Leticia," I push out before disconnecting the call. Before I can beg her not to go.

Coward. My wolf huffs over his shoulder.

He's not wrong.

Leticia

CHAPTER SIXTEEN

SELF-DISCOVERY

I hung up with Royal out of pure embarrassment. I'm running hot under the covers, yet I feel like a cold sweat has taken over my skin. I push the blankets off to get up to . . . do what exactly? Uncovered, lying on the bed and looking up into the darkness of my room, I feel every bit as alone as I am.

Mom, Dad, and Berto are gone. There are no guards in the penthouse itself. The dreaded feeling of being watched seems to have lessened. I feel too alone and miss being connected. *I miss Royal.*

Grabbing my phone, I turn the flashlight on before I put my feet on the floor. Shining it to illuminate my path, I go to the bathroom.

I blink against the blinding lights, turn off my phone flashlight, and look at myself in the mirror. My blonde hair is wild and untamed from rolling in the sheets, so I grab the brush and straighten the locks before weaving them into a loose braid.

When that's settled, I look at myself again. My cheeks are flushed, and my shoulders are moving erratically with my breathing.

Royal was such a gentleman. Letting me do this on my own and not pushing me for more. He's right though. The only thing stopping me is this expectation of what I should and shouldn't do.

This is an opportunity for me to take control. Control over a piece no one can take from me. It's a choice and something for me, just for me.

I can hide under the covers like I used to when I'd stay up way too late reading. No one ever caught me then, so no one could possibly catch me doing this.

How do I even start? I've never even watched porn out of fear of being caught, shamed, and given a lecture on Catholic values. *Twenty-three years old and I don't know how to—* I stop the beratement, and more embarrassment and shame creep in again. Royal said it wasn't bad. He reassured me it was okay.

Turning my phone flashlight back on, I turn off the bathroom light and head back to bed. I know the way, but that feeling of being watched always makes me feel like something is going to come out from under my bed and grab me by the ankles.

"So pathetic." I scold myself but climb into bed quickly. "Twenty-three, never had an orgasm, and afraid of monsters under the bed."

Lying among the covers, I stare up at the ceiling again. It feels scandalous to call Royal back. Intimate to do something sexual with another person who's not my chosen husband. But I could take that back, an intimate experience, and it would give me a semblance of my first time with someone else. Someone that I choose.

Am I choosing Royal because I like him, or am I just choosing him because he's the first man who has ever been nice to me? But the last part isn't entirely true. Ever since I turned sixteen, there have been more advances and attention from Dad's men. Many of them have been nice, and those who have been too nice don't last long. But Royal isn't the first man who has been nice or paid me attention.

He's the first man I've wanted attention from. I don't think he's just being nice either. I don't think he's like everyone else who just wants to get close to Dad and Berto.

Drawing a deep breath, I hold it while going to my recent calls and clicking on Royal's name.

The phone rings twice, and I almost hang up before he answers. "Hello?"

"Promise me you won't think this is pathetic and that you're not doing this out of pity," I demand without greeting.

"Leticia, this is not pathetic, and you'll never have my pity." His voice is so warm and affirming.

I close my eyes and fidget with the sheet with my free hand. "So . . . where do we start?"

"Well, for me, I prefer to be naked." There's a sound of leather creaking on Royal's side of the phone. "I know you're afraid that someone might be recording you. What are you comfortable with?"

"I can get under the covers," I offer.

"That's a good idea. You can use them to give you some privacy."

"Okay." My voice fluctuates more than I'd like. It's a mix of fear and excitement and reflects how they're coursing through my body.

I tug the covers up over the top of me, making sure the phone ends up close to my head. I pull my shirt off first, but the sleeves get tangled, causing me to have to sit up. I try to stay as covered as I can, clutching the comforter to my chest, while putting my discarded shirt on the pillow next to me.

I'm shuffling to get under the covers again when Royal quietly speaks. "Are you doing okay? You sound frantic."

"It's harder to get undressed lying down than it really should be." I feel a break in tension, and I laugh. "Halfway done."

"We're in no rush. We've got all night." Royal's deep voice sends a shiver through my body.

I pull at the tie to my sweatpants before hitching my thumbs into my waistband and shoving them and my underwear down. When I kick them aside, I freeze. I haven't been fully naked, outside of my bathroom, for years.

I'm warm and cold at the same time. It's like the war in my head — to be bad or to behave — rampages in my brain. I work on calming myself, but it's hard.

After settling in, I speak softly. "Can you hear me?"

"I can hear you. Am I on speaker?" Royal asks. "You're kind of distant."

"Let me get my headphones." I roll in bed, and the sheets are smooth against my skin. It's luxurious and freeing.

My headphones are right where I left them, and I snatch them off the nightstand, opening the case and popping them into my ears. After they announce their connection, I can hear more sounds on Royal's side. There's rustling fabric and a whoosh of air like he's lying down, probably in his own bed.

"Okay, can you hear me?" I check in as I nestle back under my covers.

"Yeah, I can hear you. You settling back in?" Royal hums.

"I guess?"

"Get comfortable. Lie on your back and let yourself relax. This is supposed to be good, and if it isn't, tell me to stop and we will. Do you understand?" His voice has the hint of a command.

"I understand. If I say stop, we will." Butterflies flutter in my stomach as I confirm that with him.

"That's good." Royal's voice is sultry, and I close my eyes.

I picture him in the photo he sent me. His hair was wet and wavy, and a sheen of water coated his pecs and abs.

"Take some deep breaths. Focus on how your body feels. Let your hand wander over your skin. What do you want to touch first?"

"I-I don't know." Indecision paralyzes me. I try to move my hand, but it won't budge.

"It's okay not to know." Royal reassures me. "We're not going to dive right into it. Tease your belly with your hand. Feel the soft skin and how warm you are."

Taking my hand, I drag it up from my navel to my breast.

"Don't forget to breathe." Royal's voice holds a little playful banter.

Drawing a breath, I exhale with a small laugh.

"Run your fingers in a circle around your breast, don't run straight to the nipple. Tease your body, let it build anticipation."

His directions slow me down from where I was moving straight to the nipple.

"How did you know?" I stiffen, eyes opening to the darkness of my room, and I stop my movements.

"You seem like the impatient kind," Royal answers. "You seem like you're the kind of woman who does things fast and efficiently. But this isn't something you rush. Not at first."

The more he speaks, the more transparent I feel. We haven't known each other for long, but he seems to know me so well. It's like he understands me more than I understand myself. Certainly better than I know him.

"What are you doing?"

“I’m also in bed, naked. I’m following my own instructions too. I hope you’re okay with that.” He pauses, and I think he’s going to go on to the next instruction when he adds, “We’re in this together, right?”

“Absolutely.” I find that I’m smiling, and I feel better about this. “What next?”

Royal lets out a soft groan. “Next, we’ll trace our fingers around the nipple. Feel it pebbling from the touch. How stiff it becomes.”

I close my eyes again and focus entirely on what he says and how I feel. The sensations match his words exactly.

“Trail your hand down away from your breast, to your stomach and lower. Run your fingers between your legs and then back up to your breast. What are you feeling right now?”

Touching myself like this is foreign. I try to just do it and not think too much. When I slide my fingers between my legs, the hair is soft, and I trail across my folds. My breath catches in my throat.

“I’m excited, and nervous, I guess,” I admit.

“Breathe, slow and steady.” Royal’s voice comes with exactly what I need to hear. “One more time, dip lower.”

This time as I do, a little of that shame fades away, and it’s easier.

“That’s it.” Royal is breathy, sending a chill down my spine. “Are you ready for more?”

“Mmmm.” I clench the bed sheet with my other hand. The desire for more battles with uncertainty, and I try to let it go. “Yes.”

“We’ll take it slow. Pull your feet up toward your body. Let your knees fall out to the sides. Open yourself. Don’t rush it. Go at your own pace.” Royal coaxes me along.

I move my feet together, pulling them up. They rest flat against each other as my knees go out to the side. I’m warm and protected under the blankets. *No one can see.* I remind myself as I finally settle into this new, more vulnerable position.

“Okay,” I sigh, pleased with how I’ve been able to push through my fears.

“That’s so good.” He sounds so proud of me, voice full of a heat I’ve never heard before. “Think you can use both hands to play?”

“Maybe. I kind of like clutching the sheet for dear life.” I squeeze my fist tighter. The fabric nestled in my fingers is hot and damp with my sweat.

"It's okay if you don't want to. You're already being so brave. I can tell you're trying hard."

His praise melts me into the sheets.

I'm breathing easier and feeling more self-assured. "We could try two."

"Good." Royal practically purrs into the phone, but it's not a purr, more like a pleased growl. "Go ahead and take that other hand, rest it on your stomach. It doesn't have to move, just feel it resting there. You can use it to feel your breaths, pull them deep and low."

Each breath draws a deep, warm scent of my own smell and of the fresh, laundered linens on my bed. It's cozy and safe.

"Slide your fingers back between your legs, let them slip deep between your folds. Go nice and slow."

He makes it sound so easy, but I follow his instructions. Using two fingers, I push down between my lower lips and am met with a warmth I didn't expect.

"Oh." I slide my fingers a little more, coating them with moisture.

"Are you warm and wet?" Royal's inquiry brings more warmth to my face and neck.

"Yeah, I am." The admission makes me smile, and I don't even know why.

"Pet yourself, don't focus on anything other than getting to know your body." His words come out slowly, without a rush. After a minute of silence, he continues. "You should be able to find a spot that's a little hard and protrudes from the rest. It'll be toward your pelvic bone and —"

"I found it," I gasp.

"That's your clit. It's probably extra sensitive if you've been touching it while we've been talking. You should be touching it." He groans.

"You okay?" I still, listening. His breathing is ragged.

"The head of my cock is a lot like your clit, and I ran my hand over the top of it. I wanted to experience it with you." There's a gravelly quality to his voice that I love to hear.

"Is that how you touch yourself?" I've seen the anatomy books and diagrams, but I've never put any thought into it. *Am I being weird?*

"It's one of the ways." Royal draws a slow breath and lets it out. "I like to play with the soft underside of my cock. Just below the head is extremely sensitive. As I get more aroused, it feels good when I run each finger across the bottom and then over the head."

I listen to him, trying to imagine how he'd look, but it's a fuzzy mental image at best. "I bet that feels good."

"It feels so good. But I want to focus on you. How about you take your fingers and gently rub around your clit? You might like circles around it, or you may prefer straight up and down." The encouragement in his voice is heady, and I hear the faintest shuffling of fabric from his side of the phone. "Can you do that for me, gorgeous?"

Gorgeous? My heart flutters, and I swallow before answering. "Yeah, I can do that."

"Good girl." Royal's deep, growly praise causes an all-out kaleidoscope of butterflies to take flight in my chest and stomach.

I breathe through the lightheadedness as it comes and focus back on my fingers sliding around my clit. A tingling sensation builds between my legs as I pass my fingers around the little nub.

"Oh, damn. That little gasping noise you just made. I swear I felt it in my balls. You must be feeling good?" The way he tells me what's happening with him gives me courage.

"It feels so good. It's like everything in my body is starting to relax." I try to put words to an experience I've never felt before. "Is that what it's like for you?"

"At first, it is. Then a new tension builds."

I feel what he's talking about. "I feel different. It's tight in my low tummy."

"You're doing it right. Are you working yourself slow or fast? Your breathing sounds like you've sped up. Did I say go faster?" His scolding is more of a tease.

"A little faster," I admit. "I'm so much wetter than before. It's easier to slide my fingers."

"Focus on how good it feels and follow that good feeling. You can use that other hand to run up and play with your breasts, or leave it right there on your belly and keep feeling your breathing."

His encouragement is a permission I didn't know I needed.

"What . . . what did your other partners like?" I slow my breathing to better listen to him. Like if I go completely still, maybe I'll hear what he's thinking.

"Everyone is different, but some of my femme partners have really enjoyed having their breasts played with a little more intensely than just touching. You could try squeezing your nipples," Royal says. "Or go even lighter with the touch and see how sensitive they are, what's the least amount of touch you need to feel something."

"Mmhmm." I slide my hand up to my breast. The nipple is pebbled and hard. I debate being rougher with my touch, but so far, all the light touches have felt good.

"What did you decide to do, gorgeous?" Royal's voice sounds clearer than before.

The silky sheets slide over the back of my hand while I work the tender bud. "I'm playing with my breast. It's tender, so I'm barely touching it. I like it."

As I run my fingers around my sensitive breast, the tightness grows in my body.

"That's it." Royal continues to encourage me. "Keep playing with your clit too. Both together will help you come."

I refocus on my hand working between my legs and the wetness as it coats my fingers. My body already feels tight, but needing more, I try raising my hips into the touch. A jolt courses from my toes all the way to my head, pulling a gasp from me.

"How will I know when I'm going to come?" My voice comes out lower than normal, maybe what they'd call sultry in the movies.

The answer seems obvious as my body is different, tight, and every movement feels more intense.

"I can hear you getting close. I bet your muscles are starting to tense, and you're even wetter than before. Is that true?"

"Yes," I pant.

"You'll know it when you come. Keep chasing the good feeling, focus on it and the sound of my voice." Royal's words entrench themselves in my mind.

Chase the good feeling. That little tingling sensation grows stronger.

"Mmm."

"You're doing everything right. So right. Are you going to come for me?" Royal's tone sounds rough but pleased.

It should be dirty or scandalous, but I don't care. This feels good. It feels right. It fuels my fire.

"Fuck," I gasp as a rogue shock runs through my body, but what follows draws loud moans from me.

I move my hand from my breast to cover my mouth. Gritting my teeth, I force myself not to scream, fear of being caught still present in my mind, as the tingle turns into full-power pressure, shaking my body. The tension ripples through me, and I writhe as pleasure overtakes me.

"That's it. Come so good." Royal in my ear, his dirty talk, forces my orgasm harder. "You're doing so good. Let it all out."

It feels like forever before I start to come back down and can stop gritting my teeth, my breathing still irregular and deep as I uncurl from all the tense muscles.

"I — That was — Holy shit," I pant. Even with my eyes closed, it feels like the room is spinning. "Why did I wait to —"

"Easy." He drags that word out, soothing over my babbling. "Feel it leave your body, really relax. We have all the time in the world to talk later."

I take some time to just breathe through it, but now that it's over, I feel hot and uncomfortable. I pull at my bedsheets, trying to throw the blanket off. Frustrated, I sit up and throw the covers off before collapsing back onto the bed.

I'm suddenly exhausted and can't bring myself to care about anything other than relaxing.

"How are you doing?" Royal sounds different, maybe concerned?

His voice is crisp and tense but still reassuring and good natured. I can't put my finger on it.

"Good. So good," I sigh, but realization dawns on me. "Wait, did you . . . you know?"

"No." Royal doesn't sound upset though. "I didn't come. It wasn't about me. I just wanted to be here with you." I'm starting to yawn as he says, "I bet you're tired now."

"Just a little bit." I stifle the yawn behind my hand. "My body feels all different, like I'm relaxed but maybe too relaxed, and yet I could be awake or be asleep."

"Sleep." He urges me. "Your body needs rest. Valor mentioned you're going shopping with Antonella tomorrow. You'll need energy for that."

Royal talks to Valor about me? I try to be worried about it, but my brain doesn't let me as sleepiness starts to overtake me.

"Good night, Royal. Thank you."

"Good night, gorgeous." He disconnects the call for me.

Sleep takes me so quickly I barely have time to get my headphones in my case.

CHAPTER SEVENTEEN

DESPERATELY

The sound of Leticia coming had me on the edge of climaxing. I would have come right with her. But this wasn't about me. This wasn't about us. This was all about her. For her.

But not coming with her doesn't diminish her beauty or my enjoyment of seeing her come. I couldn't see a lot with her under the covers, but the way she writhed and twisted? My view was absolutely stunning. *Perfect.*

When she moved the blankets, I was treated to a view through the camera, a perfect angle of her soft, full breasts, even after she tried to tug the sheet over her. I was awestruck staring at the screen.

Her sounds were breathy at first, nearly overtaking her voice, and then falling into heavy moans. They soaked into my soul and washed away any lingering resistance to being with her.

She's so perfect. My wolf emblazons those images into the core memory bank of our mind. *We should have been there for her, to make her come, to take care of her after.*

I wanted it too. Desperately.

I should have told her to drink water and get herself a treat, but I could tell from how she wobbled on-screen that sleep was enough aftercare for now. It's my pleasure to share this with her, and I should be there to cuddle and praise her, but I can't. Tomorrow, I'll need to be in her inbox, reassuring her that I'm proud of her.

Having her experience any emotional or physical withdrawal from me and our time together because I can't be by her side is a nightmare, one I'm trying to mitigate.

She was brilliant at taking this pleasure for herself. Unlocking this with her is an honor, and now more than ever, I want to be with her. She deserves to know I'll be here for her through everything.

Our mate. My wolf sighs contentedly.

We watch her fall into a deep sleep. Her body relaxed and comfortable among her covers.

My cock throbs, reminding me I didn't come. I want to go to bed and take care of myself to the memory of her first orgasm. But I ignore it. Exhaustion is threatening to settle in, but my to-do list is at an all-time high, and if I don't get some work done . . .

Leticia

CHAPTER EIGHTEEN

HOME ALONE

"And you're sure you don't want to come with us?" My younger cousin Sarena pouts as she looks between me and the dangerous man who is her fiancé, a member of the bratva. *No, the heir to the bratva.*

"I'm sure. I'm doing Christmas with the Cavanaghs. I won't be alone in this big empty house for Christmas." I shoo them both toward the elevator.

The last of the family who hasn't cleared out to the Italian Alps, Sarena and Nikolai, stopped by, not knowing the full truth, and tried to convince me to change my mind and go with them to Italy. No one would dream of telling Sarena that Dad has given me orders to gather intelligence. Even if they had told her, she wouldn't believe it. In part, I'm not sure I do either.

"Well, call if you change your mind. I'll send the jet." Nikolai offers me a soft smile as he squeezes Sarena around the waist before hoisting her up on his shoulder and taking her into the elevator.

She bangs on his back, giggling. "Put me down, you brute!"

I give them one last wave as the door slides closed.

It's been a whole morning of reassuring Sarena that 'I'm fine' and 'No, really I *want* to spend Christmas with the Cavanaghs' and to Nikolai confirming that 'Of course I'm not afraid of staying here alone' and 'I have three security guards and a whole security team guarding the building, how many more men do you think I need to make me safe?'

Their love and thoughtfulness are in the right place. But truthfully, I'm looking forward to two and a half weeks of freedom.

Last night with Royal on the phone, I experienced something . . . indescribable, and I'm not ready to get over my taste of what life might be like, if I were someone else.

My phone vibrates in my apron pocket. I put on my apron without even thinking about it this morning. I don't need it and should probably take it off, but it's a habit, one that brings me a bit of comfort.

It's Royal.

ROYAL:

Good morning, gorgeous. I hope you got some good sleep. Are you taking care of yourself? Food? Water?

A smile spreads across my face, and my cheeks heat. *I can't believe we did that last night.* That heat starts traveling down my neck and lower. Much lower.

LETICIA:

Good morning. Gorgeous, huh? You say that like we've exchanged more than a couple photos and that I didn't look like a gremlin in mine.

I slept SO GOOD. Thank you for asking. No food and water yet, saving my appetite for lunch with Toni in a little bit.

Royal's response is practically immediate.

ROYAL:

Please. At least get some water for me, okay?

The amount of care is unexpected but not unappreciated. I slowly make my way to the kitchen. After getting a glass, I snap a picture of the cup filling up before I send it to him.

LETICIA:

Alright, only because you asked so nicely.

I down the glass of water in a few large swallows. When I finish, there isn't a message waiting for me. My heart deflates.

Even though Royal said last night was all about me, a nagging thought persists. He's been with others before and will probably have others after me. While this was a life-changing experience for me . . . he probably only did it to be nice.

The little voice inside me whispers, *He's probably already moved on.*

Up in my room, I've showered, gotten dressed, and blow-dried my hair into large and tight curls. It's more glamorous than my daily look, but by the time I get to La Fatal Piedra, the curls will soften and the look will be less high society and more casual. The right amount for a girl's day out.

I can't get what happened last night out of my head. I want to talk to someone about it. It feels like someone should be able to tell me why I feel so . . . different. But it's not like I can tell anyone. Even Antonella isn't safe to talk to because she's now Royal's sister-in-law.

Once again, it's suffocating not having any friends.

Maybe I should just talk to Royal. We're friends. He's done this before. But it's not like I can talk to him about what I'm feeling for him. We can never be more than friends.

On my way down the stairs, I check my phone, knowing I should have at least some messages from Toni about lunch today. But my entire insides flip when I see Royal's name in the notification bar.

ROYAL:

I heard you're shopping for Christmas presents with my favorite niece today. I'd love to exchange gifts with you this year.

I wait for another message to come in. Something that would point back or reaffirm that we'd be exchanging the gifts as friends. I'm not sure why I expected it, but it doesn't come.

Maybe it's because he doesn't just see you as a friend. That thought is delusional. I know it is. An arranged marriage awaits me on the horizon, and Royal is waiting for his soul mate. Those two things don't go together.

What do I send back?

LETICIA:

Okay, but I'm warning you, I'm a really terrible gift giver. Toni is the one who always seems to know exactly what to buy someone. With me, you're likely to get three socks and a paper clip shaped like an airplane.

ROYAL:

Don't worry, I'm bad at gifts too. I'm normally more of an acts-of-service type person. I thought it might be fun to try. Zero pressure for good gifts. Just something from the heart.

I could really use a paperclip shaped like an airplane too.

From the heart? I swoon. My hand goes to my chest.

"Miss D'Medici, are you alright?"

I jump, startled by the familiar voice as it echoes through the entryway over to where I've come to a stop at the bottom of the staircase.

I look over and standing inside the elevator, one hand barring open the door, is one of my usual drivers.

"I didn't mean to startle you. Sorry. The car is waiting for you in the garage if you're ready to go?" He shuffles a little like he's moving out of the way for me to join him in the enclosed space.

"Oh." I lock my phone screen, hiding away the evidence of my emotional response. "Yes, let me grab my coat."

The ride to La Fatal Piedra isn't long, but it sure feels like it. The longer I'm in the car, the more anxious I become. My palms are a little sweaty, and I think about talking to Toni. My curiosity and awakening, if that's what you'd want to call last night, are the only things I can think about.

I don't have to give Toni any specifics. I could just ask her questions about her, it's not like we haven't talked a little about this sort of thing before. Maybe it wasn't in such specific terms, but I've always lived vicariously through her. That's all I'll chalk my questions up to being.

That is . . . if there is any alone time for us to be had. It's not like I can have this conversation in front of a child.

I close my eyes and hold my breath, making a wish. *Please let me get some alone time with Antonella.*

"Here we are, Miss D'Medici," the driver says as I'm midway through the third time saying my wish.

Snapping my eyes open, I push a smile across my face. "Thank you. I'll call when I'm ready for a ride home. I'll be with Antonella all day."

I expected an argument, but the driver nods and climbs out of the vehicle to come around and open my door. The cold wind whips off the lake down the side streets and bustles my coat in one long gust. It chills me, taking the heat of embarrassment right off my skin and freezing my face. At least I can use the cold to brush off any pink in my cheeks when talking to Toni.

Through the door and into the foyer, I see Toni sitting at a table in the front section of the restaurant.

Odd that we're not in the section reserved for family. I look toward the back of the restaurant. It's nearly empty, and the usual family tables are available, but I don't long for dark corners. Even with what I want to talk about.

Strolling over to her table, I shrug off my coat. "Wait, where's my new niece?"

Toni is quick to flag me to sit down, quieting me with her low volume. "She's coming. I may have lied to get out of the house a little early so I could pick up a few gifts she wouldn't see. Declan is bringing her in a little bit. Besides, it gives us a little time to catch up."

"It's weird sitting up front and not being squirreled away to the back room with the family. I like it." I sling my purse and coat over the back of the chair, where Toni's purchases and purse are resting. Looking outside, I steel my nerves and take the first line I thought of out on the ride here. I fan myself with my hand and give her a scandalized grin. "Oh my god. That means we can finally talk about how hot Valor is."

"Yes, he is very hot." She rolls her eyes, but I see a smile poking through.

"Leticia. I haven't seen you in forever!" Cesare, a cousin my age who used to tease me in elementary school, strolls over to the table. He smiles at me and makes a pained face, slackening his jaw. "I thought you were avoiding good food. Get you the usual?"

"Rude, but yes, my lover, please bring the usual." I giggle, teasing him right back with the ridiculous joke from the last family reunion.

"Isn't he like our fifth cousin?" Toni, perplexed, looks between me and him with narrowed eyes.

Shaking my head, I explain only half of the long story that is the inside joke, but mostly I answer her question so I can move forward with what I do want to know. "Not by blood. His mom married my mom's cousin. She had him before they met."

"Well, okay then." She raises her glass and draws a sip of water.

Cesare is quick to come with my glass of wine and leave again.

Toni breaks the silence. "It's still so weird you're twenty-three."

"Yes, well, that's what happens when you move so far away for school. In five years, your little cousin becomes not so little." I hum, taking a sip of my favorite vintage. The joys of being Italian mean a glass of wine at lunch is normal, and it can help calm your nerves if you're about to give your cousin the fifth degree about all things — okay, not *all* things — men. "Okay, Valor. Is he like amazing in bed?"

"Could you have said that any louder?" She glares before flicking her eyes to the rest of the restaurant.

I hadn't realized I was so loud. But I feel this internal clock ticking down like time is running out. Soon Kerrianne will be here, and we can't talk about this sort of thing anymore. I lean forward and whisper, "So, does he make you come?"

Redness paints Toni's cheeks, and I try not to let my mouth hang open as she answers while pressing her fingers to her temple. "Yes, okay. God, why are we talking about this?"

"Because you're getting laid, and if a man so much as looks at me, Berto gets so overprotective it hurts." I groan, thankful for the honest answer regarding anything boy or relationship based.

With a sigh, Toni sits back in her chair. "You get two questions, and that is the most I'm discussing with you today."

My mind goes completely blank. I didn't know I'd be limited both in time and number of questions. I try to come up with something that won't obviously point to what happened between Royal and me, but it feels like at any moment she'll guess what I've done. It's illogical but feels real.

"What is he like in bed?"

Toni tries not to smile. I can see her working to keep the corners of her mouth neutral. "Strong, skilled, and reciprocates well. He always tells me that he's falling into lust with me."

"Eeee!" I practically squeal. "That's so swoon worthy. Level ten swoon. I love that for you. I know you've avoided dudes before, but like . . . that sounds like he's worth the extra —"

"Oh-kayyy, cutting you off." Toni moves my glass of wine away from me. "Second question?"

"Is it all big-dick energy, or is he backing that cool swagger up?" I quirk an eyebrow. *Why did I ask that? It was a waste of a question. He and Royal are probably entirely different.*

"You're seriously asking about size?" She groans, looking longingly at my glass of wine, but she's so cautious when caring for a child that I bet she won't indulge.

I want to rephrase and choose a new question, but her answers, while informative, aren't exactly giving me anything to work with. And without giving away more about my situation, I'm at a loss.

Instead, I nod and press my hands together in front of my chest. "Oh, come on. I gotta know."

"It's not just energy," Toni deadpans.

Fanning myself, I wiggle in my seat. "I'm so happy for you!"

"Thanks, me too. As far as my theory on being married to some underling . . . I'm okay with being wrong if it means spending time with Kerrianne and Valor."

Toni's said something like that before. She always anticipated being married off to nobody important for some sort of trade agreement to join families in a business deal. But it's harrowing to hear it now. All my feelings, all this question asking, all this distraction with Royal — none of it changes the fact that I'm to be married off to someone else.

I always knew an arranged marriage awaited me, and, honestly, it didn't feel too scary or restrictive. But now that I've had a taste of freedom, a taste of choosing my own fate, even if just an eye-opening night on the phone with Royal, the idea now stirs something in my gut. It sinks deep, feeling like the concrete tied to the feet of our enemies.

After a few more moments, Kerrianne and her bodyguard come strolling down the street toward the restaurant. Toni lights up seeing her through the plate-glass window and tucks her coat over one of the bags a little bit more, hiding it.

Toni has never really expressed interest in kids of her own, but I can tell there's something special between her and Kerrianne.

I'm glad to be done asking embarrassing questions. The information I got is . . . better than nothing, but my whole perspective has changed. Hope, or maybe it's a greedy desire for more, feels crushed under the weight of reality.

I put it behind me, tucking the disappointment away the best I can, but my phone buzzes, and I look at the text message. It's one in a series that I missed the original notifications for.

ROYAL:

Don't skimp on lunch. You had a big night, and without breakfast, you're probably really hungry. I know you Italians are big on wine with meals, but maybe don't overdo it.

Wow, I sound super overprotective. Sorry.

Crossing the line back to friends.

I got called into work today. But I'm here if you need me. Don't hesitate to text.

Greetings happen quickly, and Kerrianne is busy talking about the menu with Antonella, so I take the moment to read the messages one more time.

The strongest desire to tell him I want to explore being more than friends has my fingers itching to type out a message, telling him to cross the line back to overprotective and avoid friends at all cost.

I like that he's caring for me. Wouldn't it be great if we could stay on the wrong side of the friends line?

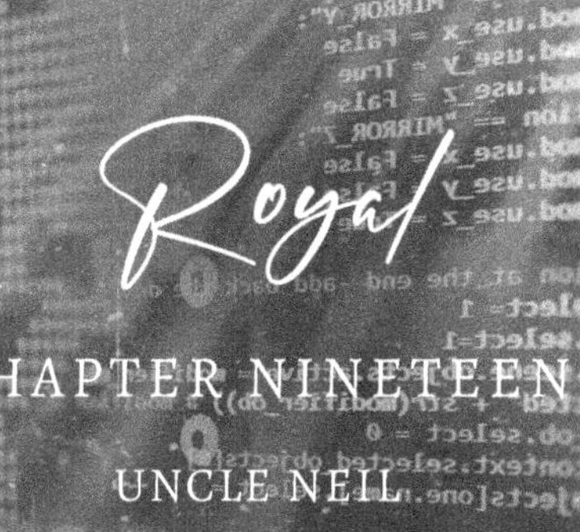

CHAPTER NINETEEN

UNCLE NEIL

"Royal?" Uncle Neil sounds surprised to see me.

I turn from where I'm pulling together a munitions order for one of our mercenaries while taking stock of what needs to be supplied at this drop location at the same time.

I pitch his name back to him in the same questioning tone. "Uncle Neil?"

Why is he here? My wolf starts questioning, his hackles raising. He's never liked my uncle.

"What are you doing out here?" He narrows his eyes at me while closing the service door to the mansion's garage behind him.

I asked that first. My wolf draws a mental map of where we are, trying to find logic in why we'd be in the same place together.

This cache, an unassuming mansion, nestled among other mansions in Barrington, isn't exactly remote, maybe seven miles from my parents' house and another ten from Valor's.

"Well, I'm here. I've got gun cases, a clipboard, and a pen." I gesture between the items as I list them off before waggling the pen.

Uncle Neil huffs. "Yes, but why are you doing that? Shouldn't you be in your tech cave working on something more important?"

I shrug. He isn't normally in my business. The technophobe is usually content to let me do whatever needs to be done and respect my work process. But the way my wolf is on edge has me pressing for information. "What's with the third degree?"

"Can't I wonder why we're not using our assets to their fullest potential?" He stands up a little straighter, the posturing meant to put me in my place.

He's not just my uncle, but he's the pack second-in-command. He outranks me not only by being my elder but by title. It won't be until Dad retires and Valor takes over as alpha that Uncle Neil and I will be on a level playing field as options for second-in-command. Assuming Neil doesn't retire with Dad. It'll be Valor's choice between us.

So . . . I really should consider backing down, but my wolf, pacing and snarling in my mind, won't let me. "Can't I wonder why the pack second is out running around to all sorts of weapons caches at all hours of the day?"

The color drains from his face.

Why is he so suspicious? My wolf snaps his teeth.

Uncle Neil tries to hide his unnerved response with a thick dose of bureaucracy. "I do work that's above your rank. You let me worry about me, and you worry about you."

I turn away from him back toward my work, fighting my eyes from rolling. "As you wish."

My wolf keeps focus on him, and in my peripheral vision, I watch as he leans up against one of the shelving units, crossing his arms. "Why is it always so tense between you and me? Valor and I butt heads, but I figure that's just him trying to take over as pack alpha soon. I'd think you'd be more laid back. It doesn't seem like you're too eager to take my place."

My phone vibrates on the table behind me, but I ignore it. "Who said I don't want to take over as pack second someday?"

"I'm just saying you're not exactly one to hang out with the pack. You're kind of a lone wolf and enjoy it that way. You maybe wouldn't like having a bunch of extra responsibility. You and I'd maybe get along better if you weren't feeling the pressure from your dad and brother to become second." He uncrosses his arms and shoves one hand into his pocket.

Danger? My wolf questions.

Neil scrubs his other hand down his face. "I just wish I'd get to know my nephew better is all."

Suspicion plagues me, but I want to get out of here and back to stalking Leticia. I can't exactly do that while holed up in this cache all day.

"Maybe some other time, Uncle Neil. I've got a busy schedule today." I wave the clipboard a little. "I'm almost done with this, and I'll be out of your way."

"Alright, I'm going to go make a cup of coffee." He pushes off the racking. "But, Royal. I can count on you if something were to happen?"

"Like what?" I furrow my brow, pinning him with my question. I set down the clipboard and pen and grab the next gun I need for the order.

"Like something happens with a buyer. You'd have my back just as much as you'd have Valor's?" Uncle Neil says Valor's name like it's distasteful in his mouth.

Now *my* hackles rise. The wolf inside me is still on edge and ready to move.

I square my shoulders and think through the movements for the easiest access to a loaded firearm. My ankle holster or managing a magazine from the table next to me. "I have always done my duty to our pack. I don't know why anyone would question that."

"No reason." He turns his back on me and heads toward the kitchen. "Want a cup?"

"No, I'm good." I watch him go, and when he's stepped through the door into the house, I snatch a magazine off the table next to me, load it into the gun in my hand, and set it down on the table pointed toward the door.

Something isn't right. But I don't know what it is. I try to soothe the angry wolf within me. Maybe I'm being paranoid. Uncle Neil has always been weird.

We'll tell Valor anyway. My wolf urges me to grab my phone and text Valor right now. But with Kerrianne shopping with Antonella, he's already stressed out about security. Adding worry about Uncle Neil would probably boil my older brother's brain.

I give up taking stock of the munitions inventory and just grab the gear for the mercenary. Before Neil's coffee is even done brewing, I've loaded the gear into the back of my SUV and am pulling out onto the road.

It's not until I'm sure no one is following me that I even dare look at my phone.

LETICIA:

I just got you the best gift ever. It's so good that if you don't want it, I'm stealing it. Not actually. I bought one for myself too.

What's hers is ours and ours is hers. My wolf is so possessively obsessed over her that he shrugs off the earlier rage and moves right into doting on her.

ROYAL:

I do believe that means we've crossed into another level of friendship.

#twinning

I'm early when I pull up in front of Mom and Dad's house. I was going to take a more thorough inventory to kill time, but it doesn't matter. The merc is also early. He's sitting in a work truck decked out as a plumber and septic services.

Pressing the button, I raise the garage door and pull into my usual parking spot. Mom and Dad's house is too far from the road for anyone to see down the long, curvy driveway, so I don't bother closing the garage door for privacy.

"You must be Royal?" the mercenary asks, leaning against his truck. "Is it true what they say about you?"

"They say a lot of things." I shrug and open the back of my SUV.

"Fair enough." He approaches and looks in at the weaponry. "You really don't mess around when hiring new contractors, do you?"

"We've found it's in our best interest to hire the best and

brightest and then make sure we've got the best tools for them to use." I lean against the garage doorframe. "I take it this is to your standard?"

He picks up the rifle from where it lies in the back of the SUV and shoulders it, looking down the barrel. "What do you offer for scopes?"

"Check the black box on the left. I brought you four options. I'm not the most familiar with them, but those are our most popular requests." I enjoy the way his eyes light up as he lifts the lid on the box.

He picks up the second most expensive one. "I had one of these when I served with the special forces. I didn't know they made these anymore."

"They don't." I fight back a yawn forced through from my wolf as he releases tension from the interaction with Uncle Neil. "We were able to obtain a large final shipment before they went out of business. It's not an unlimited supply, so treat it kindly, but they're available."

"For a price." He unnecessarily finishes for me while tucking the rifle into a case.

"Exactly." I watch as he looks over the different rounds I've brought for him to sample.

"Valor said you're the tech genius. They just let you meet with mercs alone?" He isn't threatening me, but the confusion is genuine. "Most tech guys don't know a butt from a barrel."

"I may be of most service behind a keyboard, but don't mistake me for nonthreatening. We're all predators here." I smile and then use the same line I've heard Valor use when talking to new mercenaries when they come to work for us. "As I said before, we hire the best and the brightest. You wouldn't be smart to kill me over barely ten grand in equipment. Unless you're admitting to not being all that smart."

The genuine laugh that comes from him is a little shocking. He goes back to looking over the equipment. "What they say is true, then? You have enough weapons to take down a small government?"

"If there is something you want, there is always a way to get it." I don't entertain what our warehouses have to offer.

My phone vibrates in my pocket.

Leticia? My wolf demands I take it out to look.

And because I'm trying to be nonchalant with him, I do.

LETICIA:

I'll be home alone this evening. If you wanted to have another Late Nite Byte session, that'd be cool. Totally understand if not.

Our mate wants us. My wolf wags his tail, practically bouncing for joy.

"You don't know what my first assignment is?" The mercenary draws my attention back.

I pocket my phone before answering. "Not my job. You'll receive secured communications between three and thirty days in advance for consultations and seven days in advance for direct orders."

"I was hoping for something more . . . express," he mumbles.

"I'll let them know you're hoping to get your feet wet earlier rather than later," I say to appease him, despite knowing it won't matter. The jobs are assigned based on skill and expertise.

"Thanks." He nods, looking over the last of what's left in the back of the SUV, a couple of handguns.

"You're the one who does the M-9 mods?" He indicates where the aftermarket hardware has been installed.

I nod, feeling frustrated with how long this is taking. I want to get back to stalking Leticia.

It takes ten more minutes before he's loaded the equipment into his truck and is driving down the road toward the gate.

I don't wait for him to clear it before heading into the house.

"Oh, Royal," Mom calls before I make it to the stairs to my lair.

"Yes?" I bite back a groan because she doesn't deserve my bad attitude.

"Your father and I are going out for dinner tonight. Did you want to come?" she calls from the living room.

"Depends." I walk over to the living room entryway and give her a smile but stop when I see her sitting on the living room floor with a wild number of objects scattered around her. "What are you doing?"

"Oh! I'm preparing my robot for battle." She thrusts a fork into the air for emphasis.

"That's a vacuum." I point to a pretty standard robot vacuum, clearly not fit for any sort of battling.

"Yes, Dad and I are having a battle. I'm getting some practice in. I'm going to kick his ass." She seems so proud of herself that I nod along in her excitement.

"Dinner is where tonight?" I ask, knowing that, unless it's my absolute favorite restaurant, nothing will keep me from leaving the basement where I can watch Leticia on high-def screens.

"Ellery's," she answers while picking up a hot glue gun.

"Just bring me back a half-roast duck?" It pains me to watch her hot glue a switchblade to the robot vacuum, but I stand here nonetheless.

"And sweet potato fries?" Mom asks, looking up. Her gray hair falls into her face, and she's quick to brush it away with her free hand.

"Yes, please." I turn around before I'm forced to watch her create more of this Frankenstein's monster robot.

I know it's probably against the rules to ask me for help, but it almost feels like an insult to not be included.

Leticia

CHAPTER TWENTY

PARTY ANIMALS

"Hello." I wonder if Royal can hear my smile when I greet him on the phone.

"Oh, thank god." Royal sighs dramatically. "It rang more than twice, and I thought you were standing me up."

"Don't be ridiculous." I laugh. "I'm the one who asked you to call tonight, remember?"

"I don't know, maybe this was how you were planning to end our friendship, stand me up or something." He yawns before continuing. "In all seriousness, it's good to hear your voice."

"It's good to hear yours." I keep looking at the contents of the refrigerator, like they'll magically morph into something interesting to eat.

"So, what is the cohost doing tonight?" Royal's voice changes in volume and quality, like he goes from one microphone to another. Whatever he's using now is much crisper and clearer. It's a noticeable difference with how I'm holding my phone to my ear.

"Well, I'm currently glaring at the contents of the refrigerator, demanding that they change into something delicious to eat." I give up and close the refrigerator door.

"Possibly a dumb question" — Royal pauses for a beat — "but why don't you just order food from somewhere? You're in Gold Coast. It has some of the best restaurants in all of Chicago."

"True." I think about the restaurants in the surrounding blocks. "But how do you know they're the best?"

"The awards they earn are public record?" Royal's quick to defend himself, but in a more meek voice, he says, "Listen, I'm just a man who likes to eat. A little thing like boundaries hasn't ever stopped me from finding a way to get food."

I gasp, pulling my hand to my chest as I pace the kitchen. "Scandalous! You've been coming to D'Medici territory for food?!"

"Whoa, whoa, whoa, let's not make it sound nefarious like that. I occasionally will blur the lines of who belongs where to send a delivery driver from neutral territory to D'Medici territory to bring me what I desire. But I personally have respected the boundary between our families ninety-eight percent of the time," Royal admits with such a sly tone. "The other two percent was for coffee because I wasn't about to go to that stupid fuckin' chain when a perfectly good local shop was around the corner."

"Well, I think that's probably negligible. We wouldn't want the chain stores to get too uppity about themselves." I walk over to the drawer where I keep some takeout menus hidden under tea towels.

"Decide to order in?" Royal asks, and I pause.

I get that feeling like I'm being watched again, but it's not a menacing feeling. It's kind of comforting to not be alone.

I shake my head. "Yeah, there's this Chinese place I can hardly ever order from because Dad's too racist despite being an immigrant himself, and Mom is unadventurous." I sigh, looking over the menu. There are so many options, and they all sound so good.

"My parents just went out to dinner. They're bringing me back a half duck and sweet potato fries. Maybe they'll get back at the same time as your food arrives and we can eat together." He offers, and I welcome the change in subject from my trauma dumping.

"That'd be great. But what should I order?" I drum my fingers on the counter before putting the phone on speaker and setting it in front of me.

"What are the options?" Royal tries to help.

"Should I send you pictures of the menu?" I reach for my phone again.

"Or the name of the restaurant. I bet they have an online menu?"

Moving my hand from my phone, I flip the menu over like I

haven't looked at it a hundred times just to double-check the name. "Oh, fair. It's called Lion's Den."

I don't hear any clicking coming from his side of the phone.

"This place looks delicious." Royal hums. "What was that noise about?"

"What noise?" I stop breathing, trying to listen.

"You made this little grumbling noise, like you're displeased or something."

"I don't remember making a noise," I say but now start questioning it.

"What were you thinking about?" Royal probes a little harder.

All I can do is pretty much think about you lately. My face turns hot, and I scrunch my nose up, hoping for a positive response. "I couldn't hear you typing."

"Oh, I'm using my tablet." He explains without a pause. "We could video call — that is —" he stammers, "if you want."

Is he nervous? I'm thrown off base on multiple levels. *Video call is a new step.*

"Yeah. That'd be okay. I'll warn you, I didn't look great in the photo I sent you, but now, after a day out and about, it's a lot worse." I quickly step to the drawer where I keep extra hair ties and try to wrangle my hair from the blonde mess of flyaways into a presentable pony.

"Well, I'm in sweatpants, and I think my T-shirt has a stain on it." Royal almost sounds embarrassed, maybe? "I should probably change shirts."

"Gasp!" I fake the noise. "A stain? Unacceptable. My friends can never have a stain." I'm giggling by the time I get the last word out. "Seriously." I draw a deep breath to pull myself together. "I'm not worried about a stain."

"Good, because I'm not worried about however badly you think you look. I'm sure you're perfect." Royal turns my words, the entire sentiment, back against me.

I stop trying to wrangle my hair and let it fall back loose around my shoulders because I can hear how much he means it. His honesty resonates in my bones.

"If you're sure." I tap the video call button on my phone and pick it up.

"Positive," Royal answers, and a second later, his face comes into view. "There you are, gorgeous."

He smiles widely when he says that, and it looks so genuine. He's animated and full of life.

I push past the stupid grin that wants to form on my face when he calls me that. "Okay, so you're having what for dinner?"

"Duck and sweet potatoes."

I go back to looking at the menu, but I want to be watching him. I think he has a dimple when he smiles, but I can't be sure without seeing it some more.

"Duck is like chicken. So if I have chicken, it's almost like we're eating the same meal." I look back at my phone. "Not really, but close enough."

"What's your go-to chicken meal?" Royal moves, and the background behind him spins.

I try to catch glimpses of what is in the room with him, but he fills up too much of the frame.

"Well, normally I like General Tso's chicken and snow peas or honey chicken." I look at options and try to decide.

"Order them all, then you can eat a little bit of each." Royal seems to read my mind.

"Doesn't that seem excessive?" I eye the potstickers and crab rangoons on the menu too.

"Pftt," Royal huffs. "You're supposed to order an inordinate amount of Chinese food. It's like a rule. If you don't order enough food to feed at least three people more than are attending said meal, it's against the law."

"The law, hmmm?" I shake my head and look at him on the screen.

He nods, his brown hair flopping with the movement. "Trust me, I'm a food-ordering expert."

"Okay, fine." I concede.

"Good, because I already put in an order with those three, some potstickers, crab rangoons, sweet and sour sauce, and sugar buns." He's beaming.

"What? How?" My jaw drops.

His Cheshire cat grin comes with a nonchalant shrug. "They

have online ordering, it's not exactly a secret where you live, and because we're eating together, it kinda makes this like a date."

He wants to date me? I try to hold back my excitement.

He backpedals a second. "Friend date, if we have to call it that."

"Sure." My heart falls, but I don't dare let my smile fade.

I know I'm swimming in dangerous waters. The pool of emotions is deep and turbulent. If I allow myself to be pulled away from the safe shores of friendship, nothing will save me from the reality of drowning when the time comes to marry someone else.

But Royal smiles. "Want to pick out a movie to watch while we eat?"

I'm distracted from the perilous situation again. "Absolutely."

Royal

CHAPTER TWENTY-ONE

NO SERVICE

She fell asleep three hours ago. After dinner together and one cheesy movie later, conversation slowed until Leticia drifted off to sleep. Luckily for me, she plugged her phone in before propping it up next to her.

Precious mate. My wolf sighs as he relaxes within me.

I'm in the final couple minutes of running data on a job for Valor, which luckily doesn't require a lot of paying attention, and I can watch her sleep.

Leticia softly murmurs something.

I run my hand through my hair again and rehash the conversation where I called tonight a date. *I can't believe I did that.*

I can. My wolf snarks. *We're going to keep our mate.*

The data run dumps important information into the spreadsheet, and I try to focus on it to review the findings, but Leticia snores softly, and I turn to look at her instead.

Sleepy, so sleepy. My wolf huffs out an exhale, and I can feel exhaustion slipping in.

Before climbing into bed, I grab my phone and send Valor a text, letting him know his data report needs to be double-checked but that I'll do it in the morning.

From watching her bedroom's security camera footage, I know exactly how Leticia is lying in bed. I pick the opposite side of my bed, placing my phone where she'd be lying, and watch her from this angle.

It will kill me to watch her marry someone else.

My wolf beds down inside me. He spins in a small circle, content to curl up and watch her. *We won't let her. It doesn't have to be complicated like you make everything.*

I wish it was just as simple as claiming her as our own and that a small declaration would fix the cavernous obstacle between us.

Letting my phone stay connected, I drift off the same way Leticia did.

In the morning, the video call was disconnected, and a text message from Leticia was in its place.

LETICIA:

You snore. I'm hanging around the house today, purging my closet, if you want to talk while I do so. Totally understand if you're busy.

I've sent her a couple of messages since then, but it's been over an hour, yet no response.

My pulse is pounding in my head, and a tightness in my chest has me unsettled. I was trying to behave and not spend so much time watching her.

But what if she's been kidnapped and no one knows she's gone but me? What if she's hurt and the guards they left her with don't know?

The camera feeds to Casa D'Medici are up in just a few keystrokes. The shortcut auto programmed itself with how frequently I go there.

I drop the password into the private camera feed to her bedroom after scouring the rest of the house.

On an exhale, my shoulders drop, the tension fades, and a smile finds its way onto my face.

Leticia is in her bedroom, a mountain of clothes piled on her bed, and I'm pretty sure her phone is buried somewhere underneath it.

What a mess, no wonder she can't hear us. My wolf shakes his head, preferring neat and tidy spaces. He can't imagine being in that chaos.

Unfortunately the report for Valor and a mountain of other work need to be done, so I move her room feed off to the other screen and delve into work.

It's noon before I get a message from Leticia.

LETICIA:

OH GOD. I lost my phone and totally spaced, please don't be mad.

ROYAL:

I could never be mad.

My wolf snorts. *Liar. You'd be mad if you couldn't find her. But you had a camera, so you weren't mad.*

It's not mad. I'd be scared and upset. I argue with him.

LETICIA:

How is your day going?

ROYAL:

Oh, excellent. Just the usual, work, a little more work, and a side of . . . you guessed it, work.

But then a gorgeous woman texted me and made my day better.

What are you up to, gorgeous?

I look over at the screen. Her room is . . . slightly less messy than it was before.

LETICIA:

I'm through the worst of the closet clean out. Now it's just to put everything away and get the donate-able items in bags.

Thinking about Chinese leftovers for lunch, what are you having?

The empty cup of coffee and plate where I heated up Dad's leftovers from Ellery's last night don't lend much in the way of lunch.

ROYAL:

Hadn't decided yet. I'll go take a look at the fridge while you reheat your food.

We can call while we eat and pretend we're having lunch together.

I pocket my phone and head upstairs to the kitchen.

"Mom?" I call into the quiet house.

When I decided to live at home, there weren't a lot of rules or discussions. But usually we text each other if we're leaving, just a general heads-up.

She doesn't answer, and I walk through the house to the stairs that lead upstairs to her and Dad's bedroom. Closer to the stairs, I hear her chatting on the phone with a friend. It sounds solemn and not a happy discussion.

My unsettledness could be fueled by Mom's tension. The whole house radiates with it.

Even with that knowledge, though, the anxiousness isn't fading.

First, I couldn't find Leticia, and then Mom wasn't immediately at my beck and call.

I'm being paranoid. Brush it off.

It's not paranoia if someone is out to get you. We're Mafia. It could happen. My wolf gives me at least an excuse for the tension.

I mosey back to the kitchen, rolling my shoulders with hopes of freeing up that extra tension.

It's much warmer up here than it is in my lair. Maybe I'm venting too much server heat outside rather than into my living environment.

A knock comes to the front door, and Mom and Dad's refusal to put a wall monitor in the main living area means I can't see who it is without pulling up their security system on my phone. Which would take longer than it would to just go see who it is.

I shouldn't be this on edge. They'd have to be let through the gate by the security staff, which means it's either someone on the preapproved list — family and pack members — or it's an expected contractor, which is something I'd be notified of.

But I trust the instinct. Letting my wolf rise to the surface, I grab a gun from the sofa table before heading to the door. Chambering a round, I double-check the safety before tucking it into my waistband behind my back.

"I got the door," I call up the stairs to Mom, but I don't hear an acknowledgment.

The front door is bulletproof, and I look out through the peephole, finding that the visitors fall on the list of 'family and pack members.'

Charlie Murphy is standing midway down the walk, and James Kirk is climbing out of the driver's side of the van.

They're not anyone intimidating. A couple of lower-level members of the mob, they primarily do odd jobs like deliveries and security.

I walk barefoot out onto the frozen concrete, closing the door behind me.

"James, what's going on?" I look past him at one of our work vans, normally used for odd jobs but not something I'd associate with him.

"We need you to come with us," James says from where he leans against the side of the van. He's disheveled, coat askew, and looks like he's been up for days.

Why? My wolf snarls.

"To what end?" I press for information. "No offense, but you two aren't exactly people I take orders from."

"A job went bad. We need your help. We'll explain on the way." Charlie attempts to usher me toward the van.

He's in rough shape too. In the years I've known him, he's never grown a beard, but now? Days-old scruff is paired with dark circles under his eyes.

A wicked wind whips past them over to me, and I catch a sharp nose full of acidic fear.

I shake my head. "That's not happening. I'm going nowhere."

Charlie pulls a gun but holds it low at his side as if trying to conceal it. "Let me make it easy for you, Royal. There are two of us and one of you. You shoot me, James shoots you and then goes in the house and finishes off your mom. Betty will never hear the shots. She's talking to Marge and Nancy because Derek and Alicia's son Collin was killed last night in a hit-and-run. So they're arranging the funeral. Means she won't have time to pull a weapon. Does Betty shift fast in her old age? Faster than a bullet?"

He did not just talk about Mom that way. My wolf snarls and snaps his teeth.

But while he talks, I've been running through the scenarios, and he's right. I'm a good shot, but I'm not Valor good. I'm not confident I can kill both of them and protect Mom. Shifting or not, these guys clearly have it thought out.

"Or, you can come with us, and Betty gets to live." James pushes off the van and slides open the side door without even turning away from me.

Better chance at killing them both if we're all in the van. Someone has to focus on driving. My wolf and I agree on the best course of action.

It takes everything in me to push my feet forward toward the van. As I step, Charlie tucks his gun back into his jacket. When I get close enough to him, he grabs hold of my arm and twists it backward. I try to fight him off, but he grabs my gun from the small of my back, and I know the sound of a safety being flicked off well enough to stop fighting.

"Don't make me paralyze you. One bullet, you go down and you don't get back up. Tech guys don't need to walk in order to work." He pushes the barrel of the gun into my spine. "Do as you're told, and maybe when this is done, you get to live."

"Get to live. Great," I growl.

Mom will know I'm missing. She knows I wouldn't leave without texting her. She'll call Valor.

Or instead, we kill them before leaving the front gate? My wolf conspires.

Need information. Why are they doing this? I argue with him as I'm shoved toward the van.

As I approach, the scent of stale cigarette smoke permeates the cold winter air. I choke on it and cough as I'm thrust through the van door. My knees slam against the metal floor when I fall forward. Catching myself with one hand, I try to sit upright and move toward the side of the van, but something whacks me on the back of my shoulders and neck.

Fairly certain it's the butt of my own fucking gun.

I collapse, and both arms are pulled behind my back. Instinct has me fighting back as Charlie scrambles into the van on top of me, pinning me down.

"Shit. Missed. Get the bag." A new voice draws my attention, and I get a glimpse of Tommy O'Halloran moving in the back of the van.

A canvas bag is pulled over the top of my head, and cable ties are used to secure my wrists behind my back. Then I'm pulled by the shoulders farther into the van. The door slams closed.

We ride in silence, down the driveway to the gate. My kidnappers don't mind when I move from lying on my stomach to sitting crisscross applesauce, as Kerrianne would call it, on the van floor.

It takes two minutes to get to the front gate from my parents' house. The van slows, but I don't hear the sound of the motorized gate being opened.

The driver's side door opens, and James gets out.

They killed the gate guards. So they're really not as stupid as I thought they were.

Growing up in the same house means I know the roads in intricate detail, so I follow the mental map as the van slows and takes corners. We turned left, meaning we're moving away from Barrington and the mansion-filled neighborhoods toward the country rather than right into Chicago.

We're ten minutes down the road, nearing the highway, and I can't handle the silence anymore. "So what's the plan?"

"Shut up," James snaps.

But Tommy isn't so tight-lipped. "Well, there'll be a new regime, and you can either get with the program or get dead."

"Regime change." I shake my head a little more vigorously than usual to emphasize my mock confusion through the bag over my head as the van pulls onto the highway. I lean forward to counter the physics of the older vehicle's poor acceleration, stopping myself from sliding around. "You want someone new in charge of tech? I don't know if anyone is better qualified than me. Clearly not the three of you. The last time we chatted, you still thought the dog filter on the social media apps was funny. I mean, Kerrianne likes it too, but she's seven."

"God, you're so fuckin' full of yourself," James growls from the driver's seat. "We're getting rid of you while Neil takes care of your Dad and Valor. Lucky for us, there's an easy traitor to pin everything on."

"Poor Antonella, saved Kerrianne just to be murdered by her own husband." Charlie drops his voice, and it's laced with actual empathy rather than sarcasm.

"What do you mean? I see you're doing the whole evil villain laying out their plan, so let's hear this bright idea you've got." I sigh and try not to fidget and reach for my phone. But pressing a couple auxiliary buttons would throw more than a wrench in their plans.

"Well, we're going to make it look, at least to the pack, like the D'Medicis were spying, breaking the truce." Tommy explains, but the lack of information makes it seem like maybe he doesn't really know how the framing will work.

My wolf rolls his eyes. *Low-level grunts. We're not getting enough information.*

My phone vibrates, and I raise my hip, but it's too late. The fabric of my pocket is too thin, and it rattles against the metal van floor.

"You didn't take his phone?" James snarls.

"Hand it over," Charlie tells me.

"Really? It's not like I can move with my hands cable tied together."

Total and complete lie. If I wanted out of these things, it'd be a breeze. Dislocate the thumb, and slide right out. Lord knows Valor and I have practiced enough times over the years. Even Kerrianne is pretty proficient at getting out of cable ties.

"Get his phone," James orders from the front.

Tommy, from behind me, jostles me this way and that, shoving until he finds the pocket with my phone in it. He must extend it over my head as he says, "Here, take it."

Maybe I can pit them against each other. "Why are you handing it to Charlie? You're better with tech than he is, Tommy. Though I thought there was a chance I could live through this? If so, just give it back, and no one has to get hurt."

The van is slowing, and I hear the tick of the blinker.

It's been three minutes. My wolf calculates. We're less than a dozen miles away from the house.

"You're so full of yourself. Gotta be the smartest ass in the room, don't you?" Charlie growls.

It doesn't matter that they have my phone. None of them are smart enough to access any information on it anyway.

"Better the smartass than dumbasses like you." I laugh at my own joke.

Immediate regret stings as Tommy smacks the backside of my head with an open palm. "You really don't know when to shut your mouth, do you?"

I take that as my cue to rest before whatever they've got planned next. A headache blooms. Whether from the smack upside my head or being hit earlier, I can't tell, but it only gets worse.

My phone is in a military-grade case, and it makes a really distinct sound when it bashes against metal shit. And over and over again, something is hitting my phone case. If I had to guess, the back of a gun. Probably the same one I borrowed from the living room table.

Why would he not take it out of the case first? My wolf groans, experiencing this amateur hour like it's actually entertaining.

The van takes another turn. I'm less familiar with where we are this far from the house, but we're definitely headed out away from civilization.

"Enough!" James shouts, and I'm clearly not the only one suffering from the noise. "We'll destroy his phone when we get to where we're going."

"Which is where?" I attempt to figure out more of the plan.

"Nice try, nerd." James scoffs at a normal volume now that Charlie is done trying to destroy my phone and its military-grade case.

"Again, I thought there was a way I got to live in all this. Survival of the fittest and all that? I'm just trying to figure out how to stay on this side of the grass."

I know from hostage negotiations training that I need to relate more to these guys, but I've known them forever. If there was more I could do to get on their side of things, I'd try, but we grew up playing in the same pack. We already have things in common, and they're doing this anyway.

"It's not up to us. Neil is deciding if you're worth saving," Tommy answers. "We're taking you out to the preserve and waiting for instructions."

God dammit, Uncle Neil.

"The preserve? With notoriously bad cell service?" I force myself to clench my fists rather than break out of these cable ties and smack him up the side of the head as he sputters like it's not something he considered.

There's got to be more information about what's going on. Maybe he knows it. Push harder. My wolf urges me. *Or kill them now?*

"Alright, so what?" I ease up on the pressure I was pushing with my questions and try a more casual tone. "Neil is framing Antonella, and he's going to try to kill Valor in his own house?"

"No, that'd be stupid. He's not doing it in the house. He'll do it on the lawn, make it look like the D'Medicis showed up and ambushed the place," Tommy answers with a smug scoff.

"When?" I feel sick to my stomach and start thinking through the movements.

Break the cable ties, assess, grab the closest gun from Charlie or Tommy. Shoot whoever had the gun, then kill James, then finish off Charlie or Tommy, whoever I didn't shoot the first time.

Moving van. Need to stop first. My wolf catches the flaw in the plan. *Could pull James out of the driver seat, but would we drive off the road first? Would have to kill Charlie and Tommy first.*

"They should be on their way to Valor and Antonella's soon. They wanted to make sure you were out of the way first. Couldn't have you warning Valor or shutting down that smart house of his." James draws out his words, calculating something.

That's the most surprising part of the plan. They knew I'd be watching, should have been watching. I was busy watching Leticia. *Would I have even noticed?*

Of course you would have. You get door alerts for Valor's torture chamber. If they're framing Antonella, then Valor would take her there. My wolf continues. *Leticia is not the problem. Our mate is not the problem.*

The van slows further, and we turn off the paved road onto a gravel one. Without seat belts, or even a seat, I'm jostled around, sliding on the floor, while the van drives too fast on uneven ground.

Five more minutes of plotting, my head throbbing, and suffering in silence pass before the van comes to a stop.

James shoves me out of the way as he opens the door and climbs out. "Gotta take a leak," he says, and I hear his footsteps crunch in the gravel as he walks to the right.

Another pair of footsteps approaches.

"Get out," Tommy snaps.

Tactically speaking, this is the right time to make my move. I make my lousy excuse. "Really, guys, not like I can just get up and follow. Cable ties and a bag over my head, remember?"

Tommy pulls the bag off the top of my head, taking a little hair with it. I let out a low growl but force composure.

Luckily, it's early afternoon in winter, so I'm not blinded by the sun since it's starting to set. It's still cold as fuck though, and despite running warm as a wolf, I'm freezing and wishing I had at least a pair of sandals in all this. *That'll teach me for answering the door barefoot.*

When Tommy goes to pull me up by my shoulder, I resist, pressing the cable into my left thumb socket. Almost . . . there . . .

After a painful pop, my thumb dislocates, which I time with a fall to the floor of the van.

"Are you fucking stupid?" Tommy barks, stepping into the van to pull me out.

Slipping my hand free, I roll backward over my shoulder and bring my arms in front of me. Tommy is a big dude, taller than me and built like a bus. But no amount of muscle can stop him from reacting to a painful kick in the groin. I press back on my right hand and kick out my left foot, catching him right in the balls.

He doubles over, causing him to fall forward over the top of me.

Gun, holster on his belt. Left side. My wolf sees it before I do.

I scramble and grab his gun, pointing it directly at his heart.

"Sorry, Tommy, isn't personal." I grimace as I pull the trigger, putting a bullet through his chest.

The sound is deafening in the small space, and my ears start ringing. I bite back a cry as I push my left thumb back in place, staying back out of the view of the door.

"He killed Tommy!" Charlie yowls as he opens the driver's side door before sprinting around to the side of the van. From far to the right, I hear a distant "Fuck!" from James.

Charlie cautiously approaches the sliding door, gun drawn. He peeks in just enough for me to lunge forward, push his forearm down, and quickly point my gun at his head. I pull the trigger.

No bang. Just the deadening click of empty. "Who the fuck brings just one bullet to a kidnapping?"

I press the still-hot barrel into Charlie's cheek instead, causing him to scream and pull away from the van. Jumping out, I see James running toward us, fumbling with his belt. Before James can reach for his weapon, I toss the empty gun at him, which he tries to catch on instinct. Swinging a wide barrel punch, I clock him across the cheek and then kick him in the gut.

Behind you. Charlie's up. My wolf helps.

I whirl around a second before Charlie can point his gun at me again. I grab his armed hand, forcing it to the ground. We struggle, and a gunshot fires off. I cry out at the impact on my left leg. The force dropping me to my knees.

Definitely got shot. *Isn't this lovely? Fucking Neil and his goddamned power trips.*

But no pain comes.

I assume I can buy some time with the adrenaline pumping

through my veins, so I pull myself up and ram my forehead into Charlie's nose. Might as well make the most of my headache. His nose crunches as he squeals, and he lets go of the gun. Pulling it from his grasp, I shove at his shoulder, pushing him back to the ground.

Before I can do anything, James tackles me from behind. Normally I'd be able to hold my own, but my bare feet slip on the loose gravel. White blasts across my vision as James lands a brutal punch across my face. Charlie might be a shit fighter, but James clearly has had some practice.

We're missing lunch with our mate over this? It's bullshit, my wolf snarls.

Charlie's voice is muffled under the ringing in my ears, so I can't make out what he's saying as he approaches. The sound fades, and it takes a second for me to recover.

"We're supposed to keep him alive, you idiot." James is shouting, pinning me with his weight.

"He came at me!" Charlie defends.

"Shut up!" I command, channeling every little bit of my Dad and Valor, their alpha command-y-ness, as possible.

Reaching down, I grab the gun from James's holster and buck my hips, shoving him off me. Charlie holds his hands in the air, with James joining him a moment later.

I wince as I stand, the pain in my leg starting to gain purchase. Pointing a gun at each of them, I ask, "Who else is coming out here? Why the fuck are we all the way out here?"

"You don't get to make demands." James rages at me. "You're our fuckin' hostage."

We only need one of them to talk. My wolf huffs, and I pull the trigger.

Luckily, James's gun fires perfectly. The round finds its home in his skull, and he drops to the ground, wide eyes unseeing.

I turn to Charlie, who slowly backs away from me, his shoes catching on sticks and roots as he backs toward the nearby woods.

Pitying him, I repeat the questions. "I'll give you one more chance. Who else is coming out here? Why are we all the way out here?"

"Just N-Neil and Sa-Samuel. Neil said he'd c-call with instructions after he takes care of Valor," Charlie answers. "Please don —"

I shoot Charlie square between the eyes. His body falls, and aside from my panting breaths, silence fills the space.

Suddenly, my leg starts screaming in pain, drawing my attention. My left leg has a solid bullet hole in it, blood already staining my pants.

"Fuck." I force myself to draw slow breaths. "What have I done?"

What we needed to to survive. My wolf supplies, refocusing me.

I'm not the one in immediate danger. It didn't hit an artery, so I'm not going to bleed out by the time it takes to get to civilization. I step back the ten feet that I'd made it away from the van.

Adrenaline keeps my body running, and I move, with a little pain, into the van and dig around under Tommy to find my phone.

Luckily, it's under an easy-to-move arm rather than his torso.

The phone case is toast, and I pry off the broken metal and tempered glass.

Faster. My wolf urges me. *Valor, Kerrianne, Antonella. They need us.*

Once I wrestle the phone free, I find that the damage to the case resulted in the screen breaking in inopportune places. I push the emergency dial button, trying to get it to send through a call, but it's busted and it clicks without making headway.

Try something else! my wolf snarls.

Frustrated, I try the screen again. It turns on this time but is hardly functional. I do what I can with it. Finally I get one app, the phone's basic call feature, to ring to the outside world.

It rings and then stops.

No service.

No service because, of course, we're in the middle of nowhere. I move to the driver's door of the van and yank it open.

The keys aren't in the ignition.

"Be so fuckin' for real right now." I want to scream but clench my fists instead, the shattered glass on my phone screen cutting into my hand.

Focus. Don't get drawn into the distraction. Find the keys. My wolf levels me out.

It takes slow steps to walk back over to where James lies dead. And every step, I keep trying the call button.

On the sixth step, the call connects. I freeze, holding as still as I can.

"Valor." He answers.

"Fuckin' hell. It's not Antonella. Don't hurt her. I couldn't get the damn thing to call out or answer. They shattered the damn screen. It's not Antonella." I'm talking so fast that I can't slow down. I gasp for breath, trying to make sure I'm making sense.

"You're okay?" Valor doesn't acknowledge what I've told him.

Get moving. The wolf urges, trying to drive me toward James and the keys.

"Neil and fuckin' Samuel are trying some shit. They're —" I take a step forward, and the line sounds like it goes dead. "God fuckin' damn it. What good is a fuckin' indestructible case if it breaks and destroys the phone?"

"Yes, I can hear you. Can you get here?" Valor is despondent, his voice flat, cut off from his emotions like when something bad is happening.

"Yeah. I'm on my way as soon as I fuckin' find the goddamn keys." I go to step forward again, and the phone beeps. I freeze, turning around back toward the van. "Fuck it, faster if I hot-wire it. I'm on my way. Don't hurt Antonella."

The call disconnects. It was either Valor hanging up on me or the universe giving me a big middle finger. The screen goes black, and no amount of pressing gets it to light up again. I toss it into the van before looking at Charlie and James.

Don't panic. Stop the bleeding first. My wolf draws my attention back to the wound in my leg, and focusing on it brings pain into my consciousness.

I rip the bottom of my pants on my non-injured leg, tearing the blood-flecked fabric apart and wrapping the wound tight, applying as much pressure as I can stand but not making a tourniquet. If I can't stop the bleeding, things are going to get worse, and a tourniquet is the absolute last resort.

Bandage tied tight, I survey the mess I've made. My blood is all over the place out here. Evidence of what happened is everywhere.

I'm worried, despite the time of day and year, about someone coming back and finding the corpses . . . *If there's no body, then there's no crime, right?*

Yeah, I'm more worried about that than getting stopped by a cop who isn't on our payroll. *I don't know who I can trust. Who knows where the coup ends?*

It'll be agonizing getting the bodies into the van, but a double-murder charge is a hell of a lot harder to make go away than bodies are.

Leticia

CHAPTER TWENTY-TWO

STOOD UP, PARTY OF 1

It's been two and a half hours. I ate my food in silence, and now I'm moping rather than putting my room back together.

I can't believe he joked about me standing him up for a date and then did so to me.

I'm pathetic. The first guy who made me feel something, I let him into my head and my life, and at the first opportunity, he bolts.

Worst of all? I texted Toni for at least someone to talk to, and she hasn't responded.

No, scratch that. Not the worst of all. Worst of all is that I still have to do Christmas with the Cavanaghs. That is, if Christmas still happens. Maybe I get uninvited. If I don't though . . . how embarrassing will this be? Maybe I'll get lucky and Royal won't be there. I won't have to look at his face and give him a gift. *Do I even give him the gift still?*

I don't have to look to know the matching microphone blankets, part of a 1950s-themed collection from a chic boutique, are still there. I guess I could just return those. Won't need late-night talk-show host blankets since —

What if something happened to him?

I'd been so busy wallowing in self-pity that I didn't even think of it. Maybe he can't text me back because something bad is happening. We've been so adamant about not talking about work and our families that it's been so easy to forget — Royal is Irish Mob. He could be hurt or worse.

Guilt and worry feel like two stones battling for place in my stomach.

How could I be so dense?

I pick up my phone and see the three pointedly worded messages from when I thought he was standing me up.

More politely, I send:

LETICIA:

Proof of life. At least let me know something bad didn't happen to you?

CHAPTER TWENTY-THREE

COST OF CIVIL WAR

It took almost an hour for me to get the bodies in the car. The pain in my leg fought against the adrenaline and anxiety as it made its way through my system. But, in the process, I found the keys, so I didn't have to hot-wire the ancient van. Though it would have been good practice.

"Royal." Dad meets me in the driveway of Valor's house.

"Dad." I shove open the driver's door with a wince. "I'm probably going to fall out and look really stupid. Could you turn around so you don't have to watch?"

"What happened?" Dad rushes over and opens the door as wide as it goes. He brings his hand up to cover his mouth. "You're bleeding."

"Yeah, that's what happens when you get shot." I nod.

I have to use both hands to move my left leg, the one with the bullet lodged in it, over the edge of the seat before spinning entirely out.

Despite his and my best efforts, I end up on my knees, thanks to the awkward angle and the placement of the wound, screaming at the top of my lungs in pain.

Bile rises up, reminding me I haven't eaten today, and I let the acid out onto the driveway. My body dry heaves when it's empty.

Empty, like I feel right now. The adrenaline is wearing off. Being safer than I was before lets me be vulnerable.

"Jesus, let me get help." Dad goes back to the house.

He's not squeamish and has never had a problem getting bloody, but when it comes to us, his kids, Dad's always been a worrywart. Mom usually dealt with our cuts and scrapes. That is, until Valor got old enough to learn and took over.

Should shift, let me heal. My wolf advises.

But he can't guarantee that shifting will push the bullet out without complications. I fall to my side and lie on the cool cement, letting the cold soak into my body.

"Royal," Valor says.

I hadn't realized I'd closed my eyes until I have to open them to look at him. "Yeah?"

"Quit bleeding in my driveway." He offers me his hand.

Valor is blank, devoid of anything. It's not the stone-cold killer or the calculated interrogator. He's blank like when his first wife died.

Bad. Bad. My wolf worries.

But I push myself up until I can grab Valor's hand, and, per usual, my older brother cares for me. He pulls me up almost effortlessly to precariously stand on one leg. Then he pulls my arm across the back of his neck, supporting my weight so we can hobble into his garage.

Was that garage door open when I got here? Or am I missing time? Where did Dad go? Mom? Kerrianne? Antonella?

I don't ask questions, not aloud. Answers will come if I'm patient. Black spots dance at the edges of my vision, but I fight them away.

He takes me into the main portion of the house and then straight to the stairs that lead to his lair. Unlike mine, warm and full of technology and neat gadget toys, Valor's is cold. Stainless steel wall panels, sloped floors, and drains.

Oh no. The scent of blood meets us before we even get through the secret passage to his lair.

"What did you do?" I growl as he tries to lead me through.

I stop walking and push him away from me, making him square up to me in the narrow space of the doorframe.

"It was too late when you called. She couldn't be saved." Valor doesn't explain further. He doesn't have to.

Valor sidesteps me into his lair, and I want to grab him by the shirt, haul him back, and kick his ass.

Chained to the far back wall, snarling and snapping, its jaws is a vicious, freshly turned wolf.

Poor Antonella. My wolf sympathizes but doesn't really know what that's like.

Freshly turned wolves are violent little delights. They're all animal. It can take days or weeks for them to find their consciousness.

Where he finds sympathy, I find rage. The fact that Valor wouldn't hold it together and verify . . . I try to let it go. What's done is done, but the pain for Antonella's change, forced and uninvited, weighs heavily on me.

"Oh great, you found him." Uncle Neil's voice draws my attention away from the wolf-shaped elephant in the room. He's chained to the wall adjacent to Antonella, who's still snapping and snarling.

"Oh great, he's still alive." I snark back as Valor drags me over to his stainless steel table.

"Oh great, two sarcastic assholes," Valor grumbles as he guides me onto the table.

I should take that as a sign that Valor probably isn't ready to talk about the battle that unfolded here. But he walks over to his cabinet of tools, and my lower pain threshold has my mouth running on nervous energy, patience be damned. "So, what happened? Where's Kerrianne and Mom?"

"Neil lied about Antonella being a threat. I did what I thought was best. Antonella is a wolf. Mom is with Kerrianne back at your house." Valor's recap could have been an email rather than a meeting between us. He steps from one cabinet to another before coming back to me. He thrusts a white plastic bottle at me. "Take three of these."

I don't question what he's giving me. I hope it's for pain. After dry swallowing the pills, I heed each of his instructions, from lying back to holding still.

I turn my head away to avoid watching whatever Valor is about to do to my leg.

The view I have is of Uncle Neil, and rather than look at him, I shut my eyes as tight as I can, tilting my face up to the light.

"Did you ever think Uncle Neil would be able to pull off something like this?" I say quietly as Valor places something on my leg.

"I'm right here." Uncle Neil scoffs.

"We know," Valor and I say at the same time.

"No, I didn't," Valor growls. It's a sound I've heard him make thousands of times, but now he doesn't stop. It's just one long trail of growling. "I didn't think any of this was possible. I didn't know any of this could or would happen. I would have fucking—"

"OW!" I scream.

"Oh stop, you big baby. It just barely hit the bone. Smart not to shift though. This could have been bad." Valor holds forceps up toward my face, the spent bullet caught between the prongs.

I feel sick to my stomach all over again, but I force it to stay down. I want whatever those pills were to work. Fast.

After a few more minutes of Valor packing the wound and bandaging me up, I sit upright.

The bullet out of my leg doesn't fix our family's problems.

My uncle betrayed us.

My new sister-in-law is now a wolf.

Both of them are chained up in my brother's basement.

"I missed a whole damn coup being planned inside our own organization," I say quietly.

"We all did." Valor steps in front of me, and we lock eyes. "You don't get to beat yourself up over this. That's my job. This is my responsibility, not yours."

"No one will blame you, Royal," Dad says from where he comes in through the secret tunnel entrance. "You can't possibly monitor everyone all the time."

"I should have seen this. Neil was acting weird this week. He was going to caches at odd hours, long distances, and I just assumed it was business related. I didn't verify." I spiral and close my eyes. "If I hadn't waited so long to kill them and call, she wouldn't be—"

"No." Valor's tone is deadly and cold. He points at the snarling wolf. "That. That. Is *my* fault. I have to answer to her. I have to answer for that sin. Not you."

I hear him, and I try to take him at his word. But a little bit of me is dying inside.

We're Mob. People live and people die all the time. We are the kingpins of running mercenaries and weapons. Death is no stranger as it comes knocking on our door. It's business as usual.

But this is the closest I've been to the front line in a long time.

Dad steps over to where Valor and I are, placing a hand on Valor's shoulder. "You need to get cleaned up to take Antonella to the cabin."

Valor nods. "Yeah."

Dad turns to me. "Let's go get you some clean clothes. Before those pills kick in and knock you on your ass." Dad offers me a tense smile, and in a slow slide, I move from sitting to standing on my own two feet. "We don't have to talk about any of this until we're fed, clean, and the bodies are hidden."

CHAPTER TWENTY-FOUR

"NORMAL" OR SOMETHING

"Royal," Kerrianne whispers, waking me up from a fitful sleep. "Grandma says I'm not supposed to wake you up, only see if you're awake to offer you pancakes."

"Yes, please," I whisper back without opening my eyes. "With chocolate chips."

Kerrianne flops down over the top of me in a hug before darting up the stairs, yelling, "He wants pancakes and chocolate chips. I want chocolate chips too."

With a groan, I climb out of bed. My leg is stiff, and I struggle to throw it over the side of the bed. Valor's job of packing and wrapping the wound held through the night, but it doesn't stop blood from soaking through the bandage.

It takes a monumental effort, and I hobble to my bathroom. I don't remember coming home last night. I don't remember anything after Dad set a bowl of soup in front of me.

I take a piss standing, luckily managing not to fall over. But when I'm done, I close the lid and grab the tablet off its charger from the cupboard above the toilet. After snagging the wound caddy from the shelf above that, I sit down to sort out my life.

Maybe I should take care of my wound first, but even without my wolf awake, there's one thing I need to do.

My phone is backed up to the cloud in six places, and I pull a clone onto the tablet. I ignore the fifty million notifications and home in on the only person I can't take care of in person today.

Leticia sent me seven total messages.

> LETICIA:
>
> Ready to call?
>
> Ope, did you miss my text? My food is hot, I'm going to eat.

Those two were sent fifteen minutes apart.

An hour later, I got two more.

> LETICIA:
>
> I really wish you would have told me we couldn't call today if you hadn't meant to be here.
>
> In the event you still want to be friends, I'm turning my phone to silent so I don't get distracted while studying.

I deserve a whole lot worse than those two messages. So much worse. There are only two more from last night.

> LETICIA:
>
> All done studying for my final.
>
> Proof of life. At least let me know something bad didn't happen to you?

My chest aches, and I rub at the spot before reading the last one.

LETICIA:

Good morning. Please don't be dead.

No reply is better than what I can tell her right now. I don't even know what my world looks like, and it isn't fair to beg forgiveness and swear I'll be better behaved, only to have that crushed by what Dad and Valor may have to say today.

Bloodied mess contained to my bathroom with the door closed to hide it away from Kerrianne, I get myself and my tablet up the stairs one painfully irritating step at a time.

Who thought a lair in the basement was a good idea? Why couldn't it be on the main level of the house?

My wolf wakes up, the painkillers or sedatives Valor gave me last night slowly wearing off, and he reminds me of that time in high school. I came home, missing baseball practice, to find Mom and Dad getting handsy on the kitchen counter.

Fair enough. Lair in the basement is safer most of the time.

"I told her not to wake you up." Mom sighs, looking me over. "How's the leg?"

"My trash bin needs to go out, but it's healing." I turn off the burner she's standing in front of on the stove and pull her into a hug.

Unprocessed emotions from yesterday well up with tears in my eyes, and I try hard to shove them down. But Mom wraps her arms around me and squeezes hard, and I'm on the verge of falling apart.

"Not in front of Kerrianne," I beg her.

Mom lets go, and she has tears in her eyes too. "You shouldn't have let them use me as a threat. I'm old, but I'm not that old. We'd have fought them off together. You could have been hurt." She looks down at my leg. "More."

I nod and don't argue with her. The choices I made yesterday weigh a million pounds. Had I not let them take me, would Antonella still be human? Would Mom be alive? Would Kerrianne?

"Just trying to be grateful we're all alive." I clear my throat and step away.

She turns the burner back on and resumes flipping pancakes. I pull one off the top of the stack. The heat of it burns my fingertips, but I stuff it into my mouth and breathe around it with my jaw hanging open, trying to cool it off enough that I can chew and swallow.

"At least one of my sons learned manners." Dad rolls his eyes when he sees me.

Swallowing, I snark back. "Yeah, sure, Valor chews with his mouth closed, but when was the last time he took out the trash?"

"He doesn't even live here." Mom laughs, and the tension in the room eases. "Kerrianne is playing upstairs with that old train set. So if you two are going to talk before I serve breakfast, get to it."

"What do I need to do?" I dive straight into it while pulling up a to-do list on the tablet. "Obviously, full system sweeps. Go through Neil and his family's financials and all their data usage — phones, security systems, the whole nine yards. Everything turned inside out. I thought maybe tomorrow I'd go over —"

"Royal." Dad stops me. "None of that has to be done today. I went through Neil's phone." His voice cracks, and it's then that another wave of sadness hits me because Neil is Dad's brother. "There were only text messages with those already caught and dead. I don't think he has other accomplices out there. That we need to worry about any sort of immediate attack."

I sit in the silence and the weight of that, feeling the barrage of emotions that come with now being safe and acknowledging the brush of death I'd faced. My fingers shake, and it's hard for me to turn the screen off on the tablet.

"Valor asked that we be the ones to tell Antonella's cousin, Leticia, about the family secret. Apparently, she's the one we need to worry about figuring it out. With how close they are, Antonella is likely to fail at keeping the secret from her. Unintentionally, of course."

"Yeah, she's wicked smart," I add without thinking. I scrunch up my features. "Can we pretend I didn't just say that out loud?"

"Nope," Dad answers.

I draw a slow breath, letting my face relax. "Alright, it's nothing, but Leticia and I have been talking since that first time she went over to dinner at Valor's."

"Nothing?" Mom's voice makes it clear she's doing the impossible and reading into what she doesn't know is happening.

Dad draws a deep breath. "Royal, be careful with her. I don't need to tell you, but I will anyway, we can't afford any sort of altercation with the D'Medicis, and I'm sure Gregorio would love a fight. He wasn't happy about the truce to start with."

"I am being careful. We're just friends. Nothing's happened between us." *God, do I hope that sounded true.* Neither Mom nor Dad calls bullshit on that. "I'll figure out Leticia's finals schedule at the university, and I'll bring her out to the house and show her."

"Take her to Valor's. Leticia is more familiar with it since she's been there. I'm keeping Kerrianne here. You can feed Captain." Mom delegates and decides how this is all going to go. "It has to be soon though. Your brother wants it done before Antonella gets herself together. Since they talk a lot, he doesn't want too many questions unanswered in texts."

"Yes, I'll take care of it." I nod. It's harrowing to be the one who has to show a human their wolf, and it goes against everything we're taught. With Dad telling me not to dig too much into things, at least I have something to do. "Do I need to feed the prisoner too?"

"No, Jack and Declan are taking care of that. They're both pissed off at him and promise to keep him alive but make him miserable." Dad almost laughs, and I remember that's where Valor gets it from. The unhinged.

Dad can both grieve his brother and talk about torturing him, in the same conversation, and be completely okay with it.

Lord save me if Valor and I ever come to head like that.

"You're sure about telling Leticia the family secret?" My leg throbs, and I hobble over to the informal dining room table before pulling out two chairs, one for my leg and one for me to sit on.

"Is Leticia really that smart?" Dad comes to sit with me at the table.

Probably smarter. I go with the more diplomatic answer. "Yes.

She's smart enough to work out that there's something seriously wrong or different with Antonella."

"I know it goes against tradition, but there are exceptions to rules for a reason. We'll need to control the narrative, then. Make sure Leticia knows what's at stake if she lets the secret out. It's better that we take control of the situation than be blindsided, not knowing what to do." Dad's word on it is final.

"Is it okay if I do it tomorrow? I just need the day to . . ." The truth is, I don't know what I need the day to do, but the bare minimum is to apologize for ghosting her.

"Sometime this week, before Valor and Antonella return, is the most important part." Dad censors himself as Kerrianne comes in from the living room.

"Are pancakes ready yet?" She twirls the skirt of her dress around her, spinning in a tight circle, and then frolics over to the table. "I bet I can eat as many as Royal."

"Oh yeah?" I narrow my eyes across the table. "Little thing like you going to eat more than a big thing like me?"

"My stomach is bigger. I'm still growing. Dad says you're not growing." She nods exuberantly and pulls out her chair to sit down at the table.

"You're on, pup-squeak." I smile at her and try to just be present in the moment for her like Valor would want me to be.

Leticia

CHAPTER TWENTY-FIVE

RETURN OF THE POLTERGEIST

It's been two days since I last talked to Royal. I check my phone again. Forty-nine hours, thirty minutes, and some seconds.

I open the messages and look at the last one I sent him, asking him to not be dead, and wait in the lobby of the Fine Arts building, where my final was. My driver isn't here yet, and I'm getting a little worried that something happened, but I also finished my final twenty-five minutes earlier than expected. So, he's really not even late yet. I'm just on edge.

"Leticia." My name is said from behind me.

I know that voice. I turn around and see Royal standing there with a coffee carrier and a bouquet of flowers. "Royal?"

He's taller than I expected. Under his jacket, he's wearing a teal shirt that highlights his eyes. The jacket he's wearing isn't all that thick, but it looks warm. The dark wash denim of his jeans is wrapped around his thighs, but I draw my eyes back up his body.

"Surprise?" He offers the bouquet out toward me. "I'm sure it's not customary to give someone flowers after taking a final exam because no one ever brought me flowers after a final. But I figured it's pretty much standard if you stand somebody up."

I cross the ten feet between us as quickly as I can, bypassing the flowers and drink carrier, and wrap my arms around him. I draw in a deep breath to exhale a sigh, but I get caught up in the scent of warm chocolate and something else I can't quite put a finger on.

But a second into the hug, I realize what I've done and backpedal or . . . try to . . . Royal holds me to him, wrapping his arm with the bouquet around me.

"I'm sorry. I missed you. I'm alive. I would never intentionally stand you up," he says softly and mostly to the top of my head.

When I push against him a little harder, he lets me go, and I step back. Suspiciously, I eye him. "What are you doing here? I thought you didn't cross the territory lines like that?"

"We're in a truce, territory lines are just guidelines for business. We're able to move freely through them now." He shrugs and gives an almost carefree smile. "I was wondering if you wanted to come out to our territory, get lunch, and see the countryside?"

"That sounds like something right out of a regency romance." I laugh and shake my head. "And it's crazy, there is no way my family will just let me go galivanting around the countryside."

"I mean, they did say you could come for Christmas, so think of it as a pre-Christmas luncheon." He offers the drink carrier out to me, where two cups are nestled. "I even brought peppermint hot cocoa for the occasion."

It should be a harder decision. I should be angrier with him. Shouldn't it? Shouldn't I?

But the way he's smiling, the way he showed up, with flowers of all things. I may not be dating Royal, and nothing could even come of this, but it's all swoon worthy, and I'd be a fool not to embrace it. At least for a little bit.

"Alright, I'll see if I can get it past my security." Guilt tingles in my stomach all the way through to my spine. If Dad told my security about how I'm supposed to be spying on the Cavanaghs, then they'll absolutely allow it.

I try to push it aside and act normal, pulling the cocoas off the tray one at a time. Royal strides over to the trash to dispose of the carrier before coming back to collect a cup from me. In exchange, I take the flowers. They're a beautiful mix of roses, lilies, pine boughs, and berry sprigs.

Royal leads the way over to a bench where we can watch the doors and the driving lane for my security to arrive.

"So, are we going to talk about why you just ghosted me?" I take a sip of my cocoa, giving him time to answer my question.

"We are, but not here. Thus, the lunch." Royal's stiff and rigid. Nothing like his easygoing nature over the phone.

"Ahhh. Well, if it's the usual, 'It's not a woman's place to know' speech, you can just give it to me here. I've heard it enough times." I slump a little bit, feeling defeated but also relieved that there will be nothing to report back to Dad.

Royal looks at me and shakes his head. "If I was going to tell you that you didn't need to know, then this meeting would have been a text message. I'm very efficient."

His goofy grin puts me at ease. Maybe the Cavanaghs are different. Antonella told me they are, but I didn't understand how. And maybe, just maybe, I won't learn anything at all, or I can find enough noninvasive information to make him think I tried.

"So, was that your last final?" Royal gestures broadly to the building around us.

I nod and let myself feel the weight of studying lift off my shoulders. "It was. I'm officially free until January."

"Very nice. Want me to hack into the grade system and fix anything for you?" he conspiratorially whispers.

"What? No. You can't do that." I gape at him. But he just raises an eyebrow in response. "You can?"

"There isn't a lot I can't figure out how to do with the right motivation." He takes a smug sip of cocoa.

The black SUV rolls up into the parking lane, and my driver gets out. "Alright, let's go convince the driver that you're not a threat."

Royal laughs. "Well, I wouldn't go that far, but I'm not threatening to you."

That's when I notice it. His stride is a little short for someone so tall, and he kind of weaves left to right as he walks. "Are you limping?"

He tries to hide it, stepping more forward. "It's nothing. I'll be okay."

"You're sure?" I stop him, looking at him like I'd have any clue if he's lying.

But with a soft smile, Royal steps forward and opens the door to the vestibule. "I promise."

Surprisingly, lunch with Royal out in the middle of the mansions outside Chicago is a perfectly acceptable way for me to spend my time. The driver asks a few questions about what sort of vehicle Royal is driving, but after hearing things like 'bullet resistant' and 'practical tank,' I'm excused from the normal ride home. All the driver tells me is that if I need a ride home, to give him a call and he'll come get me.

What in the alternate reality is this?

CHAPTER TWENTY-SIX

WICKED SMART MATES

What alternative reality is this? I grip the steering wheel a little tighter, then let it go. They say when you meet your mate, you'll just *know*. And holy shit, is that true. The gray skies are a little brighter. The wind is a little less cold. My cocoa tastes better than normal, and I don't feel anywhere near as nervous as I was about showing her my wolf.

Not alternative reality. Perfection. My wolf swoons. He urges me to reach across the too-spacious SUV and hold her hand. Or to brush the lock of golden hair that's fallen into her face away from her sea-blue eyes. Or to tell her that I love the way her shirt dress swooshes around her hips.

I can't do any of those things. But the more he presses, the harder it is to hold back.

"So, can you tell me now that we're in the car together?" Leticia turns in her seat a little bit so she can see me better.

"Well, I can give you a few details. There was a little coup within our ranks, and some bad things happened. I got pulled away during our lunch, and my phone was completely destroyed. I got a new one this morning, though, so we can text again." I edit a bit and censor a lot.

I'll give her all the details, but not when there's a risk of her jumping out of a moving vehicle. And when I can adequately show her I'm not making up the whole wolf shifter stuff.

She'll believe us. My wolf comforts me. *She's smart and will believe.*

"And what happened to your leg?" Leticia pushes for more details, and I love her inquisitive mind all the more for it.

"I had a little run-in with a projectile." I avoid the words 'bullet' and 'shot' in hopes of softening the blow.

"Oh *my* god. You were shot?" Leticia is too smart for me and worked that one out.

Time to lie. My wolf urges me to de-escalate.

"Yes." I don't lie to her, and my wolf practically falls over with frustration. "But —" I hold up a finger, trying to slow down the panic that's filling the car with tension. "I am fine, as you can see. I'm up and walking around like normal."

"You should be at home, resting, and I don't know . . . healing. Definitely resting," she harrumphs.

"I'll do as much resting as I can in the next couple of days. Does that sound fair?" I try to compromise.

"Fine." She crosses her arms in front of her chest.

In case she's cold and not just guarding herself against the bad things I told her, I turn up the heat.

We're finally out of the city and nearing the highway exit to turn home when, with the smallest voice, Leticia asks, "Do you think Toni had something to do with the coup, and that's why she isn't texting me back?"

"Antonella didn't have anything to do with the coup." I confirm, hoping she hears how serious I am. *But the coup had everything to do with why she's not texting you back.*

"So is her phone damaged too, or is it something else?" Leticia is so brilliant and curious that if I wasn't on the business end of keeping secrets, I'd be much happier about this.

"There are some security concerns with phones right now. It'll make more sense when we get to the house and I can explain." I chew on my bottom lip for a second. "I promise, it'll get more confusing and then it will all start making sense, and I'll answer every single question until you run out of them."

"You're making a lot of promises," Leticia says like a warning, looking over at me. "You're sure you can keep all of them?"

"I'll never lie to you." I stop myself from saying 'I promise,' but I'll keep every one I can. I mean it wholeheartedly.

Finally we get to Valor's front gate.

"Oh, we're going to Valor and Toni's?" She peers through the windshield.

"Yeah, Kerrianne is with my mom and dad. It'll be quieter here." I don't elaborate that it's because no one is here and that the guards know not to let her out if I'm not with her.

I roll down the window when we approach the guard shack. The guard is one of Valor's most trusted, and he looks at Leticia and me for almost a whole minute before nodding and letting us through the gate. Probably committing her scent to memory if something goes sideways.

Nothing bad will happen. My wolf sighs and rolls his eyes. *You're so dramatic.*

Leticia

CHAPTER TWENTY-SEVEN

WEREWOLVES OR WOLF SHIFTERS?

At the front of the house, Royal presses a button in the car for the garage door and pulls into a spacious garage.

The door slides closed behind us, and when I get out of the car, I note that the space is heated. The air is a little chilled from the garage door opening, but still rather warm and comfortable.

Inside, the house is exactly as I remember it, with the exception of how quiet it is. I can tell no one is here. The home feels stark and cold. Despite the cozy elements, it feels barren of life.

"I think it's best if I just show you what we're dealing with rather than try to dance around the subject. And then when you know what's going on, we can talk about the specifics," Royal says from where he's walked ahead of me toward the back of the house.

"Oh, okay." I follow him through the kitchen to the gorgeous sunny living room.

He opens one of the French doors to the backyard and starts pulling off his coat.

"Royal, it's freezing. What are you doing?" I zip my heavy peacoat up in demonstration against the cold, then close the door to the house behind me.

"I'm sure it feels really cold to you, but honestly, it's not that bad. Especially not compared to a couple of days ago. This is nice." He laughs, and it's not his usual laugh; this is almost a wounded sound, one that doesn't actually feel like humor.

He tosses his coat onto some patio furniture and then pulls his sweater off over the top of his head.

"Royal, you're acting really weird." I use that voice Antonella uses when she cautions younger cousins against doing something dumb.

I must get it wrong, though, because Royal moves on to unbuttoning his dress shirt. This is why Berto kept telling Dad I should know how to use a gun. But I don't really believe that thought holds merit because I don't think Royal intends to hurt me.

"I promise you it's going to get a whole lot weirder." He shrugs his shirt off his shoulders.

"Well, you could make it less weird," I say with the hope that maybe whatever this is doesn't have to happen.

"I can't do that." He runs a hand across the back of his neck.

I get a look at his body, and Royal is definitely more of a gym bro than he let on. The single picture I have of him did nothing to show how built he is.

Not the time, Leticia. I mentally face-palm myself.

"Leticia, focus," Royal says. "You can check me out later, but I have something that I need to tell you, and it needs to happen soon."

"What do you have to tell me that involves taking —" I can't believe what I'm seeing. Royal unbuttons his pants. "Taking your clothes off."

"I just need you to promise that you'll stay as calm as possible and let this process, before you do anything. Remember everything we've talked about and that we've been friends, and it feels like we've been friends for a lot longer than a week."

He isn't wrong. The long talks and nights on the phone do make it feel like I've known Royal a lot longer. It makes it feel like I'm not really meeting him for the first time today.

Royal's jeans slipping from around his waist, however, has me raising a hand to shield my eyes from view. *We're friends, but are we those sort of friends? I mean, did him walking me through my orgasm make me that sort of friend? Do I want to be that sort of friend?*

I try to focus and draw slower breaths than the words rushing in my head, but all the questions feel valid.

"I'm turning around, for your sensitivities." Royal laughs, and he makes it sound like I'm some Victorian damsel he needs to be chaste around. Though, maybe I am.

I close my eyes and draw two more short breaths.

"Okay. Royal, this is moving past weird into uncharted territory," I tell him, but when I open my eyes and look between my fingers, Royal isn't there.

I slowly lower my hand because maybe he's crouching, taking off his socks, or — *OH my god.*

"That's a wolf." I step backward away from the massive animal. "Oh, my god. ROYAL!" I shout, trying to find him in my peripheral vision, but he isn't there.

Did he get eaten by the wolf? Am I getting eaten by the wolf?

"Great job screaming, Leticia. Gonna fuckin' scare it into attacking you." I talk to myself this time, trying to keep my voice low. "Maybe I can reassure the wolf not to attack me. Nice, wolfie. Good, wolfie."

I step backward again, trying to put distance between the really big wolf and me, all the while coaching myself to not freak out. "Think of it like a dog. I like dogs."

The snow crunches under my feet, and with my next step, my heel hooks on ice.

I try to stabilize myself, but I go sliding down to the ground.

The wolf springs forward.

"Ahhh!" I try to curl up into a ball.

Is the ball the right thing? What do you do for wolf attacks in the wild? Why does the world prepare you for bear attacks and not wolves?

I wait for pain and for paws and teeth to try to tear into my jacket.

Instead, a snuffly, cold nose presses against my ear. I move my arm to better protect my head, but that leaves my middle more open, and the wolf shoves its snout into the opening near my stomach.

"Don't eat me!" I try to push it away, but the animal is massive, and my fingers slip into thick, rough fur.

But after a few seconds of not being mauled, I stop and slowly uncurl my body to look at the animal closer.

It's big and fluffy with light gray and white fur. A strip of white fur goes up from its nose between its eyes. The ears are cupped, sticking up through the fluffy coat.

"Okay." It's like my brain is fuzzy with what I'm seeing and what I didn't see.

"First there was Royal, and now there's a wolf." I keep the animal in my line of sight but turn my head. "Royal?"

The wolf barks.

I startle, scooting back on the snow.

"The wolf is Royal?" I nod.

The wolf nods back.

"The wolf is nodding back. The wolf is Royal." I shake my head.

The wolf dips its head.

"That is not — No." I push up off the cold ground, straightening my coat. I'm starting to feel more chilled, and I imagine my nose and cheeks must be turning red. "This can't be. No. Humans don't become wolves."

The wolf walks forward and bends its neck up to look at me, pretty much standing as tall as it can. Its chest is pushed against my front, and its nose is practically against my chin.

"Royal?" I question again a little louder, like maybe he hasn't heard me, maybe the wolf isn't Royal, and this is a misunderstanding.

Then the wolf's warm, kind of dry tongue licks my chin.

"Ew. Dog breath." I step backward.

A shiver rakes through my body.

"Okay, Royal, if you're the wolf, then you need to stop being the wolf. This is weird, and we need to talk." I square my shoulders at the beautiful gray wolf.

The wolf steps back and lets out a massive sneeze before walking over to Royal's clothes.

I keep my eyes trained on the wolf.

It's hard to comprehend seeing it. The wolf's body shifts and changes. It's fast and slow, and time seems to move differently as it happens.

But then Royal is back, his bare ass facing me.

"Okay, Royal is a wolf. I sound insane. God, I'm going to end up a nun." I close my eyes. *Maybe this is just a bad dream, and I'll wake up.*

"I am a wolf. My whole family are wolf shifters." Royal's voice is a little hoarse. He clears his throat. "You're not going insane. And you're not going to be a nun." When he turns toward me while buttoning his pants, he's wearing a devilish smirk. "You wouldn't have any fun being a nun."

"You can't be serious." I shake my head and gesture to him. "A wolf."

I quickly look down at the ground. Distinct paw prints litter the snow-covered earth, big like a giant dog. I pull my phone out of my pocket and take a picture. It happened. I have proof it happened.

"You can't tell anyone, Leticia." Royal's voice is low, almost threatening. "If you're going to tell someone, I have a duty to stop you."

"No one would believe me." I scoff and put my phone away. "I can barely get anyone to believe me about anything else. You being a wolf would get me locked up in one of those 'rejuvenation centers' or something meant to keep me calm but not actually called an asylum." I shove my hands in my coat pockets. "So why are you telling me this?" I shiver, and my teeth start chattering.

"Come on, let's go inside. You're freezing." He steps toward me like he's going to touch me.

I step back and dodge him, heading toward the house on my own.

Once we're inside, my coat hung up and boots off, Royal fusses over me, having me sit in front of a fireplace, which he clicks on with a remote, and looks at me with a deadly serious expression. "Antonella is now also a wolf shifter."

I freeze. "No. No, she's not. Excuse me, what?" I stare at him, mouth gaping, trying to wrap my head around the impossibilities that are apparently possible. It's one unbelievable thing for Royal to be a *wolf shifter*, but Antonella? For some reason, that's where my brain decides to draw the line at suspending disbelief. I try to remember the words he used back in the car. "This has to do with the coup? The incident where you were shot?"

Royal nods. "There was a defector among the ranks. My uncle, Neil, went a little bit power hungry. He tried to have me killed and frame Antonella and your family for breaking the truce."

"No." Stunned speechless, I roll my wrist, hoping to encourage him to keep talking.

"I'm fine, my parents are fine, Kerrianne is fine." Royal assures me.

"But Toni is a werewolf now." I reiterate his words.

"Wolf shifter." His jaw flexes as he grits his teeth for a minute, and tension further tightens his features when he furrows his brows. "Valor was led to believe that Antonella was going to hurt Kerrianne. He . . ." Royal scrubs his hand back through his hair. "He was an idiot and put her in a position where she could get hurt."

"I'm a big girl, Royal. You don't have to spare me the details. Don't be like my dad." I want to be strong, but my voice isn't exactly steady, just pointed.

"Valor strapped her into his work chair. The one where he tortures people. And because she was in that chair, she was hurt by the chair first and then further when Neil attacked her. She couldn't defend herself, and the only thing they could do to save her was to give her a wolf." Royal continues. "Valor knows he fucked up. His blind spot has always been Kerrianne, and I can tell you right now, Antonella is making him pay for his fuckup. But I know you notice —"

"The family secret." Everything starts falling into place. "We don't eat people, and he called her pup. Like wolf pup. You're not cannibals, you're not human."

"We're not human. We're not cannibals." Royal nods in agreement.

I stand up and start pacing. *Stay calm.* I urge myself, but my heart beat is only speeding up, and when I draw deep breaths, they're shaky and uneven.

"Leticia." Royal stands and steps into my path, stopping my pacing.

"You're not human." I feel like an idiot repeating it, but I can't for the life of me understand.

"I'm not human. But nothing has changed. I'm the same guy you've been getting to know. Antonella is the same person you've grown up with. It's just now you know what makes us different." He gently rests his hands on my shoulders, reaching his thumb up to brush my jaw.

"Why are you telling me?" I make eye contact with him.

"We knew you'd notice, and Valor promised that he'd let you in on the secret. You're smart and really in tune with the world around you. If we didn't tell you, then you'd figure it out. It saves Antonella from lying to you." He squeezes my shoulders a little. "You're not in any danger knowing."

"As long as I don't tell anyone." I raise my eyebrows.

"As long as you don't try to tell anyone." Royal agrees.

"How would you know if I did?" I look at where I set my phone on the coffee table.

"Uhm." Royal takes a step back, letting me go.

"Royal?" I try again to infuse my voice with the same tone Antonella uses to get information out of the younger cousins when they're misbehaving.

"I have live monitoring on your phone." He drops that information with a guilty wince.

"You *what?*"

"It's just a precautionary measure. I wanted to be sure you were safe." Royal defends himself, raising his voice a little.

"Safe for who?" I argue, my eyes going wide with the question.

"For yourself, for us." He brings his tone back down, lower than normal, and I can tell Royal is leaving something out. It's in the way he hangs his head.

"And?" I pressure him for more.

"And because I've grown fond of you and wanted to be sure your parents and Berto were treating you alright. Antonella mentioned to Valor that you don't get along with your parents all that well. I figured there was some big change. Some stressors can change . . . I'm just digging myself a hole and pleading the fifth." Royal stops talking, zipping his lips with his fingers.

"You can't just plead the fifth. You've been spying on me?" I want to be mad. I should be mad. "Wait, you said . . . what was it about my grades . . ." I close my eyes and try to think back to the conversation at school before we got in the car. "There isn't a lot you can't do without motivation."

I open my eyes, and Royal has a whole new look on his face — sullen with downcast eyes, chewing on his top lip.

"I've been getting this feeling of being watched at home. Did you hack into the cameras in the penthouse? I mean, I tried to tell Dad the security company was a Clark Enterprises subsidiary, but he didn't believe me. You've been watching me." I'm accusing him and posing it as a question, but my blood is colder than the weather outside.

He doesn't have to answer because I know.

"I found out we had access at the wedding. But I've only been watching you since we started talking. If you had feelings of being watched before that, then it wasn't me. I can dig back through the system, though, make sure everything is —"

"Stop," I snap. "The night we —" I swallow hard, trying to hold it together. "The night I . . ."

Royal nods, and his whole body deflates. "I was there."

"You were reassuring me that most cameras don't have night vision. But the one in my bedroom does?" I can't even tell if I'm angry. I feel like I should be angry, but I'm not feeling that fire heat of rage.

"It does. But if it makes you feel any better about this, when I got access to the system, I went in and disabled the feed so no one else could watch you . . . but me. They'd need to be a better hacker than me to crack the encryption on that camera." He offers a polite smile with a shrug. "So I made it safer?"

I can't believe this. I was being watched. This whole time.

I walk over to the couch and flop down, lying flat and looking up at the high ceiling. It's two stories high with massive windows that let in the glow of the setting sun. Beautiful place to have a meltdown if I do say so myself.

I've had a stalker. Sure, he was friendly, but a stalker nonetheless. I didn't even know. I mean, I thought someone was watching me, but I didn't KNOW.

"Gorgeous, talk to me. Be mad at me. Just say anything." Royal sits down on the chair closest to my head, looking down at me.

"I don't know how to feel. I know I should be mad though." I turn my head to look up at him.

"Well, you not being mad is kinda good for me, so I'm not pushing you into being mad." He takes the decorative pillow out of the chair before pulling it into his lap and lounging backward.

"Okay, so you're werewolves. How long —"

"Wolf shifter." He's quick to correct me. "Werewolves, as far as I know, are a fictional beast."

I snort because here I was thinking that humans who turn into wolves, whatever their preferred term may be, were fictional.

Royal gives me a sheepish smile, likely picking up on what I'm not saying. But he continues. "I shift when I want and am not controlled by the moon, and silver is just another pretty alloy. Bullets, as you've found out, can wound just as much as anything else. It's different, and some wolf shifters get really touchy if you call them a werewolf."

"Got it, wolf shifter. How long have you all been wolf shifters?"

I don't know why I'm changing the subject. I only know that I can't really process him spying on me, on us, and it's almost laughable that a conversation about wolf shifters being real is easier.

But is it any different from what Dad has sent me here to do? *Oh shit, did Royal hear that conversation?*

"Forever, it's genetic, or you can be turned, but everyone in my family has always been a wolf shifter. Well, now excluding Antonella, who was just turned."

"That's kinda cool. I mean, not the whole turning her part. I'm glad her life was saved, but it shouldn't have been in danger to begin with." I look away from him and back up to the ceiling, taking a deep breath. "She is okay, right?"

"Yeah, she's okay. We can check on her and Valor later. I promise," Royal says, preceding the sound of fabric rustling as he adjusts in his seat.

"My dad wants me to spy on you and report back what's going on." I wince, afraid of the backlash, even though deep down, I know Royal isn't the kind to get angry.

"I know," Royal says softly. "Which is why when they told me I had to tell you this, I questioned it. But I also know you're a good person."

"And that you've hacked into my phone and can probably stop me from texting them information you don't want them to know?" I wager.

"I'm hoping I don't have to, but ultimately, yes." His voice is lower and somber. "I don't want to be wrong about you. I hope telling me about what your dad asked you to do means that you're telling me you're trustworthy."

I sit up and look at him. "What happens if I'm not?"

His jaw twitches, and he draws a slow breath before letting it out. "It's my job to make sure you keep our secret. If that means turning you so that you share the secret and have the equal motivation to keep us all safe, then so be it."

"Oh." I was not expecting that. Taking me prisoner and locking me up or outright killing me were the possibilities my mind conjured up.

"For the record, I don't want to have to turn you. I like you human. Even if you're so much more vulnerable to the world." He cocks his head. "Though, I guess all that does is make me want to keep you safe that much more."

My heart flutters, and I fight a smile and look away before my cheeks can flame. I pretend to be examining the house. "So now what?"

"Well, lunch as promised. I have to feed Captain, and then I thought maybe you'd like to just hang out? That is, if you still want to be friends." Royal's voice is pinched, and I turn back to look at him.

The wince he wears, tightened eyes and lips pulled flat, makes me laugh. "Yes, we're still friends."

CHAPTER TWENTY-EIGHT

HE CARES

"Kerrianne really loves this little guy, doesn't she?" Leticia is in the tortoise enclosure, bending over and feeding Captain a piece of kale.

And I'm the pervert staring at the way my friend's skirt hugs her ass. *I'm going to hell for thinking thoughts like wanting to fuck her in the tortoise room.*

No hell for wanting to fuck your mate. My wolf corrects me.

But as much as I feel a mate bond toward her, the logic of it all still stands. I don't know how she feels about me, if she likes me how I love her — *Love? When did we get to that?* It feels right though, and that means we're star-crossed lovers, and I don't know a way not to draw a plague on both our houses.

Yet. My wolf is drooling over her. *We don't know how to keep her yet.*

Concerning, but comforting.

Should we worry about how well she took us being a wolf? I avert my gaze back to the feeding chart and measure out the recommended amount of food so Captain doesn't get overweight.

Our mate is smart. She believes what she sees. What more do you want from her? Screaming, crying, running for the city to get pitchforks would be a bad reaction. My wolf sighs and makes me look back at Leticia. She's close, looking over my arm at the food chart.

"Wow. Did Kerrianne do all this?" Leticia tilts her head to read the text better.

"I mean, I helped her run the program to make the charts, but she's the one who knows how to care for Captain best. She watched all sorts of videos about caring for these kinds of tortoises and gave Valor a complex about how much knowledge is too much for a kid to know about something." I laugh, remembering the way he panicked and ran to Mom and Dad because Kerrianne had hyper-fixated on the new family pet.

"She's so smart." Leticia places her hand on my forearm.

I freeze, and my wolf fixates on that spot just as much as I do. Her skin is cool compared to mine, but her touch is so delicate. *Gentle.*

"Toni would know more about what is too much knowledge, so if she's not concerned about Kerrianne, then I'd trust that everything's just fine." Leticia shrugs and smiles up at me. "We've got a younger cousin who pretty much planned a whole family vacation when he was her age. Like down to the best days of the week to do things. Sometimes kids are just extraordinary."

"True." I nod and have to clear my throat to talk. "I can adjust Captain's lighting remotely, so we don't have to hang out here since we're leaving him enough food."

"Sure." Leticia gestures to the door. "Lead the way."

I hate having her follow me down the hallway. I try to shore up my steps, but the wound in my leg is still fresh and tender. Shifting definitely didn't help, and I can smell blood.

"Do you need to use the bathroom before we head back to my place for lunch?" I look over my shoulder at her.

"If you don't mind." She steps into the powder room by the garage.

I rush to the kitchen, where I know Valor keeps a box of first aid supplies. Without much time, I grab a self-adhesive gauze pad and push my pants down. *Why didn't this heal more while I shifted?* The wound has definitely reopened, and I seal it with the gauze pad. It'll be good enough until I can get home and re-wrap it.

I'm put back together and tucking the first aid supplies away when Leticia comes into the kitchen.

"So, this is awkward." Leticia doesn't look at me as she fiddles with the belt hugging her waist. "I'm out of tampons and just got my period."

My brain slowly catches up with what's happening. "Oh. I don't know if Antonella would have any. Their bathroom is on the second floor. Want me to take you there? I mean, I assume she has some since she was human."

"Toni uses the cup. So that's out. I just need to stop by a gas station or something. They normally have some boxes." Leticia looks uncomfortable, and it's more than whatever embarrassment she's trying to hide.

"That's hardly an inconvenience." I brush it off. "We'll go back out to the shops and then home. We can even get lunch while we're out if you'd like. There are fewer choices out here than in the city, but ninety percent of the options here have really good food."

"I'm sorry." Leticia pulls her hair over her shoulder and plays with the ends. "I feel so —"

"Don't berate yourself over something your body does naturally. Mine turns into a wolf. A period is hardly abnormal." I'm assuming, since I only remember like four things they taught us about human women's periods in high school.

Thankfully the internet exists. My wolf, for once, sees the merit of the online world for more than just stalking.

"Can I get you anything else before we leave? Hot water bottle? Chocolate? Water? Soda?" I'm listing off random things I generally like with the hope something sticks.

"Uh, water would be good. I want to take some pills to help with the coming cramps." She shuffles slightly.

Pain. My wolf deduces from the movement. *How much pain? Ask,* he demands.

"I'm out of my depth. Wolves don't have periods. I'm kinda at a loss as to what is happening. So I'm just going to hover and be like one hundred percent the most overthinking best friend in the entire world until I'm satisfied you're being cared for the way you need to be." I warn her instead of asking invasive questions.

"Oh, best friend?" Leticia cants her head and follows me to the cupboard where Valor keeps the drinking glasses. "When did you get a promotion?"

"Self-appointed." I grin at her with a full smile.

"Oh, well, in that case, I want to be the Grand Poobah of friends." She smiles back, and my heart flutters.

This could have gone so much worse. So much worse.

"Uh, Royal?" Leticia murmurs while looking at her phone in the passenger seat.

She's quiet and tense, much like when she saw me in wolf form.

"Uh, Leticia?" I parrot back. "Everything okay?"

"My dad just texted me. It's the middle of the night in Italy, but he wants to know what information I learned today from hanging out with you." She tilts the phone toward me, but I only spare it a glance before continuing down Valor's driveway.

Her breathing picks up, and I focus, trying to listen for her heartbeat, but I can't hear over the road noise and through her thick coat. But she's practically hyperventilating.

"The truth is obviously out of the question."

"Tell him you found out that Valor and Antonella are honeymooning for a little bit this week and that you fed Kerrianne's pet tortoise." I give honest facts mixed with just a dash of fiction. Make it easier for her to lie to her dad.

"Okay." Leticia nods and starts typing on her phone, her fingers shaking. "Shit," she mumbles.

"Just take it easy." I try to coax her off the ledge she seems to be standing on. "Don't worry about it too much."

"He'll know I'm lying. He's going to push for more information. I don't know how to do this. I don't know how to lie that well." Her voice holds a whine of discomfort that pulls at my soul, and I want to soothe her worries for her.

Help her. My wolf whines.

"He's not going to know you're lying. When he pushes for information, you'll tell him that all we did was talk about boring stuff — the tortoise, Valor's mansion, and the original builder from the eighteen hundreds and that it looks like it needs a gargoyle on the roof."

Leticia huffs a laugh. "I definitely expected gargoyles when I first saw the place." She tries to draw a steadying breath. "Okay. He might buy that." But it doesn't work because she's back on the verge of hyperventilating.

Rather than continuing to drive down the road, I pull over, leaving a little room for someone else if they want to pass to get to the house.

"Will you look at this before I send it? I don't want anyone to worry that I'm doing something wrong."

"Yeah, I can look. My phone is going to ask to approve the message sent out anyway." I feel a little guilty about that. Like I shouldn't be monitoring her this way, not when she's being so forthcoming with wanting to keep our secret.

But I didn't think of Neil as a threat, and look what happened.

I trust Leticia not to say anything under normal circumstances. I'm not one-hundred-percent sure that I can trust her under pressure. Not yet.

Our mate will prove herself. You'll see. My wolf is still swooning over her actually being with us.

"You're a wolf shifter," Leticia breathes out. "A wolf. You turned into a wolf."

"Yeah, I did." It feels like she's having a whole other revelation about what happened. "I can do it again if you want to see it one more time to be sure it's real."

"No. I believe it happened." Leticia tries to explain as she runs her fingers through her hair. "I don't believe it happened, but I don't need to see it again."

I let her work through the emotions, but what I wouldn't give to actually be knowledgeable enough about her to fix this, to help her.

Leticia presses send on her phone, and mine vibrates less than half a second later. I pull it out of the mount on the dash and take a look.

LETICIA:

There's not much to say. We went to Valor and Toni's house, they're out of town for a few days on a honeymoon trip. We fed their pet tortoise, who is cute and named Captain. He didn't talk about any work. He just wanted to know about my finals and how school was going.

"Good touch with what I asked about." I approve the message. "See, you're way better at this than you thought you were. I didn't think to address the conversation that way."

Comfort her. My wolf urges.

I'm trying. I argue back.

But I know what he really wants me to do. He wants me to physically reassure her that she's not alone because she isn't, but she probably feels it. There's a whole species difference from the driver's seat to the passenger seat, and that's probably really alienating for her.

I move slowly, like I'll spook her, and reach over the center console, resting my hand on her mid-thigh.

Big mistake on my part. My cock twitches when I feel the softness of her skin under the control of my touch.

Leticia moves her hand to cover mine, and for a brief moment, I wonder if she'll push me away. Instead, she rests her hand on top of mine.

Her phone buzzes, and Leticia jumps.

"It's okay. I'm here." I offer my hand out to her. "Do you want me to read it?"

"N —" She pauses. "Yeah, could you?"

I open her phone, which doesn't have a security lock on it, and read the message aloud. "Your dad says: What days are you spending Christmas out there? The invitation said for the twenty-third, but it seems you and Royal are close. Maybe you can find a way to spend more time with him. We need to know as much as you can gather. Who their business partners are, things like that."

Not respecting the truce? My wolf and I are both suspicious about this demand for information gathering. *What could they need information for?*

"How does this sound: I'm spending the twenty-third, but have been invited to spend all of winter break now that they know I'm staying home alone while you're all in Italy. I didn't think you'd approve of it," I say.

She's silent, and I look over at her.

Eyes wide, she's looking at me. "Did you just invite me to spend time at your house? Like, spend the night?"

"Well, you can stay at Valor's if you'd rather, but his house is kinda creepy at night if you're all alone." I encourage her to choose to stay with us. It's not necessarily staying *with* me, but it's closer.

"Send the message." Leticia squeezes my hand.

Our mate wants us. My wolf pushes forward, and I forget to hold him back.

Leticia gasps. "Your eyes, they just changed from one color to another."

I blink and push the wolf back. "Sorry, my wolf really likes you."

Understatement of the century. My wolf huffs and settles back in.

"I mean, what's not to like?" Leticia giggles, and it's good to see her less panicked than before.

Tearing my eyes away from her, I look back at the phone, double-checking the message before hitting send.

"How are you doing, really?" I look at her, trying to get a read on what's going through her head.

Her eyes are a little sunken, and she doesn't seem as energetic as usual.

"I'm exhausted," she admits, shoulders dropping. "I need to go home and pack in case he says yes, and my uterus hurts."

I force myself not to deflate because, more than anything, I want to spend time with her. But I nod. "Let's get you a tampon, and I'll take you back to the city."

"Just one tampon? I don't think they sell them individually outside of a bathroom vending machine, and I can't even tell you the last time I saw one of those." Leticia still finds the energy to make a joke.

"Alright, well, then at least a box, but we should have some on hand at the house for human visitors, so maybe you can show me what you need as a start. Then I'll take you back to the city, and maybe we'll have an answer." I stop myself from spewing a whole plan about helping her pack and getting to see her room in person.

Take her home and never let her leave. My wolf amps up the inner rampaging thoughts of how we'll do everything we can to keep Leticia forever.

"I'd like that." She squeezes my hand again. "Thank you for not freaking out about my dad. It means a lot that you trust me. I promise I'm keeping the secret no matter what."

"I believe in you," I answer because I know she means that.

I know she means that she'll try, and even if I don't believe she'd make it through a round of serious questioning and interrogation, that doesn't change how I feel about her. I believe she intends to keep wolf shifters a secret. I believe she doesn't want to tell her dad anything about our family business. But more than that, I don't expect Gregorio D'Medici to truly push his daughter hard enough to come close to breaking her.

What the Italians don't see in Leticia is exactly what makes me love her.

Leticia

CHAPTER TWENTY-NINE

FUCK UTERUSES

"Wait, are you telling me that wolf shifters don't have periods?" I groan, rolling to my side in bed, the hot water bottle clutched to my abdomen and phone in hand so I can keep video calling with Royal. Per usual, my cramps have completely halted all work that needs to be done.

"Yeah, they go through what we call heat instead. It's kinda just like in canines." I think I can see his cheeks turning pink.

He's sitting at his computer, the camera showing me a full view of his bedroom and a lot of his desk area, rather than just the camera from his phone.

Fair is fair since apparently he watches me through the camera in my bedroom. I still can't believe I have a stalker, a hot stalker, and I'm okay with it. Maybe it's because Royal seems so well-intentioned. But it's hardly the weirdest thing that's happened to me today.

"So, what you're saying is . . . ?" I try to prompt more.

He shakes his head. "You don't want to hear about it."

"Let me be the judge of that." I argue back. "I'm bleeding and in pain."

Royal murmurs, and the microphone just barely picks it up. "Ditto."

"You're in pain?" I push and roll over to lie on my stomach. The heat of the hot water bottle presses into my pelvis, and I sigh, feeling some relief from the terrible cramping.

"Yeah, so shifters also have super-fast healing, but that bullet wound is not cooperating." He runs a hand down his face. "Do you want me to tell you about my wound or wolves in heat? Equally embarrassing topics, so you only get to pick one."

"Wolves in heat. I'm weighing my options as to which is better."

My back starts to ache from lying in such an odd position. I try to adjust by shoving my leg up a little bit to support my pelvis. It does nothing, and I go back to lying on my side.

"Weighing your options, sounds like you want to be a wolf. I think you should wait to see Antonella before you make that decision." Royal clicks on something, furiously tapping the mouse with a lot of force.

"It doesn't click better if you hit it harder." I scold him.

"It makes me feel better to click it angrily. It's like I'm telling the other person to fuck off." He narrows his gaze at the computer screen. "I mean, seriously? Who tries to hold a meeting at five p.m.? Absolutely not."

"Okay, so wolves in heat?" I hedge.

Royal leans back in his chair and looks up at the camera. "It's like one big two-person orgy. It's sex, sex, and more sex. It's the only thing that gives the female partner relief, and it's also the only time they're fertile. So it's either wear a condom or welcome a little ball of joy or two nine months later."

He's so callous about it that it takes me a second to realize my mouth is hanging open. "Oh. That's . . ."

"Mmhmm." Royal looks away from the camera, and this time, I'm positive his cheeks are bright pink with a full flush.

"But it's only twice a year that it happens? Because I could see that being not so bad in the scheme of things." I roll onto my back and instantly regret it, turning back to my side.

"Compared to the circles you're rolling in bed, I'd say so." Royal leans forward, resting his head on his hand, supported by his elbow on his desk. "There isn't an inch of that bed you haven't tried to lie on yet."

"So you are watching me right now." I accuse him.

"I'm always watching." He doesn't even sound a little remorseful.

My phone vibrates, and a message notification pops up over the top of the video call.

"Berto just texted me."

Royal picks up a phone off his desk and looks at it while I click into the notification.

BERTO:

I convinced Dad that the best thing is for you to stay at the Cavanaghs' and really get immersed in their operation. It's the only time we've had this sort of opportunity since Toni has clearly forgotten who her family is. We expect twice daily updates.

"Holy shit, they said yes!" I spring up out of bed, heading for my suitcase.

Royal doesn't answer, and I go back to the video call. He's still watching what must be my room feed.

"Unless you don't want me to come." Vulnerability crashes into me. *No, this was his idea, not mine. He wants me.*

Instead of answering right away, he looks up at the camera. "More than anything, I want you out here so we can spend time together. I've kinda forgotten what it's like to have someone I get along with so well in my life. I want to soak up every second."

"Well, then I guess I better pack. If I leave here early enough, we could get breakfast tomorrow morning."

"Better yet, I'll pick you up tomorrow. We can grab breakfast in the city before heading out this way. I need to pick up a couple parts, and we can use it as a report back to your dad." He beams at me.

"Deal," I answer and ignore the pain in my uterus to start packing.

Leticia

CHAPTER THIRTY

ROBOT VACUUM WAR?

"Okay, I'm apologizing in advance." Royal winces as he looks back at me. He holds the door to the house partially open behind him.

"Apologize for what?" I squint at him and lean, trying to see past him into the house.

"My parents." He scrubs a hand down his face and pushes the door open. "Mom, Dad, I'm home. I brought Leticia D'Medici, please don't be weird."

"No! Go back! Dammit, turn around!" a feminine voice calls from deeper in the house.

Royal takes my coat and hangs it on a hook by the door next to his and then continues into the house. His shoes are still on, so I leave my booties on and follow him from where we came in through the garage.

I stop walking, but Royal doesn't.

"Get 'em! That's it, you've got her on the run!" a masculine voice responds.

Down a small hallway, we're in the central part of the home. It's chaos. The kitchen to the left has a blue couch pushed up against the opening, blocking both the hallway and an entry into a living room. Brown living room recliner-type chairs are tucked in at the kitchen table, and there are end tables in the kitchen itself.

What on earth? As we get closer, I hear the whirr of at least one vacuum cleaner as it rolls across a hard surface floor.

Royal steps over the sofa, where it blocks the path, and looks into the living room. "So much for not being weird."

Trying to be respectful, I lean forward but can't see beyond the couch and around the wall. I kneel on the sofa's arm, keeping my booties off the upholstery, and finally get a view.

Betty and Ian Cavanagh are standing on the raised fireplace hearth, and two robot vacuum cleaners, modified with big knives and three balloons attached to each, are driving around the living room.

"You couldn't have waited until I got home? I was barely gone for three hours." Royal talks to his parents, but they don't answer. Instead, he looks over at me. "Sorry. They're on this whole 'I can do anything better than you' kick, and they've already made it past the more normal challenges like butchering chickens, field dressing rabbits, assembling rifles, and running a 5k."

"Naturally." I shake my head, pretending that what he said was even remotely normal.

A pop draws my attention back to the robot vacuum cleaners as they circle each other. One of the vacuums now only has two green balloons.

"Aha! First blood," Betty cheers. Her green sweater sleeves are rolled up, and the buttons down the front hang open to reveal a petite autumn leaf–patterned shirt tucked into her blue jeans.

The robot vacuums start driving away from each other as they auto cycle to clean the floor.

"How's it going, dear?" Betty waves over to me. "I heard you got left behind for Christmas."

"Oh, I'm well. Thank you for having me," I call back with a small wave.

"We don't have to watch this if you don't want." Royal offers, but his eyes drift from me back to the vacuums.

"This is good. Just let me take my shoes off." I smile and turn around on the arm to unzip my booties so that I can get a better vantage point.

When I get back up, the vacuums are circling each other again. Betty's vacuum, with blue balloons, looks like it's going to take out another one of Ian's green ones.

"No, go the other way." Ian coaches the bot, gesturing with his hands in a big sweeping motion for it to turn around.

He's wearing a matching green long-sleeved polo shirt with the sleeves pushed up. Almost like he and Betty coordinated outfits this morning.

"Your parents are so much fun," I whisper to Royal. There's no fighting the smile that grows on my face.

I can't even remember the last time Mom made a real laughing noise, not the ones she uses for polite society company. And Dad's never had fun a single day in his life, not even when we were children would he play games with us.

"Fun is one word for it." Royal rolls his eyes. "They're weirdos, but they're my weirdos."

I watch on, more invested in how Ian and Betty interact with each other, their lighthearted jostling and joking. And I notice that Royal and his dad share the same nose, but he has more of Betty's smile.

Ten minutes in, Betty's bot takes out another of Ian's balloons before his vacuum dares to come close to popping one of hers.

Even though it's a friendly competition, the way they're egging each other on is so full of love. Betty ribs him and makes a joke about slowing down in his old age, but she does so while squeezing his hand tight like she never wants to let go.

And twenty minutes later, Ian is cheering on Betty's vacuum as it pops the last of his balloons.

I want a love like that.

Royal is watching his parents and the vacuums as they keep running around the floor space. I lean against him just a little, and he looks over at me.

He looks at me the way Ian looks at Betty. Butterflies swarm in my stomach.

Could I have a love like that?

CHAPTER THIRTY-ONE

PLAYING WITH FIRE

Dad and I are moving the furniture back into the living room while Mom disarms the robot vacuums. She chats with Leticia about her university degree and the Christmas market. Leticia easily fits in here, and that's a massive relief. Mom doesn't get along with just anyone, but her eyebrows are relaxed, which is Mom's tell for whether she likes someone. I hadn't realized how worried I was about her getting along with two of the most important people in my life. I breathe easier.

"What are you doing, Royal?" Dad murmurs as we set the couch back down in its normal space.

"Gregorio asked his daughter to spy on us. I was planning on telling you and Valor, but clearly, there were more important things for you to worry about, and I had this handled." I keep my voice low, turning my back to the kitchen.

"Then why did you bring her here? Why did Valor authorize telling her the family secret?" Dad pinches the bridge of his nose just like Valor does when he's upset.

"Because I already have total control over her phone and because I know she's smart enough to figure out Antonella is now part of the family secret. Valor already wanted to tell her before Antonella was turned." I try to explain as quickly as I can. Clearly, Valor didn't tell Dad as much as I thought he would have. "The enemy of my enemy is my friend, and Leticia isn't friendly with her father."

Dad drops his hand from his face and eyes me. "You're falling in love with her."

Falling? Hardly. My wolf snorts. *Fell for our mate the minute we started stalking her.*

"Royal," Dad growls low. He reaches out and grips my shoulder. "You can't have her just because you're obsessed with her."

"I know," I huff.

It would be easier if I told him she's my mate, but a part of me wants to keep her to myself for a little bit longer. I want to be the one to tell her everything, not have it outed within the first hour of her being here.

"I'm controlling the narrative. Have some faith in me. As far as sons making mistakes, this week, mine have been less offensive than Valor's, where pack volatility is concerned."

Just throw Valor under the bus to distract from our mate? My wolf chuffs. *This is going well.*

"Be careful." Dad squeezes a little harder and then lets go. "Men in our family become idiots when it comes to women we fall for."

I nod, knowing better than to promise him nothing will happen and that he doesn't have to worry. He totally needs to worry.

Dad leads the way back to the kitchen to grab another piece of furniture.

I pick up an armchair when Mom says, "Oh, stop. I helped your father move them out here, he and I can move them just fine without you. Dinner is at six thirty. You and Leticia go have a good time."

"Oh, what time should I come to help cook?" Leticia immediately responds.

Mom's eyes go wide before she squints at her. "Are you a guest, or are you here against your will?"

"Uh. I think the former." Leticia looks at me.

But Dad is already cracking up laughing.

"Guests don't cook." Mom gives her a big, warm smile.

"Well, if you're sure." Leticia's cheeks are turning pink. "I'm just so used to doing it at home. I'm sorry. I didn't mean to offend."

"No offense taken." Mom steps around the kitchen counter and wraps her in a big hug.

Mom likes her. Dad will approve. My wolf calculates. *Now all you have to do is seal the deal.*

I shove him away because why did I think this wouldn't be hard? Why did I think having her here was a good idea when I can barely go ten minutes without thinking about her?

They hug for a second before Mom lets Leticia go and shoos her toward me.

I know it's wrong. I know everything about this is wrong, but until after Christmas, I'm going to live in this fantasy world. I'll believe that this . . . this could be ours.

I let Leticia go down the stairs to my lair first so she's not watching me hop down each stair to avoid straining my leg any further. At the bottom of the stairs, Leticia looks around, examining. I try to see the space for the first time with her.

There's a sitting area with a fireplace and comfortable lounge seating off in one direction, where several doors lead to a couple bedrooms and closets. Ahead is the door to the server rooms that's closed. My bedroom door is open on the left, and my bathroom is tucked around behind the stairs.

It's not all that spacious looking, but it's only half of the older house's walk-out basement. Mom and Dad's house is nowhere as big and grand as Valor's.

"This is really nice." Leticia looks up at me. "I really like how cozy everything is. Home is so . . . well, you've seen it."

"Your penthouse is grandiose and mausoleum-like." I share the observations I've gathered from scrolling through camera feeds.

"Oh, thank god someone else sees it." Leticia giggles.

Without thinking too much about it, I lead the way into my lair. It's the original living room of the basement and is spacious. Thankfully, clean. The housekeepers came yesterday morning and straightened out the usual shit I can't be bothered with.

"This is so cool." Leticia looks at my desk setup with the monitor wall and various spaces for laptops.

"But wait, there's more." I use a fake game-show-host voice and snatch my tablet off the desk. After opening the app, I turn on the LED lights around the room and dim the overhead, making it cozy and warm rather than the cold, sterile feeling the central lighting gives off.

"Whoa." Leticia looks around the room, her eyes lighting up. "This is everything a bedroom should be."

"Bedroom slash workspace, sure." I put the tablet back down and step toward her, listening closely.

Her heartbeat picks up, and her breaths come a little faster.

"Ideally, I'd have the workspace be an ensuite and keep the bedroom more intimate."

This close to her, I drink in her features. High definition doesn't compare to the real thing. She looks at me with wide, searching eyes, but her expression is open, her pink lips slightly parted. Having her in my space makes it impossible to fight the pull to her. Her eyes flick down to my mouth before returning to mine.

I don't even bother trying to stop myself. I raise my hand to her face, and Leticia doesn't object when I tilt her chin up toward me. One small lean forward, and I press my lips to hers, kissing as gently as possible.

Leticia kisses me back and then yields, letting me guide us deeper into the act. I go slow because nowhere in any of our conversations did it sound like she's had the chance to do this with someone.

When I pull away, we're both breathless.

"That was my first kiss," Leticia whispers, a huge smile pulling at those soft lips.

Fire burns through me at her confession. Thinking it and being right feel entirely different.

"I hope it didn't suck." I raise my eyebrows. "We could try again if it did."

"We could do it again just because it's fun." Leticia smirks.

This time, I wrap my fingers into her hair, bringing my other hand up to cup her chin, and kiss her like I wanted to from the beginning. It's deep, hard, and everything I'm too cowardly to say aloud. Everything that's too risky to even think about for too long.

She fists my shirt as if to pull me closer to her, but with millimeters to spare between us, there's nowhere to go, not without becoming one with each other, not without being buried deep between her legs.

If she asks for it, I don't have the power to say no.

I also don't have the ability to stop myself from pushing my tongue into her mouth.

Leticia moans and lets me explore before pushing her tongue back against mine and playing with me.

My cock throbs, and I try to shuffle away so she doesn't have to feel me pitch a tent against her, but Leticia pulls me back. Skilled little fingers pull at my shirt, untucking it from inside my slacks.

I break our kiss, breathing hard and trying to hold it together. But all I want to do is throw her down on my bed and take every last first from her.

"Gorgeous, you're playing with fire." I try to step away, my hands falling from her hair and face.

Leticia's pupils are blown wide, the beautiful sea-blue color all but encompassed. "I'm okay with that."

"I need you to give me more than four words." My voice is hoarse, and I clear my throat.

She nods, and my heart is hammering in my chest.

"First orgasm, first kiss, first everything." Leticia's voice doesn't waver, but then her body tightens. "Wait, I'm on my period. Forget I —"

I kiss her deeply again, stopping her objections. I murmur against her lips, so glad I fell into a doom spiral of research last night. "Don't worry about it. I scoured the internet last night. Orgasms and sex can help with cramps."

"It's messy." Leticia objects, but then kisses me again. "Your parents? They'll hear? Or I don't know, walk in?"

"Mmm, too bad no one invented something to get clean with. Oh, wait." I smile against her lips and kiss her again. I lean behind me and push the door closed, the hinges dragging it shut and latching with a soft thud. "My parents won't hear, and they won't venture downstairs."

"Are you sure?" She pulls away, but her fingers remain on the hem of my shirt.

"Yeah, I'm positive I know how to wash bedding and get clean," I answer.

"Not that." She sighs and rolls her eyes but also pulls me closer. "I mean about us, having sex. It'll change things about us being friends. We'll be friends with benefits. What if you don't like me anymore after that?"

"One. I see nothing wrong with friends with benefits. Two. I could never not like you. Three. Nothing will change how I feel about you." I stop myself before saying, *Four, I love you.*

We love you. Our mate, my wolf adds.

"I don't want my first time to be with some guy I just met after a wedding I didn't want because my . . ." Leticia sighs, her body deflating with it. "Please."

"Whatever you need, it's yours." I nod and try to let her lead.

Inexperienced on Leticia is adorable. She pulls at the buttons, trying to work her way up my shirt, but her fingers keep fumbling.

I wrap my hands around hers and steady her. "We'll do this together. It doesn't have to be fast."

Leticia draws a slow breath, matching mine.

When we get to the top button, I release her hands and slide my shirt off my shoulders before tossing it on the back of my chair.

My late-night doom spiral and inability to sleep until I'd thought seventeen steps ahead bring me so much relief as I pull the top bedding back. The mattress protector on my bed is waterproof, but I still have the absorbent blanket tucked on the foot to lay down as well.

Leticia watches me pull back the bedding and lay out the blanket. "It's going to get bloody."

Bloody. My wolf wags his tail, and I try not to smile.

"It'll wash." I could explain all the qualities that make it the best sex blanket known to man and wolf kind, but I don't.

I kiss her again, and she relents.

"I don't know what to do," she whispers against my lips.

We do. My wolf tries to answer her.

"I can lead." I offer, then try to find a compromise. "Or we can talk through it like we did your orgasm."

Her cheeks start turning pink first, then it floods down her neck, and I want to kiss all that warm and glowing skin, but I hold myself back, waiting for her.

"I thought I could be brave, but I don't want to talk." Leticia nibbles on her bottom lip. "Is that bad? Is it bad I just want you to take control."

"No. Your choice is valid. I'm here for you and what makes you feel safe, cared for." I lean forward and kiss her cheek, the side of her jaw, and at her ear, I whisper, "And loved."

Leticia sucks in a breath, and I don't give her a chance to second-guess as I nibble on the skin just below her ear.

I pull at the belt that's wrapped around her waist, holding the knit sweater dress tight to her frame.

When it's free from around her, I toss it onto my desk chair and trace my hands lower, bending to keep my face close to hers. I pull at the bottom of the dress, dragging it up and around the curve of her ass.

Her breathing hitches.

"You're doing so good, gorgeous."

She lets out a steadied breath.

Past the leggings, my fingers catch a few bare inches of skin before tracing up over her bra. Leticia raises her arms and helps me pull the dress over her head. She doesn't try to hide herself from me.

Is it because she remembers I've already seen it? Or is it because she's not afraid of me seeing her?

My wolf doesn't worry himself with what I'm thinking. He keeps salivating over her.

Refocusing on warming her up to sex and what is happening to her body, I quickly put her dress aside before dipping my hand into the waistband of her leggings. They're tight, clinging to her body.

I have to take a moment to slow myself down. My cock is raging in my pants, dying to get out, to get to her.

Slow and steady. My wolf scolds me when I push her leggings down around the curve of her ass, pushing her panties along with them.

Stopping and listening to him, I sit on the bed before her and kiss first under her bra, then work my way lower as I trail my hands back up.

Her scent is so strong; it's fruity, lemony, clean, and mixed with the heady scent of arousal. The desire to be buried between her legs, licking her to come, almost overtakes the task at hand.

I press my fingers into her skin, massaging her low back and then farther down, feeling that ass I've been so obsessed with. It's just as soft and voluptuous in person as it was in the video feed.

Leticia lets out a moan. "God, it feels so good when you work on my lower back."

Noted. My wolf takes that fact so I can focus on her. I run my fingers back up to her lower back again.

She groans, and I know to come back to that and help her through the discomfort.

But one thing at a time. I bring my hands back around her ass and then down her thighs, picking back up where I left off in stripping her out of her leggings.

First around one foot, pulling off the sock with them, and then the other.

From where I'm seated, I look up at her. Still clad in her bra, she's gorgeous, but I want all of her. I want to see every inch of her.

If she's reading my mind or just finding a little bit of bravery, I don't know, but Leticia reaches behind her and unclasps her bra.

Her tits bounce free as she removes the straps from her arms before tossing it aside.

I swallow hard, looking up at her. The dusky rose color of her nipples perfectly complements the light cream color of her skin. And I despise myself for the mood lighting because I want to see every inch of her flesh in the best light to commit it all to memory. But I trust there will be time for that later.

I push up off the bed to stand and drag my hands along her body.

Leticia shivers, and then she giggles.

Excitement. My wolf decides.

Wrapping my hands into her hair, I tip her mouth up to mine again and kiss her deeply.

She presses her hand against my chest, and I freeze.

"Tampon." She looks away from me.

"Lots of research, remember?" I place a kiss against her forehead. "Trust me, I know the first time brings a lot of emotions, and I'm here for every one of them. I'm here for you. We're doing this together."

"Okay." She stretches up onto her toes and kisses me.

My heart pitter-patters, all excited, and heat runs up my neck.

Cautiously, I try moving her over to the bed. Leticia walks the few feet with me and understands that she needs to lie down. With her ass squarely on the blanket, head resting against my pillow, I'm thrilled knowing my whole bed is about to smell like her.

How long can we go without washing the sheets? My wolf provides a conscious thought to the feeling I have that I can't name. Something so much stronger than love.

I undo my belt and take off my pants. For a second, I think about leaving my boxer briefs on, to give her some experience being touched before coming face to face with her first penis, but ultimately I decide I'd rather her freak out earlier than later if this is too much for her.

But to me, there's always been something erotic about a partner's cock pressed against your thigh as they kiss you. Maybe it'll be the same for her.

Leticia

CHAPTER THIRTY-TWO

ORGASM PLEASE

Royal slides his pants down, and his cock is bare to me. I look at it and almost ask if I can see it closer, but I'm pretty sure there will be time for that later. He kicks his pants aside and then slowly climbs into bed next to me.

There's a bandage on his leg, white and pristine, stuck to the skin. I want to ask about the wound and if this will hurt him. But he's smiling so big at me that I let it go. *If he was worried, he'd tell me, right?*

Lying on his side, he presses up against me, and his cock finds a home along my hip. It's warm and I feel it throb. *Why is this so hot?*

In Royal's bed, everything smells like him and fresh laundry. It's this deep, masculine scent of rich dark chocolate and something else I can't put a finger on, and I almost want to roll around in it. But the source is right in front of me, looking down at me and smiling.

"Hey," I say because I feel like I should say something, but immediately, it feels like the wrong thing.

Can you fail at intimacy? Because I'm pretty sure I'm failing.

"Hey," Royal answers and presses a kiss against my lips. After a few seconds of kissing, I already feel better about being so weird. "I want to explore your body with my hands, is that okay?"

I nod and press up to kiss him again. Apparently, I love kissing. From watching movies, it never seemed like much. Toni's recount of her first kiss never made it seem like this. Nothing like this intensity.

Royal starts out with his hand on my stomach like he'd coached me to do. He's so warm that every part of him feels like a little furnace against my skin, and I'm grateful for it. The heat of his body drives away some of the chill of being naked in front of someone for the first time.

Slowly, he moves his hand, traveling up my body toward my breasts. He pauses on my sternum between them, not making any move to pick one or the other.

Against his lips, I let out a disappointed huff.

"In such a hurry." He kisses my cheek and then down my neck, his body sliding along mine while his hand finally moves to a breast. He doesn't beeline toward the nipple; he traces his fingers around it, almost petting the soft skin and working his way there.

I arch into the touch. Everything he does, I want more of. I need more of it. I've never felt this sort of need before, and it's so ungodly intense that I could writhe from it.

Finally, his fingers brush my nipple, and it hardens under his touch. The way his fingers dance around it tickles, but not in the way I expect. The view as he takes it between his thumb and index finger is alluring. He squeezes gently, and I can't help my body's response. I do writhe, pressing up into his hand and against his body next to mine.

I want to be a part of him, to move with him, and feel every bit against him.

"More," I whine, but the word comes out breathy.

"As you wish." Royal trails the kisses he'd been placing on my neck and shoulder lower, across the top of my chest and toward my other breast.

"Oh fuck," I whisper as his kisses draw nearer to my nipple.

I can't breathe like a normal person, the air moving in and out of my body in shuddering breaths.

"We'll get there." Royal looks up at me with a smile.

I nod and watch as he goes back to lapping over my nipple. It's warm and rough but tender all the same, the saliva cooling on my skin.

"Are you cold?" Royal cocks his head to the side.

"A little, you're nice and warm, but I'm a little cold." I don't want to complain or stop what's happening.

Royal reaches behind him to the bedside table and picks up a remote. After two taps of a button, a fan kicks on. "Just diverted some heat off the server room vents. It'll warm up in here."

"You didn't have to do that." I feel like an inconvenience.

"Didn't have to, but wanted to all the same." He sets the remote down and rather than going back to my nipple, he pushes up over the top of me before moving down my body, kissing his way down my stomach and lower.

The butterflies in my stomach do somersault aerials, fluttering everywhere all at once, while he kisses lower and lower yet.

Royal is absorbed in what he's doing, and I follow his lead. With tender care, he raises one of my thighs, spreading me open to him, and I let him.

When he nudges the other aside, I push myself up. "You don't have to, there's the tam —"

"Hey." Royal looks up at me with a grin, brown eyes bright and expressive. "Let me do all the worrying, you just do the enjoying. I did hours of research last night. And I'm very certain I've become more of an expert than most human men. I wanted to know what you were going through so I could help, and while I didn't expect to get to this step of helping, I'm nothing if not prepared."

"There's going to be blood and stuff." I protest.

"I'm familiar with blood and stuff. Not to be gross, but I do have a wolf inside me that tends to like to eat furry woodland creatures that are full of blood and stuff." Royal pauses and slides back a little bit. "But I also don't want to push you. If this isn't right for you, I don't want to —"

"I want it. I want this. I want you." I'm quick to stop him. I sit up a little more, getting closer to him.

Royal rises to meet me.

"You said you wanted to make me feel loved, and I do." I close my eyes, hoping I'm not reading too far into what's happening between us, but I'm lost if not wrapped up in him.

With a deep kiss, Royal lays me back onto the bed. He climbs up along my body and keeps kissing as he comes to lie next to me. He trails his fingers back down my body and between my legs.

Stroking with the lightest touch, he delves between my folds. The way he played with my nipple at first, all tease and no deep touch.

"Royal," I gasp when his fingers brush over my clit.

"You like that?" He teases the motion again.

"Mmhmm." I draw deep breaths, focusing on the pleasure like he taught me the other night.

It feels like forever ago that I was doing this for the first time, and now here I am in bed with him.

"That's good." He presses a little harder, and I reach up and turn his face toward me.

We kiss, and I let myself get lost in the intensifying touches. Pleasure pulsing but never coming to a peak.

Minutes pass, and I run my fingers into his hair. It's soft and so grabbable. I squeeze my fingers together.

"God, that feels good," Royal groans against my lips. "Ready for more?"

I nod and expect instructions, but instead, he pulls at the string of my tampon. Before I can say anything, he pulls it free.

Embarrassment heats my face, but Royal seems unfazed, just quickly wrapping it in a couple tissues from his nightstand, followed by a thud into what sounds like a waste bin.

Okay, that was surprisingly not that bad. I draw a steadying breath.

"I know a lot of guys like to make themselves sound bigger than they are and inflate their ego, but I don't want to just force myself into you. I know things are better if you're prepared. Are you okay if I use my fingers on you, or would you prefer I get a toy?" Royal's eyes are locked on mine, and I'm lost in them for a moment.

"Fingers are okay. If you don't mind . . . It feels more connected?" I struggle for words.

There is no judgment from him, and he nods before kissing me again. He trails his hand back across my hip to my pelvis and then back between my legs. This time, his fingers go lower. They run over my entrance, and I stop breathing, everything focused on what he's doing, on what's to come.

"Breathing is a super important part of life, gorgeous." Royal kisses my cheek and then down my neck. "Please do that for me."

I draw a slow breath and push it out. On my exhale, Royal slides his fingers inside me. Two of them curl in this come-hither motion, and I raise my hips off the bed to meet it.

"Look at you, so needy. I love giving you what you want." He practically purrs in my ear with a low growly sound. "You're so warm, wet, and tight. So tempting."

He moves down my body again, kissing his way down to my breast. This time he's not as gentle as before. Royal's teeth connect with the skin in a new sensation, a slight threat of pain, but I don't hate it.

I focus on drawing another breath again, and when I do, Royal moves his fingers more as if to reward me. I close my eyes, the ceiling and the view down my body so blurry that I can hardly see anyway.

"That's it, just relax, give in to the pleasure. Do my fingers feel good inside you?"

"Mmhmm. So good," I moan, and he strokes in and out of me, his thumb finding my clit as he presses on something inside me, which drives a sharp zing of pleasure through my body. "What was that? It felt so good."

"Your G-spot. Good to know you like it."

He repeats the motion, and I shake and shudder.

It's like when I was playing with my clit at home, but twelve times more intense. I draw slow breaths, focusing on chasing the pleasure.

"Good job, gorgeous. Focus on getting yourself to come." Royal breaks from teasing my nipple with his tongue and teeth. "I want to hear you scream for me this time. You don't have to worry about being quiet."

He trails kisses back up my neck to my cheek before kissing me deeply. With his tongue, he explores my mouth again, following the same pattern as his fingers.

I can't control the pleasure as it comes. It had been building slowly, but out of nowhere, it washes over me hard and fast. My body goes rigid as it takes me. I break the kiss and cry out, unable to stop the sound.

Royal doesn't stop touching me, he repeats the movement again and again as I come, writhing on his fingers until finally, after at least a minute, if not more, I'm able to relax and my breaths come easier.

"You're so fucking perfect when you come." Royal hums, still kissing patterns all over my skin. "I could watch you come forever."

"Mmm, is that so?" I try to sit up, but Royal eases me back down.

"What's the hurry?" he murmurs in my ear.

"I don't know." I admit and snuggle in close to him.

Royal pulls his fingers from within me and wipes them on the blanket behind him.

"Oh no, it'll make a me —"

Royal kisses me silent. "It washes. It's designed specifically for this sort of situation. Don't worry about it. I promise."

"Okay, no more worrying." I sigh and try to push it out of my brain, rolling to my side until our fronts are pressed together. His cock is hard and throbs against my abdomen. "Is that painful? Should we . . ."

"As far as painful experiences go this week, my dick hard and weeping for you is definitely not on the list." He kisses the top of my head and drapes his arm around me, pulling me close.

I reach between us to where his cock presses against me.

This time, the gasp belongs to him as I wrap my hand around it.

"So good," he murmurs into my hair as I test what squeezing it feels like.

He may not want to brag about size, but the math isn't working for me as I think about this going inside me. It's thick, and I can barely wrap my fingers around it.

"Don't be intimidated by it. We'll go slow, and if you want to stop, all you have to do is say so, and I will." Royal continues to anticipate all my hesitations, seemingly reading my mind.

"I'm ready for more." I grin up at him, giving his cock another slow squeeze.

He strokes my back. "So greedy. I've turned you into some sort of sex fiend."

Biting my lips together, I shrug. "Oops?"

"In our defense, we were left unsupervised." He smiles and pulls away from me.

A brief second of panic sets in as he climbs out of bed. But he walks over to the dresser, the one he showed me in the photo. When he pushes on a portion, it opens for him.

He grabs something small from the front and comes back to lie down next to me. Holding it up, he shows it to me, a little silver thing, and pushes a small button on one end. It comes to life, vibrating in his fingers, before he turns it off again with a longer push.

"It's a bullet vibrator."

"Always with the guns and your family, isn't it?" I laugh nervously.

Royal joins in on the laugh but turns more serious. "I just want to have it as an option. I tried to do a good job stretching you out with my fingers, but this can give some extra stimulation on your clit and get you through if there are any painful parts."

When I nod, he nods back.

"I don't want to hurt you." He kisses me.

"I know you don't," I say between kisses. "I don't think you could."

Royal carefully pushes my legs apart with his as he kneels between them.

I draw short breaths, trying to focus on the excitement and not the scary feeling like this is all a mistake, or that it's going to be too painful, or all the horror stories I've heard about first times.

Royal comes to lie above me, supporting his weight on his elbows. "This is all on your time."

"I want it. I'm a little afraid, but this is what I want." I force my breaths to go slower.

"I'm taking you at your word, but remember, you say stop, we stop. It's not going to change how I feel about you." He reassures me, and I feel the warmth of his cock as it presses against me.

He rolls his hips, and his head presses against my clit.

"Mmmmm, yeah. For sure, I definitely want this." I moan, the warmth and pressure building, and the reminder of pleasure sending sparks through my body.

He slides his cock down between my folds, and it feels so much larger than his fingers did.

"Breathe." Royal kisses my lips. "You gotta breathe."

"Breathing. On it." I nod and draw a deep breath.

Once I exhale, Royal kisses me, and his cock pushes in just a little bit. My whole body tightens at the intrusion.

Royal doesn't stop kissing me though. He pushes his tongue into my mouth, deepening the kiss, and I let myself fall into a trance of his lips as they dance on mine. Slowly, he withdraws his cock and then pushes in what feels like a little more.

I gasp at the fullness I already feel, knowing there's more and not sure how it's going to work.

"You're so good." Royal praises me against my lips. He kisses my cheek and then moves to nibble on my ear. His voice is low, barely a whisper. "You're taking me so well."

As if to punctuate his point, he presses in a little deeper. I make a noise, and it's somewhere between a moan and a pained yelp. I bring my arms up and wrap them around Royal. Not to push him away but to draw him closer.

"Please. Move, I want more."

Royal pushes up a little and looks down at me, or maybe he looks into my soul with how golden his eyes are right now. "Do you want the toy to lessen the pain? This could really hurt."

Unsure, I try to think it through, but there's likely to be pain either way.

"Is it weak of me to want the toy?" I bite my lips together, afraid of judgment, even though I'm sure it's not coming.

"Not at all, I think it's so brave to be trying so much at one time. The toy is going to help, and I know you're going to enjoy it." He picks up the vibrator from wherever it had ended up and turns it on. "This is the lowest setting. It has more if you want more, but let's start low and work our way up."

"I like that plan." I agree.

It tickles as he glides the vibrator across my skin.

I jolt with the movement, and Royal laughs. "I know those sensitive spots on the pelvis always tickle. Couldn't help myself watching you squirm."

I huff and shake my head.

With deft fingers, he slides the vibrating toy between us and teases it over my clit. My hips buck of their own accord, pushing me onto Royal's cock.

I gasp and he moans, and we're lost to the movement between us.

Royal rolls his hips, pulling out before pushing back in a little farther, a little deeper. The stretching feeling turns into a painful ache that I don't have words to describe.

He presses the vibe against my clit again, and pleasure folds through me, distracting me from the next push of his cock. I gasp and forget how to breathe, the biting pain battling the arousal the vibrator brings.

Royal lowers himself over me, kissing up my neck and jawline before placing soft kisses on my lips. I push up to him, exploring his mouth with my tongue and wordlessly encouraging him for more.

We're not talking anymore, but we're communicating all the same. Our push and pull as he slowly works his way inside me is bringing me to the edge.

"I'm going to come," I pant against his mouth, the vibrator driving me right up to the edge.

"Good, come for me, gorgeous," he murmurs low, the gravel in his voice spurring me on.

I crest over the edge, screaming out in pleasure and then gasping as Royal pushes deeper. Stars blanket my vision, and I close my eyes, my orgasm still washing over me as Royal moves, now freely fucking into me.

I lose all track of time as heat continues to pulse through me, in time with his thrusts, and soon I hear his voice over my own. "That's it, you're taking it so good."

His praise fades into a low growl as his whole body shudders in release. Royal turns his head away from me, his dark hair brushing against my cheek.

After a few panting breaths, he turns his head back to me, kissing my neck and shoulder. "You're fucking perfect, gorgeous."

Royal

CHAPTER THIRTY-THREE

AT YOUR SERVICE

My leg is killing me. I definitely didn't think this through.

The discarded vibrator is still running on the bed next to me, and I'm quick to turn it off before turning my attention back to Leticia.

Our mate is beautiful. My wolf admires her beneath us.

"I'm going to pull out slowly, okay? Let me know if I need to stop." I cup her face with one hand and kiss her slowly, backing my cock out of the perfect home it found between her legs.

Before I'm even fully out of her, I miss her. With every centimeter I pull out, I miss the connectedness and the feeling of being buried in her. At my release, I had to bite the pillow to not claim her as my own, and now, withdrawing from her is brutal and testing my wolf again. I refuse to take that choice from her. If she wants to be a wolf later then we can discuss, but she won't be turned in the heat of passion.

Leticia doesn't make any pained noises or tense up, and I'm glad it doesn't hurt her, but part of me wanted to delay the inevitable, at least a little while longer.

She looks down between us, and I pull her chin back up to me. "Don't look. Don't worry about it. I'll clean you up first. Then let you go pee."

I don't want her to look because I know for sure my wound reopened, and it's not just her blood in the mix.

For good measure, I kiss her one more time before pushing all the way off the bed and rolling toward the tissues and the garbage can.

The blood trailing down my leg from my wound only made it to my knee, and I quickly wipe it up, tossing the tissue in the trash can, before pressing on the wound over the now-bloody bandage.

"Okay, it is absolutely true what they say about sex being good for cramps." Leticia lets out a wistful sigh. "I'm on day two of my period, and this is the first one ever to not have me in agonizing pain."

"Glad to be of service." I look over my shoulder at her.

The blissed-out look on her face is all smiles and a perfect after-sex glow. Her hair strewn across my pillow is radiant even in the low mood lighting.

I didn't exactly plan specifically for us to have sex, but I definitely thought she'd have an orgasm in my bed. And now I'm glad I planned ahead, just in case, because there's a fresh pack of wipes in the bedside table, and I'm able to hastily clean the blood and semen off myself.

Without facing her, I grab a new pair of boxers, sleep pants, and a shirt out of my dresser and pull them on. It's barely noon, so naked in bed all day is an option, but not one I'm positive she'll be comfortable with.

"I'll be right back," I say on my way out of the bedroom to the bathroom.

Hot water runs from the tap slower than normal, or maybe it's just my impatience, as I wet two washcloths to bring back to her.

Leticia is dozing. Her slow breaths that I'm familiar with from our video call make me smile. I gently kneel by her side and begin wiping the blood from between her thighs.

She doesn't stir.

Just one lick. My wolf whines. *A little taste. We didn't claim her when we came.* His argument, that he behaved before, doesn't hold up against violating her wishes.

Stalking her is one thing. Assaulting her is another.

"Mmm." Leticia wakes as I finish.

"Hey, gorgeous, I've got you mostly cleaned up. You gotta get up and go pee though." I'm smiling like a damn idiot at her, but it's only a third of what I want to be doing.

Leticia pushes herself up onto her elbows and then rolls, pulling her legs closed. "I should probably be embarrassed you just cleaned me while I slept, right?"

"Nope, absolutely not. Because then I'd have to be embarrassed that I cleaned you while you were sleeping, and since I was providing the bare minimum care a partner should, that doesn't make sense." I shake my head and offer her my hand.

For her feelings of modesty, and not for any fear of exposure, I offer her my bathrobe. It's long on her, almost hanging down around her ankles as she wraps it around herself and walks, with her thighs locked together, to the bathroom.

The obsessive part of me wants to stand in the bathroom with her, to ask if I can clean her up the rest of the way, but instead I say, "If you want a shower, there are towels in the little cupboard. I left one of my T-shirts in there for you, too, if you want, and there are human feminine products under the sink. I'm going to go get your bags out of the car."

"Okay, thank you," Leticia calls back.

My wolf resists with every step I take away from her.

A note on the door at the top of the stairs explains why the main floor of the house is so quiet. Mom and Dad went to pick Kerrianne up from school and to feed Captain, which means, covered in the fresh scent of sex, I won't raise any immediate red flags.

I'm gone for barely three minutes before I get back downstairs, but Leticia hasn't come out of the bathroom.

I clean up the blanket I'd laid down and take it to the laundry machine, and she's still in there.

Open the door, my wolf demands as I stare at it. *Open the door to make sure she's still safe.*

I reach for the knob but barely stop myself, raising a fist to knock instead.

"Just a minute," Leticia calls out, but her voice cracks.

This time, I can't help myself. I push open the door, and she's sitting on the closed lid of the toilet.

"Gorgeous, what's wrong?" I clear the space between us and crouch next to her.

"Royal, we had sex, without a condom and —" Her words turn into a gasp that's biting into my heart, but I don't know why. Her eyes are wide and terrified like a deer caught by the pack.

My phone is back in the bedroom. Though I don't even know what to search for to figure out what has her so rattled.

Seconds, maybe minutes, hell, it could be an hour later, and she finally whispers, "It's not a high chance, but I could get pregnant."

Relief crashes over me like a second orgasm, and I wrap my arms around Leticia, pulling her close. "Oh, that's all you're worried about. Don't be worried."

"Don't be worried?" She struggles and pushes against me. "We can't have a baby, Royal, this is serious."

I let her push me off. "You and I can't get pregnant, Leticia. Not like this."

"For someone with a lot of sex toys, you don't know how babies are made?" Her anger sharpens her words.

Made our mate angry. My wolf blames me, but it's not like he knew why she was mad either.

"We're not the same species." I shrug and try to help her feel less defensive. "Wolves and humans aren't compatible. You would need to be turned into a wolf for us to get pregnant, and you're really human right now."

"Oh." Leticia deflates, and I pull her into a hug once more.

"You're sure?" Leticia eyes me, her breathing sharp and labored.

"More sure than anything. It's why there are so few wolf shifters. We're only compatible to breed with other wolf shifters, and changing humans is a huge deal. We don't do it unless it absolutely has to happen." I spare her details, knowing the next time we talk about this or that her next question will be about Antonella.

"You said we could check on Toni and Valor?" She follows the exact line of questioning I was expecting.

"Absolutely, I'll go pull up the cabin feeds." I release her and gesture to my bedroom. "You get in some comfortable clothes, and after we spy on them, we'll watch a movie."

Leticia

CHAPTER THIRTY-FOUR

AGAIN?

Royal wouldn't lie to me.

Well, not again, right?

I shove the rampaging thoughts of pregnancy away. *Even if he is lying to me, the risk is small. It'll be fine.*

It's one thing to not flat-out tell me he's been stalking me and watching me. It's another to lie directly to my face.

Royal wouldn't do that.

I draw steadying breaths. They come easier, and my heart doesn't feel like it's about to jump through my rib cage. I love being the older cousin to what feels like hundreds of little D'Medici cousins, but kids have never been my calling. I'm not like Antonella. I don't particularly want to spend more time with children. I certainly don't want any of my own.

Not that I expect to have a choice with an arranged marriage on the books. Some asshole is going to want kids, and it'll be my responsibility to fulfill my duty.

Royal is telling me that we can't have kids because I'm a human and he's . . . not. I'm taking it at face value. We're safe.

Cleaning up after sex was a unique experience. His semen inside me sparked a whirlwind of internal screaming and what-ifs, but now that I'm clean and cozy in a pair of joggers and Royal's T-shirt, I'm more at ease. Maybe it's because I'm wrapped up in his sweet chocolatey scent again that I feel so safe.

I hug my arms around myself, the smile returning to my face.

I had sex. My first time wasn't some stupid wedding-night fuck to consummate a marriage I didn't want.

It was scary, but it was good. He cared for me, and it wasn't about what some asshole wanted. It was about me.

I chose this. Warmth floods my core.

I chose him. The butterflies are back.

When I wander back into Royal's room, he's standing over his desk, working on a keyboard that is seemingly stacked on top of one of his numerous monitors. The light from the screen he's working on highlights his features. His strong jaw, with a short beard growing over it, is well paired with his broad shoulders and muscular arms.

"So." He pulls me into his arms, kissing the top of my head.

I snuggle in tight against him, the attention and affection pushing any last thoughts of pregnancy from my mind.

A winterscape fills the screen before me, and the bright midday sun glistens off the snow. A large, imposing black wolf sits in stark contrast to the landscape, its head hung as it watches over a gray and white wolf with a red-tinged muzzle, lying flat on its side, panting.

"The one lying in the snow and panting is Antonella. The one looking like he's incredibly sorry and trying to apologize for the fiftieth time is Valor." Royal points between the two of them.

I instantly miss the way his arm held me tight to his body.

"How do you know he's sorry and apologizing?" I squint at the screen and bring my hands up to where Royal's other arm is wrapped around me, hooking my fingers on his forearm.

Like he knows what I'm asking for, Royal squeezes me a little tighter. The reassurance I'm here and still connected to him is a welcome reminder.

"Mmm, head low, shoulders hunched. It's an apology. And she is *so* not ready to hear it. She's not even looking at him." Royal gestures to Valor and then indicates where the other wolf, Antonella, is looking somewhere off-screen, pretty much anywhere that isn't Valor's direction. "I really don't blame her. Valor fucked up. He should be held accountable. I'm even mad at him for hurting her, and I don't know her all that well."

"Well, unfortunately, Antonella's temper is long. She gets really big mad. But, given some time and space, she usually forgives pretty easily, especially when she knows the other person is genuinely apologetic." I let out a huge sigh.

But it doesn't really make sense to me. That wolf is Antonella. It's a beautiful animal. She's fluffy, and white fur is intermixed with the gray and some black, giving a mottled color down its spine. But how can that be Antonella?

"Oh, he feels bad, alright. I don't think I've ever seen him so upset over something he's done, and he broke my leg in two places once," Royal says with a laugh.

My fists clench, and I glance down at his legs, wide eyed. They're obviously both there, and if the physical activity we just engaged in is any indication, they both work, but how does Valor get to behave like some sort of demon rampaging through a family?

I glower and grumble, "Is that supposed to make me feel better?"

Royal gives me a toothy grimace while wrapping his arms around me again. "Yeah, kinda?"

I shake my head and look back at the screen. "Is she safe?"

He speaks low to the top of my head. "She's an apex predator with a man who will kill someone for looking at her wrong. When they come through this, Valor is going to worship the ground she walks on."

"Swoon," I murmur, hoping he doesn't hear me.

If he does, Royal doesn't say anything. But he closes out of the window.

"I hate to address the elephant in the room, but your dad texted you wanting an update." He changes subjects.

"That's the elephant in the room?" I turn and look up at him, eyebrows raised and mouth agape.

His cheeks are red, and it's growing down his neck.

"It's the most time sensitive one?" He shrugs and interlaces his fingers in mine before leading me over to the bed.

He's made the bed in a more turned-down style, like at a fancy hotel. The covers are folded back, neat and inviting, all evidence of what we'd done cleared away. My phone is sitting atop the covers.

"What about the other elephant?" I sit down, not concerned with my phone.

"The one where we just had mind-blowing sex, and I fully plan on doing it again later?" His eyes are brown when he starts the sentence, but they turn gold — I *watch* them change color — as he finishes.

"Your eyes just changed color." I get distracted from the conversation, looking at them and how they're inhuman but soulful.

"Sorry." He blinks a few times, breaking my trance. "Did I mention that my wolf really likes you?"

"That's what that is?" The distance between us feels too far, so I pull on his hand, and Royal sits next to me on the bed.

"Yeah, he's just really close to the surface, like we're ready to shift and switch places." Royal explains with a squeeze to my hand.

I settle in, pulling up a leg and hugging it to my chest.

Royal bites his bottom lip and hungrily rakes his eyes across my body. "But about the whole sex elephant." He shakes his head, and it looks like it takes tremendous effort for him to pull himself away from wherever his thoughts strayed to be more neutral. "I want to circle back. Are you hurting? Are you okay? Do you want to talk about it? Would you maybe like to do that again sometime?"

"I'm a little sore." Pulling my leg up has stretched muscles I didn't know existed but are now making themselves known with a slight ache. "But it's nothing compared to what my cramps are normally like, so I'll take it. And that was *amazing*, so yeah, I would totally do that again, but maybe after I rest a little."

"Oh, absolutely, rest, food, water, snuggles, and probably a movie before we even consider round two." Royal reaches over and runs his fingers through my hair, pushing it out of my face.

It's a move straight out of a movie, and I let out a contented sigh. But the real task at hand nags at the back of my mind as guilt eats away at me. *I only agreed to help Dad to spend time with Royal, but now this is the consequence of my own actions.* "Okay, the awful elephant, what do I even tell Dad? Because what we just did is absolutely out of the question." I stare at my phone, not even wanting to look at the message myself.

Royal picks it up and hands it to me. "You're going to tell him enough of the truth that it's not suspicious. No embellishments that you'll have to worry about keeping straight."

"That I made it safely here, I met Betty and Ian. I noticed you keep a lot of weapons in the home?" I try for something that might appease my father.

"All of that is true and should be expected. It shows you have good observation skills. Why don't you add on there that it's an intelligent house and has a ton of security?" Royal offers while I unlock the phone.

A lonely notification sits in my inbox.

DAD:

Status update.

LETICIA:

Made it to the Cavanaghs' safely. It's beautiful in the country. There are tons of security cameras. Royal calls it an 'intelligent home' with a lot of security. They have more weapons in their house than we do.

I hit send, and the message sits spinning in my inbox, looking like I have really spotty service.

Royal's phone makes a noise, and he looks it over. "Sounds perfect."

After a tap on his screen, the message shows as sending on my end, and finally, the checkmark indicates it's been delivered.

"That's so scary you can do that." I put my phone aside. The little device that's only one part of how he's been watching me. "You can do it to everyone?"

"I mean, that would be incredibly inundating, and I'd never get anything done, but I can block just about any phone I can get access to," he admits, running a hand across the back of his neck. "The link I sent you for the first Late Nite Bytes was a Trojan horse. I admit it was wrong, but I wanted to know everything about you."

Somehow that doesn't sit right with me. But I can't put my finger on it. "Me? Or Dad's business."

"You. It's always been about you." The look in his eyes is somber. And I want to believe what he's saying. He elaborates. "To be honest, we couldn't give two fucks about your dad's business. All we cared about with the truce was stopping the bloodshed."

Does he mean that? Or am I just a pawn in someone else's chess game?

Royal reaches over to the nightstand and pulls out a remote control. He looks back at me, and whatever he sees stops him. He must see the hesitation on my face. "Leticia, I'm not joking. Yes, we're keeping eyes on your family. But I'm not supposed to look any deeper than just making sure your family is holding up their end of the truce. Me watching you was purely, *is* purely, personal." He tosses the remote aside and puts a hand on top of mine in my lap. "I've liked you since I first saw your text messages coming in on Antonella's phone. And the more I've talked to you, the more intense it's gotten."

Swoon. Tears well up in my eyes, and I blink them away quickly. "I'm trusting you."

"Good. Because I'm trusting you too. You know a life-changing secret." He leans forward and presses his lips to mine. I kiss him back, but he breaks away. "Let's throw on a movie. I'll go up and get some snacks."

After a quick how-to on the remote and a reveal of the child-proof password to watch something more than a PG-rated movie, Royal drags himself away from me. I find a campy-mystery movie that I've seen before, but it isn't showing up as watched in Royal's system.

He's back ten minutes later with a massive tray piled high with food.

"Normally, I lay this on half the bed and then lie next to it, but since I've got a much better partner to snuggle, I think if we put it on my desk chair, it'll work?" Royal pulls out his chair with his foot and makes it look easy to place the board down, resting on the armrest.

"How much food do you think I can eat and still have room for dinner?" I gape at the board.

"Well, I wanted you to have options, and really, I figured you'd only eat a quarter of it. The rest is all me. Plus, whatever we don't eat, we can put back." Royal shrugs. His hair is disheveled, but he looks so perfect. He hands over a big forty-ounce cup of water. "Drink a little, please."

The 'please' gets me. It's not a command, but it's definitely not a suggestion. It's strong yet spoken with a soft tone. I take the straw between my lips and draw a few sips. It's just ice water, but it hits the spot. I didn't realize how thirsty I was.

Royal

CHAPTER THIRTY-FIVE

BROTHERLY LOVE

"Royal," Mom growls. "Don't make a mess."

I look at the area next to the sink where I'm cleaning up breakfast dishes. "I'll clean it up."

"Not what I meant," Mom whispers. "You and Leticia?"

"We're both well aware she's someone else's bride. In the meantime, it's just fun." I shrug and run the rag over the counter for good measure to wipe up.

"You're going to get hurt." She wraps an arm around me and squeezes me to her. "I hate seeing my babies hurt, and Valor is hurting enough for the both of you."

I snuggle against her. "I know."

"As long as you know." Mom lets me go and steps away. "Can you and Leticia handle making dinner and watching Kerrianne? Your father and I are going to be at a meeting with a mercenary and his family until late, and I don't want to eat at ten p.m. because I have to come home and cook."

"Absolutely, I shall order takeout." I salute her.

"Oh, absolutely not. I taught you how to make one meal so you can impress a woman. Dust off that skill set." Mom smacks my arm before walking away. She calls over her shoulder, "You missed a spot."

I wipe the counter again to do a more thorough job and reexamine the last twenty-four hours. From picking up Leticia in

Gold Coast to bringing her here, sex, cuddles, having her sleep in my arms, and breakfast in bed, there is quite literally nothing I can think of that would make the last day better.

Footfalls make their way upstairs, and slowly, slightly damp, fresh out of the shower, Leticia comes up the stairs.

"Hello, gorgeous." I smile at her, admiring the soft blue sweater she's wearing over a pair of tight leggings. Looking to the living room, I make sure no little eyes are watching before I run my hand along her side and cup her ass.

There's a soft squeak, and Leticia covers her mouth with her hands. With a little more composure, she answers, "Hello, handsome."

"The parents are leaving me in charge this afternoon. I have the pleasure of cooking you and Kerrianne dinner this evening." I smile down at her.

Leticia quirks an eyebrow. "You, cook?"

"I do, in fact, possess the acumen and knowledge of how to cook at least one meal." I nod with proud definition.

"Mmhmm." Leticia nods along with me. "And that meal is?"

"Spaghetti." I smile at her.

"No." Leticia shakes her head, jaw dropping and eyes wide. "Absolutely not."

You upset our mate. Fix it. My wolf urges.

"What's wrong? Do you not like it?" I reach for my phone. *Cooking is just following a user guide. I can do that.*

"I'm not eating 'spaghetti' made by the next generation's suburban dad and pretending it's passable. Especially since 'spaghetti' is pasta and I'm not sure if you mean bolognese or not." Leticia shoots me down with accuracy.

I hang my head. "Yeah, that's fair."

"But I would be glad to help you make it." She tips my chin up with her finger to meet her gaze. She has this mirthful glint and a crack of a smile.

My wolf rises to the surface. Wagging his tail, he pressures me to lean into her touch.

I do, and her smile brightens. She doesn't know it's an answer, so I verbalize. "Then I'll be the greatest sous chef ever."

"Excellent, now show me the pantry. I'll need a full inventory." Leticia gestures broadly to the kitchen around us.

Our mood is soured by phones vibrating.

Leticia looks at hers and groans. "It's stupid Berto. He wants an update for Dad. But he wants to call."

"You can call." I nod and gesture toward the back screened-in porch, away from where Kerrianne is reading in the living room.

"What do I tell him?" Leticia whispers, her eyes wide as she holds the phone out to me. "I don't know anything."

"That's exactly what you tell him, you don't know anything. The only time we talked about my work, it was more about security and that we can see all of our territory with ease. Let them know my parents have a meeting tonight, but you don't know what it's about. Just that you're helping me cook because you don't want to eat suburban dad spaghetti." I rattle off ideas for her.

Leticia nods along in understanding.

We step out onto the screened-in porch, and Leticia shivers.

You should have grabbed her a sweater. She doesn't have fur. My wolf scolds me.

But it's too late for me to go back.

Leticia makes an exaggerated movement, tapping the Call button. "Berto."

Her phone volume is loud enough that I can hear without her having to put it on speaker.

Berto talks fast at Leticia rather than having a conversation. "Leticia, what is going on? What have you learned? Dad is six shades of pissed that your updates are so insignificant."

They don't appreciate her like we do, my wolf growls.

"That's because I'm not learning anything. They don't talk about work. We've spent more time talking about movies and watching his parents play with robot vacuums. You knew it wasn't likely they were going to just tell me things." Leticia handles her brother's demanding tone like a champion. "All I know this morning is that Royal said they can see all sorts of their territory with a push of a single button."

"Interesting, they're certainly focused on video surveillance. Why are they so watchful?" Berto muses, but again, the question isn't really directed at Leticia. "What else? Do they go anywhere? Do anything? Are there people coming to the house?"

"No one comes to the house, but Mrs. and Mr. Cavanagh are going out tonight. Some sort of meeting. Royal wasn't invited. We're staying back with Kerrianne and having food. Save me, Berto. They tried to make me eat boxed spaghetti."

"That's abhorrent." Berto scoffs but refocuses. "Where were they going? Who are they meeting?"

Leticia looks at me, and I shake my head. She understands perfectly. "I don't know. They didn't say. It didn't sound like a large gathering though. Just that they'd be back late and for us to cook dinner."

Berto groans, "Fine. I'll tell Father. But this sort of update isn't going to be enough. We need something substantial."

"I'm doing the best I can." Leticia argues with him.

Berto is quick to end the call with a snappy "Do better."

With as fast as Berto hung up the phone, I'm faster to wrap Leticia into a hug, the cold porch chilling her body. "You did so well. You didn't even need me to tell you how to do that. It was so natural. Let's get you warmed up."

Leticia finds enough suitable ingredients between Mom's pantry and refrigerator to cook up a feast. She looks over at me as she arranges them on the counter. "Do you think Kerrianne would want to help with the pasta?"

"Letting that girl help you with anything is a first-class ticket to being her favorite relative." I tap my finger against my chin. "The question is, am I ready to share being the favorite with you?"

Leticia rolls her eyes and starts rummaging through drawers, looking at the contents. "I could never steal being her favorite from you. I can't build robots."

"I mean, the robot we worked on this week is pretty cool." I wish I could read her mind and tell her where to find what she's looking for, but there's something graceful in the way she dances around, pulling drawers and closing them behind her.

"Hey, Kerrianne?" Leticia calls to the living room.

A book gets dropped on the floor, and the light thuds of her footfalls precede Kerrianne before she peeks her head around the corner to the kitchen. "Yeah?"

"Do you think you can help me make pasta?" Leticia cocks her head to the side.

My wolf tips his. *Mate knows our language?*

No, she's mimicking movements. She's probably doing it unconsciously. I brush it off.

She'd make a good wolf.

When he says that, I freeze. The conversation between Kerrianne and Leticia turns to a silent film.

Antonella, in wolf form, raging and fighting against Valor as he put her in the cage in the back of the van so he could take her to the countryside, plays in vivid memory in my mind. I break out in a cool sheen of sweat. There is no way I could do that to her. I'm not built like Valor. I couldn't hurt the woman I love like that.

Leticia is human, and I like her that way.

I like not thinking about what it would mean to turn her.

We can't have pups like this, my wolf growls at me, highlighting how Leticia is talking with Kerrianne.

But I don't even know if Leticia wants kids. I never thought about having them before. Why should I start now?

"Earth to Royal." Kerrianne waves her hand, trying to get my attention.

"Come in command, this is Royal." I shake myself out of it, focusing on my niece. Focusing on what is real.

"Space cadet." Leticia giggles, covering her mouth with her hand.

Trying not to be embarrassed by being caught in a random thought, I attempt to pull anything from my memory of what they said.

"Grandma's mixer with all the gadgets. Can you get it out of the closet so we can make long pastas?" Kerrianne wobbles back and forth.

Pup has energy. We should take her to let it out. My wolf warns.

I shove him down and out of my mind. He's caused enough

trouble. We don't need to add a shifted wolf puppy and a too-close-for-comfort human to the mix.

"Absolutely." I nod and leave the two of them, thankful for the second to collect myself.

The deep green mixer is right on its shelf in the closet, where it always is, but I lean against the doorframe and pull out my phone.

My relationship with my older brother may be a difficult one sometimes, but even when we're going through hell, we make time for each other if we need it.

ROYAL:

I think I fucked up. Not as bad as you did, but bad enough that I can't tell Mom and Dad.

I don't expect a text back right away, but the chat bubble pops up, indicating that he's typing.

VALOR:

I don't think that's possible. What did you do?

ROYAL:

I let a stalking obsession turn into something more.

VALOR:

If she/he/they are the one, then Mom and Dad will understand.

That's one thing about Valor I never quite understood — but I appreciate nonetheless. I always thought he'd be so uncool with me not being straight, but just like with Mom and Dad, it was a moment of 'oh' and moving on with our lives.

Telling him this feels so much heavier.

ROYAL:

She's the one. I don't think anyone is going to understand.

VALOR:

Give me a couple days. Antonella is . . . close.

Unless it's Leticia D'Medici, then you're fucked.

ROYAL:

I'm fucked.

Hope Antonella is really kicking your ass for what you did.

VALOR:

You better put space between the two of you right now or it was nice knowing you.

The one or not, you can't have Leticia D'Medici.

I mean it, Royal, the two of you can't happen. Think of the truce.

Got to go. Time to get mauled again.

Valor has worse things on his plate than my fuckup.

I've thought about the truce and how we're D'Medici and Cavanagh relationship saturated. I know it's unlikely that the D'Medicis will want to deal with us now that we have the truce. But this isn't fair. How am I supposed to just walk away from my fated mate?

I grab Mom's dark green stand mixer and the bag of attachments, then walk it back to the kitchen.

Leticia pulled her hair up into a ponytail and dumped flour out on the counter. She's teaching Kerrianne how to make a little well inside it.

Awww. Look at them. My wolf sighs. It's all love and affection for two of his favorite people.

Seeing Leticia with Kerrianne is cute, but I'm definitely not thinking about what it'd be like if Kerrianne was our kid.

If you don't want to have kids with someone, isn't that a sign you're not the right fit? I try that thought on for size, but all it does is conflict with my heart that's screaming how much we need her in our life.

Leticia

CHAPTER THIRTY-SIX

ANOTHER FIRST...

I forgot how tiring it is spending a whole day with a second grader, and to think Toni does this with a whole classroom.

With Kerrianne tucked into bed upstairs, Royal and I were mostly off the hook until his parents came home. Now we're officially 'off duty,' and the first thing I did was change back into Royal's oversized T-shirt and pajama bottoms.

I pull the fabric up to my nose, drawing in the strong masculine scent of him again. The inhale and exhale send a wave of relaxation through my whole body.

Royal is sitting at his desk when I come back, his fingers flying over the keyboard. The screen is black with green letters, like the old-school computer games on floppy disks we used to play in elementary school.

"Work?" I ask, leaning against the back of his chair.

Even seated, he's so tall that I can rest my head on his shoulder rather than on top of his head.

He hits the Enter key on his keyboard a couple of times and nods silently. I let him concentrate, just standing there content to watch as he does his work.

A few minutes later, he leans his head against mine. "Yeah, just a temporary security patch. The client had an idiot employee open an attachment for some malware. My data scrubber got it out of their system, but it left a back door wide open, so I'm just running some code to make sure it's patched."

"It's cool that you can do all that." I wrap my arms around his shoulders, hugging him.

Royal picks up one of my hands and brings it to his mouth, kissing the back of it, then along my thumb before turning my wrist over and kissing the inside of it. "It's all in a day's work. I don't know about you, but I'm exhausted. Kerrianne knows how to take it out of you."

"All out of you?" I stop breathing, wondering if he'll get the meaning behind my words.

"I wouldn't say *all* out of me." Royal's kisses turn a little more heated, and his tongue brushes against my skin. "What do you have in mind?"

"Well." Indecision hits hard as I try to ask for something but don't know how to say the words. "I-I'm not quite . . ."

Royal takes pity on me, nuzzling against my head before turning slightly to look at me. "More of what we've already done or something new?"

I dislodge myself from hugging him and let him turn to see me. "I don't want to leave any firsts for someone else to ruin."

With a solemn nod, Royal's eyes turn calculating, moving back and forth a little, like the code on the screen did. "There's a lot we could try, but some of it should be done with warming up and practice. It's not something that should be done just on a whim."

"Oh." I try not to let disappointment hang in my voice.

"How have your cramps been?" He turns his chair to face me, and god, how I want to climb into his lap.

"They're fine, not as bad as they have been." I brush it off like I normally would, like my mother and the doctor do.

"I noticed you had a bad one while helping Kerrianne. I should have offered to get you something." Royal hangs his head a bit.

"If it was really bad, I would have gone and gotten something." I reassure him. "But what does that have to do with trying something new?"

"Well, you've said you're not interested in having oral performed on you while you're bleeding. So I was thinking we could play with your luscious ass." He bites his bottom lip before slowly letting it go.

"Oh." That hadn't even occurred to me.

"When you say 'oh' like that, it lets me know I missed the mark. What were you thinking?" Royal is so unfazed by my response. It's like he's discussing the weather more so than sex.

"How did you get so good at talking about sex?" I hide my heated face behind my hands.

Royal pulls my hands away one at a time. "I've had a number of partners and found that it's easier to just ask for what I want rather than expect someone to read my mind."

I try to take his words to heart. "I feel it's been a lot about me and not enough about you. I want to make you feel good too."

Royal is shaking his head before I finish my statement. "Not how I feel at all."

"You're sure?" I try to step back from him to examine everything about him.

But he doesn't let me. He wraps his arms around my ass and drags me to him until my knees buckle and I'm pulled onto his lap.

When we're nose to nose, he answers. "We took yesterday nice and slow, but both of us had orgasms. At the end, we both expressed satisfaction."

"Okay." I settle in on his lap.

He's given me everything I've wanted, even if I haven't been able to ask.

"I don't want to push you too far too fast. I understand wanting to be able to do this all on your own terms, I respect that, but I don't want you to do things because you're feeling like this is the only chance to make it happen." He nuzzles against my shoulder, and I rest my head on his.

"This could be my only chance." I fist his shirt, disliking the way reality keeps finding its way into the bubble of false hope and the fake future I've made with him.

He doesn't say anything, not for a long while. He draws deep breaths and relaxes into both the seat and on my shoulder, and for a little bit, I wonder if Royal fell asleep.

"Some people get off giving oral sex. But it isn't hard to have a decent first time doing it. The mechanics are pretty straightforward." Royal runs a hand up my spine. "But anal is a bit of a different beast. It can really hurt if someone doesn't take the time to work you up to their cock. And I never recommend taking a cock during your first time."

I stiffen as he trails his hand back down, caressing and then palming my ass.

"What do you recommend?" I manage to get out in a whisper.

"A small toy or a finger or two," he whispers back.

Nodding, I agree. "Yes, let's do that."

He grips the globe of my butt a little tighter, and his eyes turn that goldish-brown color. "I was hoping you'd say yes."

Like I weigh nothing, Royal stands from the chair, carrying me to the bed. He gently sets me down on it and slides his hands up my pajama-clad legs, the ruffling of the fabric tickling at my skin. Once he makes it to the waistband, he slowly draws the bottoms down.

When I shiver, Royal smiles. "Let's get you warmed up." He wraps his fingers around my ankle and pulls my leg, dragging me across the bed toward him. He reaches past me and pulls the covers down before he stops and laughs. "Okay, this was way sexier in my head."

The laugh breaks all the tension. My nerves fizzle off, and I back myself up over the lump of covers he made to be more central on the bed.

"Thank you, m'lady." He tips a nonexistent hat to me.

"How do you do that?" I sigh, looking at him. The messy hair and relaxed posture, it's so effortless.

"Do what?" Royal shrugs, but his eyes are roaming my body.

"Make sex not scary." I sit up a little bit on the bed.

Royal steps over to his toy cabinet but keeps his eyes on me. "Sex isn't supposed to be scary. It's supposed to be fun. If you can't laugh every now and then during it, then what's the point?"

"Honestly, I'm not sure." I curl my knees up to my chest, a cramp hitting me hard.

"Cramp?" Royal stops opening his toy cabinet and steps back to the bed.

I nod. "It'll pass."

"It's such bullshit women have to deal with this." Royal comes to sit next to me on the bed and runs his fingers through my hair.

"Cramping during wolves' heats usually just means you're ready for another orgasm, but it doesn't sound like that for humans."

"I mean, I wouldn't turn down an orgasm." I lean into him, drawing in a deep breath of that sweet chocolaty scent I've come to find comfort in.

"Good." He aggressively kisses the top of my head with an overexaggerated smack of his lips. "Let me get a heat pad for your cramps, and then I'll make sure you're well fucked and ready for cuddles and sleep."

I'm about to argue with him that he doesn't need to get me a heating pad, that he doesn't have to take such good care of me, but Royal is gone before I can even open my mouth.

He wants to take care of me. I don't remember a time when someone wanted to take care of me like this. Tears well up in my eyes, and I wipe them away, begging them to stop before he gets back. *Not sexy, Leticia.*

Royal is back before I get my eyes to stop leaking tears.

There isn't a single second of hesitation. He plugs the heating pad in and lays it behind me on the bed before wrapping me in his arms and snuggling me close. We lie on the bed together, chest to chest, the warmth of the heating pad soaking through my T-shirt and skin.

His touch is tender as he dries my tears. Then he kisses me soft and sweetly.

But I don't want to just be comforted. I want the orgasm he promised. I want to feel relief and shed the unwanted emotions.

I tug at the hem of his shirt, hoping he understands what I want, what I need.

Royal moves, letting me help him pull the cotton over the top of his head. He discards it onto the floor.

When I start tugging mine up, Royal's hands find mine, and he helps. The way he drags his fingers along my skin pulls a heated gasp from my chest. He presses his lips against my navel, kissing as he works his way up my chest, before he finally discards the shirt. I took my bra off when I put my pajamas on, so I'm left in a pair of panties and nothing else.

Warmth envelops me on all sides as Royal pulls a blanket over me. Wordlessly, he slips out of bed and over to his toy cabinet.

Butterflies swarm my stomach as I don't know what to expect, but I'm relieved he didn't take my tears for disinterest.

He sets whatever he collected on the nightstand and comes back under the blanket with me.

When he kisses me, it's deep and meaningful. Every part of me knows how to respond, and I do. There are so many things I can't tell him. That I want to tell him but would be forbidden to speak out loud. They all lead back to how I feel and what I want between us.

Royal's hands wander. They trace imaginary lines down my body, dragging across soft skin, and when he presses his fingers under the band of my panties, I raise my hips to help him remove them. The uncomfortable menstrual cramp persists, but the pain is second to the excitement his touch is eliciting.

"It's easier said than done, but I want you to forget how to think and just focus on feeling. Okay? Don't worry about a mess, don't worry about what I'm thinking or feeling, just focus on how you feel and be present." Royal is firm with his words, but they're delivered with the utmost kindness. "Can you do that for me, gorgeous?"

"I'll try." I can't get my voice out above a whisper, but that doesn't matter.

Royal beams at me. "Good girl."

I don't know what it is about those two words. He's said them before, but they still make my heart pitter-patter, and my brain stops overthinking.

"Do you want to make choices about how we play, or do you want me to make decisions for you?" Royal asks into the side of my neck as he kisses from my jaw to my shoulder.

Immediately, the tension is back. I stiffen and try to think what it would mean to let him make decisions, but I don't even know where I'd begin.

"I . . ." I shake my head. "I don't know."

"I'll drive. You just tell me if we've made a wrong turn. If you don't like what I'm doing, say stop and I'll stop. No questions asked." Royal so easily takes control of the situation.

But his suggestion feels right, and I exhale a long breath. "I like that plan."

Royal pulls his pillow off the top of the bed and offers it to me.

"Roll over, face down. Put this under your middle and get the heat pad right where you need it. I'd do it for you, but I want you to be as comfortable as possible. Let me know if you need more pillows."

I shuffle around like he instructed. When I lie down with the pillow under my pelvis, I let out a low groan. "I never thought about lying this way for cramps. It feels so good."

"It looks even better." Royal matches my groan.

I roll my head and find him squeezing his cock through his sweatpants. He's already hard, and I shuffle my thighs apart, hoping for him to come closer.

"So needy." He tsks. "I'll take care of you. Just relax. I'm going to put some massage oil on your back. You can stay quiet. You don't have to say anything unless it's an objection if you don't want something."

I nod and pull my arms up along my side by my chest and wait. I'm surprised when warm oil is poured along my spine. I expected it to be cold.

Royal's hands go to work. I've seen them fly across the keyboard so masterfully, so it shouldn't come as a surprise that his fingers are adept at this also.

It's been forever since my last trip to the spa, and the masseuse has nothing on Royal's talent. He loosens knots in my shoulders and moves down to my lower back.

"I love the little noises you make," he says softly. "You're so good at telling me what you like without even knowing it."

He slides his hands from my lower back to around my butt, and I tense up.

Royal just keeps massaging, his fingers working through tense muscles until I'm soft and pliable in his hands.

He kneads the backs of my thighs and runs his fingers back up through my ass cheeks.

My breath catches, and I try to make myself breathe.

Royal slides his fingers back down the other direction. "It's okay if you're not ready for this."

"I am, it just surprised me." I close my eyes and force a breath.

"All you have to do is say stop and we'll stop." He reminds me.

I feel massage oil poured at the cleft of my ass and focus on how good Royal's touch feels. One of his hands works between my legs, and my thighs tremble when he hits the sensitive bud of my clit.

Pressure at my back entrance draws my attention, but as fast as the pressure came, it's gone again.

That's how he toys with me. He teases my clit just enough to make me think about the pleasure that's coming and then pushes against my ass. It's slowly building the excitement. By the third, fifth, seventh time he's teased me — I've lost count — I push my hips upward, begging him for more.

When he slips his finger into my ass, I gasp. The anticipated pain is nothing more than a little pressure, and the way he works my clit has me moaning. My body moves of its own accord, pushing back into him.

"Like that, gorgeous?" I can hear the sultry smirk in his voice. "You look so good like this. Your ass in the air. Presenting for me. I like your silent begging to be fucked."

I gasp again as he slowly thrusts his finger in and out of my ass. The pressure changes with each stroke, building my pleasure, and those strokes match the way he pets my clit. I swear I'm already seeing stars.

"Royal." I say his name as a warning.

A warning for what though? That I'm going to come? That I like this? Neither of those things needs a warning, do they?

"Be so good and come for me," he growls in encouragement.

It feels too soon, like we haven't played enough, but his words do it. They push me over the edge, and I press my hips up into him as he works my body. I grind against his hands, the pressure in my ass growing as I come. And god, it feels so good.

I grip the sheets and clench everything in my body as I come. By the time the orgasm passes, I'm panting, my toes are tingling, and I can hear that Royal's talking to me.

It takes a moment for my ears to stop ringing before I can hear him clearly.

"You're so perfect." He slows his movements on my clit. "I knew you'd have such a big orgasm. Gorgeous, you're perfect. So adventurous. And I could listen to that scream forever."

"I didn't realize I was making noise," I pant, my voice feeling a little scratchy.

"So loud. So good." Royal is moving, pulling himself away from me, and I dislike it, but I let it happen. "I'm not going anywhere. I'm just going to clean up a little bit, then we'll see if you're a 'more than one orgasm in a play session' kinda girl."

I open my eyes and see Royal pull a package of wipes out of his nightstand drawer. He cleans his hands, but I'm not focused on that. His cock is hard, and he's wearing way too many clothes. Which isn't saying much since he's shirtless.

"Why am I always naked and you're dressed? Am I a bad partner, not making sure you —"

"You're perfect and not a bad partner." Royal stops me from spiraling.

After tossing the wipe in the waste bin beside his nightstand, Royal dips his hands into his pants. Through the fabric, I watch as he fists himself.

He closes his eyes, and his head rolls back. "You have no idea how badly I want to say fuck it, be bad, and push you too far and fast with this."

"Why won't you?" I try not to take it personally, but that statement feels pointed.

"Because I want you to want me. I want you to enjoy everything there is about sex, and being shown, the right way, is what will get you just as excited as I am." He looks back down at me. "Think you want another orgasm?"

I smile, wagging my butt back and forth. "If I say no, it'd be lying."

"Well, we wouldn't want that." Royal pulls his hands from his pants before sliding them down his legs. He kicks them aside, and I'm distracted watching his cock.

I've become some sort of sex fiend or something because I can't help but look at it. I want to feel him inside me again.

Rolling to my side feels awkward. But once I'm on my back with my pelvis tipped up in the air, it feels just as good as having my butt up.

"Now that's a view." Royal bites his bottom lip.

He works liquid over the toy he'd previously gotten from his cabinet and then comes back to bed. The mattress dips with his weight as he walks on his knees toward me. His eyes turn moody, but it's not anger. It's something more mischievous.

"If I don't get your ankles around my ears really soon, I'm going to get mad."

"Well, we wouldn't want that." I repeat his words and lift my legs until they're up in the air, my calves pressing against his chest.

His cock slides over my mound, resting between us.

"Yeah," he groans as he slides one hand down my leg toward my hip and leans forward, my legs flexing toward my body with the movement.

"Yeah?" I quirk an eyebrow at him.

"I can see myself fucking you like this." He turns his head, nipping at the inside of my ankle before kissing it.

CHAPTER THIRTY-SEVEN

GOOD GIRL

Excitement buzzes through me, and I hurry to dispose of the tampon. Leticia makes this cute disgusted face, but when I kiss her ankle again, she goes back to smiling. Leticia couldn't be more perfect even if she tried. My cock is resting right above her clit, and I'm struggling to hold control and not slam into her. I haven't felt this out of control with a partner ever.

She deserves me to stay relaxed though. She deserves gentle and caring touches. But that doesn't mean I'm not above corrupting her.

"I want to teach you all about double penetration." I slide back, notching my cock against her clit, pressing into the sensitive bundle of nerves.

Her gasp and eager nod are such an enthusiastic yes that I'd be a fool to think I'm truly the one doing the corrupting. A sex-starved minx is just waiting to be unlocked inside her.

Our minx. My wolf pushes to the surface, and the way he rakes his attention down her body, I can't help but join in on the dirty thoughts about her.

"Royal, keep doing that, and I'm going to come again." She pulls in a ragged breath, her toes curling in my peripheral vision.

Testing that, I grind into her, the pressure against the head of my cock causing my balls to twitch. I'm not going to make it long myself at this rate.

Begrudgingly, I pull myself away from her long enough to take the lubricated anal plug and show it to her. "You're all warmed up, so I'm going to push this in. You'll feel some pressure. But it won't be too bad."

"I liked how it felt." Leticia worries her bottom lip.

"Good. Because I loved watching you take my finger like that. I wanted it to be my cock."

I lift her hips up just a bit more, exposing her ass to me. The toy and her hole are both well lubricated and fit together perfectly as I press the tip against the ring of muscle.

The moan she makes as it slides in has me salivating. I want to eat her out, and fuck her, and then watch her ride my cock, and the list goes on and repeats itself in excess. We'd never leave my room again if it were an option.

Play with her more. My wolf begs.

I turned on the toy's power switch before lubricating it, so now it's just a quick tap of the play button on my phone's lock screen. But it's on the nightstand, and Leticia is naked and practically begging beneath me. The toy filling her without the added vibrations will have to be enough this time.

Slowly, I slip my cock into her, testing her and how it feels to be joined like this.

"Oh," she gasps, but the look in her eyes isn't rounded and scared.

Leticia arches her back, and I slide in deeper.

She lets out a huge sigh. "I feel so full."

"Mmm, and we're just getting started." I lean forward, and my cock sinks in slowly.

"That feels so good. Right there," Leticia pants, her shoulders dropping and her pelvis lifting.

I grind my cock into her, probably pressing on her G-spot based on depth.

Short thrusts feel good, so I pump my hips, and she writhes beneath me. The view is perfect, and her tits bouncing lightly has my balls twitching.

Going slow is no longer possible. I run my hands down her legs, trailing one up her body to her tits. The other finds its way to play with her clit.

The sensation of the toy pressing against my cock has my legs shaking.

Leticia groans low, shaking her head back and forth. "Royal, this feels so good. Please give me more."

"You're taking it so good. I'll give you more. Eyes on me," I softly demand.

Brilliant blue eyes lock on mine, and I direct her gaze down to where our bodies are joined. Her mouth opens with a gasp.

Breaths turning ragged, I roll my hips, pushing my way into her, the pressure building between us.

Her eyes flutter closed.

"Come on, gorgeous. Focus, eyes on me. I want you to watch me come. I want you to watch as I fill you up." I didn't realize I was so invested in having her see what we're doing together.

Pups could be good. My wolf takes the idea of her full and runs with it.

I guess my brain does too. Maybe it's because if I'm falling over the edge of lust, or love, with her, I want her to fall with me.

Selfishly, I push the rest of the way into her. Leticia cries out, but it's pleasure and not pain. She grinds into me, her whole body tight and rigid. I circle her clit, and she tenses under me.

"Royal, I'm going to come," she pants, her eyes locked on where she's swallowing my cock. "Please, make me come."

"Asking so nicely. Good girl." I praise her and roll my hips.

Pulling in and out of her, I make sure to angle the way she likes so I press into her G-spot.

Seconds later, she screams, and her whole body locks up. With her legs pressed against my chest, her pussy pulses around me, and it drives me over the edge.

I cry out with her, my balls draining as her pussy milks me. Pushing her legs apart, I collapse forward and shallowly thrust into her. Then I claim her mouth with mine as my orgasm crashes through me. Breathlessly, she arches into me and fists my hair, holding me close as she kisses me back between panting breaths.

We're lost in a bubble, the pleasure holding us captive. We exchange gentle kisses back and forth until our breathing regulates and my cock softens.

"You're perfect in every way, gorgeous." I kiss the tip of her nose. "Come on. Let's get you cleaned up."

CHAPTER THIRTY-EIGHT

FIVE MORE MINUTES

"Royal." Leticia keeps her voice low. She pushes against my side, pulling me out of a dream. "Your phone is ringing. It's Valor."

I offer my hand out. "I'll tell him to get fucked then we can go back to snuggling."

Yeah. Since he told us to separate from our mate. My wolf yawns and flops back toward sleep.

With a little giggle, Leticia unplugs my phone before putting it in my hand.

Squinting through the dark at the offensive glowing piece of technology, I press the button to answer it.

"Good morning. Please fuck off," I groan.

"No." Valor is firm and assertive, and road noises are in the background of the call. "We're on our way home. I didn't know if you wanted to bring Leticia over to see Toni right away. I know Kerrianne is dying to come home. Mom said she'd bring her over but . . ."

Despite sounding like a suggestion, I know my older brother isn't truly leaving the decision up to me. I'm to bring Leticia over to see her cousin shortly after Valor and Antonella get home.

I withhold the attitude I want to give him. "Okay. We'll get up and ready. About an hour?"

"About an hour." Valor confirms, and the call disconnects.

I roll from my back toward Leticia, sliding my cell phone back on the nightstand and pulling her close to me. I kiss her forehead and murmur, "Five more minutes."

"Five more minutes only works if you set an alarm." Leticia yawns and snuggles into me. "Get some more rest, I'm awake."

"No, it's only fun if we're both sleepy and snuggly together," I huff but then start kissing her all over.

Ten or so kisses in, Leticia is giggling and pushing against me, trying to escape. I slowly stop and let her go.

"It's so dark in here, I could barely believe the time on the clock."

"Yeah, I customized my lair with state-of-the-art blackout curtains because I work odd hours, and it's just an added level of security for the computers when I'm working."

I yawn and reach over to the bedside table. The remote is right where I left it. I push the button, and my blinds shift a little, letting in some natural light.

She pushes herself up to sitting and runs her hands back through her hair. "So, I get to see Toni today?"

"Yeah, we're going to go over with Kerrianne." I flop back, looking up at her from a new angle.

The most absolutely perfect woman on the entire face of the earth, and I've been blessed with this time with her. It's hardly explainable.

"Should I be nervous?" Leticia uses air quotes with those words.

I shake my head, quick to reassure her. "No, she's still the same person. Was Antonella prone to being grumpy or irritable?"

"Not really. No more than most people?" Leticia slides out of bed. "Why?"

"Then she's probably not a grumpy or irritable wolf." I sit up, moving to follow her. "Wolves tend to be just more intense versions of ourselves. Mine gets even more obsessed with things, people, than I do. But he's also super loving and just wants everyone to get along."

"Like when he was mauling me?" Leticia smiles despite the negative connotation in her words.

"Yeah." I roll my eyes and correct her even though it's not necessary. "Like when all he wanted was to give you a ton of licks and keep you warm from the cold weather."

"Okay, if you say so." Leticia stretches her arms up over the top of her head, and while I love seeing her in my clothes, I'm sad I don't get a glimpse of her perfect skin underneath.

Something is wrong. My wolf and I feel it at the same time.

There's nothing wrong with Leticia and me. We're perfectly comfortable. But it's like the whole world has shifted its atmosphere, and I can't get a reading on what it is.

"Go shower. I'll meet you there. I've got a little work to do." I encourage Leticia.

But it doesn't matter what program I check; all the camera feeds seem fine, and every system turns up with perfect security protocol. The nagging feeling that something is wrong stays seated in my gut, resting against my spine.

Leticia

CHAPTER THIRTY-NINE

SUBURBAN DAD BOLOGNESE

I'm just waiting for the conditioner in my hair to set when the door to the bathroom opens.

"It's just me," Royal calls over the rushing water. "Mind if I join you?"

"I would be offended if you didn't." I'm smiling before I even get to see him.

When did I become so enthralled with him?

"Well, wouldn't want that." Royal, already naked, steps into the shower with me and lets out a deep guttural moan. It brings back memories of last night, teasing a smile to my face. He sighs. "I didn't think anyone else in the world liked showers as hot as I do."

"What's the point in having a shower if you're not boiling like a lobster?" I scoff and draw a deep breath.

The shower has gone from smelling clean and soapy to thick with Royal's natural scent — chocolatey, woodsy, and comforting. I'm salivating at the thoughts of all the things we've done together and all the ways he's made my body feel like mine.

With Royal, I'm no longer renting my body from some future arranged marriage. It's mine to use freely.

That's why this hurts so much. "About today."

"What about today?" Royal has his head tipped up, letting the water wet it. Overspray mists off him toward me.

"I don't think it's a good idea to be so forward about how much time we've been spending together and how we've been spending that time with each other." My words were meant to be so much stronger than they come out.

Royal swallows, his Adam's apple bobbing, and then he looks at me. "You're right. Valor and Antonella have a lot going on. It's probably not the right time to spring on them that I want to find a way to make us a more permanent thing."

"I'm sorry, a what?" I blink dumbly at him, my jaw falling open.

More permanent. Oh my god. That's not what I was . . .

"Leticia, I have big feelings for you, and I don't want to be on borrowed time." His eyes are that deep brown color again, not his wolf, but the soulful tone that sees me at my depths.

"I don't know what to say." The truth is that the butterflies are back and throwing a party inside me. I shake my head. "But not today. We can't get into that today. We have to be just friends or something because Toni is a wolf now, and her life has already changed enough without her having to worry about me and Berto and my dad."

"Okay." Royal closes the few inches that were between us. "Deep breaths."

I hadn't realized I was hyperventilating. I draw a slow inhale, forcing my lungs all the way full. *Borrowed time and big feelings.* Those words rattle against the cage holding my heart. The cage that was protecting it from getting hurt because I'm destined for an arranged marriage. But now I know the truth — the cage is empty. My heart is already gone.

"Today we're just friends. I'm just some asshole techy who's been tormenting you with long-winded rants about cybersecurity and robots." Royal says those words, consoling me, but I can tell he doesn't feel them.

"And I've been boring you to death about cooking when you tried to make suburban dad bolognese." I pick the most mundane and normal thing we've done.

"I promise to not think of you naked and how your ass looked propped up on my pillows." His dirty words increase the temperature in the shower. Despite the heat, I shiver. "But then you've got to promise you won't think about putting your ankles on my shoulders."

"It'll be easy." I lie because it won't be easy to break this bubble we've been living in. It's going to be hell to go back to reality and pretend like Royal means nothing to me and that my heart didn't go rogue and fall for him. I try to pull in a deep breath. "I'm just going to remember how mad I am at Valor for hurting my favorite cousin."

Royal huffs. "Yeah, okay. You're right. That's going to make this a lot easier."

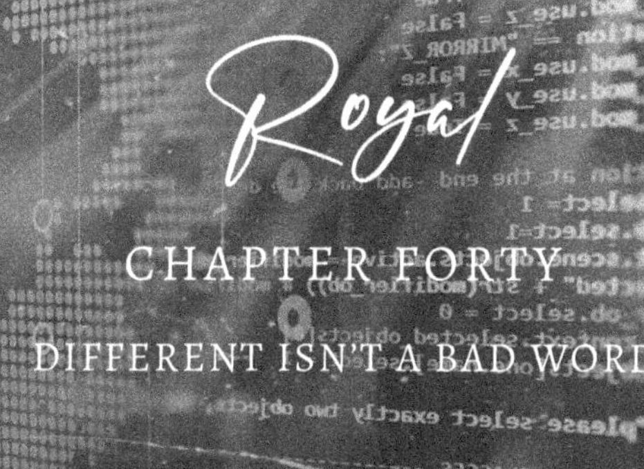

Royal

CHAPTER FORTY

DIFFERENT ISN'T A BAD WORD

We beat Valor and Antonella back to their place. Parking the SUV next to where Valor usually pulls into the garage, I look in the rearview mirror at Kerrianne. "I want you to go in right away and feed Captain. Can you handle that, or do you need assistance?"

"I can do it." Kerrianne, who gave Mom sass this morning, is still grumpy and takes it out on me with an aggravated huff.

There's gotta be something in the water this holiday season that's got everyone all squirrely. I'm not immune to it either. I practically confessed my love to Leticia in the shower this morning.

We go into the house, and Kerrianne darts off to the tortoise room, and Leticia maneuvers the hall to the kitchen. She starts digging through cupboards and pulling out a few things.

"I'm going to make hot chocolate. Do you want one?" Leticia offers as she starts a pot of water to boil.

"Yeah, that'd be good." I don't really want one all that much, but I think, like Leticia, it'll be good to keep my hands busy doing something other than exploring her body.

I open up the security surveillance on my phone to a ping for the gate, Valor and Antonella pulling through now.

"They'll be here in just a couple of minutes, better boil enough for all of us." I gesture to the pot before wiggling my phone.

A few minutes later, as predicted, the sound of the garage door rising, then closing, can be heard, and finally the door to the garage opens.

Kerrianne walks right past the kitchen toward the sound.

"Kerrianne, give them some space, come back," Leticia whispers.

But the strong-willed seven-year-old stays glued to the corner, waiting.

Valor lets Antonella lead, and when she comes into view, it's a whole new Antonella. I wonder if Leticia can sense it too. The way Antonella came across as poised and well-mannered before has turned into calculating and disciplined. She glances around the open space before there's a shift. The atmosphere of the house changes as Antonella breaks her perfect posture to stoop, opening her arms for a hug to Kerrianne.

One dancing hug with Kerrianne, and their embrace is done.

Leticia's next, and the cousins wrap their arms around each other, holding on tight.

Does she know how strong she is now that she's a wolf? Not so tight. Don't hurt her. I fight back a growl.

Not hurting. My wolf waves off my concern.

But there are tears in Leticia's eyes when they separate, and she's quick to wipe them away and smile. "It's so good to see you."

I move to Antonella slowly, not to spook her, wrapping my arms around her. My heart hurts with what I couldn't say before, the words that felt so lost. I beg for forgiveness at a whisper level. "I'm sorry I didn't call him faster."

"I don't blame you for any of this. I'm glad you're okay," Antonella whispers back. She squeezes me tight before letting go.

"Go sit, I've got cocoa started. Put your feet up, they're going to get cold not wearing any socks." Leticia shoos Antonella with a wave of her hands.

Leticia takes steps to the kitchen, and Antonella turns toward Valor. I can't see what she tries to say, but Valor nods.

"I don't think I have to worry about my feet getting cold anymore." Antonella sighs as she takes a seat in one of the chairs.

Kerrianne has been patient in waiting for more cuddles, but the second Antonella sits, Kerrianne climbs into her lap, snuggling up against Antonella's neck.

They look perfect together. Antonella is great with Kerrianne, and anger rises in me again.

Almost lost her, my wolf growls, thinking about what it would mean for Kerrianne to lose someone else.

Valor makes like he's going to sit beside them and be this perfect fucking family. And letting my anger ride, I step into his way.

Even though he's second-in-command with Neil out of the way, he's always outranked me. But I hold my ground — picking his wife, a newly turned wolf, a woman I've only known for a couple of weeks, over him — as he appraises me. It should say a hell of a lot about how angry I am at him, even if I don't obviously convey it in my actions and words. How I don't forgive him, not yet, for hurting her.

Valor nods slowly, then steps around me, keeping his distance from Antonella and taking a seat on the couch.

Tension ripples off me, and I force myself to contain the yawn that tries to escape. It lessens the tension all the same.

"Grandma says we might not go back to school after Christmas. Is that because you're part of the secret now?" Kerrianne questions.

"It is." Antonella gives her another squeeze. "You know how your wolf gets tired and cranky sometimes?" Kerrianne shuffles backward a bit to see Antonella better before nodding, which prompts Antonella to continue. "Mine is like that a lot too. So, I might not be a good enough secret keeper for a little while. I may need to take some time to make sure I'm good and ready to be a secret keeper."

"Grandma says Leticia knows the secret and is keeping it, but she doesn't have a wolf. I didn't know that was supposed to happen."

Kerrianne's statement leaves Antonella lost. Her eyes dart to Valor and then to me, trying to answer.

"There are special times when secret keepers don't have wolves, like Father Michael doesn't have one, but he knows." Valor offers some clarity, and I admire how easily he breaks down complex wolf laws into child-sized pieces. "If you're ever not sure if someone knows our secret, it's best not to tell them. Not even to test and see if they know it."

"Are we going to give Leticia a wolf like we gave Antonella?" Kerrianne turns, trying to look over her shoulder at Leticia.

"Not unless we absolutely have to," I snap. The sound of my teeth clicking makes me pause. *Don't protest too much. Remember, you're just friends today.* I try to dial back my answer, rumbling a bit, turning it into a joke. "It's kind of nice having a human around."

Leticia glares at me upon approach, a tray of mugs held in her hands, but she turns it into a mocking smile. "Hardy, har, har. Asshole."

Asshole? I'm stunned but keep my mouth shut. *What the hell did I do to get called that?*

It dawns on me slowly. She doesn't know how to play it cool. Leticia doesn't know how to act disinterested.

Adorable. My wolf sighs.

She sets the tray on the coffee table. "For the best cousin." Leticia holds one out to Antonella. "For the asshole I like." She offers one to me.

Her hand trembles for a second, and I want to forgo the agreement to be friends and question her and the new animosity. But I force myself to let it go.

Our mate is hurting like we are. We'll fix it later. My wolf consoles me.

"For my favorite little bestie." She gives one to Kerrianne and leaves Valor's on the tray on the table before sitting down with her own.

"Be nice, Leticia." Antonella warns her.

"He has arms," Leticia answers before bringing the cup up to her mouth. "I could have poured it down his shirt . . . or worse."

The threat has even me pausing to see if it's viable because this is a new side of Leticia I haven't seen before. The way Antonella looks at the ceiling and lets out a heavy sigh has me less certain that maybe there isn't something I'm missing about Leticia.

Maybe our mate has fangs and bites after all? My wolf cocks his head.

Valor, unconvinced, stands and takes the cup from the table before examining it. "Should I be concerned this is . . . different?"

"Should you be?" Leticia cocks her head. "Do you require something different?"

I lean forward, offering my mug of hot cocoa to Valor. He takes it and passes me the mug intended for him.

Would our mate poison us? To get back at Valor? My wolf rises to the surface, trying to smell the cup contents.

Would Leticia poison someone at all? I mean, she spends enough time in the kitchen, so why shouldn't she know something about poisoning?

I keep my eyes locked with her for a moment. "Speak now . . ."

Leticia rolls her eyes before leveling me with a flat gaze. "The only thing different here are the two of you."

"Manners, all of you," Antonella chides softly over the lip of her cup before she takes a drink.

Kerrianne giggles, her cocoa sloshing. "Different isn't a bad word."

"Oh, in this case, it most definitely is. They're using it as an insult." Antonella groans. She squares herself to Kerrianne. "And it's not one we'd repeat at school because?"

"Insults are bad and meant to hurt people. Even if we think they're funny, it could hurt," Kerrianne recites like she's said this before.

I lean over to Valor and use my cup to shield my mouth. "The fuck are they teaching the kids at the school?"

With a shrug and a shake of his head, Valor sits back down on the sofa. "I don't know, but maybe I should take some classes."

I snort, trying not to lose my shit at that notion.

Which is fine because Kerrianne huffs, her sassy attitude coming back out. "You can't come to class. You'd never fit at my desk. Your legs are too long."

"Excellent logic." Leticia nods and takes another sip. Her phone rings, and she groans as she answers it. "Berto, for the last time. Mind your own business and not mine."

I freeze looking at her. That seems so out of character from all the times she's talked to Berto and her dad, but maybe, with Antonella at her side, she feels more in control? Something?

"What is your problem?" Berto huffs from his end of the line.

Being farther away from her than I was on the porch yesterday, I can barely make him out.

"I'm calling to let you know an SUV is on it's way out for you. Send me your location so I can update their directions. Your time with the Cavanaghs is over. Dad brokered a deal. You're to be married to Steffano Bianchi." Berto informs her, like it's just a casual phone call and not a life-changing event. "Get your shit together, you've got to pack for Italy."

Steffano Bianchi is a trash human. He used to broker arms through us for his guards at their mining operations, but when we found out he wasn't just protecting the mines with those guns, we cut off his supply. There are hundreds of pages of reasons not to work with the guy. But most pertinent at the moment is that Leticia would be the third Mrs. Steffano Bianchi.

Antonella must hear Berto, too, because she taps Kerrianne's leg, and Kerrianne scrambles out of the way, coming over to sit with Valor.

When Antonella holds her hand out, Leticia hesitantly gives her the phone.

Antonella's voice is glacial as she rumbles, "Berto. You did not just say that."

Leticia has gone ghost white. She leans forward and sets her mug on the table.

"That's the second most ridiculous thing you've ever said." Antonella is on the verge of growling.

I set my cup down and move toward her. Placing a hand on either arm, I try to steady her, demonstrating breathing. With new wolves being as volatile as they are, the last thing we need is her shifting in the living room on a phone call.

Antonella follows my lead, taking a few steadying breaths, and the growl fades out of her voice. "I'm not letting that happen." She hangs up, raising her gaze to Leticia before repeating herself. "Leticia. I'm not letting that happen."

Threat of Antonella going rogue dissipated, I move away from Antonella, putting myself closer to Leticia. The problem now is that Leticia's dropped the act. She's no longer putting on a show by pretending to hate me. Her eyes are full to the brim with dread, and the lack of fire in her threatens to snuff out some of my own.

"Don't be silly." Leticia gives the most pained smile I've ever witnessed as she takes her phone back. "Look how well it worked out for you. Aside from, like, maybe the last week, arranged marriage can work quite well. It's time anyway. I shouldn't be putting it off."

"I'll figure you a way out of this." Antonella shakes her head.

"You've got enough on your plate. I know the man Berto is talking about. I'll keep his house in order and dinner warm and on the table. Nothing I don't do now," Leticia says and returns her attention to her phone, probably doing as Berto asked and sending him her location.

But it's all false bravado; she's terrified, and the acidic scent of fear is wafting off her.

We're all silent — Kerrianne hugging Valor, Antonella and Leticia having a silent conversation, and me trying to calculate all the ways I can make Steffano Bianchi disappear.

Don't forget poison, acid bath, and that one mercenary who feeds his victims to bears. My wolf is so very helpful.

But Leticia doesn't let us dwell on it. "Sorry for the interruption. Now, where were we? Talking about putting a Christmas tree up in here? With such high ceilings, surely we could get one at least a respectable height. Maybe ten feet?"

"Better go twelve with these ceilings." I look up, playing into her massive change of topic.

It'll be better if we wait until after they're married to kill him. I can't believe I'm thinking that thought.

After the wedding but before the consummation is a tricky timeline. You can't let someone else touch our mate. My wolf offers a solid consideration.

Tabulations run in the background of my thoughts.

Kerrianne dismisses herself upstairs to play, and the four of us sit in awkward conversations that would be better off as uncomfortable silences. But it's not long before Valor's phone buzzes.

"Leticia, there's an SUV at the front gate for you." Valor glares at his phone.

Logically, I know what he's going to do is right; he's going to send her home.

She'll be safe in D'Medici territory because of the deal. Leticia is even more valuable to them now than she was before. No one is going to be able to lay a finger on her.

But that doesn't mean I like it.

"I'll be going." Leticia stands and steps over to Antonella.

They say their goodbyes, and Leticia heads to the front door.

But I can't make myself say goodbye in front of Valor and Antonella. I know I haven't been the best at pretending we're not in love with each other. I've already confessed, in part, to Valor anyway.

The door closes behind Leticia, and Valor looks at me with that flat, dead-eyed look, the killer look.

I nod, knowing there are a lot of things Valor could say but won't.

Standing, I gesture the way she went. "I shouldn't let her stand out there alone. It'll look bad to their security."

"Good call." Valor dismisses me.

Would he agree if he knew what lightning-strike idea has taken over me? Maybe not . . . But it doesn't matter.

I only have a few minutes to explain my plan.

This is the only place where we'll be truly alone.

Well . . . after I edit the security camera footage covering this portion of Valor's driveway.

Leticia

CHAPTER FORTY-ONE

THE PLAN, THE FIRST PROPOSAL

"Leticia," Royal calls softly.

I hadn't even heard him follow me outside.

"Hey." A smile pulls at my face even though it has no right to. "Fancy seeing you here."

"I want to help. Let me help." He nods as if trying to get my blanket agreement, all the while stepping closer.

Don't get too close. You're not mine to keep. Tears threaten to prick at my eyes. *I'm married to someone else.*

I push aside all my feelings and ask indignantly, "Help? With what?"

"I can prevent them from marrying you to Stefanno Bianchi. They might have signed paperwork in Italy, but it isn't done in America yet." Royal rushes the words out.

"Oh," I try to say, but it's more of a strangled sound in my throat. I shake my head slightly, but can't seem to get my body to work.

Royal takes it as an invitation to keep talking. "I can backdate you and someone, of your choosing, into a secret marriage. I can fabricate the marriage certificate, financial records, vacations, photos, and anything else you would need to prove a marriage. If anyone questioned it beyond that, all you'd have to do is get Antonella and one of his friends or family members to give a sworn statement with recollections of your relationship."

He finally pauses for a deep breath, waiting like he's expecting me to need a minute to catch up.

He's offering me an out, and I can't take it. I knew this was inevitable. I knew playing house with him was going to hurt when the time came. I just didn't expect it to be so soon.

I've been following, but I still ask for clarification anyway. "What do you mean?"

"I mean, I can make it so that they can't marry you to Steffano because you're already married to someone else." And then, with a nod, he takes it one step further. "To me."

"I couldn't ask Antonella to do that." I start with the easiest objection, despite the clawing at my heart, begging and pleading me to say yes. "I appreciate the offer though."

"Valor would do it in a heartbeat," Royal says.

"Have you seen my older brother? Not a single man in their right mind would even look at me twice, let alone risk being killed over touching me. You should feel the same way." I warn him off as more moisture pricks my eyes, threatening to freeze over in this cold. "It's too dangerous."

"I'll do it," he casually says, no hesitation. "I'm not afraid of Berto. I'm a wolf, remember."

"Royal, I can't —"

"I'm offering because I want to. I want you. You can't help that your dad and brother are assholes. You don't deserve what they're putting you through. You deserve a choice. I want to fight for your honor. I want to fight so that you can make a choice. Give me the opportunity to fight for you." Royal cocks his head and steps closer to me. I can feel the warmth radiating off him.

"How can you do all this?" I whisper, not believing it. *Could he really protect me from them?*

"It's what I do. Don't worry about how I do it." Royal reaches toward me.

I let his fingers entwine in my hair. I let him place a kiss on my lips.

The last one. The last time. My insides feel like they're coming undone at the seams.

Headlights from the SUV illuminate the trees as it comes up the driveway.

I step away from him, putting distance between us for the sake of no one knowing what we've done.

The SUV is here to collect me, to take me back to D'Medici territory, then I'll go to Italy and meet Steffano. They'll throw an engagement party and make a big deal of me finally getting married. An engagement ring will be given, a date will be picked, and I'll find out all the plans that have already been made for me.

It's all for show. Our family loves big weddings, and I'm already dreading it.

"Leticia." Royal's voice drags me back to the present and the distance between us. "Marry me?"

I *want* more than anything to say yes. I want to jump up and down and scream yes so the entire world hears me. I want everyone to know how I feel about Royal.

The SUV pulls to a stop in the center of the driveway.

I force my feet to move one step and another. I don't have a choice. Not if I want to keep him safe. "No."

To Royal's credit, he doesn't fight or argue with me. He gives a single solemn nod. "You have my number, Leticia. Use it. Anytime, day or night. I'll answer."

"Thank you, Royal."

I try to commit how he looks to memory. His reddish-brown hair and warm brown eyes. The soft beard, the strong hands, and the comfort he brings me. But tears pour out of my eyes, and I don't wait for the driver to open the door for me. I climb in unassisted.

But I can't help but leave it this way. If I anger my father and jeopardize this deal, it won't just be me who pays for it. He's likely to do the unspeakable to Royal, and what would that do to Antonella? To Valor? And Kerrianne? Losing Royal would be a house of cards toppling all at once. I wouldn't be the only one suffering that loss.

Silent sobs form before we're even halfway down the driveway. Every roll of the tires sends another ache through my chest. The dreadful ache of my heart staying behind with Royal.

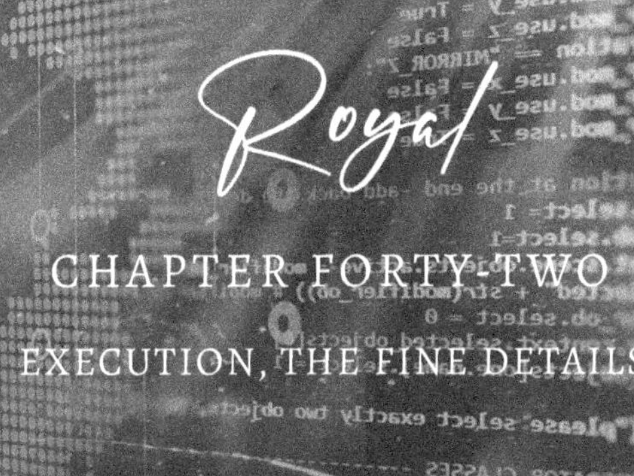

Royal

CHAPTER FORTY-TWO

EXECUTION, THE FINE DETAILS

Watching her cry tore me to pieces. My wolf is the only thing holding me up at this point. I don't bother going back in to say goodbye to Valor and Antonella. They have their own life to live, and I've got work to do.

I don't remember driving home. I only remember walking down the stairs into my lair.

Leticia didn't want me to marry her, but she's not thinking clearly. It's a shock to the system. I heard who they're going to marry her to. I know what he's like. I won't let that happen. Stefano killed his last two wives. Everyone knows it, but no one has been willing to prove it. For fear of repercussions or something else, I don't know.

I won't let the beautiful, full-of-life Leticia be pulled into that sort of darkness. I won't let her fall into a wakeless slumber, locked in a tomb in Italy. She's too bright and too beautiful.

We'll fight to protect our mate. My wolf hunkers down for what is going to be a long night.

I get to work, starting with marrying us on paper. Leticia may have said no, but I'm pretty sure there's a rule that says you're not allowed to make big decisions under duress.

Having your whole life uprooted and being married to a murderer counts as duress.

The first order of business is turning on her phone's GPS

tracking and enabling backdoor access to get locational tracking every six minutes. It's a few clicks of the mouse.

Gregorio and Berto might not be shipping her off to Italy tonight, but they will soon enough, and I want to know the second she moves.

Suitcases. My wolf points out that her two suitcases packed with clothes are still sitting in the seating area.

I pick up my phone and take a picture of them before sending it to Leticia.

ROYAL:

Missing these?

The dancing dots pop up on the screen as she types a message.

LETICIA:

The driver doesn't want to come get them tonight. We'll send a car to pick them up. Do you mind packing up for me?

Don't mind if I do. I walk over to my tech closet first and dig into the back before pulling out two identical token trackers. Then I grab a few pin-sized ones for good measure.

ROYAL:

I'll have them packed and ready for the driver to pick them up at the house. But I would much rather have you here with them.

Is it emotionally manipulative to say shit like that? I dislike that message the more I read it, but it's sent and seen, based on the viewed icon next to it, so there's no taking that one back.

LETICIA:

It's just not meant to be. There's already a Cavanagh and D'Medici truce in place. They don't need us to be together too.

I'm sorry, Royal.

My wolf is howling with heartbreak at that last text. But I push through it. I place the first two trackers, one in each suitcase, past the lining and tight against the frame. These will make it through airport security without a problem. She'll never be any wiser.

With the pin trackers, I'm a little bolder. One I shove into her toiletries bag, and the other into the insole of one of her penny loafers. Do I think she'll take the shoes to Italy? No. But she should for sure take the toiletries.

None of this is as good as being with her, but they're just a precaution if I lose sight of her.

I walk into my bedroom and pull up the tracking information and the video feeds of Casa D'Medici.

Then I sit down and stretch, settling into my chair. It's only three in the afternoon, but this could take a while.

Boundaries be damned. I'm keeping her from being married to that asshole. And I'll sign my name in big bold letters.

She wants us too. She didn't know we were unafraid. Our mate tries to protect us but forgets we're the thing that goes bump in the night. My wolf is staying present and focusing on what I'm doing, ever watching rather than hiding away while I work.

The long, tedious part is first. I stalk her cell phone's activity for the last year and find places she frequents that are right on the edge of D'Medici territory, places I may have accidentally wandered too far into. I get lucky with a market she goes to in the neutral zone.

She goes there every week, sometimes multiple times. It's a long way from Gold Coast, but she must love something about it.

That's where I start.

I create a whole bank account with the credit union nearby and start backdating entries. Small purchases from both of us. Deposits from my personal account to cover them. And then larger expenses. Any place within a few blocks of that market is fair game to get a fake purchase on our account. Next, I start branching out, working farther north toward up here in Barrington. Then I dip purchases from my card into D'Medici territory, dated before the truce.

Getting into the state's system to file the marriage certificate is going to be harder. Not impossible, just harder. And . . . a little risky if I get caught.

No risk, no reward.

Leticia

CHAPTER FORTY-THREE

WATCHED

I don't even look around me. I know the feeling of being watched is Royal through the cameras. I haven't felt alone or unwatched since I arrived home yesterday. But now it doesn't feel as spooky. It's oddly comforting.

The feeling follows me through the penthouse as I fetch my bags from where the guards left them earlier this morning, then back up to my bedroom. I open the suitcases on the stands and start unpacking just to pack all over again.

It's the silence that's killing me. I've tried turning on the television, but it's not enough noise, or rather, it's not the right kind of noise.

I've changed in the couple of days I spent at the Cavanaghs. I know what it's like to sleep next to a man, to be curled up in his arms, and I know what it's like to have a best friend.

There's nothing saying we can't be friends, though, is there?

I grab my phone and agonize over the word choices.

LETICIA:

Does this mean we're not best friends anymore?

ROYAL:

I would love to be best friends with you.

His response brings an immediate smile to my face and a sense of relaxation to my soul.

LETICIA:

Want to call with me while I repack?

The next response isn't immediate. I don't know why I expected him to answer at all, but given how fast the first response came in, it felt like the next one should follow soon after. *Right?*

It takes five minutes — me unzipping my suitcase and staring at the pristine folded clothes, the dirty laundry items washed, dried, and repacked — before he responds.

ROYAL:

I had a late night, so I might fall asleep on you. But we can call.

LETICIA:

I promise to hang up if you start snoring.

I'm still giggling when my phone starts to ring.

"I do not snore," Royal says when I answer.

He definitely sounds groggy, and when the option to video call comes through, I don't hesitate to accept it.

Royal looks worse for wear. Heavy dark circles shadow beneath his eyes, and he's almost more pale than he'd been before.

"Are you okay?" I shove the suitcase back on the bed so I can sit and look at him more thoroughly.

His hair is unkempt, more than usual, and he's lying in bed with a pillow pulled against his chest and another resting under his head. I ache to be back in that cozy warmth with him. I miss how safe it felt to be with him. Even while sleeping, I felt safer than ever before.

He nods. "Yeah, I just worked way too many hours at once, then I had to take my wolf for a run because he's pissed at me."

"Let me put headphones in!" I gasp, quickly muting my phone.

Oh my god, and he was worried about me letting their family secret out?

Once they're tucked in my ears, his voice in surround sound, he says, "Gorgeous, I'm monitoring your house. No one is hearing anything I don't want them to."

I miss you. It's on my lips, but I have to push it away. "What were you working on?"

"Some boring paperwork stuff. I had over a year's worth, and I figured I'd just bang it out all at once rather than dillydallying with it any longer," he says, but there's a smile on his face.

I almost call him out for it, but he's probably so tired he's delusional.

"Dillydallying, is that the technical term?" I lean my phone against a suitcase so he can see me and then start unpacking.

"No, the technical term is lollygagging, but for the bystanders I try to use plain language and not jargon." Royal jokes before letting out a big yawn. "I hope you don't mind that I washed your clothes. It felt wrong putting a couple dirty things back in a clean suitcase."

"You washed them?" I don't mean to sound so shocked. "I would have thought Betty . . ."

Royal is shaking his head. "No, Mom would have lectured me about not ruining any of your nice clothes with mine. But I wanted to make your life easier by not having to do laundry in case those were things you'd want in Italy."

"Yeah, I do. Thank you."

I pull one of the sweaters he washed up to my nose. It smells just like him. The warmth and sweet chocolate smell fill my nose and my lungs, and stress fades from my system.

But when I pull it away, reality smacks me in the face again, making me raw to the world all over.

"Flying out tomorrow," I say.

"I know, gorgeous." Royal sounds so sleepy. "I'm still watching you."

"Planning to watch me forever?"

His blinks get longer, and he nods a little. "Won't need to stalk you forever. Just until you're safe here with me."

"What does that mean? It sounds a lot more than 'just friends.' " I try to ask, but Royal is definitely asleep.

His head is bowed forward a little bit, his mouth parted just so slightly.

Royal looks so peaceful. I give it a couple more minutes before disconnecting the call.

I wanted him to be all my firsts, and I was able to give him so many of them. My first kiss, my first orgasm, my first time having sex. He gave me the choice and the opportunity to be myself. The choice of how my life happened was something I never thought was possible.

The offer to marry me, the way he so quickly jumped to what life would look like if we were together. It was reckless, but it was kind and compassionate. More than that . . . it's what I want. I want to choose Royal, and he gave me that possibility.

It took so much strength to say no, and now? It was so hard not to tell him to come get me. I want him to rescue me from all this. I want to find what other firsts I can give him.

But I know at my core that whatever deal my father has made for me to be married off isn't one that comes cheaply. To get between him and this deal would be deadly.

After Antonella called the truce, I listened outside his office door and any room he would go into to all the terrible things he'd say. How she disgraced the family, how she'd be better off dead, how he should milk the Cavanaghs for every penny they're worth, and how I'd better not be learning any of Antonella's headstrong ways. The threats against Valor and Kerrianne were unrepeatable. The words he used were ugly and hateful. I don't think the threats he made, although in anger, were empty.

If I thought there was a way I could be with Royal and not put his life in jeopardy, then maybe I'd give it more thought. But truce or not, if Royal gets between Dad and the deal he cut with Steffano, then there will be bloodshed.

I can't put Royal's life in danger like that.

But a little fantasy about it while packing can't hurt. I pull the sweater that smells like him back up to my nose. Long deep breaths, and I pretend I'm packing to go back to Barrington rather than the Italian Alps.

What is your life when you'd trade châteaus in the Alps for mansions in the suburbs?

Leticia

CHAPTER FORTY-FOUR

ITALIAN ALPS

The private jet touches down on the tarmac, and I'm green . . . again.

I rush to the jet's bathroom before the plane even comes to a stop and manage to hurl in the toilet. *I fucking hate flying. Every single time: take off, landing, turbulence — my stomach decides it's not happy.*

"Leticia?" Berto calls, and I rinse my mouth out using a bottle of water I left in here the last time.

"Coming." I straighten my shirt and smooth my hair before opening the door.

When I step out of the bathroom, Berto is waiting for me. Arms crossed over his chest, he's in a crisp, clean new suit. It fits him much better than the ones tailored in Chicago. Clearly, it was purchased during the time he's been in Italy.

"Thought you ran away when I came in and saw just your purse. Should have known you were throwing up." Berto looks me over, pity in his eyes. "Every time, really?"

"It's called motion sickness," I grumble and pick my purse up out of the chair next to where I was sitting.

"You're just in time. Engagement party today, doing a brunch mixer at a restaurant in town. Mom's already picked out flowers for your wedding, but they want to go into Milan to try on wedding dresses later this week."

There's no 'it's good to see you' or 'I've missed you,' and there never will be. But giving me the lowdown on the chaos my mother has already been stirring is, in his own way, showing he cares.

"And Dad?"

I wait for Berto to go down the stairs of the jet before me. I follow him, and then he offers me a hand for the last step.

"Dad is extremely pleased with this deal. I really like having you as a little sister. Be a good wife to Steffano and don't fuck it up," Berto mumbles, and I realize why.

Standing a few yards away by two luxury cars are Dad and Steffano. My stomach lurches, and I place my hand in front of it. *Please behave, don't vomit on his shoes.*

I've seen Steffano, and his previous wives, in passing before. He's always given me that snake-oil-salesman vibe. Sleazy and fake. But most of Dad's friends are that way. There's been no differentiation.

The information I could find on his wives revealed two very different women. One was subservient and meek. She looked like someone was going to hit her at any moment. The other was fiery and fought with him in public.

Two things Mafia men don't like. Women who show fear and women who show too much courage. I guess neither of Steffano's late wives passed for perfect, and now they're gone.

I'll do whatever I can to split the difference between the two. Like Berto said, *don't fuck it up.*

Berto leads me over for the formal introduction.

"Steffano Bianchi, I present to you my daughter, Leticia Alexandra." Dad sounds so pompous and arrogant. He takes my hand away from my stomach and offers it to Steffano.

I dread Steffano's touch. The second between Dad raising my hand and Steffano taking it moves too quickly. I can't pull my hand away in time. Steffano grips it, almost politely at first, as he raises it to his mouth and presses a kiss to my knuckles.

Our eyes meet. His are a deep dark shade of brown, nearly black, that eats at my flesh, gnawing to the bone.

If that was where it ended, I'd be fine, but then he turns my wrist over and kisses the inner part like Royal did. It's too much like those moments that I claimed for myself. The special piece of me I gave to Royal. And I can't help but pull away.

"I'm so sorry." I put my hand over my mouth before lowering it to my chest. "I feel sick after traveling."

"Perhaps this will help." Steffano reaches into his coat pocket and pulls out something small, pinched between two fingers. He then extends it to me.

The rock glistens in the sun. It's easily four carats of cushion-cut sparkle set in a single gold band. I offer my left hand out, and instead of sliding it on my finger, he tucks it into my palm.

I push it onto my ring finger myself. The band is a little small but not too uncomfortably so. But I know better than to complain. It would seem ungrateful and unobedient, or something Father would have to apologize for.

It's easiest if I play the perfect wife from the first minute we meet.

"Come, wife," Steffano orders like I'm a dog, turning and opening the door to the sports car for me. "We must arrive at the party together, look happy as newly engaged people should look."

Wife. My stomach churns and threatens to bubble over with bile.

Marry me. Royal's voice echoes in my head, and I regret being four thousand miles from home, I regret saying no, but I don't regret keeping him safe.

I lower myself into the sports car and wait as Steffano closes the door with a soft click.

My purse vibrates, and I dig out my phone.

ROYAL:

Be safe. Enjoy Italy

Be smart. Connect to the Wi-Fi when you arrive.

But as soon as I see that message, it changes.

ROYAL:

Be safe. Enjoy Italy.

I rub my eyes, sure I'm hallucinating the disappearing text message, but I managed a couple hours of sleep on my flight.

When Steffano closes the driver's door, his presence is suffocating. I tuck my phone away.

He looks over at me. "I can either make your life a living hell or like a princess in a castle. How you behave determines that. Do not embarrass me, and you'll get a taste of what it's like to be my princess. I'll give you everything you desire. Money is no issue."

Ew.

The latter sounds like just as much of a living hell as whatever the former implies. But my initial response, a single 'ew' when being threatened, should be a telltale sign that I'm no longer cut out for life as a made man's wife. I'm already too different from who I was before Royal. I don't have the fear I used to have. Fear that I really need to have.

But I bow my head subserviently and look away. "I understand, Steffano."

"Good. How is your Italian?" He starts the car.

The engine hums in a low purr, and the rumbles through the seat bring me a dirty yet delicious memory of my time with Royal.

"É buono o cattivo quanto vuoi che sia." I look over at him with a soft smile. My Italian is far from perfect, but the more I speak it, the stronger it gets.

"Don't be smart with me." He glowers. "Guests at this party will mostly speak in English. Until you get the accent perfect, perhaps you do the same. They're expecting an American wife. But I want one who is well rounded."

"Yes, Steffano."

No one's ever told me my accent is bad. I regularly get mistaken for a native Italian, but apparently, it offends him.

I'm just tired. I'm emotional. It's a big change. Let it go. I coach myself through every technique I've used when Mom and Dad get upset with me. I've spent my whole life learning to be neutral and passive. Now is the time to put those skills to the test.

Royal would have never made you feel like this, a little part of my heart yells.

"Ah, there she is, my new wife." Steffano opens his arms as he sees me approaching.

It's been three hours at this brunch party that's officially lapsed into lunch, and I was headed to the bathroom to decompress. But with a smile, I step into the open space, and he wraps his arm around me, the dark ruby liquid in his wine glass sloshing.

I smile and rest a hand on his chest, playing the doting, loving fiancée. "Here I am."

"Show them the ring, princess." Steffano gives my arm a little squeeze.

Princess. It grates on my nerves, but on command, I pull my left hand from Steffano's chest and present the mammoth rock to an older couple.

"How beautiful. You're a lucky girl." The woman looks at the ring over the top of her glasses.

"And the diamond isn't half bad either." The man laughs and gives me a rueful smile.

"Thank you." I smile politely.

"As I was saying." Steffano's hand falls off my back, and I'm given the space to step away.

I take it without a second thought, continuing on my course to the bathroom.

Inside, door closed, slumped against it, I finally draw a full breath of air. Out of habit, I dig into my purse and look at my phone.

ROYAL:

Ahhh, in a public restaurant, I don't need access to their Wi-Fi. I can see you just fine.

I hate how his hands are all over you.

Also, this is my first time doing some serious overseas stalking. I thought it'd be harder.

I snort reading the messages.

LETICIA:

Friends don't stalk friends.

ROYAL:

I'm really bad at being just friends.

"Leticia?" My mother's voice is like nails on a chalkboard. "Are you in here?"

"Just a few minutes, Mom. I'm not feeling too good, you know me and flying." I tuck my phone back in my purse, the message exchange with Royal tugging at my heartstrings.

This is my life, stolen moments in a bathroom, the most connection I've ever had to another human being, someone who isn't even human, with four thousand miles between us.

I start listing the usual lies to get me through this.

It'll get easier. Royal will lose interest in me. I'll be married and focused on being perfect for Steffano. It's not going to hurt forever.

Except that last lie I'm not sure I can make myself believe.

Tears well in my eyes, and this time I let them fall. I'll blame it on the jet lag, the motion sickness, or the joy of being a new bride.

Only I'll know I'm in mourning. Only I'll know it's the loss of love and what could be. I played with fire, and now I have to feel the cold from its absence. From his absence.

CHAPTER FORTY-FIVE

INTERNATIONAL STALKING AGENCY

She never connected to Wi-Fi.

I still have access to her phone, but Leticia never connected to the Wi-Fi at the house she's staying at. It seems to be owned by one of Steffano's subsidiaries, and I can tell he pays for all the amenities. It looks like his primary residence, so it surely must have Wi-Fi.

But Leticia never connected to it. Without the mirrored connection, I can't figure out what system he has. I can't stalk her. I can't —

My wolf is a wreck. I'm a wreck. I'm on the verge of shifting all the time.

It's been two days, and she hasn't gone anywhere in public, just private residences, and she hasn't connected to any Wi-Fi.

Why couldn't they be poor and worried about things like data and roaming and lack of coverage? my wolf snarls.

"Royal," Valor snaps.

"Yes?" I turn to face him.

"A little fuckin' help. This massive tree was your idea." He glares at me, and I draw my focus back to what I agreed to help with.

A Christmas tree, twelve feet of one, for the informal living room in Valor's house.

"What? You can't do it yourself?" I scoff and look over at him. "Consider it payback for the last time you did something without my help."

Valor stops trying to wrestle the tree, which is wrapped in plastic sheeting we'd normally use to get bodies to the cleaners. He looks over at me, drawing a huge breath. "Say what you're going to say and stop making snide remarks. Let's hear it."

"You know how incredibly fucked it was that you did that to her? Of all people? She literally saved your daughter's life. Why wouldn't you at least call me before taking her down to your lair?" I keep my voice down, knowing we could be ten seconds away from being ambushed by Kerrianne.

"Is that it?" Valor's voice is flat.

"She's perfect for you. If you'd pull your head out of your damn ass, you'd see that," I add, knowing this is the last time Valor will hear what I have to say on how he hurt Antonella.

Since we were kids, it's always been a 'one and done' conversation style for our grievances. Sure, we both manage to land barbs afterward every now and again, but we've both tried to stick to Mom's rule about having it out the first time.

"I know she's perfect." Valor pulls his hat off, and his shoulders drop a bit. He becomes less the family's inquisitor and more my older brother. "I know I messed up a good thing with her. I wasn't the only one who was blindsided in this, but I have to answer to her, her wolf, and my daughter on the subject. I see your anger, and it's valid, but I'm also living with it too."

Some of my anger fades. "Call me next time?"

"Don't be in the middle of getting kidnapped, then?" He laughs, breaking the tension between us. "Who the fuck gets kidnapped at twenty-six?"

"Easy for you to say. I was outnumbered, and they threatened Mom," I snap.

"Mmhmm. Yeah, you're getting more training." Valor smiles. It's a little more sadistic than loving. After a moment of silence, Valor extends the olive branch. "Are we good?"

I nod and move toward the tree, helping him heft it from the truck in the driveway, up the walk, and into the house.

It's comforting that by the time it's standing in the living room, I'm not the only one out of breath. Valor pants as he sits back on his heels out of the way of the branches now that it's secured into the stand. But his eyes are turned to me, they're calculating and cataloging what he sees. His mind is always working on angles and anticipating.

"It's so perfect." Kerrianne runs up behind me and jumps, climbing up my back until she's looking over my shoulder. Her little fingers, knees, and elbows dig into sensitive places, but I don't make a fuss about it.

"Big enough?" Valor looks up at us, his whole demeanor softening for his daughter.

He might have been crabby about getting it in the house in the first place, but she'll never know.

"Definitely." Kerrianne beams and points toward the top of the tree. "And that's where we're going to put the star. Not an angel."

"Star, not an angel." I nod in agreement.

Not sure where we got to be particular about tree toppers, but I know better than to question her if I want to get home and back to watching for Leticia's every movement.

Kerrianne climbs down my back and rushes to Valor, hugging him tightly. "Thank you! I gotta go back to finish decorating Captain's room."

Before we can object, not that we wanted to, Kerrianne sprints through the house back to her tortoise's room.

"Are you staying for dinner?" Antonella asks as she comes down the stairs. Her wolf is pressed up against the surface, her eyes golden and alert.

Would our mate look that striking? My wolf wonders, but I shove him and that thought aside.

"No, I've got to get back to working on some things." I can't even come up with a single project that hasn't been put on hold for the new year.

"He's busy stalking Leticia." Valor outs me, not that he has any real proof of what I'm doing. "He admitted to me while we were at the cabin that he's caught feelings for your cousin, and now she's in Italy, and he's heartbroken."

I turn to walk away from him before I start a fight between us in the living room and probably knock over the tree we just wrestled into place. "Fuck you."

"Royal, come back." Valor sighs. "I'm sorry."

Shaking my head, I keep going. "Got to go, have a computer update to attend to."

I have to go back to bed. The seven-hour time difference between Chicago and Italy means that Leticia's day starts at midnight, and I don't want to miss a second of it.

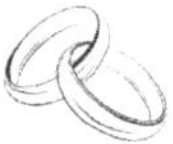

Mom is straightening the wreath on the front door when I pull into the driveway. I try to get in the garage, through the house, and down to my lair before she can stop me, but Mom's quicker than that.

She beats me to the top of my stairs. Arms crossed in front of her chest, she's who Valor gets the cutting glare from.

Mom's mad. My wolf fawns, trying to get her favor, tipping his head to the side so far that I have no choice but to follow.

I keep my eyes trained on her and cock my head aside, exposing my neck in submission.

"You cannot stalk the D'Medici girl every night for the rest of your life." Despite her gaze, Mom's words are soft. "I'm sorry she left. I'm sorry you're hurting. But you only have until Christmas to watch her every night. Then you've got to start moving on."

"I just wish she could have stayed," I admit aloud, knowing it sounds weak.

"Me too." Mom steps forward and wraps her arms around me. "I'm sorry, baby. But we all knew her place wasn't here."

The lies. My wolf whines. *Our mate's place is here with us. Forever.*

I don't argue with Mom though. I just nod. "D'Medicis and Cavanaghs already have one arranged marriage."

It doesn't feel like a lie when I say it aloud. But that's what I just did. I forced Leticia and me into a marriage. I took away a choice she made. *Am I all that different from everyone else in her life?*

I should probably have remorse. Especially standing here before Mom when she's trying to make me feel better. But that's not who I am. I made a choice, and it's going to affect all of us. I just hope it's going to protect Leticia like I think it will.

Mom lets me go with one last squeeze before shuffling aside, opening space for me to go downstairs. "Come up for dinner?"

"I'll set an alarm." I promise with a nod.

I'm not hungry, haven't been in days. But I'll make an attempt.

Leticia

CHAPTER FORTY-SIX

LONG DISTANCE BFF

ROYAL:

Good morning, gorgeous. Dress shopping today?

I'm smiling before my feet hit the ground. He's clearly going through the other text messages on my phone and still stalking me like a hawk that way.

I asked for access to the Wi-Fi but was told I shouldn't need it. 'Money isn't an issue, use all the data you'd like' is some sort of arrogance I'd never expect from Dad. He's not usually overly frugal, but they've never had any qualms about me using Wi-Fi before.

Not that there are any cameras I've been able to find for Royal to stalk me on.

I do miss the way it felt to be watched — once I knew it was him. How *loved* it made me feel. My body aches remembering the way he used that word for the first time. How he touched me like I was precious.

LETICIA:

Good night. I am sure it'll be a test of my patience.

Did you see the hideous ones that Mom said are her favorites?

I send the messages and wait for him to see them. But counting the hours back to Chicago time . . . It's well after midnight, so he should be sleeping.

But when I get out of the shower and check my phone, my messages have changed again.

LETICIA:

Good night. I'm sure it'll be a test of my patience.

ROYAL:

Send me pictures of your favorites.

Where do the messages keep going?

A knock sounds on my bedroom door. "Leticia?"

It's Steffano's voice.

I pull the bathrobe tight around me. "I'm getting dressed. I'll be right out."

"Don't be so shy, princess. Open the door." Steffano's words are sweet, but it's undoubtedly an order.

I take my hair out of the towel hat before going to open the door.

"There's my beautiful wife." Steffano smiles his greasy smile and steps forward, pushing me backward into the room. He closes the door behind him.

My suspicion grows to an all-new height, and I draw shallow breaths.

"I'm going to be late." I manage to keep my voice steady.

"They'll wait." Steffano steps toward me and brushes wet hair from my face. "I just wanted a look at you before you go."

Inspecting the goods. I grit my teeth but don't move.

"Come now, don't be shy." Steffano tugs at the robe. "I know your father promises you're a virgin, but you don't have to be afraid of me." He cups his crotch with his other hand. "Or this."

I swallow hard. Breathing isn't easy. Steffano tugs at the collar of the robe, and I hold it tight against my body.

"Don't be that way, princess. I told you we could play this two ways." Steffano warns me, his voice dropping low.

Conceding, I let him drag the robe aside, but I refuse to look at him. I don't want to watch him treat me like a piece of meat.

He hums in approval as he reveals the naked skin of my collarbone. It turns into a disgusting groan as he slowly pulls the robe back, exposing my breast and then lower. "Make sure to find a dress that shows off your figure. I love my wife shaped like a woman."

I'm not sure if that's a compliment, but I nod, barely breathing.

Steffano takes a hand and caresses along my abdomen, fingers dipping low as if to slide between my legs.

"We should wait for our wedding night." My body trembles under the tension of waiting to see what he'll do. If he'll touch me. I try to clench my muscles to stop it.

Steffano lets out a low, near growl as he pulls away. "Don't be late."

I'm frozen in place until he walks back to the door, opening it and then closing it behind him. I release a massive exhale, the air rushing out of me until I'm doubled over.

It could have been worse. I remind myself.

Steffano's touch wasn't unkind or overly lustful. But it's the first of many, and it rattles me. Maybe it was wrong to learn my body and let Royal show me what good can be.

My phone is sitting on the vanity where I left it. After I toss the robe over the towel bar, I pick it back up and type a message off to Royal.

LETICIA:

Thank you for always going at my pace.

I set it back on the counter and go back to getting ready. It still hasn't vibrated when I'm done curling my hair or when I've pulled on a sweater dress.

The longer it's silent, the more alone I feel, but maybe I should focus on distancing myself from him. Maybe I need to start a Royal detox.

The ache in my heart hits harder.

"Leticia." Mom practically cries as I step out from the fitting room into the viewing area.

It's the third dress. The first two she scoffed at and sent me back. They were both big, fluffy ballgowns. Apparently, the bridal stylist thought I would be fitting for a princess-style wedding.

This one is less fluffy, more A-line, and satin. The square neckline is not me at all.

"It sounds like we're getting closer." The stylist smiles widely. "Let's add a veil."

I stand while they primp, my aunts, Mom's sisters, Bianca and Marta, looking it over.

"It just doesn't seem like the right dress. Leticia needs something a little less subtle." Bianca gives me a coy smile. "She always wears something more modest. It's her wedding. She should get a chance to shine."

"Well." Mom considers her older sister's point. "We could do something a bit more revealing."

"Steffano did say he'd like to see my figure." It's hard not to bring back that conversation. The way he looked at me? The hunger for something that is his only in name.

"That settles it, then!" Bianca looks to the stylist, and they quickly talk in Italian about dresses and styles before darting farther into the store to find just the one.

The next dress is so tight I can barely breathe, but it's definitely fitted. I'm constricted from chest to hips in white fabric, and I have to take slow, careful steps out to the pedestal.

"Now, this would be a bit looser when it's in your size." The stylist notes how tight it is. "Unless you're looking for such an intense look."

I shake my head quickly. It's a gorgeous gown. The aunts and my mother are drawn to it like moths to a flame. A veil, a bouquet, and shoes are brought out, and my hair is pulled up out of my face.

"Is this the one?" The bridal stylist looks to me for an answer.

"It is." I agree with the consensus of the room.

It's not me. The blonde woman in the mirror isn't me. I know it's my body, my face, and my hair, but none of how I look right now is anything like me. She's getting married to Steffano, and I'm just a captive in her body.

I'm finally out of the gown, into my own clothes, but I can't shake the feeling of being trapped in a rented body.

I open my phone out of habit and find a new message from Royal.

ROYAL:

They're all beautiful, but the one you bought doesn't look like you.

I didn't even realize that there were cameras in the shop. I try to discreetly look around, but I don't notice any off the bat. *He is really good at this stalking thing.*

ROYAL:

You're flawless.

You don't need a dress to choke you in order to show off your beauty.

Tears well up in my eyes, and it's like they've come out of nowhere. I wipe them away quickly. It's too much.

I can't text him back because it hurts too much to even think about it. I tuck my phone back into my purse and go with my aunts and mother out into the city.

Down the block, cars are waiting for us.

Steffano stands near one, and he smiles at me. It's almost genuine but still too calculating to be truly caring. He holds out his hand. "May I see your phone, please?"

Obediently, I hand it over, and he begins to look through it. I wait, expecting some sort of reaction from him, but the longer I wait, the less it seems like I'll be getting one. Minutes tick by as he looks through things on my phone.

"Come, princess. Let's get you back to the castle." Steffano opens the door and offers me his hand so I can lower myself into the car. He tucks my phone into his pocket.

I set my purse on my lap and buckle my seat belt.

Steffano walks around the front of the car before climbing into the driver's seat. "Tell me, wife. What did you learn from spending time with Royal Cavanagh?" he asks, speeding through the city, out toward his villa.

"Not much, they have a lot of weapons in the home. Their security is state of the art, and Royal says he can watch every part of their territory with just a few clicks of the button." I recap the text messages I'd sent Dad, gripping the leather seat, holding myself in place as he sharply cuts around hairpin curves.

"Yes, I'm sure he can. His reputation precedes him. But I'm more wondering what he teaches you?" Steffano growls.

"I don't understand." I shake my head, watching between him and the road, fearing for our lives and what happens when a sports car crashes.

But Steffano is a skilled driver, and before he explains further, he pulls us up in front of the house.

My stomach is queasy from the erratic driving. "I'm going to be sick."

One of Steffano's servants — goons, hired help — opens my door. I'm not sure how, but I barely make it over to the edge of the driveway, lined with brown winter plants, and lose a little bit of my undigested breakfast.

"Afraid you got caught? Now you're sick with remorse." Steffano's voice is so growly behind me that I wonder if I'll see golden eyes like I did in Royal's.

I don't. Steffano's are the dark color they've always been, his glare focused on me.

"No." I clear my throat, looking in my purse for a tissue. "I'm easily motion sick. Anyone can tell you that I get sick in sports cars, on planes, and especially on winding roads and in turbulence."

I don't realize how far out of line my words are until I stop digging in my purse to look up at Steffano.

His brow is furrowed, nostrils flared, head tilted down to glare at me, and arms crossed in front of his chest.

I forgot my place, and he's surely going to put me in it. I wait for him to be explosive like Dad. I wait for him to burst into yelling or grip my arm and yank me toward the house. But he doesn't.

Instead, Steffano storms toward the house, shouting behind him, "Come, princess."

The guards stare at me like I've grown a second head.

I follow Steffano into the house, straight to a central seating area where Dad and Berto are already conversing quietly. Drinks in hand like they're none the wiser of something bad happening.

"Explain to me why you thought selling me your daughter as a virgin when she's clearly whored herself out to the Cavanagh tech nerd was a good idea." Steffano looks at Dad specifically as he grabs my shoulder and shoves me down onto a chair near him.

Berto catches my attention, eyebrow cocked. He and Antonella look a lot alike when they're pressing for information.

I shake my head, denying it. *There's no way whatever he found in my phone can prove what Royal and I did or didn't do. Right?*

"That's absurd." Dad is quick to defend, but he doesn't rise from his chair. "And furthermore, I told you she was staying with our new alliance so she could dig up information. It was hardly useful, but it proves that she does try and can observe the world around her."

"Yes, and maybe if she'd learned some helpful information, then I'd believe that." Steffano pulls my phone out of his pocket and starts reading messages between Royal and me aloud from the very beginning. All the while pacing across the space.

I never thought to delete the messages. We were just friends. They don't even sound like anything is going on between us.

"So, Leticia, what is the Cavanagh family secret?"

"They're runners. The secret is that for holidays and other

special occasions, they all go for runs in the woods together." I use the first thing I can think of that's true.

"So the sex cult, dancing naked under the moon, calling the daughter pup like she's some sort of dog?" Steffano pushes as he steps closer to me.

"A bad joke and a family inside joke that I misunderstood. There's nothing weird about the Cavanaghs. They're just a regular family. It's no different than when Berto went through that phase when we all called him Robbie, and he thought he'd be something other than a made man."

I should feel bad digging up something from the banks of my memory and using it like that to embarrass Berto to prove a point. But no way am I telling anyone what I know about the Cavanaghs.

"She's untrained." Berto defends me, standing from his chair and stepping toward me. "It's hardly like she'd know what sort of secret to sniff out. Case in point, it's not like we call anything important a 'family secret.' That would be absurd."

"Mmm, so then about this message?" Steffano starts. "Royal says to Leticia: I'll have them — he's referring to her suitcases — packed and ready for the driver to pick them up at the house. But I would much rather have you here with them."

Dad draws a sharp breath.

Berto narrows his eyes at me, and I wince.

"And our darling Leticia answers: It's just not meant to be. There's already a Cavanagh and D'Medici truce in place. They don't need us to be together too. I'm sorry, Royal." Steffano finishes. He's engaging Berto more so than my father in this conversation, but they both turn to me for answers.

"We're friends, and we were both sad that our Christmas plans had been changed. We're sad not to be able to spend time together, and it's not like anyone really needs us to be friends, so I was sorry that we needed to be less friendly." I'm digging myself a hole, and I know it. I try to stop and shut it down. "We're just friends."

"So does your friend know what you look like naked?" Steffano bends at the waist to put his face nearly level with mine. He grips my jaw as he cuts into me with his eyes. It's bruising and painful against the bone.

"Of course not." I throw my head back, pulling away from him, in shock that he'd even ask that sort of question.

"Why would he know what she looks like naked?" Dad rises out of his seat in what nearly feels like my defense.

"Well, the nerd can see every part of their territory, can he not?" Steffano makes such a logical leap that my jaw drops.

I look up at Berto, raise a hand to my chest, and turn back to Steffano. "I hardly think he was looking at me in the bathroom while I was changing or bathing. That's completely crossing the boundaries of friendship."

"I don't think you're just friends." Steffano's voice is low. He stalks away again and throws the accusation over his shoulder. "I think you whored yourself out to the Cavanagh tech nerd. You're not as pure as your father wants me to believe, and now you're worth less than the agreement we signed on."

"I didn't." I look at Dad, shaking my head, begging him to believe my lie.

The word whore should sting, but with how Royal made me feel, there's no way I can let a man who buys women influence how I feel about my body.

Maybe I'm not lying well enough because I can't be made to feel ashamed of what I did.

But Berto looks me over with a frown and shrugs, then turns back to Steffano. "There's no way to know for sure if she is or isn't a virgin without consequence. But she's still an American citizen by birth. Which is what you need in a wife."

"And? There are Americans everywhere." Steffano scoffs.

"But they're not D'Medici." Berto seems to be the one running the deal. "You can find a different bride who can get you a legal American passport, but will they be able to fence you the kind of merchandise we will? Or are you going to stop with an expansion operation?"

I don't know if I'm appalled or pleased by how well Berto is keeping me in this arranged marriage and the deal on the table. I've never seen him at the helm, and part of me thinks it's cool, but all I want is an out.

"I can't even stand to look at her knowing another man has

touched her, and I can't get rid of her because of the stupid agreement," Steffano spits and turns back to face me.

The look in his eye sends a chill down my spine, and I sit straighter.

"Allegedly." Berto corrects. "And that's fine, we'll send her back to Chicago. You can come back to Chicago after Christmas and keep the deal on as planned. You'll live in River North and officially start life as husband and wife as soon as the marriage documents are accepted by the court. You don't want her here, then fine. But you need her, and you need this deal with us."

"Send her back to Chicago where Cavanagh is? That seems like a good idea to you?" Steffano looks down his nose at me. "Just gives her more time to whore herself out."

"We can make it so she doesn't leave the apartment for any reason. There will be no way for Cavanagh to get to her. You can keep her phone so she cannot contact him." Dad so helpfully interjects.

Steffano drops my phone in front of me. I could reach out and grab it, but instead I let it fall to the floor, not knowing if the case protects it or not.

"She can have her phone, but I'll be reading the messages, Leticia. I'll be reading the messages, and you'd better be able to explain everything you say to him. If you're 'just friends,' then there shouldn't be any reason for me to punish you when I come to Chicago next month."

"I understand." I nod and don't argue.

"Send her back to Chicago," Steffano huffs and storms out.

"I told you not to disgrace us." Dad is seething, his face red. He steps over to me, pulls his arm back, and smacks my face, the slap seeming to echo in the small room as the pain shoots through me.

"Nothing happened between Royal and me." I raise my hand to my cheek.

With the way his temper rages, I'm not even shocked that he hit me. I expect worse. But I stay strong in my conviction. Berto said they can't prove anything happened between us.

"Get out of my sight. You are a disgrace to the family." Dad waves me off.

Berto grabs my phone off the floor and hands it to me before pulling me to my feet and wrapping his arm around me, practically dragging me through the house and out to the cars.

He pushes me into the passenger seat of one and slams the door behind me.

"You didn't even make it a whole week," Berto mutters once he's sitting in the driver's seat of the sports car. "I would have thought you'd at least be good enough at being a wife to make it a week."

"In my defense, he hasn't had any of my cooking." I try to joke with my brother but anticipate it going over poorly. Berto was fun once, but I don't know if he can be anymore.

"No, I suppose not." Berto sighs. The car engine rumbles as he pushes the button. "You're welcome for saving you from both Dad and Steffano."

I nod and stay silent. A bruising grip to the chin and a smack to the face are hardly the worst either of them has done. I'll be grateful for Berto even though my mind is already rushing someplace else.

I want to know if I can check my phone, if I can still contact Royal. But I know better. I just failed at the one job I've been trained my whole life to do: be a perfect, obedient wife. And now I've got to prove to them that I'm worth keeping around. I'll need to work on getting back to the girl I was before Royal. Even if it kills the woman I became.

CHAPTER FORTY-SEVEN

SCARIER THAN THAT

Leticia stopped answering my messages two days ago. One day ago, I got a notification that there was movement in Casa D'Medici, and Leticia moved back into her parents' penthouse. It was a relief from the sickening dread and obsessive attempts at finding a way into Steffano's network. His security is good, I'll give him that, but I had been close when she'd arrived home.

She has her cell phone. I've seen her carry it around. I've watched as I've messaged her, and she seemingly reacts to it.

But she never messages me back. I've tried calling too. Knowing that she's alone in their penthouse, she should have no reason not to answer.

Something happened to Leticia in Italy, but I can't figure out what.

"Royal." A soft knock comes from the top of the stairs. "It's time for dinner and presents." Antonella beckons me to come up from my lair.

Presents. I wrapped mine while waiting for messages back from Leticia. I take all but the one I bought for Leticia upstairs with me, wishing for one little message back.

I send off one final message for the night.

ROYAL:

Merry Christmas, Leticia.

It's read almost instantly, and I spare another glance up at the monitor. Leticia is staring at her phone, fingers poised like she's going to respond. Instead, she tosses her phone on her bed before flopping back and looking up at the ceiling.

Why won't our mate be ours? my wolf howls, angry and heartbroken.

I don't have answers.

"Jesus fucking Christ, Royal." Valor pulls off his earmuffs and smacks me up the backside of my head.

I lower the rifle, looking at him rather than downrange. "You said you wanted to scare the guy. I don't think I can get any scarier than that."

"I was thinking a little more finesse." Valor sighs, tossing his earmuffs aside. "Come on."

I set the rifle on the tailgate and walk with Valor downrange, the frozen ground crunching underneath our boots.

We're barely three steps away from the truck, and Valor starts. "What are you going to do to get Leticia back?"

"What do you mean?" I pretend not to know what he's talking about.

"Well, she's already married in Italy. So killing the husband would be my first move." Valor slows down his steps, falling in line with where I'm dragging my feet.

"Are you being serious? The last time we talked about her, you were pretty much in the 'let her go' category." I stop and shove his shoulder with my fist.

Valor winces, a little sore from Antonella's wolf still taking chunks out of him when she gets a chance, which is why he needed the younger brother, with the rifle, on the shooting range for this game.

"I admit that from time to time, I can make snap judgments and need a moment to reconsider." Valor blows out a breath, the exhale going up in a cloud of condensation in the morning light. "In your text, what did you mean when you said: she's the one?"

"You know what I meant." I can't even get the words out of my mouth.

Coming to a full stop, Valor turns on the ball of his feet and looks at me. "For argument's sake, pretend I don't."

Say it with your full chest. My wolf encourages me. He thinks of all the glimpses of Leticia we've been storing away in our memory bank where she looked especially pretty.

I shore up and meet Valor eye to eye. "Leticia D'Medici is my fated mate."

No ifs, no ands, no buts about it. My wolf finishes.

"Then we'll do what we need to do to get her back, but it's not going to happen overnight." Valor shakes his head and scratches a spot underneath his beanie. "Give me some time to figure it out. Obviously, killing the husband is the first step, but how to get a profitable deal between the D'Medicis and us that doesn't violate the truce is a whole other problem."

I should probably open my mouth and say I already found a way. But I don't want to be scolded right now. I'm already hurting, and if Valor finds out what I did, he's likely to tell me to undo it. I want my safety net in place.

Valor keeps thinking, and we walk the near mile to the target zone.

The man is struggling where he's tied up against the backstop. Gagged, he smells like piss and fear, and I think some feces might be mixed in there as well. I wrinkle my nose as Valor has to get much closer.

"Paulie." Valor pulls the gag off the guy, and that's when he looks vaguely familiar.

Is that the guy who designed Valor's remodel of the mansion? my wolf asks, cocking his head.

"Why is it that when I went into your office to get the plans for my house, my entire home was being circulated on your televisions?"

"It's part of the agreement. We can show off remodels that we've —"

Valor tuts. "Now I know for a fact that's not the case with our agreement. I specifically had the agreement modified that you wouldn't show any of the plans or pictures from our house, including the three-dimensional sketches and computer-generated rendering."

"I-I-I can explain," Paulie stammers.

"There's no need." Valor clearly isn't feeling the bloodlust today because that sort of behavior, putting his kid at risk, isn't normally well tolerated. "When we leave, Royal is going to be accessing your company's mainframe."

Oh joy, more work for me. I bite my tongue.

"He's going to personally scrub every inch of your computers and pull out every single project you've done for Clark Enterprises and our subsidiaries." Valor smiles, and it's scary. "Then, because I'm feeling generous, he's going to give you a software security update. It'll let us monitor who you work with, when you start and end projects, and who is paying for everything."

"No." Paulie struggles harder. "You can't. I have confidentiality —"

"I wasn't asking." Valor reaches up and taps the backstop, where the first bullet I sent downrange hit just an inch from Paulie's ear. "You've been bragging about working with Clark Enterprises for a long time, and now I'm just making it official. By the time Royal is done . . ." Valor kicks Paulie's leg over, revealing the second shot that I'd placed between Paulie's legs. It nicked his pants but missed anything important. "You're going to be a Clark Enterprises subsidiary, and well, I think the metaphor about where this shot landed speaks for itself."

We own his family jewels. My wolf laughs. *Nice.*

I'm smiling at my wolf's need to explain the nuance, which draws Paulie's attention. "What can I say, I love a good dick joke?"

The normalcy of working again will be nice though.

"I mean, a hostile takeover isn't really complete without one, is it?" Valor huffs a laugh.

"Takeover, I mean, silent partners?" Paulie starts trying to make a deal. "Surely we can come to an agreement."

"The agreement is that I've already talked to your chief architects and all the high-level staff. I picked up the plans for my new build already." Valor pulls out his phone and holds up what must be a picture to Paulie. "See, here's me and the chairman of the board." Valor turns it back to himself before showing him another one. "Me and your chief architect."

"So, what you're saying is that Paulie here is really just a figurehead CEO at this point." I deduce aloud to further the conversation for Valor.

"Exactly. Truthfully, not necessary and redundant. The chief architect could do his job." Valor stops talking to Paulie and turns to me. "Is it worth keeping him alive?"

I look at Paulie, debating Valor's words. I don't particularly enjoy killing people, and Paulie doesn't seem dangerous. "I mean, I guess. Just in case there's something I can't figure out in the system, it might be beneficial to have him alive."

"When was the last time you couldn't figure something out?" Valor casually leans against the backstop.

"I mean, never say never . . . but I can't foresee him being really all that useful."

I hate when Valor makes me determine whether someone lives or dies, but usually, if we get this far, he's already decided. He just wants someone to approve his choice.

"What, no. I've a wife and kids. You can't leave them without a father. I'll do whatever you ask. I'll step down." Paulie tries to negotiate.

"Now that you mention it." Valor pushes off the backstop and stands next to me, looking at Paulie. "There is a job Paulie here could do."

"Oh?" I look at my older brother, who is full of surprises today.

"We need a messenger. That acquisition we had out in Indianapolis needs a new figurehead CEO." Valor crosses his arms in front of his chest. "Of course, there's a salary reduction, and it wouldn't come with any of the benefits he's got now. But if he's truly begging for his life, then he won't mind."

"I'll do it. Please. I'll gladly do it. Help you get the company making more money. It'll be good." Paulie nods the little he can with how his head is fastened to the backstop.

"Good, excellent, two birds, one stone." Valor nudges my arm, and we turn to leave. Valor calls back over his shoulder, "I'll send someone for you. They'll have more information about your role. Remember, Paulie, I own you. Not the other way around."

We're well out of human earshot when Valor changes the subject. "I think the best bet is to wait for Steffano to come Stateside. It'll be easier to make it look like an accident and untraceable. If we send a hit in Italy, too many things could go wrong. Like someone claiming the D'Medicis were the ones who ordered a hit. I don't want anyone caught in the crossfire."

"Your plan makes sense." I nod and rub my chin.

I should really tell him what I've done. I bite my lips together.

The alpha will figure it out sooner or later. Let him think he's in charge. My wolf yawns and settles in. *He knows she's ours. He'll know the lengths we'll go to keep her. It's just a matter of time.*

ONE MONTH LATER

Leticia

CHAPTER FORTY-EIGHT

THE PAPERWORK

I longingly stare at the message on my phone again, taking a break from studying. Steffano demanded I finish school, which felt odd since he wants nothing to do with me, but I don't argue with a chance to get out of the house for a little bit each day.

ROYAL:

Good morning, gorgeous.

It's roughly the same message every day. Sometimes he adds some flavor to it, showing he's still watching me. Comments appreciating my new outfits, voicing frustration with the way Mom treats me, or angry jabs at my father for how he's become increasingly more physical with me.

Normally, I read it a few times and then delete it. But today I can't bring myself to do it. I want to keep these moments. Worse, I want to reply. But the days are coming when Steffano will be here. He'll read my phone, and I don't want to cause anymore pain for myself.

"Leticia!" Dad bellows from the first floor.

My bedroom door, left ajar for this exact reason, creeks open as if to beckon me further.

Picking my phone up and tucking it into my skirt pocket, I hurry out into the hallway and down the stairs to where he'll inevitably be tapping his foot about something. My stomach pits. Steffano should be arriving sometime in the next week. Is he early?

Dad is standing at the bottom of the stairwell, his face beet red and a handful of crumpled papers in his hand. "What is this?"

He shakes the papers at me before practically shoving them into my chest.

I grab them before they fall to the floor and pull them away from my body to look. "I don't know, what is it?"

CERTIFICATE OF VITAL RECORDS
COUNTY OF COOK
STATE OF ILLINOIS
OFFICE OF THE COUNTY CLERK

My stomach drops. My soul is sucked out of my entire body. *He didn't.*

Certificate of Marriage
Groom: Cavanagh Royal Alexander
Age: 25
And
Bride: D'Medici Leticia Alexandra
Age: 23

Date of Marriage: August 23, 2024

He did. He did. He did. I look at my father and shake my head. *Deny.*

Deny. Deny. My heart thunders in my chest, causing my pulse to thrum in my ears. "I don't know what this is."

"You lived in my house. You married that lowlife. You lied to me about being my little girl. For what? Months? A year?" Dad's face has started to turn purple, and a vein is popping out on his forehead. "Francesca!"

Mom appears, as she does, from lurking somewhere nearby, her slender body curling in on itself as she approaches. "Yes, dear?"

"How did my daughter manage to get married without us knowing?" Dad sputters.

"She did *what*?" Mom rushes forward and takes the marriage certificate from me. "No, no, no. This can't be right."

"It is," Dad snaps. "I went to the county clerk to file a marriage certificate, and our daughter has been married to that Cavanagh scum since before the truce was finalized."

"I didn't marry him. I only met Royal when I went to visit the Cavanaghs. I'd never seen him before." I shake my head, spinning a small lie. I don't know why I'm protecting the memory of Royal showing up at school.

"Get your coat." Dad lunges forward, grabbing my arm. He squeezes as hard as he can, and it aches, the last set of bruises not fully healed.

He yanks, wrenching my arm behind my back before he hurls me toward the entryway. My arm screams in pain, the flesh feeling like it's shredded and even the bones feeling torn apart.

I collide with a wall, my face making impact with the stone. *Ow.* I try not to cry. But I'm seeing spots and my head hurts.

Using my non-injured arm, I shove away from the wall.

Dad snaps his fingers. "We're going to go see your husband right fucking now. Since he seems to think that you're worth having, then he can pay the bride price I got for you ten times over."

I don't argue but walk, or maybe it's more like stumble, as fast as I can to the coat closet. I fish out my spring jacket and pull my phone from my pocket. My arm protests with every movement.

Pressing the emergency button on the side of my phone pulls up the option to send a text message to my emergency contact. I hit the button, and it pulls up my chat with Antonella.

LETICIA:

> Royal and I are apparently married. We're on our way to Cavanagh territory. I'm scared. Dad is really, really mad. I don't know what to do. I told Royal not to do this. Now he's messed up Dad's plan and deal. I don't know what to expect.

Antonella is in school today, and I don't expect a reply.

"Who the fuck are you texting?" Dad rips the phone out of my hand. "Let me guess. Your secret husband?"

Dad throws my phone down the hallway. It clatters, bounces, skids, and finally comes to a stop underneath the hallway table.

I don't defend myself. I keep my head down and draw my shoulders together. Keeping quiet, I make myself small while cradling my arm to my chest. He'll still be angry, but at least I won't give him any more reason to escalate.

Hopefully, she gets that text.

Hopefully, Royal isn't home.

CHAPTER FORTY-NINE

BUSTED

"Royal." Dad's voice drops off with a frustrated edge.

But I already know what it's about. I'd been double-checking my work.

I hadn't been watching the screens full-time, nonstop, but I had them up in the background. I heard muffled shouting through my speakers and pulled up the feed in time to see Leticia being forced into the penthouse elevator. The ride to the garage was silent, but before that, in the foyer, when Gregorio shouted, 'We're going to see your husband right fucking now,' I knew it was me and not Steffano he was talking about.

Tears were in her eyes, one arm clasped to her chest, and her hair was much messier than her normal gently tousled look.

I tried to text Leticia, but her phone was completely offline. That was an hour and two minutes ago. With traffic, it's not surprising it took a little longer to get here.

I climb the stairs two at a time and confront my parents. Dad is pinching the bridge of his nose, pacing, and Mom is looking out the window. She's dressed up like they were planning on going somewhere this afternoon.

"Why is Don D'Medici coming up the driveway? Why did he yell at me that you're in a secret marriage with his daughter? Why is he making demands for fifteen million dollars?"

"Well, that number is an insult to Leticia." I scoff and think about how it barely makes a dent in one of the many offshore accounts I hold.

"Royal." Mom sighs and looks at me with that mom look, the 'You disappointed me, but I love you anyway' one.

"They were marrying her off to someone terrible. I figured the roadblock would be in our best interest. You've been talking to Valor about what wars we're choosing to back now that we have damn near close to a monopoly on weapons building and shipping." I start with my pre-prepared and well-practiced defense.

"Does she even know you did this? Are you actually in a relationship?" Dad lets go of his nose and purses his lips, likely holding back a litany of other questions.

"She probably knows by now. We're friends. And on paper, we've had an ironclad secret marriage." I shove my hands in my pockets. "It's enough that even if they wanted to claim that she and Steffano are in a relationship to get a naturalized marriage, they'd be hard pressed to make that case for at least three years."

"Jesus Christ, son." Dad goes back to trying to wear a hole in the floor. "And I thought Valor was reckless."

"It's fifteen million. I've got that sitting —"

"Not the point, Royal." Mom draws a steady, calming breath. "Even though the D'Medicis are being a little cold with us, we're still working to build a relationship with them for business purposes outlined in the truce. The D'Medicis may not know the arbiters are vampires, but we should take the threat of extermination quite seriously."

"If anything, he's more bound to us now." I shrug nonchalantly, but inside, hot lava is stewing around in my gut. It heats my body from the inside out. *They don't even care that she wouldn't be safe with Steffano.*

It's because you haven't told her she's our mate. My wolf throws that out there, and it cools my anger.

The SUV pulls up into the driveway, and I spit it out. "It's because she's my mate."

"You're sure?" Mom looks at me, eyes wide. "I'll be pissed as hell if she isn't."

"We don't believe in divorce." I use logic as an attempt to drive home my point. "I wouldn't have married her if I wasn't sure."

"God damn it." Dad scrubs his hand down his face before pushing back his gray hair off his forehead. "Alright, then we'll do what it takes."

What it takes resonates loudly with my soul.

My wolf finds ease in Dad's agreement with what we want, what we need. *Our mate is coming home.*

Dad opens the front door, and Gregorio D'Medici, the man himself, storms into our home. Leticia, cowed, follows. She looks all wrong, subservient like this. Where is the brave woman who has been coming out of her shell?

She shouldn't be cowering and afraid. Not here, not when I'm so close to her. Not where I can protect her.

Two D'Medici henchmen push their way through the door before Dad can close it.

"What, you're not coming to collect your wife? The secret is out." Gregorio practically sounds wolf with the rumble in his voice and sharp click of his teeth as he snaps the words out. He reaches behind Leticia and shoves her toward me.

I catch her, pulling her to my chest, and she whimpers.

I want to whisper to her, comfort her, and tell her we're keeping her safe, but I don't dare speak. Clutching her to my chest has to be enough reassurance.

Step one, acquire mate. My wolf starts formulating a plan and checking off the quickly growing to-do list. *Step two, secure mate.*

"Because you've been married since August and no one knew. You think we wouldn't find out?" Gregorio screams.

I don't take his bait. He wants me to backpedal, and I won't. He doesn't scare me. He's a man and I'm a wolf.

We could just kill him. My wolf licks his chops.

But that's not right. That's not how we get rid of Gregorio. *Too easy to plant evidence. We can make him go to prison.* It's the first time I've had to think about what to do about Gregorio in all this, aside from copious amounts of money to pay him off. *Not a bad plan.*

"That's enough," Mom snaps with a very demure huff. She's the worst at keeping her wolf in check when angry, but that sounded more suburban housewife than I've ever heard her.

I slowly release Leticia. She stands up a little more firmly and steps beside me. But she doesn't look at me, her eyes trained on the floor. She doesn't give me any sign that she's happy to be saved.

Oh, our mate is mad. My wolf crouches inside me, wanting me to appease her but not knowing how. We know a lot about her, but nothing that can solve this.

"You have no idea how much this lover's tryst has cost me. The fact that he defiled my daughter, marrying her before the truce. It should be grounds for a call to the arbiters." Gregorio gestures between her and me.

Leticia finally looks at me out of the corner of her eye. I haven't learned every single one of her looks and the silent messages she tries to give, but I'm confident that look is trying to tell me there's no way in hell her dad knows about what we did in my bedroom before Christmas.

"I didn't defile your daughter," I say firmly. *Defiling would mean I believe having sex makes her less than. And thus not a lie.*

Her dad huffs. "Steffano suspects she's not a virgin. He'll never want her now. He'll go back on my deal."

"So, she's technically not your property?" Dad homes in on that fact, already calculating.

Not property, my wolf snaps, but I suppress him. Now's not the time to split hairs over words like that.

"We're in charge of her care until Steffano arrives." Her father is beet red in the face and tries to square up to Dad.

Dad looks to Leticia. I try to see what he sees, but my eyes get caught on the bruises forming on her arm. Then the red mark on her face. Rage seers through me, and I want to pull her to me and look her over more thoroughly. I want to catalog her injuries and then cut the body parts off Gregorio that he hurt on Leticia so he might have an inkling of the pain I'm in.

"It seems she's already banged and bruised up quite a bit. I can't in good faith say you're caring for her well." Dad leverages. "I think it's in our best interest that she remains here and we deal with Steffano directly."

"Don't be stupid." Gregorio postures.

The front door opens, and Gregorio's goons raise their weapons.

Valor joins our standoff, eyebrow cocked in surprise, but he doesn't move for his weapon.

"Do you plan on letting Berto come in, or is he supposed to stand out in the cold and keep guard?" Valor huffs with a laugh, clearly unaware of what he's walking into. "It's below zero. Even I'm cold out there."

No one says anything, and Valor looks back over his shoulder. "Berto, quit being a dumbass and get in here."

A few seconds later, Berto trips coming in the door behind Valor.

"As I was saying." Dad takes control of the conversation. "Leticia is married to my son. She's part of a deal you struck with Steffano, and he left her in your care. That care is arguably not sufficient. She'll remain here with us until Steffano can be reached for a better negotiation."

"So your son can defile her more? I think not." Gregorio turns to Berto. "Get your sister in the car."

Berto stands frozen in place.

Surely he didn't actually freeze to death. My wolf scents the air.

It takes a good thirty seconds before Berto shakes his head. "This is between the Cavanaghs and Steffano. You shouldn't have brought her here to start with, but they have more claim on her than we do. If we called the arbiters, what would they tell us?"

"To quit squabbling since we're in a truce and deal with it like adults," Valor deadpans, walking over to the coatrack to hang his coat. "I for one don't want to give them any opportunity to say either side is not withstanding the truce."

"They were married before the truce." Gregorio brings up that detail again.

Such a smart idea. My wolf praises me for it.

"So you really had no right to marry Leticia off to begin with, then." Berto glares at his father. "I told you it was a bad idea to marry her to Steffano."

Whose side is he on? I raise my eyebrows at Valor, who shrugs.

Gregorio makes a big deal out of reaching into his pocket and pulling out his phone. It's afternoon, making it nearly nine o'clock in Italy, but it doesn't seem to bother Gregorio as he announces, "I'll just call Steffano now."

"Great idea." Mom sighs. She gently touches Leticia's shoulder as she turns. "I'm going to make coffee. Join me?"

CHAPTER FIFTY

WHAT IS REAL?

I'm shaking. Maybe it's just my hands, but it feels like my whole body. I'm barely holding it together. My arm hurts, the world feels like it's ending, and I can't seem to draw a deep breath. But showing weakness isn't an option. Not in front of Dad.

Betty takes me into the kitchen and starts pulling coffee mugs from the cupboard before she stops, sighs, and turns to face me.

She pulls me into her arms, gently wrapping me up into a hug like Royal did when I was thrown at him. Betty speaks softly. "It'll be okay."

Her hug feels so much more comforting than any I've ever received from my own mom. I let the tears fall that I'd held back. She squeezes me a bit and then, when I'm ready, let's go.

Betty wipes away my tears and gives me a partial smile, but it's a calculating look.

"Do you need something for your head and arm?" she asks, stepping toward the cabinet where I'd seen some medications.

I shake my head, not wanting to seem weak. But with the movement, something in my neck aches, and I gasp.

Betty pulls out a bottle of over-the-counter pain relief and hands me two pills before pouring a glass of water. I don't instantly feel better — pain relief doesn't work that way — but by the time I've swallowed the pills, the water glass doesn't feel so heavy. The world doesn't feel like it's ending. My head and arm still hurt though.

The coffee machine on the counter gurgles, making a full pot of coffee. The glass carafe is nearly full by the time it's done. Betty places it on a pot holder in the center of a tray before adding the mugs around it. She makes another tray of things like creamers and milk, sugar, and some other sweeteners.

"Is that too heavy for you?" Betty nods to the second tray.

"I'm sure it's fine." I smile softly in reply.

It's agony carrying the tray, but I follow her with it, items rattling on top, back to the living room.

We've been gone for maybe ten minutes. Ian is seated in one of the large recliners, and Valor sits on the stone hearth by his side. Royal stands, feet apart, arms crossed over his chest. He watches me enter, and it elicits the same feeling of being watched that I've grown accustomed to.

On the other side of the room, Dad's men are standing with their hands clasped together before them while Dad sits in the other chair and Berto sits on the couch. The clearly drawn lines don't leave Betty and me much room to pick and choose where to sit, but Betty sets her tray on the coffee table before pouring a cup for Ian and then herself. She sits next to Berto, leaving me room on the far end of the couch, closer to the Cavanaghs than my own family.

Tucked in with the Cavanaghs, I feel safer than I have in a long time. No, I feel safer than I have since I left Valor's house. It wasn't that long ago I was here in Cavanagh territory, but it feels like forever when your whole world is uncertain.

Royal is across the room from me, but just having him close, I know I'm safe.

Dad's phone lights up where it's sitting on an ottoman, Steffano's name flashing on the screen.

"The daughter you promised me, that I paid you for, is married to a Cavanagh," Steffano says like he's repeating it for the third or fourth time, the implication setting in. "I am flying to America. We will meet in person tomorrow. You'll explain to me how this happened and how all of you can make it up to me. I've already invested. The money is transferred. This is unacceptable!" Steffano shouts.

I flinch, and Royal nearly starts moving but holds himself back.

"We'd be glad to discuss how this will work out. This is clearly unexpected, and we'll happily negotiate a fair price for your inconvenience." Ian sips his coffee. "But given the damage done to Leticia, she will be staying here in our home."

"Damage?" Steffano spikes that word up as its own question. Like he can't believe that would happen. "Surely you don't think I damaged her."

"No, but she's bruised up quite a bit and favors one arm," Betty casually answers, like it's her place to join the conversation. "She'll be seeing a medical professional, and we'll be taking any damages he attributes to her mistreatment as part of payment in this deal."

Do I look that bad? My arm hurts, but I don't think I'm really favoring it all that much. I look down at the bruising. It's significantly deeper in color than I expected, and compared to my other arm, it's definitely swollen.

"Fine." Steffano concedes. "I don't want to do business with the D'Medicis. I'll only work with the Cavanaghs. Gregorio, you can make this up to me in other ways, and we'll discuss it after I negotiate with the Cavanaghs. She's an object of value, and despite her being tarnished, we'll negotiate for her."

I want to be disgusted that he thinks so little of me, but what do I care what an asshole like him thinks?

The line disconnects, the phone screen turning black.

Dad glares at me before assessing the room. "This is unacceptable. You should be negotiating with me, not Steffano."

"Gregorio, Steffano already paid you for Leticia." Valor says my name less harshly than every other word in that sentence. "You gave up your claim on your daughter. Now we have to deal with the person who actually has a legal vested interest." Valor stands, rising to his full height. "It's best you leave. Now."

Dad goes red in the face all over again, and he stands. "Are you throwing me out?"

"No, we're telling you to leave, and you'll do the right thing and vacate the premises. This is supposed to remain civil. Let it be civil."

Ian remains seated, sipping his coffee like there isn't enough tension simmering to boil water.

"Come on, Dad." Berto can barely handle looking at him and spits his words with disgust. When he stands, he extends his hand to Valor. "Thank you for your time."

Dad and I are both slack jawed. *Is Berto taking over? Dad will allow it?*

But Dad gets to his feet. Making a point of looking anywhere but at me, he snatches up his phone and storms out the door.

Berto gives me one last smile. It's small and apologetic, but he doesn't say anything. Then, gesturing to the other two men to follow, he leaves.

The brush of cold air sweeps through the room and takes with it all the tension.

The most surprising part is that Betty laughs. "What a blowhard."

Ian cracks up and joins in. "I thought he would turn purple with how little he was breathing. Do you perform CPR on someone if they're actively choosing not to breathe? Or is there something else you're supposed to do?"

Valor lets out a yawn. "Well, that was eventful. We better figure out what Steffano Bianchi will want, though, so we're not caught negotiating with our asses hanging out."

"I've already been going through what I could uncover. His tech is surprisingly well set up, but the maintenance is a little lacking. From what I can find, he's still up to some bad shit." Royal looks at me, and his gaze is weighted with heavy emotion. "I'll fill you in, but I want to get Doc to look her over first."

"Already sent him a text. He'll be here soon." Betty reassures him. "Why doesn't Leticia help me figure out what to have for dinner, and the three of you go look over some inventory numbers and be productive."

She's practically dismissive with them, but they don't argue . . . Well, Valor and Ian don't. They make their way out toward the garage while Royal remains in place.

"Can we have a minute?" Royal gestures between him and me.

"The last time I let you two have a minute, we got into the middle of an Italian deal. Is that really the best idea?" She huffs.

I'm really taken aback by how strong-willed Betty is with the men of the house. She doesn't concede or bow to any of them.

Royal looks at the floor and mumbles, "No."

"I'll do it anyway since I'm sure I'll find her in your bed in the morning, but you're not off the hook. Fated mate or not, you know this wasn't the way to get what you want."

Fated what? I have to assume that's a wolf thing but not exactly something I need to expend brain space on at the moment with everything else going on.

Betty stands, crosses the room, and pats him on the shoulder. "But when the dust settles, know that we'll be extremely happy for you both."

As soon as the door to the garage opens and closes one more time, Royal rushes to me. He kneels at my feet and gently reaches for me. "Are you okay?"

"Am I okay?" I repeat. "Am I okay? I told you not to do this. It's too dangerous. What if something happened? What if Dad got mad and hurt you? Your family could be in so much trouble. Even though they're acting like this is just business as usual. It's weird. No, I'm not okay."

"I'm so sorry he hurt you. I had no idea he'd — I should have assumed he'd have done this to you, and I didn't have a better plan in place to protect you when he found out." Royal has tears in his eyes, the deep brown intensified by moisture. "Forgive me?"

"Of course I forgive you." I lean forward, trying to get closer to him.

"Take it easy." He brings his hand up and lightly brushes at my hairline.

The barest pressure sends a sharp sting through my skull, and my right arm aches. *Maybe I'm more hurt than I thought?*

"I can't wait for the doctor to get here and get you checked out." Royal's nostrils flare. "I want to hurt Gregorio the same way he hurt you."

"I don't like that." I shake my head. "I don't like the idea of you stooping to his level."

"Fine." Royal leans forward and places a soft kiss against my lips. "I'm glad you're back home, where you belong."

I nod because somehow, despite how wrong and weird everything is, I do feel at home. I do feel a sense of belonging. *Is this what family is supposed to be like?*

"I have one last confession." Royal squeezes my hand lightly, and I look up at him again to find his cheeks turning pink. He takes a deep breath and holds my gaze. "Leticia, I love you. I've loved you for a long time."

My stomach flips, and I think what's most surprising is that I'm not surprised at all.

I cup his cheek, wishing I could throw my arms around him. "I love you too. But I don't know when it happened," I whisper, but I mean it. I feel it. "I knew you loved me. I hope you knew that I loved you too."

His lips tug upward, trying to smile, even though unspoken tension and conflict still hang heavy in the air.

I sigh. "But I'm still mad at you. I'm still not okay. I still don't know how I feel." I try to be firm with him because this is Royal. I don't need to censor myself or be afraid of him. He makes it easy to share my truths, as unpleasant as they might be.

"That's okay. You can be mad at me. I accept that I fucked up." He nods before gently pulling me to his chest for a hug. "I can own doing something bad and let you have space to process it. But I needed you to know how I feel. I needed you to hear it."

I draw a deep breath, his scent filling my nose, and with the exhale, a lot of my anger fades. Fear stays with me though. There's so much uncertainty that it keeps me on edge.

The pack doctor, who simply introduced himself as Doc, is an adorable older gentleman. He's average height and kind of generic looking with white hair on the sides of his head and bald on top. Doc wears a light blue denim button-down shirt with the medical symbol on the breast pocket.

"Now, does this hurt?" he asks with a thick accent that I can't place.

Doc prods tenderly on my arm near my wrist.

"Ow, yes." I want to pull my arm away from him but hold as still as I can.

Royal, however, starts to growl from where he's leaning against the doorframe.

Betty comes up behind him and smacks him upside the head. "Stop it. I taught you better than that."

The interaction distracts me until Doc pushes harder. I let out a pained yelp, bringing my other hand up to stifle the sound.

"I definitely think something is broken." Doc nods. "It would be best to get an X-ray and take a closer look. I have the portable machine here, but if it's broken, the supplies for a cast are back at my workshop. Would be best to see you there. I think that's what we do."

I'm nodding along because Doc is talking to me, but I don't feel like I have any say in what's happening to me anymore. And since he thinks my arm is broken, it's just one more thing to add to the pile of problems I've accumulated and feel helpless under. But for the first time, the people making decisions care. They're taking over but doing so out of compassion, not for the sake of being in control.

"Alright, we'll drive her over. Are we your last stop?" Betty smiles at me, but she's addressing Doc.

"Yes, I was going to the O'Sheas', but Tim isn't answering his phone, and I'm not working with that ass of his alone." Doc nods resolutely before picking up his bag and getting ready to leave.

"Alright, come along, dear." Betty holds out her arms and gestures for me to get up from where I'd been seated at the dining room table.

"I'll take her. You can stay here and war room with Dad and Valor," Royal says, and without any argument, his mother agrees.

Out in Royal's SUV, I struggle with the seat belt, and Royal reaches over from the driver's seat to pull it across my lap with ease. He mumbles, "Sorry, I should have gotten that for you."

I hum. "But Doc is a vet, isn't he?" I try hard not to sound judgmental.

Royal nods. "Yeah, award winning. He's best known for his work with — oh. I bet you're kinda wanting to see a human doctor, huh?"

"I've never broken a bone before, so I don't know." The

emotions I've been shoving down, bottling up, and ignoring erupt, spilling out in tears and sobs until I'm shaking.

So lost in my breakdown, I don't even see him get out of the car, but he opens my door, unbuckles me, and pulls me out, holding me to his chest. The sweater he's wearing is soft against my face, and it feels comforting until I remember that, in part, this is his fault.

"I can't believe you did this." I choke out the words into his chest.

Royal runs his hand up and down my back. "I'm sorry. I thought I was protecting you. I never anticipated that they'd hurt you like this. I'm so fuckin' sorry. I know you said no, but I didn't see any other way to keep you safe. I was selfish, and I should have talked to you more about it."

I don't know that anyone has ever apologized to me and meant it like this. The way he's holding me and resting his head against mine is comforting, but beyond that, there's this connectedness I can't explain. I'm enveloped in his arms, his scent, and the warmth and safety he provides.

Giant emotions crash down in waves over me. Heat of anger and frustration mix with the coolness of sorrow and tangle with the chill of relief. It takes a few minutes of sobbing and sweet comforting reassurances from Royal until I'm able to hold it together.

I push back and look up at him, wishing I had something profound to say. "Alright, let's go see the vet."

"I will absolutely get you to a human doctor if you prefer. Doc won't be offended." Royal brushes my hair back.

"I'm good." I nod, swiping at my face. "But I need a tissue."

"In the car. Let's get you all warmed back up and over to Doc."

Royal tucks me back into the vehicle, going so far as to pull out a blanket from the back of the SUV and draping it over my lap after buckling the seat belt for me. In the side pocket of the door is a car-sized box of tissues, and he makes sure I can reach them.

I'm snuggled in with the seat warmer on and the vents blowing warm air right at me.

When Royal settles in behind the wheel, my eyelids are heavy.

He looks over to me and reaches up to what I'm sure is a goose egg growing from where I hit the wall. “We’re a good half hour from Doc’s place. It’s okay if you rest.”

CHAPTER FIFTY-ONE

WHITE GETS DIRTY

I want to kill Gregorio D'Medici, truce be damned.

I want to do to him everything he did to Leticia but tenfold, and then when I'm done, I want to . . . *Shit. I'm starting to sound like Valor.*

Drawing another deep breath, I clench my fist again as Doc has Leticia take off her shirt for the X-ray. It's a catch-22. I'm used to being naked around people. It happens all the time with shifting. But she isn't. Her discomfort is putting me further on edge.

Doc X-rays not just her forearm where the break is likely, but also her upper arm and shoulder to be on the safe side.

He's already poked and prodded her bruises and confirmed that she doesn't have a concussion.

Doc turns the monitor to face us and points with the end of his pen at one spot on the screen and then another. "There are two small fractures. We'll definitely need to put you in a cast and sling. It'll need to be casted for a good six weeks."

"Mmm." Leticia bites her lips together. "Okay."

I squeeze her non-injured hand. "Are you just saying that or are you really okay?"

"Well, there's no changing what's happened. And because I've never had a broken bone before, I'm trusting Doc," she says with a shrug.

Kill them with fire. My wolf pictures a flamethrower as an option to take out Gregorio D'Medici.

"That's good." I smile at her. "First time for everything, and hopefully this'll be your last time too."

"Do you want a pink cast?" Doc asks as he goes to the cupboard of supplies. "Or I have lime green or white?"

"Is it weird to get a pink cast as an adult?" Leticia's voice is small and low, like she's talking to herself rather than Doc and me.

"Nah, if anyone is judging your pink cast, they don't deserve to be in your life anyway." I lean over and kiss her cheek in reassurance. "Besides, white gets dirty faster."

"Pink it is." Doc starts bringing over supplies.

The silence feels uncomfortable between us as Doc starts bandaging her arm. He gives me a stink eye, clearly telling me to comfort her when she squirms under his touch.

"I've got your class schedule, and I'll work with Dad to get you a dedicated security team so you can keep going to classes. Laptop and new books are already in my cart to order."

It feels like the most awkward conversation to try to start. Will she even want to talk about school? Is that stressful?

"Really?" Leticia's gaze darts away from where Doc is wrapping to meet my eyes. "I didn't expect . . ."

"Of course. No one will stop you from getting your degree and graduating. If that's what you want."

I try not to be offended that she thinks we would stop her, but I force myself to remember that her dad would have pulled her out of school without a question or conversation. That she was married off to a man who might not have cared what she wanted. It's too easy to think of her as never being anywhere else ever.

"I can condense my classes. There's still time to move them so that I don't have to go to Chicago as often." Leticia chews on her bottom lip.

"That's not necessary unless you want to change your schedule so you're in the car less," I say, but I smile a little wider, knowing we don't need to focus on the details right this second. "I am warning you, though, my parents can be a bit obnoxious about graduations."

My wolf so helpfully retrieves the memory of the two of them wearing royal-blue shirts with silver crowns and party hats to my college graduations. As if being named Royal wasn't enough, they sure had to make a big deal out of it.

"Mom and Dad couldn't care less about my schooling, and Berto would rather I not 'drain security resources' to go to class." Leticia shrugs one shoulder, holding still for Doc. "It must be nice to have someone care that you do well."

"Well, now you have a pack of us." Doc smiles between the two of us. "We all care if another does well. It's a village."

Our mate is pack, finally. My wolf approves, wagging his tail.

"A big, fancy, expensive village." I laugh, thinking about the vast numbers of acreage, homes, schools, and businesses we've amassed. None of that will matter to Leticia though. She's not impressed by those sorts of things. "With a pack, it's impossible to deny the sense of community. They might not be all related to you, but it's one big family."

"That might be nice. It's hard when you have to calculate which degree of cousins you're talking to." Leticia sighs, a soft smile taking over her face. "The fifth cousin on your mother's side is not something I appreciate having to math out regularly."

"There." Doc gestures to Leticia's arm when he's finished wrapping. "I'll find a sling. You let it dry."

Leticia looks at the cast with something I don't know how to interpret.

"I'd say it's not so bad. But casts kinda suck." I try to spin it into a positive but fall short of something truly meaningful. "But at least all you have to worry about is your school work and letting my mom dote on you."

"Having someone else take care of me is so weird." Leticia runs her free hand through her hair, pulling it out of her face.

"You let me take care of you." I helpfully point out.

"Uhm." Leticia's cheeks flame bright pink in an instant.

"Get your mind out of the gutter and back on the sidewalk with the rest of us civilized people," I whisper, hoping Doc doesn't hear. "Though, we should probably wait a couple days for me to take care of you like that."

"Okay, you two happy kids have a nice night. I've got to get home for dinner." Doc tosses a sling at me and starts cleaning up. "Welcome to the pack. Now, shoo, shoo." He waves me toward the door.

Guess he heard that. My wolf snorts.

Leticia is fighting back a laugh, but she lets me help her into the sling before we're hustled out of the clinic.

CHAPTER FIFTY-TWO

A DEAL IS A WISH YOUR HEART MAKES

After getting Steffano's information from Berto, Valor set up a place to meet and put together a whole three-course meal of backup plans if needed.

Option one, where we started, is out here at the airfield. The quiet early morning hour allows for some privacy and keeps would-be bystanders away. A decent-sized private jet pulls up in front of one of our hangars.

The jet taxis over to us, and Dad looks to me. "And what are you *not* going to do?"

"Insinuate that I'm smarter than he is? Even though it's true." I shrug, tucking my hands into my jacket pockets, trying to warm up from the late January deep freeze.

"Close enough." Valor pinches the bridge of his nose.

Dad shakes his head as our ground crew quickly maneuvers to help chock the plane and prepare for Steffano to disembark.

It's killing me not to look at my phone to check in on Leticia and Mom. I know they're at home and I know they're safe. The fifteen alarms I have that would alert me to trouble are silent. But I just want to be able to see her.

A black SUV rolls up along the driving space toward us.

"Expecting company?" I ask Dad and Valor.

Valor is already reaching for his gun. "No, I sure wasn't."

Rustling comes from behind us, easily mistaken for the wind to human ears, and I know the sniper just adjusted positions. I feel a little better knowing we brought backup firepower. But my fingers still twitch, ready to draw my weapon.

Or we shift and tear them all to pieces. My wolf wags his tail with nervous excitement.

I suppress that thought but keep him on the surface. He makes me faster, helps me focus, and if it came down to his idea, he'd be ready.

The SUV rolls to a stop, and the driver's door opens first, revealing one of the goons Gregorio and Berto showed up with yesterday. He opens the back passenger door, and I'm surprised to see Berto step out.

"Great," Dad sighs. "I thought they understood we weren't dealing with them anymore."

Berto steps toward us. With his arms at his sides, he's not quite unthreatening, but he certainly isn't showing any signs of wanting to go to bullets as a form of communication.

Valor growls low but silences it when Berto gets within earshot.

"Gregorio is dead. I'm the new head of the D'Medici Mafia. Steffano's deal with me isn't as ironclad as it was with my father. I'll be much more flexible, given our working relationship, than he would have been. I thought you might like to use that in your negotiations." Berto stands rigid, addressing Dad.

From the corner of my eye, I see the jet door open and people descending the stairs.

The three of us look back and forth, the questions more numerous than the answers and the time needed to get them.

Did Berto man up and kill his old man for the seat of power, or was there something else at play?

"There's a treaty between us, and I'd like to keep that and honor it to the full extent. I would like to stand in with your negotiations with Steffano and offer what we can to get Leticia the best possible deal and keep her safe with you." Berto turns to me. "I think you'll treat her better."

I don't argue with him because he's right. I keep my snide comments about how good she'll have it with me to myself and just nod. Berto can't be trusted, not yet, but I'm willing to entertain the idea for now. An olive branch is being extended. Especially since Valor hasn't ripped his throat out yet.

Steffano Bianchi is shorter than I expected for an Italian Mafia boss. Then again, Berto isn't all that big either.

He stalks toward us, well-tailored suit but no winter coat. His body is rigid against the balmy Illinois air.

"What is it with Italians and thinking they're impervious to the cold?" Valor mutters.

"Where is she?" Steffano makes a show of looking around.

"Leticia is someplace safe," Dad answers.

Safe at home. Where she belongs. My wolf snaps his jaws, frustrated and angry.

"You didn't even bring her to negotiate. Bold of you." Steffano postures, raising his chin.

Dad doesn't rise to the occasion; he remains relaxed and calm. "She's not up for negotiation. We'll be keeping Leticia, and you'll find we're agreeable to a number of terms that are favorable to you."

"Which is why you've brought Berto D'Medici here? I'm looking for a green-card bride. Bride being the keyword. I don't want Gregorio's son." Steffano looks Berto over, but his gaze almost seems hungry.

Don't protest too much. I struggle to hold back my laugh and hide it behind a cough.

"Berto is here as the new head of the D'Medici Empire." Dad smiles, and it's almost one of his happy ones. Almost, but not quite. "Berto informed us of the recent passing of his father, and as the truce between our families isn't tied to a singular generation, we're all here to work together."

"I already paid the D'Medicis off." Steffano points heatedly at Berto. "Gregorio accepted the deal. That's not my problem."

"I never said it was." Berto adjusts his tie ever so casually, but something about it makes me think he's doing it as a way to keep himself still and anchored to the ground. "I just think there might be room for improvement so that everyone walks away from this happier. I can cut you a better deal on transportation than my father could."

"Plus, I'm sure you were buying guns from us to sell to Steffano.

We can cut out the pricing of the middleman by extending a deal" — Valor lets out a low growl of displeasure — "jointly."

"I want double the number we talked about." Steffano looks at Berto and then to Valor. "That'd be fifty fully automatic rifles delivered to any location of my choosing. I want an additional shipment of thirty in the spring."

"Eighty fully automatic rifles, no problem." Dad widens his stance and crosses his arms. "I'm sure Berto will help us with the transport, given he already has knowledge of your operations."

Berto gives a single nod.

I reach for my phone to take notes. Steffano's henchmen, who came to stand behind him, draw their weapons.

Holding my hands out, I make a show of slowly reaching for my phone in the breast pocket of my jacket. "Someone should take notes, shouldn't they?"

Steffano waves his hand, and the guns are lowered.

"Well, if that's all, then." Dad shrugs. "That's an easily done deal."

"No, no, that's not all." Steffano laughs. "I also want access to a mercenary, at my discretion, no charge, for three full years."

"Six months." Valor scoffs.

"Two years." Steffano counters.

"One year. Firm. And you're still mandated to abide by our normal screening procedures for each job." Dad takes over.

At a minimum of twenty-five thousand dollars per job, that could be very expensive. Though I can't imagine that Steffano has that many enemies he needs an outside hand to murder. Though, that's not to say all mercenary jobs are killing either. Sometimes you just need the best in the business for surveillance and protection.

Steffano thinks about it, running his tongue across the front of his teeth. After a long moment, he answers. "Acceptable." But he's not done. "I also want access to your tech geek." Steffano looks at me but pretends not to know my name. Or at least he thinks 'tech geek' is supposed to be offensive to me.

"For what?" I close the screen on my phone.

"I need a project done, setting up a new safehouse. My last contractor . . ." — Steffano chooses his words carefully — "met an untimely end after using my upgrades as his new standard for all business."

"Don't I feel that," Valor huffs, and I know he's thinking about Paulie and the architecture for his own house.

"Where?" Dad clearly wants to keep this conversation moving.

"Undisclosed location." Steffano snipes back.

"I'll know when you get me there, you might as well tell me now." I shrug.

Steffano crosses his arms in front of his chest. "Moldova."

"You can't have him full-time. He's crucial to our business. I'll give you two weeks." Dad offers.

"Can you get a whole house done in two weeks?" Steffano drops his arms, and this is starting to feel more and more like a conversation rather than a negotiation.

"New build or a retrofit? Square footage? How many outbuildings? Am I fortifying the house or the attached land too?" I ask for as many specifics as I can off the top of my head.

"New build. One thousand one hundred square meters. One outbuilding, a garage. You'll be integrating the existing land security into the system," Steffano rapid-fire answers.

"Two weeks is doable. I'm guessing you want me to bring everything necessary." I'm already trying to come up with a list.

"Yes, I'll provide you with the specifications that I'm looking for, and you'll provide all hardware, software, and supplemental materials." He nods.

"I want the electric pre-wired before I arrive. I can mark out on blueprints where you —"

"Already done." Steffano waves me off.

We're leaving our mate for two weeks? My wolf practically riots.

Shhh. I console him. But there's no way I'll ever be able to explain the separation in a way he'll find acceptable. *It's for the best. It's for a short time to secure forever.*

We just got her back. He protests.

Dad turns to get my consent, and I nod.

"Done, you can have Royal for two weeks, but he comes back in the same condition as we sent him to you. Any damage or harm that comes to him will nullify the agreement, and you'll get none of the remaining contract of the mercenary or of the guns. Is that understood?" Dad squares up to Steffano, making one of his henchmen twitch.

Valor sees it too, and he subtly rolls his shoulders back to accommodate a quick grab for his gun.

"I won't harm your precious geek." Steffano gives me a pitying look. "But I want him available for updates for a full year too. Those first-year ghosts in a system as they work themselves out."

"While I'm appalled that you'd think I'd leave ghosts to pop up in the system, I accept one year of tech support. But it must be done remotely."

"On-site." Steffano shakes his head. "I don't want this system accessed anywhere but locally."

Paranoid much? My wolf scoffs.

"One trip a quarter, no more than three days at a time." Valor cuts in. "We're not flying him halfway around the world just because you can't figure out how to turn on the security system."

"Once a month." Steffano tries to argue.

"No." Dad shakes his head. He makes that 'disappointed in you' look that he's never once used on Valor and me but uses on other people all the time. "One trip a quarter. Three days at a time. Best we can do."

"Fine." Steffano huffs. "Then I want to up the cash from fifteen to seventeen million. To get back the money I already paid the D'Medicis for her."

"Done." I don't even try to negotiate that.

I know Dad wanted to negotiate the amount down due to Leticia being hurt, but the money is just sitting there doing nothing anyway. The whole concept makes my gut ache. Exchanging money for the woman I love isn't something I want to do, but it seems like it's necessary. I just want to move past it.

"That's it? Are we done with this?" Valor looks around our small group before addressing Steffano. "You'll get the marriage annulled in Italy, and we'll arrange the rest of the details."

Steffano looks at me one last time. "Can't see what she sees in him, but yes. I'll take this as payment for Leticia and process the annulment in Italy."

"Well, that was much more civil than expected." Dad sighs. He steps forward to shake Steffano's hand. "It's a pleasure doing business with you."

Steffano shakes, and when they let go, he adds as if it's an afterthought, "I'll expect Royal in Moldova tomorrow, then?"

"Tomorrow isn't enough time to get everything together, even if you had the specs list in hand right now. I need a week to make sure I can source everything we need." I'm quick to argue.

"Excellent, one week." Steffano turns his back on us, walking to his jet. "Now, if you'll excuse me, I have another bride to find."

We wait until the henchmen and Steffano are on the plane and it's turning around to head back to the runway before moving from where we stood to negotiate.

A cool wind whips by, and I shudder.

That's it. In three weeks, I'll be home with my mate, and this nightmare will be behind us.

Leticia

CHAPTER FIFTY-THREE

HAPPILY EVER AFTER?

"So, what? That's it, then?" I can't believe what he's telling me.

"Yeah, that's it." Royal guides me to sit down on his bed again, where I'd been resting before he came home. "In a week, I've got a private flight to Moldova for a job. I'll get his house up and running, and I'll come home."

"Then what?" I feel dumb asking, but I have nothing, and no one is making a big deal about it.

"Happily ever after?" Royal shrugs. He sits down facing me before grabbing a pillow and offering it to me. "To prop your arm up."

I take the pillow and put it under my casted-up arm. "What does happily ever after look like?"

"Well, we should probably have a real wedding. Then move out of my parents' basement, or do a renovation to make it a true mother-in-law suite." Royal looks around. "I have no problem with either of those options. I sold the place I'd bought and moved back in here because I was lonely living alone and ended up spending all my time here anyway. But for the two of us, we could make our own home."

Home. It's such a funny word. I know what it's like to have a place to live, but the penthouse in Gold Coast was much more prison than home.

"Your parents won't mind us living here? I mean, surely they want some privacy. They hardly need another person around." Something in my voice has Royal moving.

He slides closer toward me on the bed, rotating and sitting alongside me. We're shoulder to shoulder, and he rests his head against mine, then picks up my good hand and gives it a squeeze. "My parents only want what's best for us. If that's a mansion in the territory, a cottage in the woods, or staying right here with them, then they'll be more than happy for us either way."

"Aren't they mad? It feels like someone should be mad." I try to explain. "It all feels so easy. My dad's just letting this go? It's over with?"

"Uhm." Royal tenses, and he speaks more softly. "I've never been good at saying this sort of thing. Mom's normally the one to do this, but I feel like I should be the one to say it."

"Royal, you're scaring me. What?"

"Your dad is dead. I don't know the details, but I know Berto is now in charge, and he's approving of this deal between our family and Steffano." Royal squeezes my hand. "I'm sorry."

"Dead. He's dead." My head is buzzing as I try to process that information.

Dad is dead.

He's dead, and I don't feel anything.

Maybe it's the painkillers that Royal picked up from the pharmacy.

Maybe it's . . . relief.

"We can call Berto if you want. I know your phone is probably toast. I'll have a new one ready for you tomorrow. But we can use mine to call him." Royal is so quick to try to make it better. "We can call your mom too. I still have your phone cloned."

I shake my head and lean against him. "No, that's okay."

"Antonella?" Royal offers, and it's the sweetest thing.

"I'm okay." I reassure him. "My dad is dead, but I don't feel anything about it. Relief, maybe."

"I'm trying to put myself in your shoes, and it's easier to see why you'd feel relieved the deeper I look."

Royal draws slow breaths, and I mimic them. My eyelids are getting heavier by the second.

"Come on." Royal shuffles, carefully supporting me while also helping me move to lie down. “Let’s get you all snug as a bug while I pack. You can rest up before dinner.”

“I should go help your mom.” I yawn and try to push up.

“She’s got it just fine. She wants you to rest.” Royal tucks a blanket up over the top of me.

I can hardly fight sleep as the feeling of being the safest I’ve ever been settles over my body.

Royal

CHAPTER FIFTY-FOUR

GO AND HURRY BACK

I'm desperately trying to make myself go. But I've run through my 'one more thing' checklist with Leticia almost twice now.

Leticia cocks a brow, showing she's frustrated with me double-triple-checking that she knows how to navigate the computers we've worked on all week together.

"Royal, I promise. I know how to do the things and get in touch with you. Valor also knows how to do all these things and can help me if I get stuck." She waves her phone. "I'm also quite competent at using this to call Valor and Antonella."

But . . . no objection comes. I nod and give her another kiss. "Alright, be safe. Don't overdo it. I know you've never broken a bone before, but it's a lot of healing. You should sleep a lot and get rest. Mom can handle cooking, and we have people who do the cleaning."

If we stayed, we'd make sure she wasn't doing unnecessary things with the injury. My wolf points out, but I shove him away, trying to concentrate and make sure Leticia promises to behave.

"I know. I'll be bored. It'll be fine." Leticia pushes my suitcase with her leg, and it rolls toward me without any effort. "Go so you can hurry up and come back."

I want to argue with her that the contract is for two weeks, so it doesn't matter how fast I get there. I'll be back at the same time. But I don't.

Begrudgingly, I take the suitcase up the stairs, Leticia's little footsteps following me. I roll it across the floor and wave to Mom, who is reading a cookbook at the kitchen counter.

"Fly safe," she murmurs, then leans toward the cookbook as if a closer proximity will make it make more sense to her, or maybe she needs reading glasses.

I want to ask, but a little tug comes to the back of my shirt.

I turn around, and Leticia looks up at me with her big, beautiful blue eyes. "Ask me again?"

My heart flutters a beat, and from the corner of my eye, I catch Mom giving up discretion and turning to shamelessly watch us.

She wants us! My wolf doesn't seem surprised, more so excited by the question.

I pick up her left hand and squeeze it gently. "Leticia Alexandra, will you marry me?"

"Yes." She nods, a soft smile lighting up her features even through the bruising.

I cup her chin and gently kiss her with as much love, commitment, and what I hope feels like a promise to keep her safe. If a kiss could talk, then this one should tell her how much I love and cherish her.

When we part, her eyes are a little glossy, and she wraps her good arm around me, holding the one in the cast and sling between us. I want to squeeze her tight but refrain to protect her from any more injury.

"Royal," Dad says from the door by the garage, "are we leaving or not?"

"Ian, so fucking help me, shut up," Mom snaps. "They just got engaged."

That doesn't end the moment, but Leticia and I break out in a laugh. Somehow, each of us finds it funny.

"What do you mean engaged?" Dad says over our ruckus. "He already married them."

"It doesn't count. There were no witnesses." Mom scoffs, but excitement laces her voice. "We can actually plan a wedding this time. The pack will be thrilled."

Leticia's eyes go wide.

I lean forward and whisper in her ear, “It’ll be fine. I promise. We can talk all about it when I come home. Love you, gorgeous.”

“Love you too.” She pecks my cheek, and I force myself to move away from her.

My wolf drags his feet, trying like hell to hold me back. But this is the price I have to pay to keep her. I’ll fulfill that promise.

Leticia

CHAPTER FIFTY-FIVE

ASTROPHYSICS TO A CAT

"He'll be just fine." Betty looks over at me from the kitchen. She leans a hip against the counter and crosses her arms in front of her chest. "He's the baby of the family, but I raised him right. He's strong enough to protect himself."

"Well, I wasn't worried about that until just this second." I look at the door Royal left through.

"Come, sit, walk me through this recipe." Betty nods to a chair pushed into the kitchen island.

I sit and talk through a recipe for chicken and dumplings as she cooks. It feels good to at least kind of help, but I keep wanting to get off the chair and just join in. *It'll be a long five weeks.*

"Tell me, what kind of wedding were you thinking about?" Betty smiles coyly at me.

"Well, I hadn't really been thinking?" I smile back, trying to appease her. "My mom and her sisters were planning my wedding to Steffano, and we found a dress they really liked on me but . . ."

"But the wedding wasn't about you, it was about them?" She glances at me, stirring the pot to keep it from boiling.

"Very much not about me." I absentmindedly flip the page of the recipe book.

"Well, as much as I'd like to say this one will be all about you and Royal, it won't be entirely. The pack will want to celebrate. On the first full moon after your wedding ceremony, there will be a big gathering and a pack run. But they'll be respectful of your wishes." She dips a clean spoon in the pot and hands it to me over the counter.

I blow on it before tasting it. The flavors are a little muted, but it's delicious. I hand her back the spoon. "Could use more of everything, but on the right track."

"You've got a real knack for this." Betty sets the spoon aside and starts seasoning.

"Thank you." I flip the page in the cookbook back to the recipe. "What's it like being a wolf?"

"Oh, considering becoming one of us?" Betty steps back from the stove to grab some spices.

"Not really? I don't know. Royal and I didn't talk about it a lot other than how . . ." My cheeks are turning pink, and I feel the heat as it runs down my neck.

She's just so easy to talk to, but you shouldn't talk to your fiancé's mother about sex.

"How?" Betty tries to encourage me.

"How different we are anatomically speaking." I try to downplay the interaction.

"How he can't get a human pregnant." Betty surmises. She looks me over and must see my red face because she says, "Well, there's nothing to be ashamed about, dear. We all do it."

"I just never, uhm." I clear my throat. "Never really had someone to talk to about these things, and maybe I'm talking to the wrong person."

She smiles, brushing her bangs out of her face. "You can come to me with anything. I've always told the boys I'm a place of knowledge, not of judgment. Though sometimes some judgment does happen when they do some really messed-up things."

"Like marrying a woman without her knowledge to prevent her from being married to a mafioso in Italy?" I giggle.

"Precisely." Betty seasons the food and keeps stirring. "Well, being a wolf has its positives, healing more quickly for one, and I would love more grandchildren. But there are dangers that come with it. What if we're found out by humans?"

Silence passes between us for a few moments. *Why is it that the idea of kids isn't so scary with Royal?*

"But that doesn't have to be a discussion for now. Let's get another college grad in the house and a married couple. Then we can talk about being happily mated and grand babies." Betty is all smiles. It's bright and lights up her eyes. Her happiness reminds me of how Royal looks when he's happy.

"What does that mean, fated mates? I heard you say that to Royal, but I didn't ask. We were a little busy." I think back to just barely a week ago, when I found out I had a second, but more wanted, arranged marriage.

"Well, I should really let him explain it to you, but since he's not here . . . We believe that there's a person out there for everybody and that one person is fated to be with you. You're a matched set, and nothing is stronger than that bond." Betty offers me another tasting spoon.

I taste and nod. "That's it." Then I hand her back the spoon. "So is it common to find your person?"

"Usually mates are easily found, though sometimes people get impatient and settle before they find the one. Like Valor did with his first wife. They were head over heels in love, but not fated mates. But he most certainly is fated with Antonella." Betty adds, "Ian and I are fated mates."

"How did you know?" *What if I'm not really his?*

"It's a feeling you get. Well, your wolf usually recognizes it first, and then you come to understand it. It's an intense connection. And once it hits you, you don't know if you'd be whole without it. I've heard it's not as strong between humans and wolves, but you should still feel a really strong connection to Royal." Betty tries to explain, but I imagine it's like explaining astrophysics to a cat.

But what she says . . . I feel that. I do feel a connection to Royal. It's why I couldn't say goodbye when I was shipped off to Italy. It's why I let him text me every day and didn't block him. I didn't want to be without him.

So that's what this is. Fated mates.

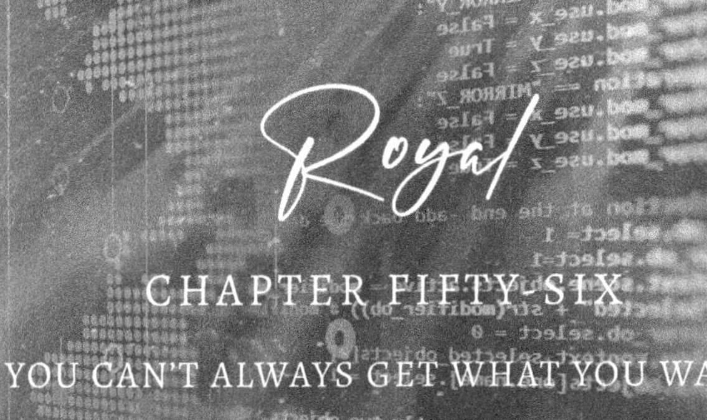

CHAPTER FIFTY-SIX

YOU CAN'T ALWAYS GET WHAT YOU WANT

I plop down on the 'bed,' which is an old military-style cot that's not exactly comfortable in the house's tech room. The stacks of boxes filled with computers and technology that I've spent the last two days rummaging through and working on aren't disappearing.

I started with the coding projects. Getting the computers ready to accept all the hardware and setting up a server to run it all through. It's the bulk of the work that only I can do because any idiot can install cameras and sensors.

My phone rings, and the three daily calls from Steffano have me gritting my teeth, bracing myself to hear his next ridiculous request. But one glance at the screen and my shoulders relax. Leticia's name glows, and the reminder of home soothes me.

"Hello, gorgeous," I answer, bringing the phone to my ear. I wait for her reply while opening the clamshell case to get my earbuds out.

"Hey, handsome." She sounds perfect, safe, and happy.

"Everything going okay at the house?" I switch from the phone against my head to earbuds before pushing up on the cot and moving to my personal laptop. I bring up the house feeds, and it takes me just a few seconds to find her in my — our — bedroom.

"Yeah, your mom and dad have been great. I think Betty really likes me. Class has been challenging with one arm, but my teachers are all super understanding and accommodating." Leticia wanders around my room, nearly pacing.

"That's good. I'm glad to hear it." I reach for my water bottle, left near the wrapper from the protein bar I had for dinner, and take a sip.

"Sooo." Leticia pauses nervously. "At what point in a relationship do girls get dick pics from guys?"

I shouldn't have taken that sip of water. I cough, holding it back in my mouth to avoid spitting it out over the thousands of dollars' worth of equipment in front of me. "I'm sorry, what?"

"Yeah, that was a stupid question. Never mind." Leticia berates herself, and I hate it.

Why is she so hard on herself? My wolf feels equally offended that she seemingly wouldn't trust us with this.

"Not stupid. I just —" I sigh and wipe up the little water I didn't keep contained in my mouth using my sleeve. "I just forget how lucky you are to never have gone through the awkward teens and early twenties with dick pics and all the drama that goes with it."

"Ahhh, I'll add that to the column of things I missed out on." She doesn't sound happy about missing that phase in life. "Unless . . . you'd send me one. You know, to be another one of my firsts?"

"You don't want a dick pic, gorgeous." I shake my head and look over at the phone.

My heart aches knowing she's at home, standing awkwardly in our bedroom, not sure what to do with herself, and I'm stuck halfway around the world, practically a prisoner, unable to take care of her.

"How am I supposed to know that?" She lets out a tiny, agitated sound that's kind of like a growl. "I've never gotten one. Maybe I'd like one."

You've made her so mad she's growling. Give her what she wants, my wolf growls at me, the implication that I'm stupid going without saying.

Great, now I've got two of them growling at me. I'm smiling, though, because her growl is nearly playful in sound, even if it's from frustration.

"No, Leticia. No one likes dick pics. It won't satisfy you in the way you're looking for." I close my eyes as my cock throbs when I think of exactly how I've satisfied her before.

"Fine," she huffs, frustrated, her tone taking that sharp, cutting edge.

Mate is pissed. You should give her what she wants. My wolf, unhelpfully, advises.

I watch on the monitor as she walks over to my bed before plopping down on it.

She lies looking up at the ceiling. "I don't understand it, then, why do guys send them and girls talk about them if no one wants them?"

"Leticia." I draw her attention away from the rant. "Do you really want a dick pic?"

"No," she huffs. "You told me I wouldn't want one."

"You don't. You don't want a dick pic because it's a flat image of something. You're more complex than that." I pause and then just lean into it. I let the distance be a buffer for the awkward. I embrace the way we've already done virtual exploration once before. This isn't new. It's just a different step. "You don't want a dick pic because you crave more."

"So what you're saying is there's something better than a dick pic, and that's what I want?" She groans, and I hear the swoosh of my blankets being pulled back on my bed. Then I watch on-screen as she climbs under the covers.

Quit being such a coward. You know she wants us. Don't let the distance win. Give our mate what she wants. My wolf urges me.

"Get cozy. I'll hang up with you and show you why you don't want a dick pic." I pinch the bridge of my nose, looking again at my phone sitting on the bed.

I still have hours of coding to get through, but it's not like I can focus if I'm rock hard in my pants anyway. I stand up and stretch out, trying not to get ahead of myself. She could still say no.

"You don't have to hang up to send a picture." Leticia yawns. "I'm sure you've got one saved or something you can send me."

"One, no. I don't." I turn off the auxiliary monitor on the makeshift desk and pull my T-shirt off, dropping it over the webcam on the laptop Steffano insisted on. "Two. You're right. I don't need to hang up. But if you want to get the full effect of getting a dick pic from a guy, then you deserve the whole experience."

"Three?" I hear her settling in, fabric shuffling and the gentle creaking of the bed.

I look at my personal laptop, seeing Leticia reach for the remote to turn off the lights in the room.

"Three, you'll have to forgive me, but I don't have the best equipment here for this sort of thing. It'll be basic, but at least it'll show you the difference." I unbutton my jeans and feel the sweet relief of the easing pressure.

"I didn't talk you into something you didn't want to do, right?" Leticia's voice is small and hesitant.

I debate turning the night vision on for the camera in my room, but instead, I embrace going lower tech, back to a time when there weren't cameras everywhere, and you couldn't just watch the person you're infatuated with.

"My wife asked me to get hard for her and show her." I simplify to the lowest rational line of thought. "She didn't realize I'm half hard every time I see her name come up on my phone. Hang up with me, gorgeous. Let me show you the difference between a dick pic and what you really want."

Leticia

CHAPTER FIFTY-SEVEN

MY FIRST …

"Good night, Royal." I do as I'm told and hang up the phone.

I swear to God I'm possessed. There's got to be some sort of demon inside me making me crave all these dirty things, especially because I keep saying them out loud.

In the dark, I stare up at my phone screen, lying on my back. *Gonna drop it on my face doing this.*

I roll to my side, and it buzzes with a notification.

ROYAL:

IMG.01

My first dick pic! I'm quick to open it up. And I can't tell if he's trying to be funny or if this is really what a dick pic is. It's quite obviously his penis. It's hard, veiny, and looks like what I saw before. But . . . I turn off the screen, not wanting to live through the I told you so just yet.

He was right. This doesn't feel anywhere near as exciting as I was hoping. I wanted to feel close to him. I was expecting to see something erotic that would help me quench the growing thirst for him.

My arm has been bugging me, and I don't know why I thought an orgasm would be the answer to make it feel better.

My phone buzzes again. And I tip it up, squinting through the darkness at the screen.

ROYAL:

VID.01

Hesitantly, I click play.

Royal is stroking himself. He's no longer standing; he's lying or sitting in bed with his legs stretched out. I pause the video and pull the covers up close around me before I turn the volume on. Not loud, well aware that I'm not alone in this house, even if Royal claims the soundproofing is enough. This . . . this feels dirty and yet exciting. In just the half second I saw, I immediately know it's what I was yearning for.

I back the video up and, with the volume on, hit play.

"Fuck, Leticia. Do you see how hard you make me?" Royal's voice is gravelly, deep and heavy.

The movements of his hand on his shaft are mesmerizing, and I catch the glint of pre-cum forming at the head. My mouth goes dry wanting to taste him again.

"I know you're thinking about how good it feels when we're together," Royal murmurs. "Touch yourself for me, wife. Get yourself wet and watch as I come for you."

I'm hot under his thick covers, and the video pauses when another message notification beeps.

I click out to look at it.

ROYAL:

Want more?

My fingers shake as I type out the three letters.

LETICIA:

Yes

ROYAL:

I feel like I should ask this time.

I know I've already seen you touch yourself. But I should get better about consent. Is it okay if I watch you play?

I want to see my wife come.

Play. I love how he makes this fun and not so serious. It's play. It's fun.

LETICIA:

I don't mind.

For a second, the bubbles show that he's typing, but they stop and then my phone rings instead.

I answer it, not needing to double-check that it's him calling.

"Come out from under the covers. Fuck." His breathing is heavy. "Fuck."

I push back the covers. The room is still dark-ish, the low glow from the electronic lights filling the space.

"Strip for me, gorgeous." Royal moans, and it sends a shiver down my spine. "You have no idea how hard I am for you. I miss being inside you."

My breath catches. *Why is that so hot?* Hot and relatable. My pussy squeezes like it's looking for his cock but comes up empty.

I sit up on the bed, pulling his T-shirt out from under my butt, then off over the top of my head, and down around my cast-covered arm. Next, I shimmy my underwear down my legs before kicking them off to land on the floor somewhere.

"How's that?" I ask, looking around the room, trying to figure out where the camera is.

"The camera is one of my security cameras. It's on top of my computer stack, but don't worry about me. It's enough to just have a little look at you," Royal says softly. "Do you see why a dick pic is grossly overrated?"

I reach for my earbuds on the nightstand, and Royal waits while I tuck them into my ears.

Lying back on the bed, I slowly trail my fingers down my body. I don't know the first thing about being sexy, so I try to remember how Royal touched me. "It definitely wasn't what I wanted."

"Did you like what you did get?" His voice wavers lightly.

"I did. Though . . . I'd really like to see . . ."

"See what, Leticia?" He hums. "Be a good girl, say the words, and I'll give you everything I can."

"Can I see you come?"

I can't believe those words just came from my mouth. It's shameful, but it's not like we aren't married. And it's not like we haven't had sex before. But why is it so hard to ask?

"Lie back and play with my pretty little pussy, and I'll send you a video of me coming. But you have to promise to make yourself come lying right where you are right now." Royal doesn't hesitate to coach me through this experience with him.

I lie back as he instructed. It's a little awkward using my opposite hand to trail my fingers down my body and between my legs. I send them straight to my clit in search of relief.

My body jolts at the touch, but I settle into the feeling of pleasure.

"Don't be so shy, gorgeous. Let me see you. Enjoy yourself for me. That's it, doesn't it feel good?" His voice is low and gravelly.

I wonder if the irises of his eyes are gold like I'd seen them before. I pet my clit, working over the small nub, feeling myself grow wetter, but I fumble as I get closer.

"What was that huff about?" He hums, waiting for me to respond.

"Nothing, it's just weird using this hand. I'll make it work." I hate the frustration ruining the moment between us and try to refocus.

"Then let me take over," he says unhelpfully from the other side of the world.

"I don't want to wait until you come home," I grumble and slide my hand away from my center, defeated.

"Leticia." Something about the way he says my name has me looking up to the security camera. The watched feeling intensifies as he pauses. "Gorgeous girl, I have a whole box of toys perfect for us to play with. Can you open my toy cabinet?"

I push my way out of bed.

"Damn, your ass is perfect." Royal's voice is breathy in my ear.

The compliment flames my cheeks as I open the compartment. "Okay, I'm looking at the toys."

"The second one from the left or the third one from the right. I can control either of those with my phone. Pick whichever one feels right for you." Whatever bed or cot he's lying on creaks as Royal adjusts.

I look between the two toys, not even sure really what they do. I grab the one on the right. It's teal and smaller overall.

"Excellent choice," Royal murmurs. "Press and hold the top button, and it'll turn on with a little burst of vibration. Then it'll stop. When you lie back on the bed, insert the larger end, and the smaller nub should press against your clit."

I follow his instructions by pressing the button to turn it on. Despite his warning, the vibration startles me as it comes to life in my hand. Then it stills as if waiting patiently for me.

Back in bed, it's another kind of awkward inserting the toy, but it isn't as big as Royal, so I know I can take it.

"Oh." I gasp as it effortlessly slides in, surprised by how wet I am. My pussy clenches around it, and I feel some of the relief I've been chasing.

"Feel good?" When I don't respond, Royal seems alarmed. "Talk to me, Leticia."

"Good. I didn't expect it to feel so good. But it's not you," I pant.

"It's so sexy hearing that you want me. I love knowing that you trust me to take care of you." He's smiling. I can just tell by his voice. "Now, lie back, relax, and let me take control."

"I still want to see you come," I moan.

"Yes, gorgeous, you can see me come." Royal laughs. A second later, the toy vibrates inside me. I twitch, startled. "We'll go nice and slow. Tell me if it's too much."

"Mmhmm." I close my eyes, focusing on the feeling and adjusting to it.

The nub against my clit starts to vibrate, and my whole body shivers. I squeeze my legs together, the feeling so good.

"Royal." I try to caution him. "That feels almost too good."

"So sensitive. I love that." Royal groans, and the vibration lessens. "I've turned it down a little, make it harder for you to come. I'll leave the setting right there. I'm hanging up to start sending you videos. Are you ready to watch what you do to me?"

"Yes," I gasp while trying not to move, but each breath I take shifts the toy just a little bit, and I'm struggling to wait to come.

"I'll talk to you in a little bit, gorgeous." He hangs up, and I pick up my phone, waiting for the first message to come in.

It takes longer than I expected. But when the video comes in, it's almost a full minute long.

Royal is lying just like he was before. His hand is wrapped around his cock, and he moves it slowly. The movement isn't straight up and down but in a curve, wrapping and turning around his cock as it works up and down.

My muscles tense, and the vibrations of the toy feel more amplified.

I let out a slow breath, watching him and listening to his heavy breathing.

"Fuck, Leticia. You've got me so hard. Every time we play, I'm so hard it hurts." He squeezes the head of his cock a little bit, and his hips buck up into his hand.

The memory of his hips bucking into me like that sends a wave of pleasure through my body. I moan, and Royal lets out a low groan at the same time.

Stupid assignment halfway around the world. I want him so bad.

I'm nearly drooling as I watch his hand work around his shaft. A bead of fluid forms on the head, and he wipes it away with his thumb. I have a feral idea that I want to be the one to lick it away.

I swallow hard.

Another message comes in just as the first video finishes.

Without hesitating, I click into the new video.

Royal's hand is moving faster in this one, his hips still thrusting up into his hand.

"Leticia. Fuck, I'm going to come. I want to be inside you so bad." His voice is growly.

I squeeze my legs together. The vibrations intensify, and I draw a sharp breath. I feel like I'm on the verge of an orgasm right there with him.

He lets out a stifled yell, and cum practically explodes out of his cock, coating his stomach in short bursts. He groans and keeps working himself until he finishes.

I can't hold myself back any longer. Realizing how tightly I'm gripping my phone, I drop it on the bed beside me. Every one of my muscles is tense, and I fall over the edge all at once. It cycles through my body, radiating out from my core. I writhe under the intensity of it.

"Royal," I call out, knowing he can hear me through the camera. I swear the vibrations get more intense, drawing out the pleasure. "Royal!"

I'm trying to relax as my orgasm wanes, but it's too much. I'm nearly overstimulated. My body tightens, and another orgasm rolls through me. I arch into it, holding myself together by a thread before it snaps.

I lose track of what I say, moan, or incoherently babble. My body feels too good to focus. The vibrations start to lessen, and finally, I collapse into a heap on the sheets.

After a couple minutes, my phone rings next to me, and I fumble picking it up. "Hello?"

"Gorgeous. I'm hard again after watching you come." Royal's voice is practically a purr. "You did amazing for me. It was so intense watching you come all over that toy."

His praise relaxes my body further, and I slump into the bed. "So good. Your videos, I've never seen anything like it."

"I'm so glad my wife likes what she sees." He sounds like he's smiling.

I pull the phone away from my ear and press the video button.

A second later, his face comes into view. "Such a good girl. Let me stay on the line while you get cleaned up, then you can get a little post-orgasm nap in."

He talks me through removing the toy. It's like he reads my mind, knowing about the tiny hint of shame wiggling at the back of my brain. Royal continues to praise me, saying how sexy I was and that he's proud of me.

By the time I lie back down and we've said goodbye, I miss him like crazy, but I feel closer to him than ever before.

CHAPTER FIFTY-EIGHT

SOMETHING ABOUT SCREWDRIVERS

We should be back at home with our mate. My wolf yowls with frustration as I unpack the fiftieth high-tech camera into the big crate so that I can just carry it from room to room with me for the install.

I've been at this for seven days, and while the time I've been able to connect with Leticia has made this much more bearable, we'd both rather be home together.

Do you think I don't know that? I growl as I unbox one more.

My crate is full, so I start up toward the top of the house.

The floor plans are meticulously designed. It's clear Steffano knows what he's doing when it comes to security. Really, any idiot could be doing this, but it's his way of exacting revenge for taking Leticia from him.

I'm ahead of schedule with everything and hoping to negotiate going home early if I finish it all up.

"Royal." Steffano greets me as I climb the last stair to the top floor of his new house. "Aren't these views incredible?"

I take a minute to look around us. It's hilly, and there are trees, but given the time of year, the foliage is sparse and the landscape kind of barren.

But it's not worth my effort to argue with him. "It certainly is."

"I can't believe she'd rather be with a tech geek like you than with a man who has all the power in the world. You work for *me*, but she chose you." Steffano huffs and leans against a nearby wall.

His obsession with power and a social hierarchy is obnoxious, and yet I'm the one in a wolf pack.

To stop myself from smarting off, I hold the screwdriver in my mouth while I start working on the cables.

We could do what Dad did with his screwdriver? My wolf suggests, picturing the day back in the garage while I cracked the safe.

The easy way I consider violence should scare me, but I'm getting more used to thinking like Valor. It's easier to protect Leticia if I'm willing to kill without remorse for her.

"Nothing to say to that?" Steffano crosses his arms in front of his chest.

I take the screwdriver out of my mouth. *Try to behave.* I let out a slow breath. "Sometimes it's not about power. Not all women are attracted to it."

"So they claim." Steffano raises his nose in the air, and I force myself not to roll my eyes.

"Well, I'm going to get to it. Big project and all." I gesture to the box of cameras. "Unless you want to help."

Steffano scoffs. "I'm letting you know that it'll just be you in the house the rest of the week. I don't want my men knowing of all the security procedures I have. Do not tell anyone what you do here."

"Got it. I take what we do seriously. I'm not about to fuck up your house because I'm mad at you for how you treated Leticia." That might have been a little too bold of me to say.

"She had the chance for me to treat her like a princess. Then I found out she was a whore for the Cavanaghs."

He did not just say that. My wolf snaps his teeth, growling, tossing his weight into each lunge, and trying to break free.

"You know, if you'd prefer not to have such an easy woman like that for yourself . . . I know a guy who doesn't have the same rigid rules your organization does for getting rid of someone unwanted." He shrugs, unaware of the rage coursing through me. "It would be quick, and her body would never be found. I'll give him a call right now."

Steffano's offer to kill my mate snaps my threads of barely contained restraint.

I lunge forward, my logical brain gone, survival instinct on high gear.

My wolf helps guide my movements. With the first jab, the screwdriver misses a rib, neatly lodging into the space between.

My next movements become a blur. I pull the screwdriver out and plunge it into the side of his neck. I yank it toward me, ripping it out just like Dad had done in the garage, and Steffano falls to the floor, clutching his neck.

It was so easy. And it happened so fast. It takes me a minute, drawing deep breaths full of copper-scented air, to get a handle on what I just did. The screwdriver coated in crimson now lies at my feet.

Steffano gasps and sputters, coughing blood all over me. *Great.*

He reaches for the gun strapped to his waist, his bloody fingers slipping against the metal.

"That won't save you." I shake my head and reach for it myself.

He fumbles trying to take it out of my hand, and I'm definitely going to need a shower to wash off the evidence of this altercation by the time I flick the safety off.

Too noisy. My wolf warns me. *Someone will hear it.*

I hate that he's right. Killing Steffano just got more personal. I click the safety back on and lower the gun to the floor out of his reach before picking up the screwdriver again.

It's messy but not as hard as I thought it would be to impale his skull through his eye with the screwdriver.

Steffano's brain shuts down fast, his body slumping to the floor.

"No one talks about my wife like that," I snarl at his lifeless body.

No one talks about our mate like that. My wolf snaps his teeth in punctuation.

Leticia

CHAPTER FIFTY-NINE

THE WILD LIFE OF ROYAL

"So there I was, dragging his body, wrapped in one of those construction drop cloths, down the stairs, when in walks his second-in-command." Royal sighs. He runs his fingers back through his hair. "Obviously, I hadn't thought that far ahead, so I reached for my gun when the guy says, 'That won't be necessary.' "

"I mean, if you hate your boss, and someone else takes care of the problem . . ." Valor hums, adjusting how he's sitting next to Antonella on the sofa. He wraps his arm around her, holding her close.

I'm sitting in a chair with a blanket thrown over my lap, Royal sitting next to me on the ottoman he pulled over.

"Exactly. So Emilio, his second-in-command, worked on disposing of the body while I sent Steffano on a virtual world-class vacation, jet-setting around the Caribbean. It'll look like he fell overboard in a few weeks, and Emilio can take over the organization." Royal is smiling. "He still wants the guns, and I said I'd throw in a few modifiers to sweeten the deal. Which he was amenable to."

But I'm still in shock. "You killed Steffano because he insulted me."

"No, it started with wanting to kill him when he insulted you, but I waited until he threatened my wife to actually do it." Royal's smile falters when he sees that I'm upset. He places a hand on my blanketed thigh and gives it a little squeeze as if asking for forgiveness.

"At least one of them has self-control." Betty sighs, drawing me away from the tender moment. She's sitting on the arm of Ian's chair, leaning against his shoulder.

"You call that self-control?" Ian asks, looking up at her with bewilderment.

"Obviously," Valor huffs. "I would have killed him at the first mention that my wife is a whore."

Antonella smacks him in the stomach with the back of her hand. "Don't be cute. You're still in the doghouse."

"Are you ever going to let him out?" Betty asks.

"Mmm, maybe when the renovations to the house are done. Not a moment before." Antonella looks Valor over, but they don't know her like I do. I see the softness in her gaze and how her eyes aren't pinched tight. She's not really mad.

Royal squeezes my leg a little harder. "Forgive me?"

"There's nothing to forgive." I place my non-injured hand atop his. "I'm just glad you're back safe."

CHAPTER SIXTY

THE WHOLE ROOM

Leticia's family boxed up her entire room and sent it over with a moving truck. Bed, dresser, nightstands, drapes, and anything else you can imagine. I'm pretty sure if the wallpaper could come off the walls, they would have sent it too.

"This is a nightmare." Leticia pulls at her hair near the roots, her features pinched together as she looks at the back of the moving truck.

It arrived unannounced this afternoon with a work order signed by Berto.

"So, where do you want it?" the delivery guy harrumphs.

Rightfully so, he's a little pissed off that we're not ready to receive a full room of furniture. What we had expected to be a few dozen boxes of clothing, accessories, shoes, and books turned into a bigger dilemma than anticipated.

But my wolf doesn't like his tone and keeps demanding I step between him and Leticia.

"I'll back my SUV out. We can put it in the spare garage stall." I shrug and head to the house for my keys.

Leticia follows me. "I'm so sorry. This is —"

I stop short, and she runs into me. Turning, I put my arm around her and lead her with me into the house. "It's not a disaster, it's not a nightmare, it's a mild inconvenience at best, and truthfully, it's kinda funny. I'm sure we can find a home for everything they sent. Stop worrying about taking up space. Remember that we're a family and we're better together."

Leticia sighs, her shoulders relaxing, and she shivers with the change in temperature as we step into the warm house.

"Did they send her bed and everything?" Mom calls, probably from the living room where she's looking out the window.

"Everything," Leticia groans loudly while scrubbing her hands down her face.

"Devious. I like their style," Mom shouts again. I hear her, but Leticia probably doesn't. "I'll have to remember that trick for revenge someday."

"Stay in here with Mom. I'll take care of unloading the truck, and we can sort boxes in the garage after it warms back up." I kiss her forehead before grabbing the keys off the rack and heading back outside.

It took the moving company guys less than twenty minutes to unload the whole truck into the garage stall and for me to sign the paperwork. After leaving the heat on in the garage for an hour, it was finally warm enough for us to sort boxes without Leticia needing to be bundled up in more than a sweatshirt.

"Oh!" Leticia gasps and then folds the lid back on the box she's looking at. Her eyes are wide with shock or surprise.

Danger? My wolf questions, scenting the air.

"Oh?" I encourage for more information.

"We never exchanged Christmas gifts, and yours is in this box." She folds the lid back over, trying to seal it up.

"No way, it's my gift. I wanna see it." I step over to her and teasingly try to lift a flap to peek inside.

Leticia bats my hand away. "No way, it's not even wrapped."

"So?" I shrug. "Neither is yours."

"Oh." Leticia worries her bottom lip, and I bring my hand up to her face, gently cupping her chin. I brush my thumb across her lips, freeing the one trapped between her teeth, and she turns those intense blue eyes on me. "I guess we could have Christmas in February."

"I'll go get your gift and put it in this box." I pick up one of the boxes we already emptied. "While I'm gone, you can put my gift in another box. We don't need fancy wrapping paper."

She nods and nuzzles into the touch of my hand. "Sounds good."

I rush through the house, down to the basement, and into my storage room. The safe, where I hid Leticia's presents, is on the far wall, and I spin the dial through its combination like the thousands of times I've done it before, but it still feels slow compared to how fast my heart is beating.

There, stacked on one of the shelves, sit the presents. Various blue phone cases and computer cases sit stacked on top of each other, and the top box is a blue velvet ring box. I wasn't planning on giving it to her today, but . . . we're giving gifts, and this is the one that matters most.

No. My wolf riots. *She deserves a better proposal. The garage is for killing people, not that.*

He makes a valid point.

I tuck the ring box back into the safe and pull out the other presents, placing them into the box for her to open. After closing the safe, I head back upstairs.

"You better be proposing to her. With a ring!" Mom calls from where she's reading in the living room.

"According to my wolf, we can't propose to her in the same place we kill people." I back up from the hallway to the garage to look at her.

"So?" Mom puts the bookmark into her book. "Take her someplace nice. Tell her you heard there are swans down on the pond and that you want to go see them. It's true enough."

"The swans or me wanting to see them?" I clarify.

"The swans, Royal," Mom growls, shaking her head like I'm smart enough to know better. "That girl has been here, pining over you while you were gone, and now she's living here and being the absolute sweetest, and even starting to get to know people in the pack. You're obviously utterly obsessed and in love with her. Why wait?"

I put the box down in the entryway. Retreating down the stairs, I go back to the safe. More intentionally this time, I spin the knob.

She deserves to have it all. I agree with Mom.

Swans are stupid. My wolf disagrees. *They're just birds.*

They mate for life. I argue, trying to find the romantic nature of a half-frozen pond and swans. *Maybe it doesn't have to be entirely romantic. It just has to be pretty and peaceful? I just want it to be perfect, and nothing seems perfect, especially not compared to her.*

My wolf concedes with a sigh. *At least it's not where Dad killed someone with a screwdriver.*

I grab the small box, taking the stairs two at a time until I'm once again standing in the hallway in front of Mom. I shake the ring box at her, demonstrating that I have it before tucking it into the pocket of my jacket. I stack Leticia's jacket on top of the box with her presents and take them out to the garage.

She's sitting on top of one of the work stools, digging through another box of items, when I come in, and she looks up with a big smile. "Ready?"

"So ready, and then after . . ." I remote start my SUV with the fob so that it warms up while we open gifts. "I just heard there are some swans down on the pond. We should go see them."

"Ooooh, I've only seen swans at the zoo. That'll be fun!" Leticia's excitement comes with a genuine smile.

Mom was right. Swans it is. I toss our coats over the hood of Mom's SUV, and the ring box in my pocket makes an extra thump. My heartbeat goes a million miles a minute. Trying to play it cool, I look at Leticia, but she doesn't seem to notice the sound.

"Who is opening their gift first?" Leticia suspiciously eyes the box I brought with me.

"Same time, on three?" I offer the fairest, in my eyes, option.

"Deal." She pushes up from the shop stool, and I set her box on it before positioning myself in front of the box she put together for me.

"One." She starts.

"Two." I count with her.

"Three," we say together and open the boxes.

My box is arranged nicely — a blanket, a pair of plaid pajama bottoms in the local hockey team's colors, and a little card with three airplane-shaped paperclips on it.

I quickly disregard it to look at Leticia and watch her open her gift, only to find her doing the same thing, looking at me for my reaction.

"Maybe this wasn't a good idea since clearly we're both too interested in the other person and what they're doing. You go first." Leticia points to me.

I make a big deal of looking into the box, trying to figure out where to start. Picking up the paperclips, I smile wide. "I've been looking for these everywhere. They're perfect for all my paper collating needs."

Leticia giggles. "I couldn't resist."

I pull out the pajama pants next, holding them up and admiring how cool the pattern is. "How did you know I wear plaid pajama bottoms? Before we slept together?"

"You seemed like a plaid guy. Kinda quirky, open to tradition, but all about comfort." She shrugs as I set them aside.

The blanket is pretty much the softest thing I've ever touched, and I pull it out of the box to find a second one underneath. "Two blankets?"

"Well, I had gotten one for each of us, but now I live here, so we could share."

"No way." I shake my head and nuzzle the super soft fabric. It's white with ribbon microphones printed on it. "This is mine. I'm hogging this blanket. You can have your own."

"Do you like it?" She laughs. "They're old-school microphones from our very own podcast Late Nite Bytes."

"Like?" I shake my head, pretending to be disgusted. But my smile cracks through. "I love my gifts. I just wish I had been as creative and as thoughtful as you."

"Really?" Leticia laughs again as she starts pulling the cases and covers out of her box. "A bunch of blue covers? I don't have hardly any blue. I love these."

"Well, you can hardly be married to someone named Royal and not have a bunch of blue things." I shrug. "I bought so many because I wasn't sure I got the styles you liked. It was hard to tell from the camera angles."

"They're perfect." She strokes a finger over a glossy one with silver stars embedded in it.

"You're perfect." I correct her. "Come on, let's go see those swans before they decide it's too cold and migrate south like the Canada geese cousins."

Leticia sets down the computer cover but grabs a phone case. She changes out the current green one for the blue one before putting on her jacket and heading over to the warmed-up SUV.

Leticia

CHAPTER SIXTY-ONE

THE ONE WITH THE RING

Like the gentleman he is, Royal opens my door for me and makes sure I'm tucked inside before closing it behind me. Then he goes around the vehicle to his side.

Something's a little off. It's like he's nervous or something. Which seems weird because I don't think swans should be that intimidating, but his nervousness started before we left the garage and has me on the edge of anxiety by proxy.

We're only down the road, maybe ten minutes, before we pull off at a pond. It's not all that small but not quite as large as what I'd consider a lake. Out among the frozen reeds are some ducks and two larger white birds floating in the water.

"Ohhh." I lean forward, getting a better look at them while unbuckling my seat belt.

Royal tries to come around and open my door, but I beat him to it. I'm too excited to see more of the white puffballs on the water. But I link hands with his and trudge out into the snow. As we get closer, the swans must know we're there to see them because they start swimming in our direction, their bodies bobbing back and forth as they make their way toward us.

They swim around each other a little bit, and one dives into the water and comes back up.

Royal raises my hand and kisses it, squeezing my fingers. "Did you know they mate for life?"

"I didn't. That's so romantic." I can't take my eyes off them. They're so graceful floating along.

I go to take another step toward them, but Royal's hand wrapped in mine keeps me stationary. *Right, probably best not to approach wildlife.*

I sigh, starting to feel my nose getting cold. "They're just so beautiful."

"Nowhere near as beautiful as you." Royal beams down at me, eyes focused like I'm the only thing that matters, while he laughs at the easy compliment. "I know you've already forgiven me for marrying us on paper, and you've agreed to be my mate, but something is still missing."

He squeezes my hand and brings it up to kiss my knuckles. That's when something catches my eyes, something sparkling. On my left hand, my ring finger, is a diamond engagement ring.

"Royal," I gasp, looking between him and the ring in awe.

It's a princess-cut stone, easily three carats, and it's sparkling in the early afternoon light, almost glowing. *How did he get that on my finger?*

"It's too big? If you don't like the cut or the size . . ." Royal flounders, his cheeks turning red, and I don't think it's just from the cold. "We can get some —"

I snatch my hand away from him, glancing between him and the ring. Tears threaten to spill from the corner of my eyes, but they freeze against my lashes. "Absolutely not. Do not say that. It's perfect."

With everything going on, we never discussed a ring. I guess because we were already married, I didn't see it as a priority. But our relationship has never been conventional, so this tracks for us.

But Royal knows me better than I know myself, and I couldn't have picked out something more beautiful.

He pulls me back to him, one hand on my shoulder, the other raising my chin. The kiss is sweet and so sincere, but he breaks it quickly. "You're freezing."

"I guess a little." I downplay the way my toes are going numb. I honestly didn't even notice until now.

Before I can say anything else, Royal scoops me up into his arms and carries me out of the deep snow and back to the SUV. He tucks me into the passenger seat and covers me with a blanket. The drive back home is enveloped in quiet contentment with my hand clasped in his. Every so often, Royal rolls his finger over the stone decorating my finger.

He blasted the heater at full throttle, trying to warm me back up. The joy radiating through me helps take the edge off the chill, along with the warm air thawing my nose.

"You're really not cold?" I ask as we pull through the gates.

"Being a wolf shifter has its perks. I'm chilly but not cold and certainly nowhere near as frozen as you are. The pond was a bad idea." He sighs and shakes his head.

"It was absolutely perfect." I thwart his attempt to belittle the experience. Picking up his hand off the center console, I squeeze it. "I mean it, Royal."

He squeezes back before putting the vehicle in park outside of his garage stall. Turning in his seat, he cups my face, stroking my cheeks with his thumbs. "What did I ever do to deserve you?"

"Well, you hacked into my phone, made it easy to be your friend, saved me from a fate possibly worse than death, and managed to get us married without a witness or hell, even a bride." I laugh and nuzzle into his palm.

He smirks. "And I'd do it all again."

EPILOGUE

NOT A PRINCESS

"Leticia Cavanagh." My name is called, and a portion of the stadium erupts in cheers.

Most of my peers turn to look where a whole section is standing up and clapping, hooting and hollering. I don't think it's the whole pack, but a large majority of them.

The clapping and cheering don't stop until I've crossed the stage and made it back down the stairs on the other side.

My cheeks hurt from smiling so much, and while part of me is embarrassed that the rule breakers are my friends and family, my heart is warm from the love.

"Please remember to keep cheering to a minimum as we make it through the list," the announcer says over the loudspeaker.

I return to my seat quickly and pull my phone out of my clutch.

There's a picture from Royal, taken from his vantage point of me walking across the stage, and another of him and his parents wearing blue shirts with little crowns and the words 'Not a Princess' stitched underneath them on the right-hand side.

I was able to talk them down from big, in-the-center-of-the-shirt logos to the smaller version. But I wasn't able to convince them not to put Cavanagh across the back with pictures of Royal and me together.

I'm laughing, and the guy next to me doesn't look so amused, but I hold myself together and settle in for the rest of the graduates to cycle through.

I text Royal a heart and click into the message from Berto. It's small, just one word, 'Congratulations,' but our communication has pretty much always been single-line texts. Nothing has changed now that I don't live with him. I send him back a quick thank you.

Maybe someday he and I will have a relationship, but baby steps.

Mom hasn't reached out, and I don't think she will. But I look back up to where the Cavanaghs sit . . . It's her loss, not mine.

"Who knew graduating was so much work?" I plop down on our bed, looking up at the ceiling.

A second later, the bedroom automation that Royal set up projects the night sky above me.

"Oh, me." Royal yawns as he comes to lie down beside me, resting his head against mine as we look up at the faux night sky. "Was dinner after too much? I tried to warn Mom that it might be better if we kept things small, but what started out with dinner for the four of us turned into the seven of us, and then pretty soon the whole pack was wondering why they couldn't come."

"It was good. But I missed cuddling with you." I nuzzle in against him, drawing deep breaths of his sweet scent and closing my eyes.

"I would always rather cuddle with you than go out to eat." Royal's voice sounds devious.

But I don't engage in the innuendo lurking in his words. I'm too tired for the multiple orgasms he promised over text messages this week while he was out in the field working with Valor, setting up some new mercenaries.

"I did find it interesting . . ." Royal pauses. "That when the conversation of 'what's next' came up at the table, you seemed unsure about the future."

"Well, my life was planned out exactly this far: graduate with my bachelor's degree and get married. I've never thought about it a whole lot past today. Well, I guess I've never thought about it beyond our wedding next month." I kiss his cheek.

"We'll have to fix that. You've got a whole life to live, and I don't want you thinking small." Royal turns his head, and our lips meet. "Back to school for a more advanced degree, another bachelor's degree in something you're passionate about, a job at Clark Enterprises, a stay-at-home mate, a volunteer with the pack, and anything else you can dream up . . . The sky's the limit, gorgeous. You tell me what you want to do, and I'll support you one hundred percent."

"I just have to get used to looking at the big, wide world first." I move my hand and entwine our fingers together. "Promise that you'll be with me every step of the way?"

"I promise that even when we're not together, I'm always watching you." Royal smiles at me, and my heart flutters.

THE END

OTHER TITLES

By Jaeger Rose:

The Mafia Arrangement

My Solemn Vow

The Eclipse Verse

Omegaverse + Morally Black + Motorcycle Club

Against the Hollow

By Sarah Jaeger:

The Ardelean Bloodline

Wolf Shifter + Found Family + Emotional Damage

Smoke

Haze & Blaze

Scorch

Smog

Stay up to date on all things Sarah Jaeger & Jaeger Rose.

Follow me on social media:

www.ingramcontent.com/pod-product-compliance
Lightning Source LLC
LaVergne TN
LVHW010628110826
845149LV00014B/2810
9781971642987